Snow Fall

Having worked as a police officer and head of investigations before becoming a full-time writer, Jørn Lier Horst has established himself as one of the most successful authors to come out of Scandinavia. His books have sold over two million copies in his native Norway alone and he's published in twenty-six languages. The Wisting series, produced by the team behind *Wallander* and *The Girl with the Dragon Tattoo*, is now a major TV series starring Sven Nordin and Carrie-Anne Moss.

Snow Fall

JØRN LIER HORST

Translated by Anne Bruce

MICHAEL JOSEPH

PENGUIN MICHAEL JOSEPH

UK | USA | Canada | Ireland | Australia
India | New Zealand | South Africa

Penguin Michael Joseph is part of the Penguin Random House group of companies
whose addresses can be found at global.penguinrandomhouse.com

First published in Norway as *Grenseløs* by Strawberry Publishing, 2021
First published in Great Britain by Michael Joseph, 2023

001

Set in 13.5/16pt Garamond MT Std
Typeset by Jouve (UK), Milton Keynes
Printed and bound in Great Britain by Clays Ltd, Elcograf S.p.A.

The authorized representative in the EEA is Penguin Random House Ireland,
Morrison Chambers, 32 Nassau Street, Dublin D02 YH68

A CIP catalogue record for this book is available from the British Library

HARDBACK ISBN: 978–0–241–53382–6
OPEN MARKET PAPERBACK ISBN: 978–0–241–53383–3

This book has been published with the financial support of Norla

www.greenpenguin.co.uk

I

The email appeared on his screen at 15.37 on Friday 8 December.

William Wisting was expecting a reply from the district court, having spent most of the day at a remand hearing. The prosecutor had requested four weeks' custody and he was anxious about the outcome.

However, the onscreen message was about something completely different.

A forwarded email, it had gone to four other recipients before Mikkelsen at the criminal proceedings unit had passed it on to him.

The subject field was filled out in English. *Inquiry re: possible incident or accident.*

Glancing at the clock, Wisting understood that as far as the superintendent at the unit was concerned, it was simply a matter of clearing his desk and emptying his inbox before the weekend.

Answered locally was the brief endorsement.

The sender's name was Michelle Norris and she had also provided a foreign phone number. She wrote that she was worried because she had not heard from one of her friends since 30 November. Prior to that, they had been in touch online several times a day, until this came to a sudden halt with no warning of any kind.

In the Internet forum where they had met, her friend used the nickname Astria. She had given Norway as her homeland and her age as thirty-two. Through her own investigations,

Michelle had discovered the woman was probably from Stavern and she was keen to make contact with the local police because she feared something had happened to her friend.

Messages like this, expressing disquiet, were far from unusual. They came in many guises, arising from various circumstances, but this one was different. The sender did not actually know the true identity of the missing person.

Wisting read through the message once more. He would have known if a thirty-two-year-old woman had met with a serious accident during the past week, but he made a rapid check in the records all the same. Two deaths had been notified to the police. One was a fatal overdose by a known drug addict – the case lay in one of the bundles of paper in Wisting's office awaiting a post-mortem report. The other was a suicide. Both these cases related to men.

There had been a number of accidents, mostly road traffic incidents at the time of the first snow fall, but one was a work accident at the harbour where a man had been crushed between a machine and a container, and another had been at the recycling depot when caustic fluid had spilled on a woman's hands.

In other words, nothing of any relevance to the message from Michelle Norris.

The latest news from the district court now popped up on his screen. They had been granted a fortnight's custody. The court had upheld the defence counsel's claim that investigation would necessarily be limited over the Christmas and New Year period and it would be disproportionate to keep the accused in prison during the holidays.

A remand cell was already reserved for him in Ringerike Prison. Wisting dashed off a transport order before returning to Michelle Norris's email. Composing a short, reassuring reply in English about the inquiries he had made, he told her there was nothing to suggest anything untoward had happened to her friend.

He sent the reply and logged off the computer system.

Outside, it had begun to snow again.

Collecting his jacket from its hook, he wrapped his scarf around his neck. Before he shut the office door, as he cast one last glance at his computer it crossed his mind that he should really have added that nothing had happened to give grounds for concern, at least not as far as he or the police knew.

2

The snowplough lumbered along the road, clattering and scraping through the piles of snow, tossing aside a curtain of white.

Arnt Skaret had a hard job with the steering and gears. The road through Askeskogen was narrow and the old banks of snow were now blanketed in a fresh layer. In some places the high piles at the verges had slid back on to the road again. Fat snowflakes fluttered in the darkness in front of the headlights, seeming to sparkle in the orange glow from the beacon on the cabin roof. Flurries of snow spread across the windscreen before being swept aside. One wiper blade was worn, reducing visibility, but he knew the road and scarcely needed the marker poles to find his bearings.

Music played at low volume on the car radio. The Boss.

The lights from an oncoming car appeared in the distance, further ahead. Arnt Skaret took his foot off the accelerator and pulled out to the right. Twigs pummelled the side of the massive vehicle and, as they passed, the headlights of the other car made it difficult to see anything ahead of the snowplough.

Then he was alone on the road again. His right hand reached out for his Thermos mug but found it empty. He would have to wait for a straighter stretch of road before he could refill it.

Before he reached the Helgeroa road, he encountered yet another car, this time a small delivery van with one broken headlight.

At the Foldvik intersection, he slowed before turning left and the chains dug into the snow-covered roadway. A fox crossed the road in front of him, turning its head towards the snowplough. The front lights were reflected in its eyes before it leapt away, disappearing on to the footpath beside the road.

The grey VW Caddy was still parked in the bus bay beyond the Manvik farms. He had spotted it on the first evening he had been out with the plough. Now it had been almost completely obliterated by snow.

Arnt Skaret swung into the bus bay and drove up behind the van. It was difficult to decide whether it had driven off the road by accident or been pushed to the side to avoid impeding other traffic. No matter which, with the snow hard-packed around it, it would be difficult to move it back on to the road again.

He put his mug between his feet as he unscrewed the lid before reaching out for the flask on the passenger seat and refilling the mug.

The temperature gauge on the dashboard read minus three degrees Celsius. It had become milder in the last twenty-four hours. Without dry, fine weather, there was a danger of the snow turning to rain.

After two mouthfuls, he realized he also needed to pee. He scrambled out of the driver's cabin and stood in the shelter of the plough as the warm jet of urine bored into the snow.

He raised his eyes to the forest, where the trees at the roadside were plump with snow. It was virtually impossible for his eyes to penetrate beyond them.

A bus passed on the road as Arnt Skaret finished up and washed his hands in the deep snow.

The parked Caddy jutting out of the bus bay was the type

with a long cargo space. A Caddy Maxi. One of the Hofstein brothers used to have one like that, though that had been a while ago.

Skaret had worked on the roads for almost forty years. From time to time, he had come across stolen cars – that could be the explanation here.

Taking a flashlight from the cabin, he strode into the snowdrift and waded through to the van. Sheets of snow slid off as he brushed the side window. He shone the torch beam inside and squinted through the frosty glass.

The vehicle was empty. He played the beam of light over the steering column and ignition lock. No keys, but no sign either of the lock having been picked or bypassed.

A crucifix dangled from the rear-view mirror and a plastic carrier bag lay on the passenger seat. As the torch beam danced around, he spotted a blanket and some empty bottles on the floor.

The cargo space was sealed off and there were no side windows. Arnt Skaret walked around behind the vehicle and tried the door. Locked. Crouching down, he wiped the snow from the licence plate. Although it was coated in mud, he could make out a foreign registration number.

Not so strange that things had gone wrong, he thought.

He skirted around the car again and checked the nearside rear tyre. As he thought, worn summer tyres. In that case, the four-wheel drive would not help much. He shook his head. The vehicle would sit here until spring if no one towed it away.

3

Six slices of a frozen pizza he had cooked the previous evening lay wrapped in clingfilm at the bottom of the fridge. Wisting took out three of them and put them on a plate.

While the microwave was working, he stood at the window looking out. Children were playing with a sledge in the street.

Line's house was cloaked in darkness. She had been away for three days now and should be coming home tomorrow. When it stopped snowing, he would go across to do some shovelling so that she could drive her car all the way up to the house.

As he carried his meal into the living room, it occurred to him that the house was quieter than usual – the snow muffled all external noise. He switched on the radio just to escape the feeling of being completely alone.

Once he had eaten, he took out his iPad to read the online newspapers, and while he was engrossed in them, an alert popped up to announce a new email from Michelle Norris.

The message was a reply to the email he had sent her an hour ago, but the text in the subject field had been altered to read *Regarding Astria*.

She began by thanking him for his speedy response and wrote that before she had made contact, she had used Google Translate to read machine-generated headlines in the regional media outlets without finding anything to suggest something untoward had happened to her friend.

However, I would like to present you with further information to support my reasons for disquiet, she wrote.

I became acquainted with Astria through an online community investigating the murder of Ruby Thompson in Sant Joan de Palamós in Spain on 16 April. Ruby was a friend of mine. The provincial police in Girona investigated the homicide, but their inquiries have been inconclusive. Three months ago I set up a crowdsolving page in which I gathered all the accessible information about Ruby's murder. I wanted to reach out via social media to people who might know something, but also to attract the expertise of individuals to the case. More than a hundred people have now become involved with no expectation of payment. A core team of around ten citizen detectives is particularly dedicated, and Astria is one of these. She worked on the analysis of a comprehensive trove of photographic material. Her last communication with the group suggested that she had come across something interesting but needed time to draw a conclusion.

Many of these contributors to the investigative forum are anonymous. In her user profile, Astria states she is Norwegian, aged thirty-two, a professional analyst who works on the simulation of industrial production processes. Through Internet conversations it has emerged that she lives alone. She has also intimated that her family has a holiday house in Palamós. She was staying there over Easter when Ruby was killed and stumbled upon the forum when she was later looking for information about the case. She probably took the name Astria from Greek mythology. The email address she provided (realAstria@gmail.com) is nowhere to be found in other Internet sites.

Michelle Norris had also attached the profile picture Astria had uploaded when she registered on the investigative forum. One of the members, who had undertaken an analysis of the background, had come to the conclusion that it had been snapped in Stavern.

Along with the profile picture, an image from Google's street view was included as documentation. It showed parts of the same picture clip, but from a slightly different angle. Wisting recognized it immediately. The photograph had been taken down at the harbour on a rainy summer's day. The woman at the centre of the picture was wearing shorts and a sou'wester, a rain jacket and wellingtons. The dark green sou'wester was pulled down over her face, shielding her eyes from the camera.

Wondering how they had reached the conclusion that the picture had been taken in Stavern, he peered more closely at the background. He could see the stone tower of the fortress out on the island known as Citadelløya. A local landmark, it was only familiar to people who had lived in or visited the town. A few yachts lay at anchor in the fjord behind her and the old passenger ferry that plied out to the islands in the summer season was passing through the sound.

By pinching his fingers on the screen, he was able to enlarge the picture to reveal the capital letters on the wheelhouse. M/S Viksfjord.

Googling the name himself, he generated a long list of results, all leading to Stavern.

Michelle Norris concluded her email by writing that, although the photo had been taken in Stavern, this did not necessarily mean that Astria lived there. She repeated her concern and asked if Wisting could possibly make further inquiries.

Wisting read the email again. Some of the expressions were new to him. 'Citizen detectives' and 'crowdsolving'. He had heard of crowdfunding, the type of popular funding in which people club together to give financial support to a project. Michelle Norris had done something similar. She had set up an Internet site where what she called citizen detectives could come together to help solve the murder of her friend. The very fact that they had traced the picture to Stavern showed a certain level of competence.

The principle of assembling amateur sleuths in this way was not unlike the idea behind TV programmes that discussed unsolved cases and showed CCTV videos. Wisting's experience with the latter had been very positive. No matter the quality of the film footage, there was always someone able to say what kind of car and which year of model was being driven, who had produced the clothes being worn, or even identify a masked individual from their movements.

He sat mulling over the information he had now received. There was probably no reason for genuine disquiet. Norway was not a large country and all murders were picked up by national media. A female in her thirties, missing for over a week, usually provided good fodder for the newspapers. However, nothing had been reported.

There was little to go on to help him discover Astria's identity. If the IP address of the computer she had used had been logged in the discussion forum, it could help him progress a little. In addition, Michelle had provided the information that the family had a holiday house in Palamós. That could help substantially.

He started to formulate a response. Michelle Norris's sender address ended in .au. He had initially assumed she was Spanish, but that could not be correct. She had also provided a phone number. Wisting googled the country code and discovered that Michelle Norris lived in Australia.

He looked at the time and worked out that it must be the middle of the night there now.

He undertook another search: *Ruby Thompson* plus the name of the town where she had been killed. The top results were from Spanish and Catalan newspapers, but he also found a number of references in the English and Australian media.

Ruby Thompson, a young, slight woman with blonde hair, a round face and attractive blue eyes, was from a town in southern Australia and had been on holiday in Europe when she was found murdered on a beach in Catalonia, an autonomous region in the north-east of Spain. A British backpacker she had met en route had been arrested but released after three weeks in custody.

He read several articles, but there was little information to be gained from them. Palamós was a small coastal town on the Mediterranean, more than an hour from the border with France. The body of twenty-five-year-old Ruby Thompson had been found early in the morning by a group of surfers. It had been washed ashore and the initial presumption was that she had drowned. However, the cause of death turned out to be strangulation. The most recent article was three weeks old and reported that the police there still had no suspect in the case.

Michelle Norris's website also appeared among the search results. He tried to access it, but only an account of the case popped up. In order to enter into discussion with others, he had to set up a user profile and apply for admission.

Returning to the police computer system, he searched through all missing-person reports and suicides recorded in the past week, but found nothing matching sex and age. He checked road traffic accidents and fires with fatal outcomes, as well as all cases in the entire country that had been entered under code 9701 – suspicious death. These were incidents in which death had been sudden or unexpected, triggering police inquiries to exclude any criminal activity. Some of these cases had been reported in the media. One of them concerned a drug addict who had caused problems on board a bus in Elverum. Finally the driver had thrown him off. Next day, the guy was found frozen to death at the roadside.

It took him almost an hour to go through everything, but the conclusion was obvious. Astria, or whatever she was called, was not among the reported victims.

He sent a formal reply in which he also asked for an IP address and asked if Astria had given any specific details of her family and the holiday house in Spain. Then he put on warm clothing to go outside and shovel some snow.

4

The first snow had come sweeping in on a bitterly cold north-easterly wind less than a week ago. Overnight, more than half a metre had fallen. Since then, banks of low-lying cloud had hung in the sky, bringing fresh flurries.

Wisting pushed the shovel into the hard-packed snow left by the snowplough, blocking Line's driveway. The snow must have come at around the same time as the last sign of life from Astria, he mused.

He could hear the roar of a snow blower somewhere nearby. Wisting adjusted his cap before first making a path to the door and then starting to scoop up the snow, tossing it to either side.

A family with children had moved into a house further up the street. Although Wisting had not spoken to them, he often saw the children out playing. They were probably a bit too old for Amalie. There was a boy of ten or twelve and a girl who was most likely a couple of years younger. Amalie was only five.

Straightening his back, he watched them for a while. They were building a snowman but kept squabbling, throwing snow and knocking each other to the ground. There were no other children in the street and he did not know whether Amalie had been properly introduced to them.

All of a sudden the girl burst into tears. She stomped off up the steps and disappeared inside.

Wisting continued to shovel, aware of the perspiration on his scalp as he worked steadily. It crossed his mind that it was summer in Australia.

Between the lines of the email he had received he had read misgivings that something had happened to Astria because of what she had uncovered or was in the process of tracking down.

Such fears were excessive, really. He found it impossible to imagine how deskbound investigations by an anonymous woman in an obscure location in Norway could expose anyone to danger.

Two questions absorbed him all the same: who was Astria and why had she gone totally silent?

These thoughts kept churning in his brain, but he was none the wiser.

Wisting completed his task and returned to his own house. After a hot shower, he heated up the remaining three slices of pizza. His back was aching when he sat down in front of the TV, his muscles tender after all the strenuous effort.

Reaching out for his iPad, he opened it and saw another email from Michelle Norris. She thanked Wisting for following up her inquiry and wrote that Astria, like many other users, was logged into the investigative forum through a VPN-server. This meant that all data traffic was encrypted and it was impossible to trace her original IP address.

Astria has given few details of her family and their holiday house in Palamós, she added. *I've provided the text in which she introduces herself to the other members of the forum.*

A few lines were copied into the email, in which Astria wrote that no one in her family liked snowy winters or skiing. Instead of a cabin in the mountains, they had a holiday house in Palamós. She had gone there several times a year since she was little and knew the town well. On the morning of Monday 17 April, she had been out jogging when the police were cordoning off the beach. The body of Ruby Thompson had washed up at the water's edge. Astria stood there until the police had finished their investigations and the dead body had been carried away. She had initially thought it was a case of accidental drowning and when she realized that a murder inquiry had been launched, she became afraid. She was upset that the killer had not been caught and the whole affair sparked her interest. She was keen to contribute and would be able to do some digging in Palamós next time she was there.

Wisting glanced up from the screen, gazing at the living-room windows and the snow outside. Maybe Astria had travelled to the Catalan town. That would at least explain why he had not found any information in the records.

Nothing in the email necessitated a reply from Wisting.

When he conducted a search and read the articles about the murder, a picture of the beach, snapped while the police were still present, had been included in several of them. On further examination, he saw it had been taken from a distance. Two police cars were parked on the sand and the corpse had been dragged up from the water's edge and lay, covered, between the vehicles. A police officer was talking to a group of teenagers carrying surfboards. Further off, a huddle of spectators stood watching. Wisting enlarged the image to see if Astria was among them, but the segment was too small and indistinct, making it impossible to decide if they were men or women or pick out anyone in running gear.

The last piece of pizza had gone cold and a hard crust had formed. Wisting chewed it down while he found the email with Astria's photograph. Something about it suggested she was a summer visitor rather than a resident. Standing in the middle of a puddle in waterproofs, she gave the impression that her pose was intended to create an amusing memento of a rain-soaked summer holiday. In addition, she had said she worked as a process analyst in industry and there was very little industrial employment in the Larvik and Stavern area. On the other hand, it sounded more like consultancy work that could be carried out anywhere. At the same time, it would be unusual for a visitor to pack a sou'wester in their luggage. A rain jacket and wellingtons would be a good idea when heading to Norway on holiday. However, a sou'wester, not so popular these days, was typically an ancient relic hanging on a peg in a summer cabin.

Astria was thirty-two, slightly younger than Line. He wondered how many thirty-two-year-old women lived in the district. The total number of inhabitants was almost 50,000, which meant about 300 of each sex in every annual cohort. If this had been a formal investigation, he could have obtained the exact number and a list of names from the population register. At any rate, there were probably a few people of similar age who might recognize her from the photograph, even though the sou'wester partially covered her face. Maybe someone who worked with her or met her frequently. If he published the picture on Facebook, he may well receive a few answers in the course of the evening.

The idea made him feel like an amateur sleuth himself.

Another email popped up, this time an invitation from Michelle Norris to join the investigative forum.

A Norwegian name features in the case was all she said.

Wisting laid the iPad down on the table and picked up the TV remote control. He had already become too involved.

5

On Saturday morning he woke unusually late, even though it was still dark outside when he got up.

The radio droned in the background as he read the online newspapers, starting with the local ones.

A picture of Ellinor Brink featured in one of the stories. Wisting knew her from his schooldays, and she now worked in the property business. The article was a report on a new project aimed at young people who normally found it difficult to get a foot on the housing ladder.

Although she looked careworn in the photograph, she came across as eager and enthusiastic in the text.

He knew she had been married twice. In such a small town, people picked up these things. First to a car salesman called Moberg – that marriage had not lasted long. She had married again, this time to a banker, and had taken his name, Isaksen. They had two sons but had divorced before the boys were grown, and Ellinor had reverted to her maiden name. The elder son worked in a finance company in Oslo, but the younger boy, called Trond, had caused some concern. Yesterday Wisting had had him remanded in custody.

Ellinor had visited him in his office and asked if he could keep her informed about what was happening in the case against her son. Strictly speaking, this was contrary to his duty of confidentiality, as her son was an adult, over thirty years of age.

'Did his lawyer phone you?' he asked. 'I requested that he do that.'

'I haven't heard anything,' she replied. 'There's nothing about it in the newspapers either.'

Wisting told her that her son had been remanded for a fortnight.

Her voice sounded on edge. She did not want her son to be released. Instead, she was keen for him to stay behind bars at Christmas so that she at least knew where he was. When she paid him a visit in his office, it was because she wanted Wisting to make sure her son was convicted to ensure that he would obtain help afterwards.

'What happens after fourteen days?' she asked.

Wisting explained that he would draw up a plan of action with the police prosecutor. They would apply for an extension of custody until the trial and try to make an arrangement with Kriminalomsorgen, the criminal justice social work service, for drug addiction treatment during his sentence.

Ellinor Brink told him how grateful she was, even though what Wisting had promised to do for her son was nothing out of the ordinary. Everyone would benefit from him finding a way out of addiction and crime.

After ending their conversation, it occurred to him that she used to have a dog called Milos, named after the Greek island in the Aegean Sea. He had never been there, but thought he had heard somewhere that Milos meant apple.

He wondered why Astria had chosen that particular nom de plume. When he looked it up, he saw it was a name from Greek mythology, just as Michelle Norris had written. Astria was the goddess of justice.

He had no time to meditate any further on the choice of name, as there was an unexpected knock at the front door. Line called out hello as she stepped inside.

Getting to his feet, Wisting moved to the cupboard above the sink and took out a coffee cup.

'Was it you that cleared my driveway?' Line asked, her cheeks glowing.

Wisting confirmed this with a smile. 'Where's Amalie?' he asked.

'I'll collect her later,' Line answered, taking a seat at the table. 'I just have to do something first.'

Amalie was with Sofie, who had a daughter of the same age. Line and Sofie had come to a reciprocal arrangement to help each other out. They were both single mothers and at times took on a lot of work. Line had scaled down her career in journalism after having Amalie and now worked freelance. She still wrote a few articles but was now contracted to a production company, working on a documentary series about an old missing-person case. This meant her working more than ever.

'Did it go well?' Wisting asked.

He did not really know what she had been doing in the past few days, other than that it had to do with a recording and interviews on the south coast.

'Yes, thanks,' Line assured him. 'We're nearing the end.'

He poured her some coffee.

Ellinor Brink's business card was still lying on the table. Line picked it up and ran her thumb over the estate agency logo. 'Were you thinking of moving house?' she asked.

Wisting shook his head. 'Her son's been remanded in custody,' he replied. 'I promised to help her with a few practical matters.'

Line put down the card and looked around the room. 'You should put up some Christmas decorations,' she said. 'We're well into December now. You used to have lights on the bushes in front of the house.'

'They stopped working last year,' Wisting answered.

'Buy some new ones, then,' Line suggested.

Rising from the table, she disappeared in the direction of

the room where the Christmas decorations were stored. Very soon she returned with a large cardboard box. The top of an Advent candle-holder was sticking out of the top.

'Shall I help you with them?' she asked.

Wisting shook his head. 'Just put the box down there,' he said, pointing at the worktop.

Setting it down, Line took out the candelabra. She dusted it off and placed it in the kitchen window.

'Would you like to eat with us tonight?' she asked as she sat down again. 'It'll be some kind of casserole. I'll go shopping with Amalie.'

'Yes, please,' Wisting replied.

'She'd like an iPad for Christmas,' Line went on.

'Is she getting one?'

'Not from me,' Line said.

Wisting drew his own iPad across the table and located the photo of Astria. She and Line were not far apart in age.

'Can you see who this is?' he asked.

Taking the iPad, Line looked at the picture and enlarged it. 'Should I know her?' she asked.

'It was taken in Stavern,' Wisting told her.

'I can see that,' Line replied, but ended by shaking her head. 'It could be anyone at all,' she concluded. 'What's it about?'

Wisting took a gulp of coffee. It was far too complicated to start explaining. 'Probably nothing at all,' he answered.

Line handed him the iPad but did not let go. 'There *is* something,' she said.

'I don't know yet,' Wisting told her. 'I've received some kind of missing-person report.'

'What does "some kind of missing-person report" mean?'

Wisting was unsure how to explain it to her. 'She's gone missing from the Internet,' he said, going on to describe what it was all about.

20

Line put her hand to her face, the way she usually did when she grew pensive. 'What are you doing about it?' she asked.

'There's not much I can do,' Wisting replied.

His daughter sat back in her chair. 'Many people these days live the better part of their lives online,' she said. 'That's where they hang out, where they work and meet other people. I'm sure you'd launch an investigation if an employer was worried about an employee who'd been absent from work for a week.'

'That's different,' Wisting told her.

Line drank her coffee and shook her head. 'Not really,' she insisted.

'The problem is that nobody knows who she is,' Wisting said. 'Anyway, I've done some investigating. I can't find anything to confirm that she's gone missing.'

'So you think something may have happened to her?' Line asked.

Wisting shifted in his seat. 'To be honest, I'd like to know who she is,' he said.

'Have you gone into the case and taken a look?' Line demanded.

'What case?'

'The Spanish murder case.'

He shook his head. 'You have to be logged in,' he explained, 'with a username and a password.'

'Can't you do that?'

'Sure,' he replied. 'But I don't need to do that.'

'But isn't that how you investigate missing-person cases?' Line asked. 'Visit the last-known whereabouts and talk to the people she last had contact with?'

He laughed it off. 'This isn't a criminal case,' he said.

Line stood up. 'Not yet' was her parting shot.

6

Wisting ended up buying both outdoor Christmas tree lights and an iPad for Amalie. He had no idea what else he could get her. It was expensive, but she was the only grandchild he had. While he waited to pay, he tried to remember what Line and her twin brother had received at Christmas when they were little. He recalled the Christmas celebrations but not what lay beneath the tree. Ingrid had been the one who had taken care of everything, both the decorating and the preparation of food. The Christmas presents were usually bought by the beginning of December.

He hummed a Christmas carol he had heard in the car as he decorated the small tree in front of the house. The youngsters who had recently moved into the neighbourhood were out playing in the snow. They had propped a ladder against the wall and were diving down into the snow.

All of a sudden, Amalie appeared. 'Have you come to help me?' he asked.

'Yes, let me do that,' Amalie replied.

Handing the string of lights to his granddaughter, he helped her reach the top branches.

'Have you said hello to our new neighbours?' he asked when they heard a gleeful shout from their game.

Amalie shook her head.

'You'll have to get to know them,' Wisting suggested.

'I will,' Amalie promised before launching into something completely different.

She told him about everything she had done since the

snow came. They had built a snowman at nursery and gone sledging and skating.

When the bulbs were lit, they walked across to Line's for dinner. Afterwards, Amalie disappeared with a bowl of crisps to a seat in front of the TV while Wisting helped Line clear the table.

'Have you taken a look at that Spanish murder case yet?' Line asked.

Wisting shook his head. Astria and her story had filled his thoughts throughout the day, but he had not yet ventured on to the website. He was not entirely sure how to respond to the whole idea. It gave the impression of being something occupying a grey zone, somewhere between police and press work. A zone in which random private citizens stepped into the police arena with the ambition of tackling cases the police were unable to crack.

Line put her laptop on the table and flipped open the lid. She quickly searched for the page about Ruby Thompson's murder and clicked on the button to join the web community.

She entered *Darby* in the space for her username. 'That's from a film,' she said before he had a chance to ask.

Wisting formed the impression that this was an alias she used on other Internet sites.

Line set up a personal password and moved on. Before she gained entry to the forum, she had to give her year of birth and nationality. In addition, there was a blank field where she was invited to say why she was interested in the case and what qualifications she had that meant she might have something to contribute. Line stated that she had a general interest in unsolved crimes. In principle, she could have written anything at all. She was completely anonymous and no one could check the information she entered.

In the end she was asked to upload a photograph. Line

chose an image of a snowman that Amalie had built with the friend she had stayed with.

On the main page, a counter in the top-right-hand corner showed how many days had elapsed since Ruby Thompson was killed. It now read 238.

Michelle Norris introduced herself as the site's host, but had shuffled the initial letters of her name so that she appeared as Nichelle Morris, with the username Nichelle. She described her friendship with Ruby Thompson and related how Ruby had saved up to travel on a dream trip to Europe. The final destination on her journey had been Scandinavia. One month after she had left Australia, the dream had come to a brutal end.

Her profile photo showed a young, red-haired woman with greenish eyes.

The website itself was divided into two sections. One part was purely a discussion forum in which diverse theories were presented and discussed and the various leads considered. The other part homed in on the ongoing investigation and was divided into an assortment of projects. Many of the project names did not tell her much. These were names of individuals, restaurants or other locations, while some of the projects appeared to relate to CCTV footage and witness observations. Each project had a named person in charge. Astria had set up a photographic project, which involved gathering all the photos taken in Palamós in the twenty-four-hour period prior to Ruby Thompson being found dead. The idea was that Ruby and her killer could be depicted in one of them. The collection was part of the work on charting her last movements.

The project seemed to have started by collecting all the photos already available on social media, with the photo-sharing platform Instagram as the main source. An inbuilt function meant that the photos were automatically marked with their geographical location. Astria had made contact with people who had posted these pictures. She had explained about the murder case and asked for original photos as well as pictures that had not been published online and had asked if they knew of anyone else who had taken photographs. Almost every single person she had asked, without exception, knew of others who also had photos. This had led to exponential growth in the amount of material collected. The project folder had not been updated for the past ten days, but already included nearly 2,000 images.

The pictures were sorted in chronological order according to the time they had been taken and marked with a street or place name. Everything had been entered into a database in which selected photos could be arranged in sequence in a timeline or placed geographically on a map. Wisting had to admit he was impressed. It was always a challenge to manage a steadily increasing volume of information and difficult to organize it in a way that was easy to follow.

Line was the one who navigated around the website, bringing up a separate list of images in which Ruby Thompson had been identified, a total of sixteen from the last day of her life. With a single keystroke, these were transferred on to a town map. Most of the pictures had been taken on the beach between one and two o'clock that day. Some kind of event had taken place, with hundreds of people running out into the water at the same time. Ruby Thompson was pictured among the spectators. Wisting recognized her from the newspaper report, but her name also popped up in a text box when Line ran the cursor over the image. She was wearing a loose-fitting pair of cotton trousers, an open khaki shirt with a T-shirt underneath and had an ochre-yellow knitted hat on her head. Beside her was a man of around the same age with tousled shoulder-length hair and a takeaway coffee cup in one hand. *Jarod Denham*, according to the text box that appeared across his chest.

'Who's that?' Line asked.

'No idea,' Wisting replied. 'She met an Englishman and travelled with him. He was charged and jailed but later released. It could be him.'

Ruby Thompson was pictured in a total of seven photos taken at the event on the beach, in four different settings. Probably taken by four different photographers. Three of the images had been taken from a distance and it was the yellow beanie hat that made it possible to recognize her. In one of the pictures, a third person was identified: *Mathis Leroux*, a dark-skinned, athletic boy in his early twenties.

'Show me the timeline,' Wisting told her.

Sixteen miniature images were displayed in a series. The last of these was marked *Hotel Nauta* and had been taken at 19.46. Line clicked on it. The photo had been taken by an outdoor CCTV camera mounted somewhere fairly high and filmed at an angle looking down on the street. The quality was good, with high image resolution. Ruby Thompson was wearing the same yellow beanie and clothes as earlier that day. Walking on her own along the pavement, she had a white cable attached to each ear. Her head was raised and turned a little to one side, as if looking up at something in the high-rise buildings that lined the street.

Wisting pointed at the previous image in the series. *Catalonia Pizza – 19.42*. This was from a surveillance camera behind a bar counter. Ruby Thompson was making her way out of a door on the opposite side of the premises with a bag slung over one shoulder and the distinctive hat on her head.

'Looks as if she's on her own,' Line commented.

She returned to the timeline and opened the picture taken almost an hour earlier in the same segment. Ruby Thompson was pictured in the same doorway and the image from the CCTV footage was frozen mid-movement. Her face lit up as if she had seen someone she knew further inside the restaurant.

'When was she killed?' Line asked.

'I don't know,' Wisting replied. 'She was found on the beach around half past eight the next morning.'

Line moved back through the timeline to a photograph taken from a car's dash camera. Ruby Thompson was strolling on her own along the pavement. Before that, there was a picture of an unknown woman, smiling at the camera, beside a pram in a marina. Behind her, Ruby Thompson was walking past with two boys. Jarod Denham and Mathis Leroux. There was also a photo from a mobile coffee kiosk in which Ruby was caught in the background. After that, they were back to the pictures from the event on the beach.

'She's most likely also in some of the pictures,' Line said. 'I mean Astria. After all, she was there at Easter. There are sixteen images of Ruby Thompson. If Astria was out and about that day, it would be odd if she didn't appear by chance in some of these pictures.'

Wisting nodded. 'Probably,' he said, his eye moving from one face to another on the computer screen. 'The killer too,' he added thoughtfully.

7

Username: Nichelle

Michelle Norris drew her chair up to the desk. The fifteen-inch screen in front of her was an open window on the rest of the world. There was always someone out in the ether with special skills or access to information she was seeking.

Between two and five o'clock at night, when it was afternoon in Europe, was the most active time in the forum. This suited the job she had – the bar closed at one a.m., but she was seldom home before two.

Seven other users were online. Regulus, Effie P., MrsPeabody, Opala, Kenzie, Shelook and ApopheniaX.

ApopheniaX was the only one of these who had contributed information, but Michelle was unsure how to deal with what he had come up with. Meanwhile, she had not commented on any of his posts. Plenty of others had. His theories shifted the entire project in a different direction, towards something far more extensive and larger in scope, pointing towards a perpetrator who had killed before and would do so again. Michelle was opposed to that idea as it pushed the focus away from Ruby, turning her into nothing more than a number in a long series.

She had heard nothing further from the Norwegian policeman and he had not enrolled in the forum either. Only one new member had joined since she last logged in: Darby.

She was Norwegian but did not give much more information about herself than that.

Michelle frowned, wondering if there could be a connection. The only other Norwegian member was Astria. Twenty-four hours after she had made contact with the police in Norway, another Norwegian member had appeared in the forum.

It must be a coincidence, she decided.

The policeman who had answered her message had seemed trustworthy. She had looked up his name and obtained numerous hits in the coverage of murder cases and other serious crimes. In several of the photos he had been pictured behind a row of microphones. His gaze was steady and authoritative but at the same time contained a certain warmth. The crop of wrinkles at the corners of his eyes softened his rugged face.

A number of the pictures she had seen were from old cases. The facial features were more prominent in the recent photographs. The lines had deepened over the years, as if marked by every single tough decision he had taken in his life.

William Wisting.

It surprised her that she had received any reply at all to her imprecise email, even more so that he had followed up with questions and supplementary information in his response.

Someone padded across the floor on the storey above. Michelle stood up and walked to the balcony door. She needed a cigarette before she turned in for the night.

The heat had begun to release its grip and the air was now cool.

She lit her cigarette, thinking of Ruby as she took the first drag. Two days before New Year's Eve, she would have turned twenty-six.

The noise of the city around her rose and fell. Somewhere in the distance, music was playing. Fast rhythms, but too far away for her to identify the tune. In a street further off, she could see the flickering red and blue lights of an emergency vehicle. It accelerated away without using the siren.

She leaned over the railings. Twenty metres below, she could see a man with a dog on a lead, doing its business on a patch of grass. The man looked around before moving off without picking up after it.

Turning around, she peered in through the balcony door, towards the computer screen.

The Catalan investigators must be aware of the details ApopheniaX had posted. She was unimpressed by the work they had done so far, but they must have systems in place to note similarities in the same way that ApopheniaX had done.

Taking another drag of her cigarette, she pinched the end and tossed it over the railings.

When she sat down in front of the machine again, ApopheniaX had logged off without posting anything new. He was a mathematics lecturer at the university in Barcelona but had not given any motive for becoming involved.

His first post had been about another murdered woman in Palamós, a twelve-year-old case in which there were some similarities. The same age, both backpackers, strangled, found on the beach, in a state of undress. However, that did not necessarily mean it had been the same perpetrator.

The police had arrested Jarod Denham for Ruby's murder but had been compelled to let him go when the DNA analysis had arrived. In the twelve-year-old crime, there were no biological traces as the body had spent too long in the sea.

Jarod had a user profile too. He called himself Jade. She knew this because she had invited him in and he had uploaded many of the police reports from the case against him. His nickname was composed of the initial two letters of his first and second names. Jade. She did not think anyone else in the forum had twigged that. One discussion thread presupposed that he was guilty anyway, despite the police releasing him from custody. The theory was that the DNA traces found on Ruby had come from contact with another boy and Jarod had lost his temper when he discovered she was going with other men.

It could well be that Ruby had found a new boyfriend. Always keen to move on, to meet different, new people, she was not meant for long-term relationships. In their chat, Ruby had told her she had slept with Jarod on the night she met him and this was not the first time she had had sex with a casual acquaintance. The boys often wanted more than she did. This was one of the reasons she had been keen to go away and travel for a year. She wanted to leave behind all the complications.

Jarod did not comment on any of the posts himself, but when the discussion became most heated, she had sometimes found it necessary to intervene in the discussion thread and remind them that Jarod had an alibi for the evening of the murder. He had FaceTimed with friends at home in London and been active on the Internet. The counterargument was that the Catalan pathologists had fixed the time of death as somewhere between 10 p.m. and 2 a.m. After midnight, all the police had was Jarod's own word for it that he had been in bed.

If the crime had not been committed by a random attacker, other names were of more interest. One was the son of the couple who ran the campsite where Ruby had been staying. Another was Leo Pérez at the beach bar, and then there was Olaf, the Norwegian from whom Ruby and the others had bought marijuana.

She had been working on the case for three months now and felt she had a good grasp of the details, but she was still unable to piece together all the fragments of information to form a picture of what had happened to Ruby. Much of it was striking and suspicious and there were countless rumours swirling around. It was difficult to distinguish between speculation and what was actually of significance for the case and could point to a specific solution, in the way trained investigators did.

8

Username: Darby

Wisting was sitting in his office on the first floor, in front of his computer. He had closed the door behind him, even though he was alone in the building.

Line had sent him log-in information for the Internet forum even though he had not asked her for this. No explanation or any further details. When it was time for him to go home after dinner, Astria and the Spanish homicide case had not been a topic of conversation. They had chatted about the weather and the planned Christmas lunch with her grandfather on Sunday. However, the case had been on his mind when he arrived home.

Inside the website was a world of its own. The digital conversations covered not only the murder case but also everyday matters. The users wrote about what they had done since the last time they had logged on, about their jobs and about the weather wherever they were located. One had baked a cake and shared a link with the recipe; another needed advice for dealing with a rash and had an ointment recommended. New members were welcomed in a friendly manner. It resembled a workplace where people not only talked about their jobs but also developed social relationships. It seemed as if they all knew one another even though no one really knew who lay behind the anonymous usernames. In fact, Astria had no need to be who she claimed to be.

One of the project folders on the website contained police

reports. This was unfortunate and almost certainly illegal, in Spain and Australia as well as in Norway, or whatever country the website was registered in. The murder of Ruby Thompson was still an open case and publishing police reports could give the perpetrator access to crucial intelligence.

The documents had been translated into English, probably because Ruby's English travelling companion had been charged. It was most likely through him that the documents had ended up on the forum.

He began with the report from the discovery site. She had been found on the beach in the town, part of the same beach where she had been pictured at the local event the previous day. The discovery of the body was initially reported as a drowning accident, but the police patrol that had arrived on the scene had been quick to call out the forensic technicians. The body had been only partially clothed, wearing nothing but a blue sweater with a black T-shirt underneath. She had several cuts and lacerations in addition to unmistakable bruises around her neck. The cuts were attributed to injuries sustained after she had been thrown into the sea, probably from the rocks further north along the coast. The autopsy concluded that strangulation had been the cause of death. There was no mention of rape, but it was stated that the victim could have had sex in the course of the forty-eight hours prior to her death.

Wisting had not read much of this before he rose from his desk and picked up some paper to make notes.

Ruby Thompson was originally listed as an unidentified victim. The story was reported in the media and the owner of the campsite where she had been staying had alerted them to a possible identification. By then three days had elapsed without anyone having seen her. Her Australian passport was still in the bungalow she rented, and she was first identified from her photo. Later, this was confirmed with the help of DNA from her toothbrush and finally from a family member in her homeland.

It was slightly difficult to understand why Jarod Denham had been charged, but it emerged that he had suspected Ruby of stealing money and marijuana from him. He had told two surfers he was going to confront her with this that same evening.

Wisting nodded as if confirming a suspicion. Investigators always looked for inconsistencies. Experience suggested that a violent incident often stemmed from a conflict involving deceit or similar provocation, arousing a passionate response.

Jarod had failed to mention these suspicions of theft in his first interview but had confirmed it when confronted with what the surfers had said. However, he claimed he hadn't had an opportunity to take this up with Ruby, as she hadn't returned to the campsite by the time he went to bed.

During an official search, a bag of marijuana was found under Ruby's mattress. Jarod's fingerprints were on it, but this corroboration of his suspicions had little evidential value.

In the bungalow, a number of items that did not belong to Ruby also turned up, articles that had been stolen from tents and other camping cabins.

He clicked on further, reading statements by people she had met in the days when she was staying in Palamós and jotting down names, places, times and key words. He drew lines of connection, underlined what he felt might be important, and circled things that remained unexplained. This was what he had been trained to do. It had been his job for more than thirty years – absorbing all the component parts of a case. Sorting, understanding and digesting information.

Outside, it had started to snow again. The flakes fell

through the darkness, becoming visible in the yellow glow of the streetlights.

Wisting got to his feet, fetched himself something to drink and sat down at the screen again.

It was primarily the statements from Jarod Denham and Mathis Leroux that sketched a picture of Ruby Thompson's movements on the day she was killed. Jarod had met Ruby in a French coastal town ten days earlier and they had travelled together across the border into Spain. Neither had been to Palamós before, but the beaches there had been recommended to them by Dutch surfers heading in the opposite direction.

They arrived by bus on the afternoon of 8 April and found their way to the campsite the Dutch surfers had used. It was off-season, and they had each been allocated a cheap room in a bungalow beside the beach. Jarod had suggested they could save money by sharing a room, but Ruby wanted a room to herself. Fairly soon they had got to know a boy from Paris of the same age, Mathis Leroux. The day before Ruby was found dead, the three of them spent most of the time together. They had slept in after a late night. The waves were bad, so none of them had ventured into the water. As Mathis had heard about an event on the town beach to mark the start of the swimming season, they spent a few hours there and at the harbour before going their separate ways, but they had agreed to meet up again at a pizzeria around six p.m. Ruby had turned up half an hour late and left on her own an hour later. She did not say anything about where she was going.

Mathis Leroux's statement agreed with Jarod Denham's, but he also said that Ruby had seemed cold and dismissive towards Jarod, as if something had come between them.

These statements were supported by the photos he had seen at Line's house. The images from the CCTV camera at the pizza bar were included in the police material. Astria must have collected them from there and inserted them into her timeline.

In the police documents, the photo from the bar was presented as the last definite observation of her, but on Astria's timeline there was also a photo taken four minutes later.

He clicked on the map on which the photos were plotted geographically. The last image was taken outside the Hotel Nauta, two blocks away from the pizzeria. Ruby was walking on her own along the pavement and the white cables showed she had earplugs in.

In cases such as this one with Ruby Thompson, the last observation was always pivotal, the starting point for finding other witnesses and clarifying the direction she had taken when she met her fate.

The final secure observation of Ruby Thompson was at 19.46. According to the post-mortem report, that was at least two and a half hours before she was killed.

Wisting tried to find information about her phone. Where it had been and who she had last been in touch with. From the police reports, it emerged that she owned two mobile phones, one with an Australian number and another with an unregistered subscription. The Australian phone was left behind in the bungalow and looked as if it was only used for data. Her surfer friends had a Spanish phone number for her. It was last used at 18.17, when she had replied to a message from Jarod, who had been waiting at the pizzeria. This phone had not been found and had been disconnected completely from the Spanish telecoms network at 20.02. It had either been switched off or had run out of battery. This was only twenty minutes after she had left Mathis Leroux and Jarod Denham at the Catalonia pizza bar.

Wisting straightened up in his seat and reminded himself that this inquiry of his was not actually focused on Ruby

Thompson. He had logged on to try to find out more about Astria. Who she was and why she had vanished from the Internet.

The last message from her was posted as a reply to a question in the discussion thread about the photo project.

MrsPeabody: Have you found more photographs?

Astria: Have collected 97 photos that have not been posted yet.
  Coming soon.

Then almost twenty-four hours had passed before another user followed this up.

Ned B.: Are there photos of Ruby there?

Astria: Need a bit more time, but think I've found something
  interesting.

This response was posted on 30 November at 21.37. That was nine days ago.

The user who asked this question called himself Ned B. Wisting delved into his profile and found that he had not been active for eight days. He claimed to be a nineteen-year-old criminology student from Madrid.

Others had linked up to the thread and asked when the new pictures were coming and what she had found out, but no one had received an answer. The last person to have contact with Astria was the man with the pseudonym Ned B. At the same time, the conversation was there, open for all to see. *Think I've found something interesting* was the last comment she had made.

Wisting stood up. It was now past midnight and it was still snowing heavily outside.

9

'Are you not getting much sleep?'

Wisting glanced up at his father. 'Hmm?' he asked.

'You look tired,' his father said. 'Out of sorts.'

Wisting senior had invited them to the Sunday buffet at the hotel in Stavern. They had been there once before at the tail end of summer, but apart from that they had not had a family gathering for a while.

'I stayed up a bit too late on the Internet last night,' Wisting replied. 'Afterwards it took me a while to drop off.'

His father nodded. 'It's better to read a book,' he advised, pushing prawn shells on to a side plate. 'The blue light on the screen prevents you from falling asleep. It disturbs the body's production of melatonin. That's why teenagers are so listless. Their sleep quality is badly affected.'

Wisting senior had worked as a GP. He had retired twenty years ago now, but he kept up to date. Screen use and sleep disturbance must have been something he had read up on in one of the magazines to which he subscribed.

'Both physical dexterity and creative problem solving are improved by long, continuous sleep,' his father went on. 'And of course, that's important for you. Creative problem solving.'

Wisting agreed with him even though it had been his thoughts rather than his computer use that had kept him awake long after he had gone to bed.

Line and Amalie were also seated at the table. Amalie had found some sausages and mashed potato, while Line had helped herself to a portion of fish.

'You're supposed to eat the cold food first,' she said, taking a look at Wisting's plate. 'It takes up less space in your stomach.'

Wisting shrugged.

'I've tried to tell him that,' Wisting senior said. 'Eat right and sleep well.'

'Ketchup,' Amalie requested.

Line got up and brought back a bottle.

Apart from her brother, Thomas, who was absent, the whole family was gathered. There were no more of them. This was how they would sit together at Christmas too, in the living room of Wisting's home.

Amalie went straight from her sausages to dessert. Her great-grandfather leaned across the table and gave her a serious look.

'Well, Ingrid Amalie,' he said. He always used both her names. 'What would you really like for Christmas?'

The answer came in double-quick time: 'An iPad.'

'One of these computer screens?' he asked.

Amalie nodded eagerly.

'Me too,' said her great-grandfather solemnly. 'I'd like the Internet.'

Amalie glanced at her mother, as if unsure whether her great-grandfather was joking.

'Do you really mean that?' Line asked. 'Were you thinking of going on the Internet?'

'That's where everything happens these days, isn't it?' her grandfather replied. 'I can't even check my pension without computer access. They've stopped sending out the pay slips. And I'm charged a fee on my bills because I have them sent through the post and don't have an online bank account. The news is old by the time I read it in the paper. And when they're discussing something interesting on TV, they tell me

40

I can read more about it online, www dot something or other. Or Facebook. Everything's going on there.'

Wisting was sceptical. His father had used computers at work and used to have one at home, but that had been a long time ago. He belonged to the generation that had been left out when society became increasingly digitized, but he had never regarded that as a loss.

'The Internet has obviously come to stay,' Wisting senior added. 'For good or ill. So it's about time I joined the World Wide Web too.'

'I've already bought my Christmas presents,' Line said. 'For both of you.'

Wisting gazed at his father. He had a few friends who dropped in from time to time, but spent lengthy spells on his own. Weeks could pass without Wisting making contact, apart from the occasional brief phone conversation. Line saw him more often than he did. The Internet might well fill a void and ease Wisting's guilty conscience about his own busy lifestyle.

'You'd have to go on a course,' he pointed out.

'They have one at the adult education association,' his father replied. 'I've picked up a brochure. It starts in January.'

Wisting smiled. 'Excellent,' he said, pushing out his chair to go for some dessert. 'Then you shall have the Internet.'

10

Username: Shelook

The window in the small room had been left open all day. Celia threw her bag down on the bed, found a blanket and slung it around her shoulders before closing the window and sitting down in front of her computer.

Astria had still not answered her question. No one else had heard from her either. In fact, Nichelle had posted her missing.

Astria's timeline comprised still images, but several of these had been taken from CCTV footage. Celia wanted to look at them to compare the movements with her own recordings.

She opened the computer file and played the first sequence. In full HD, the film was of far better quality than the images from the pizzeria in Palamós.

The figure appeared in the twilight on the right of the picture and must have entered the garden through a gap in the hedge. Whoever it was wore a thin, grey hoodie with the hood up, ankle-length leggings and trainers. They approached the first window and peered in, moved on to the verandah door and tried the handle before walking to the other side of the house, where there was no outdoor surveillance camera.

The alarm was triggered three minutes later. Celia had been working on the switchboard when the images popped on her screen. The alarm company had almost 70,000 subscribers in her area alone, but all the same it was rare for any of the operators to witness a live break-in. Most of the alerts were false alarms, triggered by mistake by one of the residents being forgetful. And not everyone had the comprehensive alarm package with full CCTV coverage.

She had challenged the housebreaker through the call function, making it known that the person in question was being filmed and the police had been notified. This had not produced any reaction. Through the various cameras, she could see the intruder moving quickly from room to room, taking a glass full of coins from a shelf in the kitchen, a tablet computer from the coffee table in the living room and a few bottles of alcohol from a shelf.

The entire burglary took less than a minute. The security guard she had dispatched had arrived eleven minutes later, while it took another seven minutes for the police to show up.

Celia turned away from the screen and glanced up at the door. She could hear her mother and brother quarrelling in the living room. She was about to get up from her chair to ask them to tone it down but instead tucked her legs under and concentrated on what she was doing. She would have to put up with it for a while longer. Soon she would move out and enrol at the Police College in Barcelona. She wanted to be a detective. It would be a long road to achieve that, first with basic courses and practical work, but the past few months had made her even more certain that this was the right choice for her and something she would excel at. In the description of criminal investigation studies at the college, it stated that they were looking for recruits who were methodical, logical thinkers, able to spot connections.

It was more or less by chance that she had taken an interest in the case of the Australian girl who had been murdered in Palamós. However, nothing was sheer chance. All things

43

were interrelated. Her link to the unsolved murder was her cousin Leo. He lived in Palamós and worked at a beach bar beside the campsite where Ruby Thompson had been staying at the time of her death. Aunt Arlet had told her he had been interviewed a number of times by the police.

On looking up the case, she had stumbled upon the investigative forum. All the intelligence on the crime was there, including the interviews with her cousin Leo.

Leo was one year older than her and it was a long time since they had had any contact. Some of her childhood memories involved playing in his room. He had shown her his willy and wanted to see her naked. She had let him pull down her underpants and had not protested when he touched her. This had been repeated and had gradually escalated, continuing into puberty, when she had finally done everything in her power to avoid him. Eventually Leo had found himself a girlfriend, but that had not lasted long. When they attended senior high school, she heard stories about parties where he had tried it on with girls who were drunk and fast asleep. This was something she had never spoken of to her mother, but there had been rumours of a police investigation. She had never heard of any legal action taken, but around this time he had moved to Palamós.

However, she found it impossible to believe he had anything to do with the murder of Ruby Thompson.

To begin with, it was strange to read what he had said to the investigators. It felt invasive, as if encroaching on something not meant for her to see. Fairly rapidly, though, she had been able to distance herself from the personal elements and come closer to the case itself.

Her cousin Leo had met Ruby Thompson on the very first day she arrived in Palamós, when she had turned up at the beach bar. Hardly anyone had been there, and Ruby had arrived on her own. Unabashed, she had asked for a beer, claiming she had left her money in the bungalow she had just rented, and promising to pay him the next day. That one beer became three as they chatted and got to know each other.

The following day, she had turned up again and offered him the money she owed. At the same time, she had told him it was almost all she had. She was waiting for her father in Australia to transfer some money. At that point she had been with an English guy, who had paid for their food. Leo had said it was OK, that she did not need to pay for the beer.

They had eaten at the bar counter. The Englishman was called Jarod Denham. When he disappeared to the toilet, Ruby complained about him and said how clingy he was and that she had hoped to get rid of him when she moved on from a beach in France, but Jarod had insisted on travelling with her.

Gradually a picture emerged of how both Leo and Jarod Denham were being used by Ruby Thompson. She had served them up the same story about a father who had never bothered about her, and who did not send her money as he had promised. It could well be that the story was true, but both boys were lured into spending money on her. Leo calculated that his outlay had come to around 200 euros, much of it in the form of food and drink, for which he had not been paid back.

Leo had made some inquiries and discovered who Ruby's father was. Celia had also looked him up, finding his name mentioned when the Australian media reported the murder. He was a well-known businessman and multimillionaire.

The police reports stated that the surfboard found in Ruby's bungalow had been reported stolen. They also came across bank cards traced to a theft from a vehicle as well as computer equipment from two housebreaking incidents.

None of the owners were clients of Prosecure, but the information had given Celia the idea that Ruby could also have been behind other break-ins. On the night Ruby Thompson was killed, a total of three alarm call-outs had been logged in Palamós. There was no video footage from the other burglaries, but security guards had submitted reports on these incidents, all of which had taken place in the same neighbourhood; the modus operandi had been identical in all three locations. The perpetrator had gone in through a small window to a utility room or a storage cupboard. Money, alcohol and small electronic devices had been stolen before the intruder made an exit.

Celia looked at the video recording again, growing even more certain that the figure was female. A slim, slightly built woman who was able to enter through a utility-room window with a diameter of fifty centimetres. A woman such as Ruby Thompson.

Celia found the printouts of the security guards' reports. Another operator had responded to the first two alarm call-outs. The security guard sent out had been diverted to the residence, where the CCTV cameras had confirmed a break-in. The guard and the police did not visit the first two houses until after the owners had returned home and they could ascertain what had triggered the alarm.

The neighbourhood was 1,500 metres from where Ruby Thompson had last been spotted, in the direction she was headed. The final picture had been taken at 19.46 and the first alarm was set off at 20.07. Celia had used the Google Maps platform to follow the route. It took nineteen minutes.

She peered at the picture of Ruby Thompson and the bag slung over her shoulder. It did not figure in the images from the beach earlier that day but initially appeared in a photo from a dashcam immediately before Ruby entered the pizzeria.

If she had been the one to interview Jarod Denham and Mathis Leroux, she would have asked if they knew what she had in the bag. It was roomy enough to contain a change of clothes.

The murder of Ruby Thompson need not have been sexually motivated, as she had the impression everyone believed. At least, it did not say anywhere that she had been raped. It could have been a break-in gone wrong. A resident attacking an intruder.

She had spoken to Guillermo at the local office about it. He had been doubtful but agreed she should write a report and send it to the police. Afterwards she had heard nothing. Of course, the police must be aware of the same information that she had. It could even be that multiple break-ins had taken place that evening. Most places had alarms, and Prosecure served 80 per cent of the clients in the area, but not everyone activated the alarm when they went out. And a housebreaker usually moved on to the next-door neighbour when he saw that a house was equipped with an alarm. In fact, it was one of their selling points.

If only she could get in touch with Astria, she could point out the route Ruby Thompson must have taken from the last picture to the first break-in. She had studied the Google Street View images and found three CCTV cameras. The onscreen counter told her that 239 days had now elapsed since the murder, but the footage need not have been erased. The standard setting on the equipment Prosecure installed was for recordings to be controlled by the movement sensor, and these were not recorded over until the storage capacity was full. The same almost certainly applied to other kinds of equipment. In practice, she had experienced that the cache could last up to ten months, depending on the amount of activity within range of the camera.

47

Anyway, she had to persuade Astria to look for someone in dark sportswear instead of a yellow beanie.

In one sequence of the film, the intruder was pictured from the front. The hood was tied tightly around the face and the person depicted had a scarf wrapped over both mouth and nose. The image was good quality, but it was still impossible to use for purposes of identification. Not even someone who knew Ruby Thompson well would be able to say for certain whether she was the figure in the photo.

She could not post anything about what she knew in the forum. Even though she was anonymous, it would be a breach of the confidentiality clause she had signed. If it came out, it could cost her her job and her place at Police College.

A door slammed. Her brother had fled to his room.

Just as Celia rose to go to the kitchen for something to drink, a Facebook alert pinged on her screen. A message from one of her friends. The text box hovered for a few seconds before disappearing.

An idea struck her.

Maybe there was an underhand method of posting her suspicions on the forum. A roundabout way.

She sat down again and located the name of the client in the first security guard report. If she had been the one to experience the break-in, she would have told others about it.

Enzo Gael Arzate Sandoval was on Facebook, but the profile was private and only friends could see what he posted. The only part that was accessible was the profile picture and some obligatory details about work, education and domicile. And spouse.

Maria Silva de Sandoval's profile was public.

Celia scrolled down the screen, past the shared newspaper articles, birthday celebrations, family visits, special occasions, trips and other life events, both major and minor. Back to April.

There it was.

Three images from the CCTV footage. In capital letters, Maria Silva de Sandoval had given voice to her despair at what had happened to her.

The post was published the very next day, containing a description of what had occurred and a request for others to get in touch if they knew anything.

The first comments expressed shock and sympathy but changed to speculation about who could have been behind it. Eventually there was virtual agreement that it must have been immigrants from Africa.

One of the people who had made numerous comments was also able to say that there had been several break-ins in the area that same evening. There was also a link to a report in the local newspaper.

She was elated by this discovery. It was exactly what she needed.

Once she had downloaded the pictures, she hurriedly copied the text. Then she changed the screen image back to the crowdsolving page and posted her first contribution: *Thefts in Palamós*.

Username: Darby

Steam was wafting from the teacup. Line dipped the tea bag in and out a couple of times before leaving it to steep.

She had actually made up her mind not to visit the website about the Australian woman in Spain, knowing that once she started to read, she would linger and it would steal time she really could not spare. She ought to be working on the documentary script. Nevertheless, she went on sitting there.

The missing Norwegian user was more interesting than the murder case itself. The journalist in her sensed a story there. No matter what had happened, there would be an interesting tale to tell.

What primarily captured her interest, however, were the posts by ApopheniaX. He proposed the theory that the person who had killed Ruby Thompson was also behind seven other unsolved murders of women on the Mediterranean, along the northern coast of Spain. One of the victims had been found on the same beach as Ruby Thompson, twelve years earlier.

Line dropped two sweeteners into her cup and stirred the tea. She cocked her head towards Amalie's bedroom but could hear nothing. Probably she had fallen asleep.

The man who called himself ApopheniaX had drawn up a synopsis of every single case and posted pictures taken from newspaper reports. The female victims had all been found in the sea and were more or less unclothed. Two of them, just like Ruby Thompson, were dressed only on the upper body when they were discovered. Six of them had been strangled but, in the seventh case, drowning had been given as the cause of death. A comment was made to the effect that strangulation had been attempted and she had been unconscious when dumped in the sea. Another aspect the girls had in common was that they were all visitors, either from other towns or other countries. One was British, one German, one Belgian and one Swiss, in addition to three resident in Spain.

In a gallery, the portrait image of Ruby was included with the seven other victims, and the visual effect was striking. They all had short hair, though the colour varied, and the same build: slim, almost androgynous.

They had all disappeared in the hours of evening. In some cases, weeks had gone by before they were found; in others, only a few days. Ruby Thompson stood out from the rest in that fewer than twelve hours had elapsed. What they had in common was that they had only a loose connection to the location. They were travelling alone and had no relatives nearby to express concern and report them missing or who could give the investigators information about their habits, acquaintances or known disputes.

The oldest case was sixteen years previously, when Rachel Jenkins from Derby in England was found murdered on a pebble beach outside Benidorm. Four years later, German Bertine Franck was killed in Palamós, and after that a Span-ish girl was murdered in Barcelona. The intervals between the homicides were increasingly close, which several reports used to support the idea of a link between the murders, say-ing it was also likely that the perpetrator had a shorter and shorter cooling-off period before the urge to strike again. One of the questions asked was when he would make his next move. Eight months had already passed since Ruby Thompson had been killed, only ten months after the previous victim.

One of the users commented that Palamós was a geographical mid-point along the coastline where the serial killer had wreaked havoc and at the same time the only place where he had struck twice. This might suggest that he came from there.

Astria was one of the users who had commented on the theory. Line had to check the date and found it was only two days before she had fallen silent. She had wondered whether there was any DNA evidence that could be used to prove whether or not it was the same perpetrator. ApopheniaX referred to newspaper reports saying that the time the bodies had spent in saltwater made it difficult to find biological traces. In only one of the cases had a DNA profile been secured, but there was no information about where it had come from. This was in the murder of the Swiss girl, near the border with France four years earlier.

Speculation was rife about whether or not this profile had been compared to the evidence found on Ruby's body. No one seemed to know if the Catalan police had procedures for this kind of thing or if special measures were required.

Line knew that Spain had been a trailblazer in the use of DNA and that the forensics institute in Santiago de Compostela had the reputation of being world-leading in their practice. In the early noughties, the Norwegian police had used it to detect traces that Norwegian laboratories were unable to isolate. Later, admittedly, questions had been asked about their quality assurance procedures, but there was no reason to believe that Spain did not have a satisfactory DNA register and a system for searching among unsolved cases.

The discussion continued, and there was talk of having a

perpetrator profile drawn up. If the same man were also behind the sixteen-year-old murder of Rachel Jenkins in Benidorm, then he would have to be at least thirty-five, and mobile. Other clues were more difficult to pin down. What was needed in order to make progress with the idea of a serial killer was a name. A suspect whose movements could be tracked to see if they intersected with any of the various crime scenes.

Line read everything with more than a pinch of scepticism. Through her work as a journalist, she had delved into numerous criminal cases. To begin with she had allowed herself to get carried away with sensational theories, but gradually she had found they quickly fell apart. As soon as you started to check the details, these theories usually disintegrated.

She removed the tea bag and sipped her tea. It had gone cold and bitter while it had been left untouched.

Outside, the snow was plastered on the window. Line decided not to spend any more time on the case. Getting to her feet, she moved to the kitchen and poured her tea down the sink.

I 2

A snowplough was clearing the back yard of snow. Wisting peered up at the police station building as he waited for the opportunity to park. Nils Hammer's office was the only one in which a light was showing. Probably it had been left on over the weekend. At any rate, his car was not in the parking area.

Maren Dokken arrived on foot with snow in her hair. Finally managing to leave his car, Wisting accompanied her in. The newest employee in the department, she had become an important resource. Following the reorganization, there were not so many personnel left in the criminal investigation department. The forensic technicians were now concentrated in the north of the region, just as tactical investigators with special skills in different fields were organized into units in various locations throughout the district. The result was that Wisting and the other officers left in the department had ended up with mundane tasks, a wide spectrum of minor crimes, though not in the least mundane to the people who had fallen victim to them.

At eight a.m. they assembled in the large conference room, a gathering of investigators, office staff and officers from the patrol section. They continued with their daily meetings even though they were noticeably fewer in number. These morning sessions were a crucial arena for the exchange of knowledge.

Wisting led the meeting, picking out messages from the log covering their geographical area of responsibility, as well as a few incidents worth mentioning from other towns. None of the assignments had required any particular input or follow-up investigative resources. He ran through a selection of newly reported crimes, issued fresh instructions on the handling of impounded computer data, reported on some intelligence about a group of itinerant thieves from Eastern Europe and finally listed the planned assignments for the coming week.

They had one person in custody, he told them. Trond Brink Isaksen by name. He had been arrested after stealing from a building site in the town centre. The night patrol had followed his tracks in the snow through the town to a council house in Torstrand, where they had found the man and his loot from several break-ins. So far, they had traced the items to eight thefts committed in the past month. Most likely he was responsible for many more and his arrest would contribute to raising the clear-up rate by the end of the year.

Nils Hammer was in charge of that case. 'We're working on a list of all the stolen goods,' he said. 'He's been extremely active. I'm turning up instances all the way back to summer.'

Wisting nodded. The case was going to build into something big. He felt sure they would succeed in extending the custody period and achieving a considerable sentence. After the meeting, he would go across to the local authority headquarters and talk to people in the drug addiction team about setting up a future plan of action for Trond Brink Isaksen. Rehabilitation cost money and depended on municipal guarantees.

'Anyone have anything?' he rounded off in his usual way, running his gaze around the table.

Chair legs began to scrape against the floor. Wisting got to his feet and headed for the coffee machine on his way back to his office.

At the end of the day he would phone Ellinor Brink, but by then he would like to have some news to tell her.

For many years, the motivation in his job had lain in the thrill he derived from police work. Without warning, an ordinary working day could change direction. Quickly and unexpectedly, routine tasks could be interrupted by dramatic events. He had to face each and every day prepared for anything and everything. The desire for a varied profession with both physical and mental challenges had been what had led him at one time to apply to Police College. Since then he had not looked back and, despite everything he had encountered and all it had cost him, he had never regretted his choice in life. The unpredictability meant he still looked forward to every working day with pleasure. However, as the years had gone by, aspects other than excitement were what had become important to him. He had always thought of the expression 'to make a difference' as achieving something extraordinary, but experience had taught him it was often the small things that were meaningful to the people around him. Helping where he could was something that had become important to him. He may have inherited this from his father, who always said that helping was good for the heart, meaning that helpful people were happier than those who were content with looking after themselves.

His working day progressed towards its close with no out-of-the-ordinary interruptions. Wisting had returned from his meeting with the local authority drug addiction team without securing any guarantees: Ellinor's son had reached an age when younger drug addicts were given first priority. After all, Trond Brink Isaksen had had his chance. He had been given treatment but had not completed the course.

He stopped outside Hammer's office. The police radio on his desk was crackling, something about a road traffic accident. His radio was always switched on, scanning through the various frequencies.

Maren Dokken was sitting in the visitor's chair with her laptop on her knee. Scattered on the floor were labelled items that had been taken from Trond Brink Isaksen's apartment. Mobile phones, cameras, tablet computers, larger computers and other electronic devices.

'Made any progress?' Wisting asked.

'I'm sure all this is stolen,' Hammer replied. 'But it's not so easy to find out where it all came from.'

He lifted up a games console.

'Very few people give a serial number for what they've had stolen,' he explained. 'Now I'm phoning round everybody who reported the theft of a PlayStation to get some information, but people are not really interested in helping. They've had a settlement from the insurance company and bought a new one. They don't want old, used equipment back.'

'It's different with cameras, though,' Maren said. 'People like to get their photos back.'

There were four cameras on the floor, all with telephoto lenses.

'I thought everybody used their mobiles these days,' Wisting commented.

'That's probably why he hasn't managed to sell them on,' Hammer said.

'This is professional gear, though,' Maren interjected, nodding at the cameras on the floor. 'But they're not marked with a name or anything. I have to look at the pictures to try to find the owners.'

She lifted a camera bag from the floor in front of her.

'This one was stolen from a boat in the marina in Stavern last summer,' she said. 'I found the owner by looking up the registration number of the boat. It featured in a number of the photos.'

She turned her laptop screen towards him and showed him an image of a rain-soaked man tying up a cabin cruiser at the jetty in Stavern.

Wisting showed some interest. 'When was that picture taken?' he asked.

The police radio crackled again. A patrol had received a message to take a look at an abandoned vehicle at a bus stop near Manvik. Hammer switched it off.

'The last photo on the memory card was taken on 25 July,' Maren replied. 'The date and time are on the image file. The camera was stolen that same day. I've found the report.'

'Can I have a look at the other photos?' Wisting asked.

'I don't have them all here,' Maren answered, nodding towards her laptop. 'They're on the memory card.'

'Could you transfer them to a folder on the media server, so that I can have access, please?'

Maren nodded. 'What's on your mind?' she asked.

Wisting cast a glance at the cameras on the floor. 'Were all of these stolen last summer?' he asked.

'We haven't checked them all yet,' Hammer replied.

'Give me all the pictures you find,' Wisting said.

'OK,' Maren agreed. 'I just have to finish something here first . . . what do you want with them?'

'Come into my office when they're ready and I'll explain,' Wisting said before dashing back to his own domain.

13

Astria's picture brought back last summer as Wisting remembered it: bleak and rainy. The visitor berths behind her in the photograph were crammed with boats that had sought shelter from the foul weather. He looked for the cabin cruiser from the image on Maren's laptop, but it was nowhere to be seen.

He studied the other boats. The contours and contrasts grew indistinct when he enlarged the picture too much. Through trial and error, he found the best focus setting.

Behind Astria, the closest boat was a fibreglass vessel of around twenty-four foot, from the seventies. The ID number was located high on the side lantern: *A-19091*.

After looking it up in the boat register, he jotted down the phone number of the owner, who lived in Nesodden.

Further out along the jetty, he spotted a larger boat. *Absolute 42* was the name he could see on its side. The number on the prow was difficult to make out. What looked like a seven could also be a two. The same applied to three and five. Wisting ended up with nine possible combinations of numbers and looked up each one of these before coming up with a result for a forty-two-foot Absolute cabin cruiser. The owner was from Flekkefjord.

None of the other ten or so boats in the marina had visible registration numbers, but a yacht on its way in had not yet sailed all the way down. The sail number was legible: *NOR9692*. This boat was from Kragerø.

That gave him a list of three names, all people who had

been in Stavern on the day Astria's profile picture had been taken.

He began with the yacht he had seen entering the marina. This could well give him a date for when Astria's photo had been taken.

The owner turned out to be a thirty-two-year-old woman from Kragerø. Wisting introduced himself and received confirmation in turn that she was the owner of an old twenty-two-foot Junker and that they had been visiting friends in Stavern. She told him they had arrived there on Monday 24 July but had been out sailing almost every day.

'What's this about?' she asked.

'We're investigating a series of thefts from the marina and another incident there last summer,' Wisting replied without giving further details. 'How long were you berthed in Stavern?'

The woman had to give this some thought but reached the conclusion that they had sailed onwards on Saturday 29 July.

'But we didn't see or hear anything about any thefts,' she added.

'Did you take any photos while you were here?' Wisting asked.

'Loads.'

'Could you possibly send them to me?'

'I'm sure I could, but I can't really comprehend what you're looking for.' The voice of the woman on the phone had taken on a sceptical tone. 'What sort of incident are you talking about?' she asked.

Wisting understood her reaction and realized he would have to elaborate in order to obtain what he was looking for.

'It has to do with a slightly unusual missing-person case,' he said.

'But this all happened last summer, didn't it?' the woman objected. 'It was almost six months ago.'

'I can't go into details,' Wisting said apologetically. 'But we'd like to look at all the photos you have of Stavern marina from the last week of July.'

Finally, the woman accepted this explanation and agreed to send the images.

Next on the list was the man with the fibreglass boat. The conversation ran on similar lines. Wisting learned they had come to Stavern on Tuesday 25 July and moved on to Strømstad in Sweden three days later. He was more doubtful about sharing photographs but promised to see what he could find.

The third person was a fifty-four-year-old man from Flekkefjord. He and his family had been in Stavern from 21 to 27 July. They had already posted a lavish selection of pictures on Facebook, but he promised to collect some more.

These three boats had been in Stavern in overlapping periods near the end of July.

Wisting had written down the dates in question:

25 26 27 28
21 22 23 24 25 26 27
24 25 26 27 28 29

This gave three possible days – Astria's photo had been taken on 25, 26 or 27 July.

In the background, the passenger ferry was making its way out of the sound.

He looked up the webpage on which the timetables were listed. Daily departures from the Dampskipsbrygga in Stavern, from which the island-hopping tourist ferries depart in the summer season, were at 10 a.m. and 2 p.m.

If the skies had been clear and sunny, they could have told

him something about what time the photo had been taken, but since the yacht was making its way into harbour, it was most likely to be afternoon.

Maren Dokken appeared at the door while he sat staring at his notes.

'I've transferred the images to the media server,' she said, giving him the name of the folder he would have to search for. 'What do you want with them?'

Wisting hesitated. It had seemed like a good idea when the thought had first crossed his mind, but now it felt a bit far-fetched. 'I was going to look for her,' he answered, pointing at the screen.

Maren sat down. 'Who's that?' she asked.

'I don't know,' he replied, going on to tell her about the approach from Michelle Norris in Australia. 'The idea is to find a picture of a woman in rainwear and a sou'wester, one where we can see her face,' he concluded.

Maren was full of questions, and he had to tell her more about the website and the murder in Palamós.

'All the same, it's a needle in a haystack,' Maren told him, glancing across at the image on the screen. 'And besides, you can't be sure the photo is from this year,' she added.

Wisting ignored her last comment. 'I've arrived at three potential dates,' he said, explaining how he had done this. 'The search needn't be extensive.'

'But it's quite a stretch to think she might feature just by chance in the photos on the stolen cameras,' Maren protested.

'I'm having photos sent in from the boat owners as well,' Wisting said.

Maren shrugged. 'It's worth a try,' she conceded. 'Have you checked the weather reports?'

'What do you mean?' Wisting asked.

Maren nodded in the direction of his computer screen. 'Was it raining on all three of those days?' she queried.

Wisting had not thought of that. He located the historic weather data on the Meteorological Institute's webpages. The rain had started in the early hours of 26 July and eased off by midday on the 27th.

The time range had now narrowed to a day and a half.

Maren remained seated as he looked through the pictures from the stolen cameras. Initially he dismissed the ones not taken on 26 and 27 July. After only a few minutes, he had to admit there was nothing of interest.

'Go back a little,' Maren suggested once he had reached the last photograph.

Wisting clicked his way back through three images.

'There,' Maren said.

These were pictures of two children standing on a pavement eating ice cream. Maren stood up and pointed at the registration number of a motorhome driving up behind the two youngsters.

'I can find the owners of that vehicle and see if they have any photos,' Maren offered. 'There were a few cars in the other images too.'

Wisting had doubts about how much time they should spend on this angle, as the chances that they would randomly find a picture of Astria were minuscule.

'We can do it tomorrow,' he replied, with a glance at the time.

'Just let me know, then,' Maren said as she left to return to her own work.

Wisting looked through the images once more after she had gone and found eight car registration numbers. It was tempting to start phoning round, but he let it lie for now. Instead he called Ellinor Brink.

'The case is expanding,' he said. 'Some of the thefts he's charged with go all the way back to last summer. We're working on demonstrating a continuous chain of crimes so that we can persuade the judge of a serious danger of repetition and ask for him to be remanded in custody until the main proceedings.'

He was using words and expressions that many people might find confusing as he explained this, but Ellinor Brink had stood by her son's side in the justice system for a long time and knew what he was talking about.

'Thanks,' she said.

Wisting went on to explain further about his meeting with the addiction team in the local area and what was required for her son to be allowed to spend part of his forthcoming sentence in a treatment facility.

'Besides, he has to want it himself,' he concluded.

Ellinor thanked him again.

Wisting began to close down the open windows on his computer screen. The Meteorological Institute's website was still accessible and he checked the weather forecast for the next few days. More snow was predicted.

Before he switched off the machine, he looked through the operations log as a matter of routine to see if anything had happened in the course of the day that he ought to know about. He scrolled through various reports of traffic accidents, shoplifting incidents, chimney fires, a lost dog and complaints about the lack of gritting on the roads. One notification stood out from the others: *Abandoned vehicle (Spanish registered)*.

He clicked on the report. The regional bus company had forwarded a message from one of their drivers. A delivery van had been parked at a bus stop near Manvik for the past few days. A patrol had been sent out to take a look at it. They reported back that it was a Spanish-registered VW Caddy fitted with summer tyres. It was not obstructing other traffic and the assignment was signed off with no recommendation for further action since the owner could not be contacted.

Wisting sat with his eyes fixed on the screen before pushing his chair slowly back from the desk.

14

The light was already fading – in the winter months, there were only a few hours of daylight in the middle of the day. It was dark when he went to work and darkness had usually fallen again by the time he came home.

Wisting leaned over the steering wheel as he peered out. The Spanish van was only visible as an outline in the snow.

He turned into the bus bay and directed his headlights towards it. His wipers scraped across the windscreen. He could detect tracks left by the patrol earlier that day. The snow had been swept off the side window on the driver's side as well as the number plate, but both had been covered again by fresh snow fall.

The driving snow lashed his face as he stepped out. Leaning back into the car again, he grabbed his gloves from the passenger seat and pulled them on.

A bus passed on the road as Wisting plodded towards the van. His low-cut boots quickly filled with soft snow as he trudged forward to the driver's door.

It was locked.

He brushed off the snow, but a layer of frost made it difficult to see inside. Returning to his own vehicle, he fetched an ice scraper and a pocket torch.

The driver's cab did not tell him much. Between the seats he spotted a paper cup with a lid, and there was a plastic bag on the passenger seat and a rug lying in the footwell. A few newspapers and magazines were tucked in behind the seat backs and the rear wall of the cabin.

He skirted around the van. The door on the passenger side was also locked, as were the sliding doors to the cargo space and the double doors at the rear. There were no windows to look through.

Wisting knelt down in the snow and shone his torch underneath the van. There was clearance between the undercarriage and the ground. Stiff blades of grass poked out through the snow. The van must have arrived here immediately after the first snow had fallen.

Scrambling to his feet, he brushed the snow off his trousers.

The registration plate was attached to the offside back door, level with the lock and handle. He wiped it clean, noting the combination of numbers and letters before making his way back to his own car.

The number of the local patrol was stored in his phone. 'Fox 3-0,' was the swift response.

Wisting recognized the voice of Kittil Gram, one of the most experienced and senior patrol officers.

'I need help to open a vehicle,' Wisting said, and went on to explain where he was. 'Could you come here with some equipment?'

'We're free,' Gram replied, confirming that they could assist. 'Is it the Spanish van that's reported in the log?'

'That's right,' Wisting answered. 'It's an old VW Caddy with a mechanical lock.'

'Be there in ten minutes,' Gram said as he broke the connection.

Wisting rang the number for the twenty-four-hour desk at Kripos, the National Criminal Investigation Service. All inquiries regarding international cooperation had to be relayed through their contact point.

A woman, whose name Wisting did not catch, answered.

He told her who he was and that he needed information on the owner of a Spanish-registered vehicle.

'I'll contact Madrid,' the woman replied, as if this were a totally run-of-the-mill task. 'I'll call you back.'

The police patrol turned up at the specified time and Wisting got out to greet them.

'It's been parked here for a while,' Kittil Gram commented, gesturing towards the snow-covered van.

His colleague remained seated behind the wheel.

'Since the first snow fall, at least,' Wisting agreed.

'Summer tyres, I'll bet,' Gram said. 'If it's been driven here from Spain.'

Gram produced the set of lock picks from the patrol car's boot. Wisting followed him out into the snow and across to the van. Neither of them said anything more.

The pick was only a thin, flexible steel blade with hooks and spikes at one end. Kittil Gram pushed it down between the rubber weather strip and the glass of the side window. The technique involved grabbing hold of the door lock's latching mechanism.

He had to work at it, guiding the steel blade up and down and moving it sideways. Wisting heard it scrape on metal inside the door.

'Hmm,' Gram said, taking hold of the handle. 'I don't think it's locked, just frozen.' He gave it a forceful tug and the rubber trims tore apart with a loud ripping noise. 'Be my guest,' he said with a smile, sweeping his hand in a gallant flourish towards the opening.

Wisting clambered in. There was little space for his legs between the seat and the steering wheel, but he didn't bother to adjust it. The carrier bag on the passenger seat was from a Spanish grocery chain. It had been used to hold rubbish, mostly fast-food containers from various locations.

When he leaned forward and lifted the rug from the footwell, he found a number of empty bottles underneath, as well as a pair of grubby work gloves.

'Do you need us for anything else?' Kittil Gram asked.

Wisting did not answer. He had opened the glove compartment to look for the vehicle registration document and saw a transparent plastic bag there. The top had been sealed with brown parcel tape. Inside the bag was a yellow knitted hat.

Wisting felt a nerve clench somewhere in his back. He took out his mobile and recorded his find with a photograph before removing the bag, backing out of the van and straightening up to his full height.

'Do you need us for anything else?' Kittil Gram repeated.

Wisting looked at him. 'Can you get the cargo space open?' he asked.

'Then I'll have to tackle the lock itself,' he replied, opening the lock-pick kit again. 'There are no windows, so I won't get anywhere with the steel blade.'

Kittil Gram walked around the van and Wisting heard him set to work on the lock.

The brim of the yellow beanie was turned up, showing a small black label with the manufacturer's name, Billabong. Through the plastic he could see a couple of strands of hair.

He folded up the bag and tucked it into his jacket pocket. Then he sat in the van again and went through the contents of the glove compartment more methodically but found no papers to tell him who owned the vehicle.

The other officer had left the patrol car and now took over from Kittil Gram. A younger man; Wisting could not recall his name. He filled the keyhole with de-icer spray to defrost it and oil the lock before he got to work with the lock picks again.

It was really cold. Wisting stamped his feet on the ground and knocked his boots together. Somewhere along the road, a snowplough was approaching. He could hear the blade scraping on the road surface. As it came closer, it slowed down and stopped in the middle of the carriageway beside the bus stop. The orange glow from the roof lamps skimmed over the falling snowflakes and was reflected in tiny sparks.

As the driver emerged, he stole a glance at the Spanish van. 'Anything wrong?' His breath was thick and white as it left his mouth.

'I don't know yet,' Wisting replied. 'We're trying to find out who owns this and what it's doing here.'

'I'm the regular driver on this route,' the man said. 'That van's been parked there for days.'

'How long would you say?'

The snowplough driver had to think for a moment or two. 'Since Saturday night,' he decided and, to make himself clear, went on to say: 'The early hours of Sunday, in fact.'

'Sunday 3 December?'

'That's right,' the driver agreed. 'That was when I first noticed it.'

'Did you see anyone?' Wisting asked. 'Either in or near the van?'

'No.'

Wisting's phone buzzed. The number for the Kripos desk shone on the display. He thanked the driver and excused himself.

It was the woman he had spoken to earlier. Her name was Svensson, Ida Svensson. She read out the registration number he had given her and told him it belonged to a Volkswagen Caddy, 2009 model.

Wisting looked across at the van and confirmed this.

'The vehicle is registered to a firm in Palamós,' she said,

making an attempt at the Spanish pronunciation: 'Navis Servinauta.'

Palamós, Wisting echoed to himself.

'It was reported stolen three days ago,' the Kripos operator added.

Wisting shifted the phone to his other ear. 'Stolen?' he repeated.

'Yes,' Ida Svensson confirmed. 'I require some documentation for SIS,' she added, referring to the Schengen Information System.

'Do you have any more information about the theft?' Wisting asked.

'No,' Svensson answered. 'Has the vehicle been used in connection with another crime?'

'It's just been abandoned,' Wisting replied. 'But it could be linked to another case we're investigating. Could you possibly get me more information on the vehicle theft?'

'I can send a request at any rate.'

Wisting thanked her and wrapped up the conversation.

The snowplough driver had not moved away and must have listened in to the exchange.

'It's stolen,' Wisting told him anyway.

'Heavens,' the driver replied.

Wisting took his name and thanked him for having stopped, mostly to let him understand that he could drive on now. He was not keen to have him there if Kittil Gram and his colleague managed to open the rear doors of the van.

Taking the hint, the driver clambered into his cab and drove off.

Kittil Gram stood with his torch beam aimed at the door lock on the rear doors of the Spanish delivery van. His younger colleague was fiddling with the lock pick.

'Nearly there,' Gram said.

His colleague kept working at it, blowing on his fingers to warm them. Then the longed-for click came.

Wisting moved closer as Kittil Gram opened the door and shone his torch beam into the darkness of the cargo space.

It was empty.

Along one wall, there were shelves with small drawers containing tools and engine parts, but apart from that there was nothing in the back of the van to tell them what had become of the driver.

'I heard you say it was stolen,' Kittil Gram said. 'I expect you'll want us to bring it in. We can arrange for a tow vehicle.'

'Yes, please,' Wisting said, thanking him. 'Put it in the basement garage.'

15

Username: Darby

Sitting in his workroom on the first floor, Wisting let Google Maps show him the fastest driving route from Palamós to Larvik. It took twenty-six hours, travelling through five different countries. The journey took a bit longer if you wanted to avoid ferries.

Just over an hour after leaving Palamós, the van would have crossed the border into France. The motorway north through Europe traversed Lyon, passed over the border into Luxembourg and on into Germany. After twelve hours the van would have been in Cologne, continuing thereafter through well-known cities such as Dortmund, Bremen and Hamburg. Once in Denmark, there were a number of alternatives. Either up to North Jutland and the ferry across to Norway, or via Copenhagen and the Øresund Bridge to Malmö in Sweden. From there, it was five hours to the Norwegian border.

There were many checkpoints along the way, toll stations and border crossings; plenty to get hold of if that proved necessary.

He switched screens, back to the website about the investigation of Ruby Thompson's murder. He had studied the photos of her and was now certain: the yellow hat in the glove compartment was the same kind as the one Ruby was wearing.

For a long time he just sat there, collecting his thoughts on how best to communicate the information to the Catalan investigators.

There was a Norwegian connection, of that he was sure. However, the only thing pointing in this direction on the website was the Norwegian name Michelle Norris had mentioned – Olaf.

He scanned through the police documents again. There was no Olaf on the list of witnesses, but three people had alluded to the name: Leo Pérez in the beach bar, Jarod Denham from England and the Frenchman, Mathis Leroux. Ruby was the one who had first encountered him, but she had not told the others where or how she had come across him. She called him Olaf, but they did not know whether this was his real name. Maybe it was just something she called him because he was from Norway, like the snowman in the Disney film *Frozen*.

Olaf had shown up at the beach bar with marijuana. Both Jarod and Mathis admitted buying from him. They described him as pale, with round eyes black as coal, a very different character from the surfers who hung out on the beach. He wore a pair of dark, tight-fitting trousers and a T-shirt or sweater from some heavy-metal rock band or other.

It was odd that the Catalan detectives had not done more to find out who Olaf was, but the documents accessible on the website were from the initial phase of the inquiry, when Jarod Denham was being held in custody. Olaf would have been an obvious clue to follow up when they were forced to release Jarod.

Another thing he thought lacking in the Catalan investigation was more information about the campsite where Ruby Thompson had been staying. This was her only fixed locus in the town on the Spanish coast and was where she had spent most time. Cheap overnight accommodation usually also attracted a certain type of clientele, often restless transients running from problems in one place who quickly moved on.

The owner had been interviewed and had given an account of Ruby checking in but had little else to add. A young couple staying in the adjoining room on Ruby's final two days had also given statements. They had seen her last on the morning of the day before she was found dead. Apart from them, it looked as if no one else at the campsite had been interviewed. Probably this was a part of the investigation that had been resumed when Jarod was released and would be included in subsequent documents not available here.

The restricted time frame of the police documents gave a strong indication of who had leaked them. It would not surprise him if Jarod Denham was a member of this forum, hidden behind one of the anonymous usernames.

He scrolled down the alphabetic list of imaginative aliases and stopped at one: Jade. This nom de plume could be an amalgamation of the two initial letters of his name.

Clicking on the username, he saw that the potential Jarod Denham had been a member since the very beginning when the website was established but had posted no comments.

The total number of members had reached 186. At the foot of the list, there was someone who called himself xChange, with only a capital X as his profile picture.

Wisting scrolled up again. Some members were open about their identities, while others hid them. He had never made up a nickname like this for himself. He could have used Buster, after the cat he'd once owned, or Koppen, a Norwegianized version of the word 'cop', containing a hint about who he was and what he was doing. Just something that sprang to mind. Line had chosen the name of a character from a film she liked. He could call himself Serpico, from the old film starring Al Pacino, and use the logo of the New York Police. The idea brought a smile to his face. The point was that these unusual usernames in the forum were hardly random choices. For the people hidden behind them, they had some kind of resonance. For all he knew, whoever had killed Ruby Thompson could be among them.

16

Username: Nichelle

The only light in the room came from the computer screen. The new post about the thefts in Palamós had sparked some interest, but Michelle did not like it. Setting up a website as a collection point for information about Ruby's murder had been a bit like rolling back a stone without knowing what lay concealed beneath it. All sorts of things crept out, including people lacking any kind of awareness or appreciation of what was acceptable.

However, the discussion down through the thread had not drifted off in the direction she had feared when the post was first published. It could easily have led to dwindling sympathy for Ruby and diminishing interest in solving the case. Instead, several contributors leapt to her defence and reminded the others that she had been stranded in the middle of Europe with no money and a father who refused to help her as he had promised.

Most of the comments came straight to the point. The surveillance images of the masked intruder were compared with the photos available of Ruby. A man whose alias was Zagut claimed to be an engineer and had carried out a mathematical calculation of the housebreaker's height. He had used the picture in which the masked figure was standing in front of the large living-room window, assuming a standard window height of 180 centimetres and estimating a given distance between the figure and the window. With the help of formulae from trigonometry, he had determined the person's height to be five foot five, with a margin of error of 3 per cent. If it were Ruby standing in front of the window, it was an excellent result, as she was around this height.

Others had conducted more amateurish calculations. One image was superimposed on the other to compare the length of various body parts. One of the members had visualized it convincingly with the assistance of three-dimensional computer graphics. A recurring theme was the need for moving images to make it easier to compare gait and motion.

One user reminded them of the contents of the police reports. The surfboard Ruby had used had been stolen from a holiday house just outside the town centre, and both drugs and stolen credit cards had been found in her bungalow. This supported the idea that it really was Ruby in the new photographs. Probably she had been acting like this throughout her travels in Europe, he wrote. Got high and stole whatever she needed. Flaunted herself, slept with any boy she fancied, and moved on.

Shifting her eyes from the screen, Michelle fumbled for the packet and fished out a cigarette.

She did have the facility to delete comments and posts but had promised herself she would not do that. Everything should come out, even if this painted a different picture of Ruby from the one she had in her own mind.

Ruby was considerate and generous and faced everyone with an inquiring mind and a ready smile. She paid attention to the people around her and always had something nice to say to each of them. All the same, the truth was that it could easily be Ruby in these photos.

Michelle inserted the cigarette between her dry lips and lit it without bothering to move out on to the balcony.

Ruby had always been rebellious and headstrong, opposing established mores and unafraid to swim against the tide. Against everyone else. She was soon at odds with her parents, especially her father, and this came to a head when she met Frank. She was seventeen, he was three years older, with no education, job or income, and lived in the basement of his grandmother's house. This was where she had used marijuana for the first time. Her parents had attempted to force her to break up with him, but the relationship had lasted for six months before she moved on.

Her thoughts circled with the smoke rings as they rose to the ceiling.

She and Ruby had known each other since they had met in nursery at home in Adelaide. Ruby could be egotistical and never considered who she risked hurting through her behaviour. In many ways, it was her parents who had shaped her. She was an only child and used to having her own way. For a long time her father had been an instructor in the military police before starting up a private security company a few years before Ruby was born. Later he had sold the business to one of the major security firms, but he remained in a management post and climbed higher. Nowadays he was the CEO of the Australian division of an international security company and spent most of his time in Canberra and Melbourne.

She had said a few words to both parents at the funeral. Flynn and Elena. She had met Ruby's mother once before, but Elena had been numbed with medication and it was far from certain that she remembered anything about her. That had been a while ago now, before she had set up the website.

The thought of Ruby's parents filled her with pangs of guilt, both because she had not visited them and because she had not told them about the online forum.

A new post from Ariel popped up while she sat in front of the screen. *The currents on the Costa Brava.*

Michelle stubbed out her cigarette in an empty glass.

Ariel had broached this subject before, writing that she had a contact in the Institute of Marine Science in Barcelona who had studied the sea conditions along the coast outside Palamós. The underwater topography and prevailing wind currents from the south made the area popular with surfers. She thought the researcher she was in contact with could find out where Ruby's body had come from when it was washed ashore on the town beach.

Her contact had worked for four weeks on scientific calculations, using historical data about wind strength and tidal conditions. Assuming that the body had been thrown into the sea from the shore somewhere, and given the relatively short time in the water, he concluded that the dumping spot was somewhere along the cliffs on the coast between Palamós and Cap Roig, a few kilometres further north.

The map link provided showed a road snaking along the stony strip of coastline, with fairly scattered settlements. In a few spots, the hillside was broken by bays with sandy beaches. In only a couple of places did it look as if there were tracks leading to the sea.

Michelle changed the display to the satellite image of the desolate area. One of the side roads ended at an open space. She moved as far into the image as possible and saw how the hillside sloped down towards the clear waters. If a body were thrown from here, it would be badly injured on the way down, if it even reached the water at all.

She slumped back into her chair.

Even if this had been where Ruby was tossed into the sea, it did not take them any further towards a solution.

It felt hopeless, sitting thousands of miles away, peering at photos and maps.

She remained in her chair for ages, her eyes fixed on the screen. Then she leaned forward and searched for the airport nearest to Palamós.

17

As more snow was forecast, Wisting got up half an hour earlier than usual. At some point during the night, the blizzard had eased off, but there was already so much new snow that he had to clear it so that he could drive his car out.

His phone buzzed as he started on the bank of snow left by the snowplough at the roadside. The call was from the Kripos desk. He pulled off his mittens and answered at once. The caller introduced himself as Jon Harring.

'We've changed shift here,' he began, 'but there's a log entry about an incident to do with a Spanish-registered vehicle.'

'That's right,' Wisting replied, standing with one hand on the snow shovel. 'It was reported stolen.'

'We've managed to get some additional intelligence sent over,' the Kripos operator went on. 'The report was made in connection with a missing Norwegian woman.'

A bird had landed on one of the fence posts. It hopped on to the next one before taking off and flying away. Wisting followed it with his eyes.

'Who was that, then?' he asked.

'Astri Arctander, aged thirty-two, from Asker.'

Wisting stood breathing through his open mouth, aware of a drop of sweat trickling from his neck all the way down his back.

Astri A, he thought. *Astri Arctander.*

The operator continued: 'Her family have a property in Palamós, in northern Spain on the Mediterranean. Her brother reported her missing on 5 December. Other members of the family went down there and discovered that the van was gone. It's owned by a boat workshop where her uncle works.'

'I see,' said Wisting.

'Do you have any information on her?' the Kripos operative asked.

Wisting hesitated, reluctant to share information about his contact with Michelle Norris with a stranger.

'No,' was his response.

'She was probably the one who drove the vehicle to Norway,' Jon Harring added.

'Did you say she's from Asker?' Wisting asked.

'Her home address is Heggedal,' the man said. 'She may have come by ferry to Larvik if she's driven up through Denmark.'

Wisting shook his head, thinking to himself. The spot where the van was parked did not suggest that the driver was on her way to Asker. It was more likely she was making her way to the coast.

'I'll follow up on that,' Wisting said.

He looked at what was left of the pile of snow stretching out to the road. If he accelerated hard, he would have little difficulty ploughing through it.

'Can you send me what you've got from Spain?' he asked, walking back to the house. 'The names of the brother, uncle and other family members?'

'No problem. What should I report back to the police down there?'

'Find out who's in charge of the investigation and I'll get in touch.'

18

Wisting skipped breakfast but took time to shower and change. When he strode into the police station, he was still first to arrive in the department.

Nils Hammer regularly deputized for Wisting. As soon as he turned up, Wisting asked him to take the morning meeting.

'Has something come up?' Hammer asked.

'There's a case in development,' Wisting replied without giving any further details. 'I'm trying to get a handle on it. Come in and see me as soon as you're free.'

Wisting headed for his own office and closed the door behind him.

Some of the documents from the missing-person report and the vehicle theft had already been sent over, but everything was in Spanish or Catalan. He read the name and date of birth for Astri Arctander and understood that Morten Arctander must be her brother. On the form relating to the Spanish vehicle, the name Bernard Arctander was given. Her uncle.

He found the same Astri Arctander in the population register and quickly mapped out the family. Morten Arctander was eight years older than his sister, and there was also another brother who was two more years older. The parents, in their sixties, lived in Sandvika. On the mother's side, she had no other family, but on the father's side she had three uncles. The youngest of these was said to have emigrated to Spain. Bernard Arctander. The two others were listed with the same date of birth, Fredrik and Henrik. There were no entries in criminal or intelligence records for any of them.

According to the employment records, Astri Arctander worked for a technology company in Kongsberg, but there was no employee list on their website.

Her Facebook profile was private, but her profile picture was open. A woman in a summer hat pulled slantwise down in front of her face. It did not make her easy to recognize, but this method of partly concealing herself was identical to the photograph of Astria in the rain.

Wisting found a photo from the passport records. It seemed as if she was holding back a smile from the camera. The black-and-white picture was seven years old but it looked as if she had colour in her cheeks, and a few freckles sprinkled over her nose gave extra life to the image. Her eyes were large, with dark lashes, and her hair was gathered into a pony-tail, probably for the occasion, to avoid it flopping forward to hide her features.

An alert about an email from the Sirene office in Kripos appeared on the screen. This was the section responsible for coordinating international contacts. The acronym had something to do with supplementary information.

The Spanish and Catalan police reports had been hastily translated into English, the international language of cooperation, making the contents immediately comprehensible.

One of Astri Arctander's work colleagues had been first to suspect something was wrong. Astri worked from a home office whether she was in Spain or her apartment in Asker. This style of working was practical and functioned well on both sides. She was always prompt with regard to deadlines and quick to answer emails. At the beginning of December, however, the responses had failed to materialize. She had not answered her phone either, nor had she linked up to participate in an important video meeting. Her colleague had got in touch with her parents, who were listed as her next of kin. They were in Norway but had phoned their son in Palamós.

This son had his own apartment in the same neighbourhood as his parents' holiday house, where Astri lived. He confirmed her absence but was unable to find out anything to tell him where she might be or what had happened. The last time he had spoken to her had been at the end of November, when everything had been fine.

The police had contacted a few neighbours, none of whom had noticed anything untoward. Her brother had also made a list of people his sister associated with in Palamós. It was relatively short. There was a Swedish woman friend, an English teacher couple who worked in the international school in a nearby town and a Spanish couple who ran a restaurant. A barman who worked there had dated her a couple of times. Also, she had friends in the local gym, in a local chess club and an organization that took care of homeless cats.

Her parents had travelled down on the first available plane, along with her uncle, the one who had reported the van stolen. The theft was dealt with in a separate report.

Astri's uncle worked in a Spanish firm that dealt with the repair and service of pleasure boats and used their own tow truck, parked in a fenced area at the harbour. Astri had access to the keys for both the vehicle and the gate. It was explained that the property in Spain was owned by Astri's grandmother and comprised three residences. Astri had used the largest apartment while she was there on her own but kept an eye on the other two. The car keys were in a kitchen drawer in the smallest apartment. Not until twenty-four hours after the parents had come down had it been established that these were missing.

Wisting had now filled a page in his notebook, but the

computer registers and reports from Spain provided only limited intelligence. In the course of the day he would have to contact her parents, tell them about the most recent developments in the case and ask more exhaustive questions.

There was a knock on the office door and Wisting called out, 'Come in!' Having expected it to be Nils Hammer, he was taken aback to see Maren.

'I've collected a whole load of photos,' she said. 'Thought I should show you something if you've got a minute.'

Holding her laptop in her arms, she made her way to the vacant chair.

The previous day, Wisting had been searching for random photos of Astria, but now he had found her.

'It's no longer relevant,' he said. 'I know who she is now.'

'It's not to do with her,' Maren told him.

She turned the screen to face him. It was a picture taken on a rainy day. Two children sat under an awning, eating ice cream. Maren pointed to a black van in the parking space behind them with its rear doors open. A similar van to the one snowed in near Manvik, but this one was a Peugeot.

'I phoned the owner to try to get more pictures,' Maren said, pointing at the number plate. Attached to one of the rear doors, it was easy to read.

Wisting nodded but was becoming impatient. One of the things he had grown used to as head of the department was interrupting his own work to listen to the preoccupations of the other investigators.

'Do you remember the dog theft?' Maren went on.

He smiled, recalling a lot of talk about it last summer. Strictly speaking, it had not been the theft of a dog but of a painting with a dog as its subject. It had been stolen from a local artist's vehicle while he was transporting his paintings to an exhibition space. By definition, it was in fact an art theft. This was always good material for the press, especially in an otherwise sparse period for news during the summer months. The painting had never been recovered but, for the obscure artist, the theft had provided excellent publicity.

'This is his van,' Maren explained. 'The photo must have been taken just before or after the theft, on the same day Trond Brink Isaksen raided other vehicles and boats in the area.'

'Is he captured in any of the photographs?' Wisting asked.

Maren shook her head. 'Haven't spotted him up till now,' she replied. 'And the painting wasn't found at his home. But all the same . . .'

She flipped the lid of the laptop and got to her feet. 'Who was she, then?' she asked. 'The girl in the photo?'

Nils Hammer appeared at the door before Wisting had time to answer. He signalled for them both to sit down.

The report of a stolen Spanish vehicle had been listed in the operations log, but it took time for Wisting to explain the totality of it and the connections. His colleagues listened without interruption until Hammer summed things up in two questions: 'Why did she leave Spain? And why did she come here?'

'She was here last summer too,' Maren pointed out. 'Maybe her family have a summer cabin here or a caravan out on one of the campsites.'

Although Wisting had not got as far as considering the possibilities, Maren offered to find out.

'Where's the van now?' Hammer asked.

'In our garage for examination,' Wisting replied. 'I've asked a technician to look at it.'

'What are you expecting to find?'

Wisting raised his shoulders in an ambiguous gesture. He had no idea of the implications. 'Something to point us in some direction,' he answered. 'To take us further somehow.'

19

In addition to the translated police documents they had been sent, there were also the name, direct number and other contact details for one of the investigators on the inquiry who could speak English. Officer Malak Rendón was attached to the local police force in Palamós.

Wisting dialled the number. Not until the call was answered did he realize that Rendón was a woman. He introduced himself and understood from the initial conversation that the local police had not initiated any significant investigation. Beyond what had emerged from the documents sent to him, passenger lists of planes and ferries leaving Barcelona had been examined and a search had been made on the missing woman's phone in the Spanish telecoms network. Neither of these efforts had yielded results.

The Catalan police officer was keen to learn whether the missing woman had been located or whether there was reason to assume from the circumstances that she was in Norway. In that event, the Catalan police could close the case.

'It's a bit too early to draw conclusions,' Wisting answered.

He refrained from mentioning Astri Arctander's involvement in the investigations into the murder of the Australian tourist in April. Anyway, that case had been investigated at a higher level. What he needed to know was whether the Catalan police had been in contact with Astri's parents after the van had been found in Norway. He had no wish for them to step on each other's toes, and they would have to come to an agreement about who should relay information.

'The most appropriate thing would be for you to speak to them,' Rendón said. 'You speak the same language and have full details about locating the vehicle.'

'Do you know if they're still in Palamós?' Wisting asked.

'I'd assume so,' she replied. 'After all, they believe their daughter is still here.'

They agreed to keep each other up to date and exchange any new information. Rendón seemed unconcerned and Wisting did not anticipate any further dialogue with her. The case would soon be raised to another level.

He sat with the phone numbers for Astri's mother, father and brother in front of him and decided to call her father first.

A man answered without identifying himself. Just a slightly quizzical 'Yes, hello?'

Wisting gave his name and rank. 'Am I speaking to Walter Arctander?' he asked.

When the voice on the phone confirmed this, Wisting continued: 'It's about Astri. I understand she's been reported missing.'

'Yes?'

Picking up the pen from his desk, Wisting turned to a blank page in his notebook.

'I'm calling because the van reported in connection with her disappearance was found here in Larvik yesterday evening,' he said.

There was a fleeting silence at the other end of the line. 'What about Astri?' her father asked after clearing his throat.

'We don't know anything of her whereabouts,' Wisting replied. 'We're examining the van more closely but so far we haven't found any personal belongings.'

'I don't understand . . .' the father began, but no question was forthcoming.

'Have you any idea why the van's been left here?' Wisting asked. 'In Larvik?'

Words were spoken in the background. A woman's voice. Walter Arctander being told something.

'Are you still in Palamós?' Wisting asked.

'Yes. I have my wife here, and my son, as well as one of my brothers.'

Wisting repeated the question about whether any of them had any idea why Astri had driven to Larvik.

'She had a boyfriend there,' Walter Arctander answered. 'But I don't understand why she should leave here all of a sudden to visit him. Without saying anything to anyone.'

Wisting touched the pen to the notebook. 'What's his name?'

'Ulrik Stene.' He had to refer to his wife to be sure he had the right name. 'But they broke up last summer,' he went on. 'He was a few years older than her and had been married.'

'Do you know if they were in touch with each other after last summer?' Wisting asked.

Walter Arctander hesitated. 'No, but Astri wasn't very communicative about such things. Nor about other things, either, to be honest.'

Someone asked a question in the background and Walter Arctander passed it on: 'Where was the van found?'

Wisting explained the location of the bus stop. 'It had probably been parked there for a few days before it was reported to us,' he said. 'It was snowed in.'

Again something was said in the background that Wisting did not catch. 'What was that?' he asked.

'Well . . . we have an old summer cabin near there,' Walter said. 'At Eidsten, on the road out to Helgeroa. But it's closed for winter. I can't imagine for a minute that she's been there.'

Wisting jotted down the directions and quickly realized

that if Astri had been unable to drive any further on the slippery road surface, she could have gone on foot to the cabin. The distance was only about three kilometres.

'We'll check that out,' Wisting said.

'The key's in a box on the wall,' Walter Arctander added, giving the code.

'Did she take anything with her when she left?' Wisting asked.

'She had two mobile phones. One Norwegian and one Spanish. They're both gone. And her laptop. I've no idea about clothes and suchlike.'

Additional information came from the others in the room. 'She's taken a bag, with her bank card and so on,' Walter told him. 'Morten has spoken to the bank. He's my younger son. They wouldn't disclose anything to him.'

Wisting wrote down the two phone numbers and the name of the bank. These details had been omitted from the Spanish missing-person report.

'Have you spoken to any of the people she mixed with down there?' Wisting asked. 'There was something about a Swedish friend and someone who ran a restaurant.'

'Morten has talked to them,' Walter replied. 'She hadn't said anything to them about going anywhere. It had been a while since they'd heard from her.'

Wisting asked a few more questions before assuring them he would keep them posted.

When the conversation had ended, he opened a formal missing-person case, entering the intelligence he had gathered into the Norwegian police computer system. This provided the basis for embarking on the work of procuring electronic data from the telecoms network, toll stations and banks.

Ulrik Stene had racked up a number of cases in the

criminal records, the majority of incidents involving drunken brawls. There were several reports in which the police had been called when he had altercations with bouncers and customers in licensed premises. He had also been fined for various traffic violations.

Wisting noted where he lived and saw that he was listed as being employed by the Colorline ferry company. He could phone and clarify quickly whether he had heard anything from Astri but preferred to visit anyone he wanted to speak to. There were nuances in a face-to-face conversation that were not discernible over the phone. Not so much in what was said but rather in how the person behaved when the questions were posed.

Maren Dokken appeared in the doorway again, this time with a printout from the property register. 'Her grandmother has a summer cabin in Eidsten,' she said. 'That's not far from where the van was found.'

Wisting avoided mentioning that he had already discovered this, instead simply rising and grabbing his jacket from the hook on the wall.

'Let's go out there,' he said.

20

The Spanish van was in the garage, unexamined, with a damp patch on the concrete floor beneath it from the melted snow and ice. A yellow sign warning that it should not be touched was tucked under one of the windscreen wipers; one of the forensic technicians was due to come and examine the van.

Wisting let Maren drive while he phoned to remind them. Sickness absence and a break-in at a jeweller's shop were the reasons given for the delay.

On the way out to the summer cabin, Wisting told Maren about his conversation with Astri's father. As they approached, he pointed out the spot where her van had been parked. As they passed, Maren switched on the trip meter so that they could ascertain the exact distance to the cabin.

After just over two kilometres, they turned off from the main road on to the side road leading to Eidsten. Maren found her bearings from a printout of the municipal map of the area and, another 860 metres later, she drew the car to a halt.

The summer cabin was situated between old pine trees with snow-covered branches. Painted red, it had two storeys and a conservatory at the front with small panes of glass, all coated in rime. The other, larger windows were closed off with white shutters.

The property extended all the way down to the sea, where there was a jetty and a boathouse, as well as a small annexe built in the same style as the main house.

The driveway had not been cleared and they were forced

to park the car out on the road and walk the last fifty metres, wading through the deep snow.

'It doesn't look as if anyone's been here for a long time,' Maren commented as she moved forward, lifting her knees as she trudged along. Wisting followed in her footsteps.

The entrance was at the side, the word *Sommerro* carved on a plaque. Icicles hung from the porch roof.

Maren checked the door and found it locked. Locating the key box in the designated place, Wisting entered the code and opened it. He took the key that dangled from a little hook and handed it to Maren.

Unlocking the door, she kicked away some snow and let it swing wide open. 'Hello?' she called out. 'We're from the police.'

Wisting tapped his feet on the door frame, knocking snow from his boots, and followed her inside. On the floor he could see a pair of sandals and a pair of trainers. A cupboard door was slightly open, and he peered inside but found nothing of interest.

Maren grabbed a flashlight from a chest of drawers in the hallway. First she shone it up the stairs to the first floor before directing the beam straight ahead to the living room.

'Hello?' she shouted again. Neither of them expected any answer.

The floorboards creaked as they moved on inside. The air was dry and cold.

Wisting found a light switch and turned on the chandelier hanging from the living-room ceiling. Outdoor furniture was stacked up in one half of the room. On the other side, two comfortable armchairs stood in front of the fireplace with a chessboard set out on a small table between them.

The kitchen was clean and tidy. Nothing but a glass beside the sink. In the bathroom, there was no sign of any use since last summer.

Returning to the hallway, they moved upstairs, finding it colder on the upper floor than downstairs. The landing had doors leading into four bedrooms, where the beds were stripped of linen with quilts neatly folded.

In one of the bedrooms, several faded pictures hung on the walls. They looked as if they had been taken in the sixties. A man and a woman appeared repeatedly. The couple looked to be in their thirties at that time and Wisting assumed this must be the bedroom belonging to Astri's grandmother, the owner of the summer cabin. The other rooms had no personal touches, and it was impossible to tell which room Astri was in the habit of using when she stayed overnight.

They went downstairs again and Wisting took another look in the living room. On the wall behind the outdoor furniture, there was a bookcase and some pictures that looked fairly recent.

He manoeuvred his way through the garden chairs to study these, evocative summer photos from the area surrounding the cabin. In one of them, the entire family seemed to be gathered around a long table with an old woman seated at one end. Apart from her, most of the people were men. Astri sat closest to the camera with a little fair-haired boy on her knee, possibly a younger nephew or some other family member. He was pale and it looked as if something was wrong with him, but he was obviously laughing at something Astri had been doing to make him smile while the picture was taken.

Wisting backed out between the chairs again.

On the seat of the chair on top of the four in the pile lay a leather-bound book. He had the impression that this was a guest book, but when he picked it up he saw it was a photo album. Written on the spine was *1996–2015* and it was full of summer memories. Photos taken on the smooth coastal rocks, sandy beaches and strawberry fields. Bike and boat trips. Under each image, the date, year and names of the people depicted had been written. In some places it also gave the location where the photo had been taken, with a brief comment. Astri was in a number of them. On one of the first pages she sat playing chess with a man in a T-shirt. *Astri beats Uncle Fredrik* was the text below. In the final photograph she was grown up, lying in a hammock with her face partly hidden behind a book.

Wisting shut the album and left it lying there. Maren emerged from the kitchen with a glass in her hand. 'How long does it take for water to evaporate?' she asked. She tipped the glass to let the remaining contents slosh around at the bottom.

'That probably depends on the temperature, humidity and how much water there was in the glass to start with,' Wisting told her.

Maren lowered her hand. 'It could have sat there since summer,' she conceded. 'Or it could be the only sign that someone has been here.'

She put it back in the kitchen and they let themselves out.

Wisting stood on the steps outside, lost in thought, as Maren made her way back to the car. When she had gone halfway, she turned and looked at him. 'What's wrong?' she asked.

Wisting began to walk towards her. 'She could have arrived just as the first snow fell,' he said.

'All traces are gone now,' Maren pointed out.

Wisting realized she did not understand what he was suggesting. 'It's unusual,' he went on. 'It snows more often and more heavily when the weather is mild than when it's extremely cold. On the night the snow came, the temperature was minus twelve.'

'Something could have happened along the way,' Maren said.

Wisting let his eyes roam across the banks of snow that flanked the road. On the other side, he could see a hump in the otherwise flat, white landscape: the outline of something beneath the snow.

Neither of them said a word.

Wisting stepped over the snowdrift, sinking up to his knees. He waded forward, scraping the snow away with his arm.

Only a boulder.

Maren had arrived at the bank of snow beside the road. 'We need dogs,' she said, 'the kind trained to find avalanche victims.'

The examination of the Spanish vehicle was in full swing when Wisting and Maren drove back into the basement garage. Two forensic technicians were working in the light from bright floodlamps. One of them put down a notepad and pulled off his facemask when he caught sight of them. Wisting recognized him as one of the young, new members of the team. David Eikrot.

'What is it you're actually looking to learn from this?' he asked. 'I know it was stolen in Spain, but the assignment description was a bit sparse.'

'Any trace evidence that can tell us who arrived here in it,' Wisting replied. 'Fingerprints, DNA, documents . . .'

'Well,' Eikrot began, 'it's key ignition, but you probably knew that already.'

Wisting nodded.

'And it's covered in fingerprints,' Eikrot went on. 'After all, it's a works van. Many of the prints have been left by oily fingers, both on papers and tools. We'll secure DNA in the usual way. Traces from the steering wheel and the necks of the empty bottles. There are also a few stray hairs inside the vehicle. We'll secure them and see what we can send off for analysis.'

Labelled bags of material secured were laid out on a workbench.

The other technician joined the conversation. 'I thought there was a suspect?' he asked.

Wisting explained why they had reason to believe it had

been Astri Arctander who had driven the van and they were afraid something untoward had happened to her.

'Well, she hasn't left any personal possessions in the vehicle,' the technician said. 'No bag, phone, purse, bank card, luggage or anything else. What we do know is that she stopped at a twenty-four-hour petrol station along the motorway somewhere called Mâcon in France.'

He walked to the workbench and lifted a bag containing a receipt.

Wisting looked at it. Fuel and a variety of food items had been purchased. The date and time given were 1 December at 15.12.

He was not sure where Mâcon was, but when he had perused the map he had calculated it would have taken her ten hours to drive through France. That suggested she had departed from Palamós on the morning of that same day. The way he interpreted the French receipt, it looked as if only one bottle of something to drink had been bought, suggesting she had been alone in the van.

'There are a few more receipts,' the technician continued. 'You'll probably be able to piece together a fairly accurate travel route.'

Wisting approached the bench and peered at the receipts. Food and fuel. Various sums in euros. One of the receipts was in Danish kroner, from a Shell station in Karslunde on 2 December at 12.44.

'Where's that?' he asked.

No one could answer. Maren used her phone to check.

'Near Køge Bay,' she answered. 'Outside Copenhagen.'

Wisting nodded. Then she had driven across the Øresund Bridge and up through Sweden. They would not need to check the ferries from Jutland. The timeline made sense. She would have arrived in Larvik around midnight on the evening the snow began to fall.

'Will it be long till you're done?' he asked, indicating the van.

'Half an hour, and we'll be packing up,' Eikrot replied. 'You'll get a report tomorrow with a list of what we've secured. Then we'll make a judgement about what should be analysed. We're not talking about an unknown perpetrator here.'

'I've got something in my office I'd like you to take with you,' Wisting said. 'A hat I found in the glove compartment.'

Turning on his heel, he headed for the stairwell. The yellow beanie raised the entire case to a level only he knew about.

22

Two dog teams could be there in a couple of hours. By then there would not be many hours of daylight left, but the dogs worked equally well in the dark, Wisting was assured, and the dog handlers could manage with head torches.

Much of the search would take place along the roadside. He arranged with the patrol section to have Kittil Gram appointed leader of the search party and for them to provide another three officers to deal with the associated traffic issues.

He had reservations about logging into the crowdsolving site from the police network but was keen to take a printout of Astria's profile picture with him when he paid a visit to her ex-boyfriend. As he sent it to the printer, he also checked for any news. The discussion zipped back and forth under the post about whether Ruby Thompson was responsible for the burglaries and whether the police had looked into this possibility. Nothing had come of it – it was merely another detail tossed in among all the others.

There was also a post with retrospective calculations of how the sea currents and waves had conveyed the body to the shore. A limited geographical area was suggested as the dumping spot, but this did not take the case any further forward.

At some point he would have to inform Michelle Norris about the recent developments. She was not in any way part of the case, but he thought all the same that she deserved a return message.

He fetched the printout of Astria's photo taken on a rainy day and inserted it into a plastic sleeve before leaving by car.

Ulrik Stene lived in Dronningensgate, in the centre of Stavern, in a corner apartment above a clothes shop that was closed for winter. The entrance was via a passageway into the back yard. The stairs leading up were covered in lumps of ice and Wisting had to use the railings for support. On his way to the door, he fished out his police ID from inside his shirt and hung it so that it was clearly visible.

A tied bin bag lay outside and he could hear music from inside the flat. Heavy beats that disappeared when Wisting rang the doorbell. A dark-haired man with a well-groomed beard appeared at the door, dressed in jeans and a turtleneck sweater. His eyes dropped to the ID card and glanced up again, and he nodded when Wisting introduced himself.

'Could I come in?' Wisting asked.

'What's this about?'

'Astri Arctander,' Wisting replied. 'She's gone missing.'

'Astri?' the man repeated. 'I haven't spoken to her for months.' He blinked a couple of times, but his face gave nothing away.

Wisting remained silent, waiting to be invited in. The man hesitated slightly but took a step back and ushered Wisting into the kitchen. Ulrik Stene cleared away a few glasses as Wisting slung his jacket over the chair back and sat down at the kitchen table.

'Can you tell me about your relationship?' Wisting asked by way of encouragement.

Stene seemed to squirm a little before he began to speak. 'We actually met in Spain,' he said. 'I already knew her uncle slightly. Astri and her family really live in Palamós. My parents have a house further south, but I've been to Palamós a lot in connection with my work. A couple of friends and I ran a company importing second-hand boats. The financial crisis had a serious impact down there and it was possible to find some good bargains. I drove up and down along the whole coastline, seizing the chance of the best offers. Some of the boats were brand new and hadn't even been put in the water. Even with the cost of transportation, we made a good profit. Astri's uncle worked on marine electronics, in Norway in the summer and in Spain in wintertime. He arranged a few sales for me. That was how I met her, and then it turned out that she'd stayed with her grandmother in Stavern every summer since she was little.'

Wisting asked him to tell him more about her family.

'The Arctander clan,' Stene said, curling his lip. 'The grand-mother's still the one who runs the show. Gerd Arctander. She must be almost ninety. Nothing happens in that family without her involvement. She's the one who holds the purse strings.'

Wisting had not checked the tax returns to ascertain the family assets, but having both a summer cabin in Stavern and a holiday house in Spain spoke for itself.

Ulrik Stene told him that Astri's grandfather, in his time, had inherited a construction company from his father and had invested the profits in property.

'The construction firm was sold when the grandfather died,' Stene added. 'Now it's purely a property company, with several blocks of rental apartments in Oslo. Fredrik runs that. He has a separate property company in Spain as well. Probably did the same with property as I did with boats.'

'Fredrik's one of the twin brothers, is he?' Wisting asked, trying to place him.

Stene nodded. 'Astri's father is the eldest, sixty-something, I think. Then you have the twins, Henrik and Fredrik. Ber-nard's the youngest. I think he turned forty-eight last summer. But only Walter has children – two sons in addition to Astri.'

The entire family was described as very close-knit.

'Sometimes all the brothers would be in the summer cabin at the same time. In Spain they have three apartments built close together, but it gets cramped down there as well. The grandmother's the one who owns them, but I think it's been ages since she was down there.'

'How long did your relationship with Astri last?' Wisting asked.

It looked as if Ulrik Stene found it difficult to answer. 'What can I say . . .' he began. 'We never really became properly established. Everything was sort of semi-detached. She had the apartment in Asker and spent long periods in Spain. The bottom fell out of the boat market and I started working in Colorline, two weeks on, two weeks off. And I have a son from a previous relationship I had to take care of. And then there was the age difference, you see, even though six years is not really much when both partners are in their thirties. But after the summer it foundered, in a sense. We both probably realized it wasn't something to build on. By then we'd been together for about two years.'

It seemed as if he wanted to add something, and Wisting kept silent while Ulrik Stene fiddled with a spoon lying on the table.

'Bernard was OK,' he continued after a lengthy pause. 'But I never felt entirely welcome with the others in the family. As if I wasn't good enough somehow.'

'In what way?' Wisting asked.

'As if I should be totally perfect,' Stene replied. 'Or at least look perfect to the grandmother. In my family I'm used to speaking openly about everything, especially if one of us has problems. But in Astri's family, they almost never spoke about one another or to one another.'

'When did you last have contact with Astri?'

'Sometime in September.'

'What was that about?'

Stene looked embarrassed. 'I invited her down here,' he replied. 'Suggested we could have a spa weekend.'

'Nothing came of it?'

Stene shook his head. 'She was behind with some deadlines at work. I suggested a later date, but then she was going off to Spain.' He sat up straight. 'I thought she was still there,' he added. 'What's happened to her?'

'We don't really know,' Wisting answered. 'She drove up from Spain last week. Since then, no one has heard from her. The van's just been found here now. That's why we thought she might have been in touch with you.'

'Did she drive all the way from Spain?' Stene asked.

'That's how it looks,' Wisting told him.

'She enjoys driving,' Stene said, mostly to himself. 'But it's a long journey . . . where did you find the car?'

Wisting specified the spot.

'That's not very far from her grandmother's cabin,' Stene pointed out.

'We've checked there,' Wisting said. 'Can you think of any other reason for her driving here? Anyone else she might want to meet up with?'

'None of my friends,' he answered. 'The people Astri knows around here are summer friends. Girls of the same age who come here in the summer holidays, the same way she has.'

His gaze wandered out through the window. Wisting let him sit and think.

'The only thing I can envisage is that she had to get something from the summer cabin,' was the suggestion he arrived at.

'What could that be?' Wisting asked.

Stene shrugged. 'No idea.'

Wisting produced the photo of Astri in her sou'wester and waterproofs. 'Is this Astri?' he asked.

Ulrik Stene nodded his head. 'Where did you get that?' he asked.

'She'd posted it on a website,' Wisting told him.

Stene frowned. 'A dating site?' he asked.

'No,' Wisting said, 'it's kind of job-related.' That wasn't too far from the truth.

'I was the one who took it,' Stene said, pointing at the picture. 'Right down there.' He tossed his head in the direction of the harbour.

'Do you have any other photos of her?'

Stene took out his mobile and flicked through to another image taken in the same place but more of a close-up. A smiling Astri was taking the sou'wester off her head. Her eyes were shining and she was looking straight into the camera lens.

'Do you think I could have that?' Wisting asked.

'I've probably got something more recent as well,' Stene said.

'Send me the one in the rain, please,' Wisting asked. Taking out his own phone, he gave the number to Stene, who pinged it over.

'Who else does she have in her circle, apart from the family?' Wisting pressed on. 'What female friends know her best?'

'She has no one close,' Stene replied. 'She's thirty-two. All the friends she grew up with have moved on in life. They're married and have started families. Astri's flitted around, never settling down. She's lived in different places, done different jobs. Never really established any social network around her. In the job she has now, she doesn't even need to turn up and meet her colleagues. She can sit wherever she likes at a computer screen.'

'Do you have *no* names at all?' Wisting insisted.

'She had a childhood friend who got cancer and died,' Stene replied. 'That affected her greatly. She became heavily involved, fundraising campaigns and all that. But as I said, she's dead now.'

'Are there any friends on Facebook?'

'Yes, but she's not particularly active there.'

'Could I take a look?'

Ulrik Stene opened up Facebook on his mobile. He was right. The last post was an atmospheric photograph from Spain of palm trees and sunshine. Apart from that, there were a few shared posts from a local organization that took care of stray cats and found homes for them. One name recurred in the comments and likes in what little had been posted on the page. Else Hagen.

'Do you know who that is?' Wisting asked.

'I think she's a friend from childhood,' Stene answered. 'She became single again a year or so ago. They had some contact in connection with that.'

Wisting jotted down the name and address before closing his notebook and getting ready to leave.

Ulrik Stene also rose to his feet. 'What do you think has happened?' he asked.

'I really don't know,' Wisting replied. 'I don't know her. What do you think?'

Stene hesitated. 'She's a bit different,' he said. 'You could say she's a nerd. It's pretty mad to suddenly take it into your head to drive from Spain to Norway. I mean . . . it looks as if something's made her freak out.'

'Has she had any mental health problems in the past?' Wisting asked, shrugging on his jacket.

'No, but it's hard to tell, I think.'

Wisting was also finding it difficult to see anything rational about setting off on a road trip, as Astri Arctander had done. She might even have been fleeing from something.

Ulrik Stene saw him out. Daylight was already failing and the temperature had fallen significantly. His car was chilly and he switched the heating on full blast before driving out towards Manvik.

Three hundred metres from the bus stop where the van had been found, a police car was parked at the roadside. A warning sign had been set up and a police officer signalled for him to slow down.

Wisting cruised calmly past.

The search party must have just arrived. They had gathered in the bus bay and taken the rescue dogs out of their vehicles. Kittil Gram was standing beside them.

Wisting swung in and let the engine idle. The snow crunched under his boots when he stepped out.

He greeted the dog handlers, who explained how they intended to conduct the search.

'We'll search both sides of the road at the same time,' the older officer told him. 'Ten metres in on either side. If that gives us no results, we should undertake a search in the area of the woods.'

He nodded towards the trees near the side of the road. Wisting understood his thinking. After skidding off the road, an injured and confused driver might start to walk in a haphazard direction. The dog handler had probably also come across this before. It sounded sensible to carry out a more thorough search in the area around the spot where the van had stopped even if there was no reason to believe that Astri had been injured.

One of the dogs began barking and seemed eager to get started.

'More than a week has passed, and there's been frost all that time,' Wisting pointed out.

'The advantage is that the snow's not too deep,' he said. 'In avalanches people can lie buried under five or six metres of snow, sometimes even more than that.'

The officer had attached a head torch while he spoke and was now ready to set off.

Wisting stood for a while, watching. The dogs darted in every direction, continually using their muzzles to push aside the loose snow. From time to time they came to a sudden stop, retracing their tracks before suddenly swerving off in another direction. In some places they sank into the soft snow but scrambled up again to continue the search.

Kittil Gram followed them, down on the road. Putting his hands on the small of his back, he gave Wisting a backward glance. 'I'll call you if we find anything,' he said.

23

Username: Shelook

Celia allowed herself the luxury of feeling smug. A total of seventy-three comments had rattled in beneath her post about the thefts in Palamós, as many as seven new ones in the last hour. The first response lauded her discovery. She received support for her view that Ruby Thompson was behind them and credit for drawing attention to something that presented the victim in a bad light. It was important to have transparency. Nothing should be kept hidden.

Celia had hoped that a comment from Astria would appear, but she was still inactive.

The discussion beneath her post zigzagged in different directions and provoked a variety of theories. An obvious possibility was that Ruby had been caught red-handed by a house-owner who had then gone too far in defending his property. Another suggestion was something that had not crossed Celia's mind: if Ruby were behind the thefts, she would have to sell on the proceeds. This could have brought her into contact with shady characters. Several felt she had probably swapped the games consoles and alcohol for drugs. The man called Olaf could be the person who received the stolen goods, and it was crucial to identify him. Some contributors disputed both theories because they did not fit the idea of a serial killer.

She felt the thought of a serial killer on the loose was simply wishful thinking by the most ardent of the forum members, a fanciful attitude. To find answers, you had to use what you knew as your starting point rather than beginning with a wild theory and choosing facts to suit.

What was known was that Ruby had made contact with a man called Olaf, or at least someone known by that name. They knew he was a criminal, since Ruby had bought marijuana from him. Jarod Denham, Mathis Leroux and her cousin Leo had all met him, and they all described him in the same terms. Leo thought he had worn a sweater with *Metallica* emblazoned on it. All three were sure he was from Norway, the country that had been the final destination on Ruby's itinerary. She had planned to spend the summer in Scandinavia before flying back to Australia, to experience the midnight sun and meet the liberal-minded inhabitants.

Celia clicked on Astria's bank of photographs. Among the two thousand or so images, Ruby had been identified in sixteen of them. It was entirely possible that Olaf too was in at least one.

The pictures were displayed in chronological order. She began by scrutinizing the photos from twelve o'clock onwards. It had been the *Primer baño del año* that day. The start of the bathing season was marked by an event in which a multitude of people took part in a communal dip. Thousands gathered on the beach, most of them spectators.

Ruby, Jarod and Mathis had also been present.

Shifting to full-screen mode, she leaned forward and studied every single person in turn, peering more closely at anyone in long black trousers. After half an hour she had been through 300 images and moved quarter of the way through the timeline, with no result.

Ruby had been easier to find. Jarod and Mathis had described her outfit in the police interviews. The yellow beanie had been easy to spot.

Ten minutes later, she came up with a candidate. Someone in black trousers and a black long-sleeved sweater with printing across the chest. He stood in the second row of bystanders, wearing sunglasses. She spotted him between two other onlookers, his face half turned away, and at quite some distance from the photographer.

Even if she succeeded in finding other, better photos, it was a far stretch from that to discovering who he was. It would be easier if she had been in Palamós itself, where she could ask around and go to the places Ruby had frequented, perhaps on the pretext that she was interested in buying some marijuana.

The idea became fixed in her mind. She had two more shifts before a few days off and it was three hours by bus to Palamós. She could probably stay with her cousin Leo.

Taking out her mobile to send him a message, she stopped mid-sentence and deleted what she had written.

She'd prefer to rent a bungalow at the campsite, the one where Ruby had stayed. The phone number was listed in the police reports.

In fact, the campsite had four stars on Tripadvisor, and the cost was reasonable.

The decision was quickly taken. In the course of five minutes she had booked both her bus ticket and an overnight stay.

24

Username: Darby

Wisting was alone again in the department, seated in front of his computer with the door open. The lights in the corridor were switched off.

Astria's disappearance from the forum had generated comments galore. A lengthy discussion was kicked off by someone who thought it outrageous for her to simply abandon the online community without completing the task she had taken on. Two other contributors supported this opinion and felt that the least she could do was sign off and hand the photo project to someone else. Several of them were willing to take on the assignment. The discussion changed direction when Shelook pointed out that something could have happened to Astria. She could have fallen ill or had an accident. Those who had initially been critical of Astria were accused of thoughtlessness for not realizing how inconsiderate and hurtful their comments could be. A written conversation of sorts emerged from this, with six members arguing the point. A new member intervened in the ongoing exchange of views, wondering if Astria could have come across something that had placed her in danger, that through her investigations she had come too close to the truth. This was rejected because Astria lived in Norway, but the continuing chat took on a conspiratorial tone. One user reminded them that the last thing Astria had written was that she thought she had found something interesting, around the same time as a theory was introduced that the killer could be in the forum, reading everything about the case. This was laughed off to some extent, but another suggestion was that someone ought to make an analysis of the work Astria had done to see if anyone had shown a conspicuous interest. Shelook took on this task and the thread ended with a jokey comment that Shelook could easily be the rapist and murderer who had now infiltrated the online group.

The phone buzzed in his pocket. The sound was switched off and he felt it only as a pulsing on his thigh. He saw it was an unknown number but answered, simply stating his name.

The caller was a woman. 'You've been trying to phone me,' she said. 'I'm Else Hagen.'

Wisting sat bolt upright. This was Astri Arctander's childhood friend who had been in contact with her on Facebook.

'Thanks for calling back,' he said, explaining who he was. 'It's to do with Astri Arctander. She's been missing for over a week.'

Else Hagen reacted with astonishment but had no idea what could have caused Astri to travel back from Spain. 'I don't think I've spoken to her since last summer,' she said.

'Was that before or after she and Ulrik Stene split up?' Wisting asked.

'Around that time,' Else replied. 'Both before and after.'

'Did you have any idea why they broke up?'

'Not really. I don't think it was a single incident or anything in particular that caused it, it was more that she came to realize he wasn't the man for her.'

'Why was that?'

'What was it she said . . . that he was so uninformed. You see, Astri's so bright and knowledgeable. Ulrik wasn't really on the ball, if you know what I mean. What bothered Astri was that he always tried to make out he was smarter than he actually was. He just created the impression that he understood what she or other people were talking about. In the long run, that doesn't work out.'

Wisting nodded. He knew the type.

'Of course, I've never met him,' Else Hagen continued. 'But I got the idea that they were very different. He was superficial, interested in appearances, cars and boats. Going out to restaurants. Astri's never been like that, though the rest of her family are very concerned with outward appearances.'

She stopped suddenly. 'Do you think Ulrik has something to do with her disappearance?' she asked.

'At present we don't know what's happened to her,' Wisting replied, avoiding the question. 'He was the one who mentioned that you had been in touch with her. I wanted to find out if you might know something.'

Else Hagen apologized for being unable to help. 'I just hope you get to the bottom of it,' she said.

Wisting thanked her again for phoning him back and was rounding off the conversation when another call came in. The display showed that it was from the central switchboard.

'I have the local paper waiting on the line,' the operator said. 'They're asking about the search taking place at Manvik. You're listed as having responsibility for the case. I don't know how much I'm able to say. Can I transfer it to you?'

Wisting had anticipated this. 'OK, go ahead,' he replied.

Garm Søbakken was the reporter on the line, and he came straight to the point when Wisting answered. 'We've received a reader's photo of a search party with dogs near Manvik,' he said. 'What are you looking for?'

'It's to do with a woman reported missing from Asker,' Wisting replied. 'She's been unaccounted for since the beginning of December. The vehicle she was driving was found parked out there yesterday.'

'What are we talking about?' Søbakken asked. 'Suicide?'

Wisting understood his reasoning. The information Wisting gave him bore certain signs of personal tragedy. Indirectly the journalist was asking if it was appropriate to print a small notice or whether the story demanded greater attention.

'There's nothing to suggest that,' Wisting told him. 'The vehicle was driving on summer tyres. She could have abandoned it and continued on foot. We're looking for observations from the late evening and night of 2 December. That was when the snow came.'

'So the car's been parked there for more than a week?'

Wisting confirmed this and told him the type of vehicle involved.

'Where was she going?'

'She's familiar with the area and has holidayed for years at a family cabin in Eidsten.'

'Is it possible for you to release her name?'

'Not yet.'

'Age?'

'Thirty-two.'

'Do you think she may have been knocked down?'

'There could have been an accident of some kind,' Wisting conceded. 'For now we're primarily concentrating on locating her.'

He provided details of the number of officers taking part in the search and the assistance received from the rescue dog teams.

'How long do you intend to continue with the search?' Søbakken asked.

'That depends on the dogs, really,' Wisting replied. 'To start with we want a thorough search of a stretch of three kilometres on either side of the road. Then we may extend the radius after that.'

Garm Søbakken summarized the information he had received and rang off.

Wisting now phoned Walter Arctander's number. When he answered, the anxiety in his voice was evident.

'There's no news,' were Wisting's opening words. He explained that contact had been established with the Catalan police and that he had spoken to Ulrik Stene. He also mentioned the receipts found in the van and said that he had paid a visit to the summer cabin.

'We've launched a search with dogs along the road between Eidsten and the spot where the van was left,' he said. 'It's been picked up by the media and we're making an official statement to confirm that she's missing.'

'With her name and photograph?' Walter Arctander asked.

'Not yet,' Wisting replied.

Arctander was imagining the same course of events as Garm Søbakken. 'Do you think someone could have run her over and driven on?' he asked.

'That's one possibility,' Wisting admitted. 'The driving conditions were difficult that night.'

Walter Arctander had a list of questions and Wisting answered them to the best of his ability.

'We're flying home tomorrow,' Arctander said when the conversation was winding up. 'Irene and I. The others will stay down here.'

Once the conversation was over, Wisting was left with a feeling of not having been entirely honest. He had held back everything to do with Ruby Thompson's murder. Until now he had not included it in any documentation of his own investigation either.

It took almost an hour to write a report gathering up all the threads from Spain and the Ruby Thompson homicide, but for the meantime he only saved it on his own computer.

By the time he had finished, the local paper, *Østlands-Posten*, had updated their website with the story about the search for Astri Arctander. He read it without finding any errors.

The search out at Manvik had continued for more than two hours. In Australia it would soon be four a.m. All the same, he referred back to his last email exchange with Michelle Norris and wrote that Astria had been identified as Astri Arctander. He told her about the abandoned vehicle, described the ongoing search operation and attached a link so that she could read the news for herself in automatic translation.

He did not mention the yellow hat in the glove compartment but wrote that he had spoken to the man who had taken Astria's photograph. He attached the photo he had obtained but asked her not to share the image or Astria's true identity until this had been cleared with the family.

His phone buzzed again. This time it was Kittil Gram.

Wisting glanced at the time, thinking that Gram was probably calling to let him know they were ending the search for the day.

'Yes?' he answered.

'We've found something,' Gram said. 'I think you should come out here.'

25

Username: Nichelle

The constant drone of the aero engines made her drowsy. She had bought a surprisingly cheap ticket on the night flight from Adelaide and had only been in the air for six hours but already felt jetlagged. When she changed planes in Qatar, the time would be just past midnight. At that point, she would still have nearly twenty-four hours before she arrived in the Spanish town.

The onboard Internet connection was unstable and it took time to download even pages that contained nothing but text. Michelle Norris gave a deep sigh. Craving nicotine, she glanced up from the screen. The connection was probably better further forward on the plane.

At last the page was updated. It was six o'clock in the evening in Europe, probably the time of maximum activity, but there were no new posts or comments.

She had had the same thought as the one that appeared in the thread below Astria's disappearance. It was unthinkable that Ruby's killer could be a member of the forum. She had gone through all the usernames without finding anyone suspicious, but she did not like the idea that he might be there, either as a silent lurker or an active participant.

The thought was fleeting, but it triggered disquiet. Journalists writing about current murder investigations must feel some of the same emotions, or police officers making statements at a press conference. The killer could be paying them rapt attention.

The man in the window seat had begun to snore. Michelle would have to try to catch some sleep too. The laptop felt hot on her knee and the battery power had dwindled.

An email alert popped up, from the Norwegian policeman.

She realized from the first few lines that he had discovered who Astria was and expected to read that he had made contact with her, but the initial sense of relief quickly turned to concern. Astria was missing. She really had disappeared. She hadn't simply dropped out of the forum – something had happened to her.

A photo was attached. The woman she knew as Astria stared straight into the camera. Her eyes seemed to burn right into her. Eyes shining and full of life.

The local newspaper in Norway had covered the search operation. Wisting had pasted in a link to the report. It took time to download. The translation was not grammatically correct, but she understood the gist of it. There was a suggestion of a possible hit-and-run accident. The images were grainy, taken in the dark using a flash – a man with a head torch and high-vis waistcoat trudging through the fresh snow behind a dog. The police were directing the flow of traffic on the nearby road. Wisting's name was mentioned in the text, but she did not spot him in any of the images.

She read the article one more time before publishing a new post: *Update – Astria Missing*.

26

One of the dogs had shown interest in a spot on the eastern side of the main road, beside a tree trunk about three metres from the verge. Kittil Gram used his flashlight to indicate the location; a spade had been left embedded in the snow.

Wisting took his torch and walked along the tracks that had disturbed the fresh snow. A circular hole had been dug, around the size of a car tyre. Aiming the torch beam into it, he saw the stiff, frozen hand and partial arm uncovered by the search team.

The dog handler who had made the discovery stood on the road. His vehicle was parked behind Wisting's car. The emergency lights were flashing erratically and one traffic lane was closed off.

'She must have been hit by a car travelling at top speed to have been thrown so far from the road,' he said.

The dog was barking in the cage at the rear of the vehicle.

Wisting let his gaze slide along the roadway. It was fifty metres from the turn-off to Eidsten. The summer cabin was half a kilometre further on. She had almost reached her destination.

'There could be traces of paint on her from the car,' Kittil Gram suggested. 'I thought it'd be best to leave it to the technicians to uncover her.'

With a nod, Wisting glanced down at the blue-grey hand before walking back to join the others.

'It could have been the snowplough,' the dog handler said. 'It would have tossed her quite a distance.'

As a delivery van drove past, travelling far too fast on the narrow road, fresh snow from the verge was whipped up by the side draught. Averting his face, Wisting returned to his own car. He called the forensic technicians, who confirmed they were on their way but would not arrive for more than half an hour.

The windscreen was misting up. Kittil Gram, having sent the dog handler away, now got into Wisting's vehicle. 'You don't need to wait,' he said. 'This is going to take a few hours. We'll have to stay here anyway and keep one traffic lane closed.'

'I'm staying until they've dug her out,' Wisting told him.

'The boys have gone to get some food and hot drinks,' Gram went on. 'As soon as they're back, we'll start on the top layer of snow, so that it's a bit easier for the technicians when they get here.'

A few snowflakes landed on the windscreen, melting almost at once. Leaning forward, Wisting peered obliquely up at the sky. The darkness made it impossible to see anything.

'They'll be here for a while,' Wisting said. 'It might become necessary to close the road completely to make room for them to set up their equipment. Vans, tents, floodlights, generator . . .'

Gram stole a glance at him, sizing him up, as if he had realized Wisting had not told him everything about the background to this assignment.

'There's more to this,' he said. 'Something tells me it might not have been an accident.'

'She must have had a reason for setting out on this long drive,' Wisting told him. 'Either she was fleeing from something or else she was coming here for some particular purpose.'

'Maybe to see someone,' Gram added.

'At any rate, it must have been important for her to make

this journey,' Wisting said, but added nothing further about what was preying on his mind. If it had been important for her to come here, it could have been important for someone else to prevent her.

A police car drove up behind them. The two officers who got out approached them with paper cups and a flask of fresh coffee before setting to work with the snow shovels.

Wisting was halfway through his coffee when the forensic technicians arrived. He took his cup with him as he went out to meet them. They were not the same ones who had examined the van. He thanked them for coming so quickly and gave them a brief status report while traffic continued to be directed past.

'She also had a travel bag, a laptop and two mobile phones with her when she drove from Spain,' he said. 'They weren't found in the van.'

The eldest of the technicians nodded.

'I'll let the on-duty police prosecutor know and arrange for a post-mortem,' Wisting added.

He lingered at the roadside while the forensic technicians ventured out across the snow for a recce. Then they moved back to their vehicle and unpacked their gear. A heated tent was set up in the roadway, a generator produced and cables extended all the way to floodlights out in the snow.

'The road traffic HQ will see to the closing of the road and the signposting of a diversion,' Kittil Gram came to tell them. 'In the first instance until six a.m.'

'That will give us peace to work,' one of the technicians commented. Zipping up his overalls, he indicated with a nod that he was ready to make a start.

Wisting followed them out into the snow. At the discovery site he thrust his hands into his pockets and, shoulders hunched, watched them work. Gradually more and more of the body was revealed: a woman with shoulder-length hair. Her face was glazed with frost, making it unrecognizable. She lay on her side with one arm stretched out slightly from her body, knees bent and legs tucked up. She was fully dressed in a sweater, jacket and trousers buttoned at the waist. That was at least something.

The stiff body was carefully broken free from the frozen ground and then made ready for lifting across to a black body bag made of thick plastic. Transport to Forensics was already waiting. Both Wisting and Gram assisted with transferring the body to the bag and carrying it to the van. Exhaust fumes from the generator and the engines running in stationary vehicles lay like a filthy fog between the two banks of snow flanking the road.

Garm Søbakken from *Østlands-Posten* had shown up half an hour earlier. He stood at a distance, taking photographs. When the corpse was placed on a stretcher and slid into the van, he called Wisting over.

'You've found her,' he said.

'We've made a discovery, yes,' Wisting confirmed. The exhaust vapour tickled his throat and made him cough. 'The identity won't be established until the post-mortem tomorrow,' he added.

'Can you say anything more about what's happened?' Søbakken asked.

'It's too early,' Wisting replied, adding a few stock phrases about a wide-ranging investigation and not excluding any possibilities.

Søbakken seemed satisfied and asked no further questions. Wisting returned to the technicians, who had now withdrawn into the heated tent. Kittil Gram had arranged for hot drinks.

'We've not found her luggage, though,' Wisting said,

helping himself from the Thermos flask. 'A laptop and two mobile phones. They should be lying somewhere in the same area.'

The two technicians had already formed a plan. They would clear the expanse around the discovery site to search for traces and had already requisitioned thermal tarpaulins and fan heaters to melt the snow.

'Maybe they'll turn up there,' one of the technicians said, 'and if not, we can try using a metal detector along the road. But we may have to clear more snow to get a result.'

'Her clothes seemed intact,' Kittil Gram commented.

He, as well as the others, had experience of hit-and-run accidents: even at relatively low speeds, a car could tear the victim's clothing to shreds.

'The snow beneath her seemed clean,' said the technician. 'No traces of blood. It almost looked as if she had just lain down there.'

They drained their cups in silence before returning to their tasks, while Wisting went back to his car to call the parents.

27

Username: Darby

Line sat in front of the large computer screen in her office down in the basement. The door at the top of the stairs was left open in case Amalie woke up. A fan heater sat in the middle of the room, blowing hot air towards her legs.

She had written her first post. She should really have been working on the documentary film, but she had been drawn into the Spanish murder mystery. The more she read, the stronger a hold the story had on her. In the past two days, she had scarcely done anything other than study the case. Not only through what she read on the dedicated website but also through material she had found in other sources. She felt she had gained a good picture of the Australian murder victim – she was familiar now with the streets she had walked through, the place she had lived in and the people she had met. Having worked her way to a comprehensive overview of the cast of characters, she was fully aware of all the theories in circulation and had a clear grasp of what was factual and what was mere speculation, rumour or pure guesswork.

The conclusion she came to after this exhaustive analysis was that Ruby Thompson had been killed by someone she did not know and who was most likely not referred to in the police documents or mentioned anywhere in the forum. The idea that the same person was responsible for several of the unsolved murder cases along the northern coast of

Spain was no longer alien to her. A man given the nickname The Coast Killer by ApopheniaX.

The sound of a car reached her: the snow muffled the thrum of the engine but made the noise travel differently. Line turned her head and sat listening. The vehicle drove past, moving further down the street.

She had sent a message to her father, asking him to call in to see her after work. This had been before she had read in the online newspapers about the search operation and discovery of a body near Manvik. His response had been brief, simply *OK*, without stipulating any particular time. A plate of leftovers from dinner was waiting for him in the fridge.

Her gaze lingered on the computer screen. She had not yet published her post, mostly because she wanted to check for linguistic errors one more time. She was not used to writing in English. Also, she was keen to discuss the contents with her father before she made them public.

On the noticeboard in front of her she had pinned up the chart ApopheniaX had drawn up of the seven unsolved homicides. Since the first murder almost seventeen years ago, the intervals between the crimes had become increasingly short. In the forum, a number of people had pointed out that this was a well-known pattern for serial killers, but there was something about the incidence rate that made no sense. Prior to Ruby Thompson, it had been ten months since a Spanish girl was killed in Torrevieja, almost 700 kilometres further along the coastline. Before that, two years had elapsed since the Swiss girl was found dead in Empuriabrava near the French border, while a Belgian girl had been killed in Blanes less than a year before that again.

She had ApopheniaX's map on the screen, with the various points marked: discovery site, year and name of each victim. The map extended for miles southwards along the coast, but in the north it stopped at the border with France.

Line had studied French at senior high school, but that had been a long time ago and she was far from fluent in the language. She knew that woman was *femme* but needed help to translate the other search terms. Murdered, beach, naked and unsolved or unexplained.

Assassinée, le rivage or *la plage, nue, non résolu* and *inexpliqué*.

She had found another case. Two years ago, a Danish girl had been found murdered on the beach outside Perpignan on the French side of the Mediterranean coast.

Danish newspapers had been awash with reports, making access to information easy for her. Three weeks before the murder, twenty-three-year-old Lone Sand and a female friend of the same age had set out on a round trip through Europe by car. Somewhere in Italy, they had parted company. The friend had received a message that her grandmother was seriously ill and she had flown home to Copenhagen. Lone Sand had travelled on alone to meet up with a student friend who happened to be in Spain, but she never made it that far.

The *Berlinske Tidende* newspaper had published several pictures from her Instagram account and wrote of how the entire trip had been documented. Several times a day, Lone Sand had posted pictures of herself, with blonde, almost white hair, blue eyes and a tentative smile, in the various locations she had visited. The series of photographs began immediately after she had dropped her friend off at the airport in Florence. She had travelled to famous places such as Genoa, Monaco, Nice, Cannes and Marseilles. After Montpellier, this came to a sudden end. Her parents had reported her missing two days after the last photo was published online. The Danish police had forwarded the report, but the case had been given scant attention in France: her personal details and vehicle information were merely entered into a register. Five days later, a half-naked female body was found in the French city of Perpignan. The car was found near the harbour a further four days later. The cause of death was strangulation, but the killer was never caught.

Timewise, this placed the case between the Swiss girl in Empuriabrava and the Spanish girl in Torrevieja. The circumstances were identical to all the other crimes. A young woman with no local affiliation. Strangled and dumped in the sea. The saltwater had washed away all forensic traces.

She was keen to share her discovery with the other forum members. The work of gathering facts and formulating her post made her nostalgic for her days as a journalist, when she had worked on cases where she could communicate information no one else knew.

She read through the text one more time, adjusting a few sentences before pressing the 'post' button.

The Coast Killer – a ninth victim?

Eight other users were logged in. It would not take long for her to receive the first responses. She sat waiting, on tenterhooks, before going upstairs to check on Amalie.

Her daughter lay curled up in the middle of the bed. Lifting her slightly, Line planted a kiss on her cheek and laid her down again so that her head was lying on the pillow.

A vehicle stopped outside. Just after that, she heard a dull thud as a car door slammed.

This time it was her father, and she went to open the door for him. 'I saw you'd found something,' Line said. She spoke in hushed tones, even though there was no danger of waking Amalie.

Her father hung up his jacket in the hallway. 'It's her,' he said.

'Who?' Line asked.

'The woman from the website,' her father replied. 'Astria.'

This thought had not even entered Line's head when she read about the ongoing search operation.

'There was an update on the forum,' she said, 'but it simply confirmed that Astria was officially reported missing and more information would follow in due course.'

She put her hand to her head and ran her fingers through her hair. 'Have you spoken to the woman down in Australia?' she asked.

'I did, but that was before we found her,' Wisting replied.

He sat down at the kitchen table and began to explain. When he had finished, she realized he was holding something back.

'What has really happened?' she asked.

'It's too early to say,' Wisting told her. 'It could be like the case of the guy who was thrown off the bus in Elverum. The one who froze to death at the bus stop.'

Line nodded. There had been copious coverage of that in the newspapers. The driver who had ejected the drunk, quarrelsome passenger had lost his job but had also received a good deal of support on social media.

As Wisting reached out for the cup she had put down in front of him, Line studied his face. 'You don't think we're talking here of a tragic accident,' she said firmly.

'It could have ended up like that, but there are various circumstances that need to be explained,' he said. 'The very fact she chose to drive from Spain, for one. And why did she come here, of all places? What did she want to do here?'

'Could it have had something to do with the murder in Palamós?'

It looked as if her father had something on the tip of his

tongue, but then he changed his mind. Instead he finished by shrugging his shoulders.

'Have you been on the website again?' Line asked.

Wisting said he had. 'After all, it's relevant because, so far, that's where the last sign of life came from her,' he answered.

'I've written a post,' Line said, explaining her discovery. She could see he was growing increasingly sceptical as she did so. 'I know,' she said, before her father had a chance to say anything. 'It's conspiratorial, and could well be down to coincidence, but there's also a good possibility. Spain has a huge population. It consists of many different provinces and an assortment of police forces. No one sees the connections until you start looking for them.'

Wisting did not contradict her. 'I have to concentrate on my own case,' he said. 'Trying to find out what happened to Astri Arctander.'

Line smiled. 'That's exactly what makes it possible for one and the same person to keep going,' she said. 'The fact that no one lifts their eyes and looks beyond their own desktop.'

Wisting smiled back at her as he got to his feet. 'Do you think the serial killer followed her all the way from Spain?' he asked.

'Are you saying she was murdered?' Line countered.

'Well, I won't find that out until after tomorrow's post-mortem,' he replied.

Line accompanied him to the door.

'Have you received any comments on your post?' he asked.

'I don't know,' Line answered. 'I posted it just before you arrived.'

With a brief nod, he hugged her and set off into the snowy streetscape. It occurred to her that she had forgotten to offer him the leftover food, and she shouted after him. Shaking his head, he clambered into his car.

After heading back down to the basement, Line refreshed the webpage. Eight comments.

This is terrifying was the first reaction. The others shared this opinion, and several posed the same question: *What should we do with this information?*

Line remained in her seat. She had no idea.

28

Username: Nichelle

Michelle Norris woke when the passenger beside her stood up, wanting to get past. She made room and took her bearings. The screen on the ceiling informed her that the plane would land at Hamad International Airport in Qatar in forty minutes' time.

Her laptop was under the seat in front of her. She retrieved it and sat it on her knee, but it took ages to access the Internet.

The only email of interest was an automatic alert that Darby had published a new post on the website.

The other passenger had now returned. Moving out into the centre aisle, Michelle put her laptop down on her seat and took the opportunity to visit the toilet.

Her inactivity on the computer had caused her to lose the Internet connection, so she hooked up again and saw that the post concerned the possibility of a serial killer. Darby had discovered a new victim who fitted the modus operandi and pattern – a tourist, a Danish woman travelling on the French side of the coast.

The post was well written and summarized the main features of the story as described in the media. In the comments, there was general agreement that the information about a possible link among the many victims should be reported to the police.

It dawned on Michelle that she would have to play a more

active role. As soon as she arrived in Palamós, she would have to request a meeting with the investigators. ApopheniaX had introduced the theory that whoever had killed Ruby could have been behind a number of murders. He was from Barcelona. Maybe she could take him with her.

She embarked on a post to tell the others she was on her way to Spain. An announcement over the loudspeakers informed passengers that the plane was starting its approach and to prepare for landing. The Internet connection was abruptly switched off, but she managed to finish writing her post and save it on the machine before closing down the window.

The front page of the Norwegian online newspaper that had reported on the search for Astria had been updated in the background, with a new headline story. She did not understand any of the text, but the picture told her everything she needed to know. Four men were hoisting a stretcher over a bank of snow. One of them was William Wisting.

29

Overnight, grey winter fog had drifted across the landscape. It froze as it met the cold ground and made the roads dangerously icy.

On his way into the police station, Wisting drove via Manvik. The road was still closed to ordinary traffic but no further work had been done at the discovery site. However, a police patrol stood on guard in expectation of further investigations being carried out. In the course of the morning, a team would arrive to shovel the top layer of snow from the spot where Astri Arctander had lain and thereafter the remaining snow would be melted. The technicians had suggested they would probably be unable to do anything more until the next day.

Wisting drove slowly past, giving a nod to the two police officers in the patrol car and continuing at the same speed along to the spot where Astri had left her vehicle. En route he struggled to collect his thoughts. He could not shake off the idea that the case for which he had been assigned responsibility was somehow intertwined with the story of the Australian girl's murder in Spain eight months earlier. All the same, it felt premature to contact the Catalan police officers investigating her death. He needed something more specific. The only thing he had, strictly speaking, was a yellow beanie hat and Astri Arctander's interest in the crime.

The detour took him almost half an hour, but there was no one in the department when he arrived. On the way along the corridor he heard a phone ringing and realized it was coming from his office. As he threw his jacket down on the chair, he recognized the internal number of the Crime Response Centre.

Centralized criminal response centres were part of the police reforms. All cases were registered and sorted there, before either being dismissed or forwarded for investigation. In principle the work comprised much of what had been Wisting's job over the past twenty years or so. He ensured that all reports were properly prioritized and dealt with in the initial phase. The difference was that the CRC handled all the cases in the whole of the new police district.

The investigator calling was Mikkelsen, the superintendent who had forwarded the email from Michelle Norris. 'I've gone through the details,' he said, without reference to the email. 'There's nothing to suggest anything criminal has taken place.'

'There are a number of strange circumstances,' Wisting said.

'You're using a lot of resources,' Mikkelsen commented. 'Forensics has reduced capacity because of staff illness.'

Wisting sat down. He had responsibility for the case, but the forensics section was a shared resource over which he had no say.

'All that snow is certainly a challenge,' he replied. 'I'm using my own personnel to do the clearing, but we can't avoid the necessity for a competent examination of the area.'

'When will you get the post-mortem results?' Mikkelsen asked.

'By the end of the day,' Wisting told him.

'Then I'll instruct the forensics team to prioritize other tasks in the meantime,' Mikkelsen said. 'Until you know whether anything criminal has taken place, and whether we're talking about a crime scene at all.'

'That's fine,' Wisting answered. 'But we've lost a lot of time already. She's been lying there since the first snow fall.'

'Then half a day more or less won't make any difference,' Mikkelsen concluded.

The conversation had irritated Wisting. Mikkelsen had obviously not only read the dispassionate case documents but also the online newspapers in which the death was presented as a tragic accident. That the vehicle had come to grief in the snowy weather and the driver had left it and frozen to death on the way to summon help.

Noise out in the corridor told him that the other investigators were coming in. He ran through the reports in the operations log and prepared for the morning meeting.

The room was silent when he entered. Wisting took a seat at the head of the table and looked around. They were increasingly few in number. As well as Nils Hammer and Maren Dokken, there were four other police detectives present, in addition to Bjørg Karin from the CID office and Kittil Gram from the patrol section. None of them were close friends of his, but they belonged together. They were a team, working together, and he relied on them completely.

He decided to share what he knew about Astri Arctander. About the murder in Palamós and the yellow hat in the glove compartment. Not in extensive detail, but enough to let them all glimpse the big picture. The possibility that the young woman had been carrying a secret when she returned to Norway.

He wrapped up the morning meeting by assigning Maren Dokken to take and follow up whatever messages came in as a result of the public announcement, as well as talking to the bus driver working on the route past that stretch where the Spanish-registered vehicle had been abandoned.

One hour later, reports began to tick in – electronic

data and answers to messages sent after the van had been found.

Astri's bank account had been debited in accordance with the receipts they had found in the van and there were also another three purchases of fuel, food and drink they had not previously known of.

The Spanish van had also been recorded at Norwegian toll stations. The first transit was at 18.43 on the E6 directly north of the Swedish border. Less than three hours later, the vehicle was registered on the E18 immediately outside Larvik. This told them she had driven the fastest route, probably without stopping. She must have turned off for Larvik just before ten p.m., just when the snow had begun to blanket the ground.

The information drew a clearer picture of Astri's movements on that last evening but added no new facts of any significance.

Wisting had greater expectations of the telecoms data, but this turned out to be a concise summary. Her Norwegian phone number had scarcely been in use in the past month, but the printouts confirmed that she had taken the mobile with her when she left Spain. At 18.42 on 2 December she had received a text message from Telenor. The location showed she had just passed the Norwegian border at Svinesund. After that, no activity was recorded on it.

Just as the entry into Norway was documented, Wisting could follow the phone all the way down through Europe. Every time it passed a new national border, she received a welcome message from the telecoms provider in the country she had just driven into. The overview confirmed that she had driven from Spain and entered France just before ten a.m. on the day after she had written her last post in the online forum.

One detail aroused his interest. The evening before she left, Astri had called a Norwegian number registered to a woman in Oslo called Mona Brandt. Wisting searched her name. One year older than Astri, she was married with two children and employed in an energy company with offices in Lysaker.

The phone conversation had not lasted longer than a minute or so.

He had not yet had time to fully map out Astri's social circle, but Mona Brandt was not a name that had cropped up so far.

He keyed in the number. A woman answered in formal terms and gave a company name as well as her own.

Wisting introduced himself. 'It's to do with a current case. Astri Arctander has been missing for more than a week,' he went on to explain. 'Yesterday a woman was found dead in the search area, and we anticipate that it's her.'

The breathing on the other end of the line sounded tense. 'She's dead?' Mona Brandt asked in astonishment.

Wisting told her how Astri had been found under the snow. Mona Brandt had heard of the case in the news but was taken aback to find it had to do with someone she knew.

'I can see from her phone calls that you were one of the last people to speak to her,' Wisting added.

'She called me from Spain,' Mona Brandt replied. 'We grew up in the same street, but I hadn't talked to her for years.'

'Why did she phone?' Wisting asked.

'She wanted to speak to my father.'

'Your father?' Wisting repeated.

'He works at Kripos. Halvor Brandt. I gave her his number.'

Wisting knew Brandt, a forensics technician of many

years' standing who had co-authored a textbook on crime scene investigation.

'Did she say what it was about, or do you have any idea why she wanted to contact him?'

'No. She just said she had to speak to someone in the police about something. Dad was the only person she knew. I haven't spoken to him about it.'

Wisting scanned through the phone data on the screen. The call to her childhood friend had not been followed up with a call to the father.

'Did she say anything else?' he asked.

'I was a bit busy when she rang, so there was no time for chat. Just the sort of thing you say when it's been a long time since you saw somebody. That we should meet up sometime soon. That kind of thing. You can always phone my dad.'

Wisting took the number. Halvor Brandt answered at once but could not offer any assistance. 'I remember Astri from when she was a wee girl,' he said. 'But she hasn't phoned me. Do you think she'd got mixed up in something?'

'It's too early to say,' Wisting replied, telling him about the impulsive car journey from Spain.

'It almost sounds as if she'd fled the country,' Brandt commented.

'The circumstances give us cause to do some investigating,' Wisting said. 'We've already sent in material from the vehicle for examination. It's probably ended up at your labs.'

'Did you find anything in particular?' Brandt asked.

The way he spoke suggested he might have the opportunity to speed up the investigations.

'Well, considering she sought contact with you . . .' Wisting replied, tailing off. 'I found a knitted beanie wrapped in plastic in the glove compartment. It was packed up and sealed, almost as if she'd intended using it as evidence. We've requested a DNA analysis.'

'I see,' Brandt said. 'That sounds intriguing. Have you any idea whose hat it is?'

Although Wisting did, he gave an evasive answer, withholding the information about Ruby Thompson's murder.

'I'll check how far the request has processed through our system and see what I can do,' Halvor Brandt promised.

30

Username: Nichelle

Michelle Norris found a seat beside a socket in the transit area and plugged in. The airport in Doha offered two hours' free Internet. She entered the necessary personal details and logged on.

A mixture of confusion and sorrow had taken root within her. The dreadful feeling showed in deep furrows on her forehead as she read the translation of the Norwegian newspaper article. It contained no more information than she had already understood from the images she had seen on board the flight. A woman had been found dead.

She checked her email to see if Wisting had sent her more details but found nothing from him there. However, the automatic search engine reported a number of Internet hits on the key words *Ruby Thompson*, *killed* and *Palamós*. There was something about a reward.

One of the links was to an online newspaper at home in Australia. Ruby's parents had offered a reward of 25,000 euros in connection with their daughter's murder. They had also engaged a private detective, who had already gone to Spain.

There was a photo of Ruby's father, Flynn Thompson, dressed in a dark suit that must have been tailor-made for his overweight body. Michelle felt rising irritation. Flynn Thompson had opposed his daughter's travel plans. When she defied him and left despite that, he had punished her financially, telling her she would have to manage on her own. This had had consequences. Ruby had come into contact with people she would otherwise have had nothing to do with. Indirectly, this could be the reason she was killed.

The private investigator, Ethan Mahoney by name, had formerly been a detective with the Victoria Police in Melbourne. He had already been in Catalonia for more than a week and had met with the investigators responsible for the case, which had been at a standstill since the release of the only suspect. The private detective claimed that no active investigation was ongoing and the case had been suspended in anticipation of the perpetrator committing further crimes and his profile appearing more or less at random in the DNA register.

Ethan Mahoney, a man with an angular face and a grey buzz cut, was pictured on the beach at Palamós. The sleeves of his white shirt were rolled up and looked tight on his upper arms. His investigations had uncovered an error in the Catalan police's information about the last sighting of Ruby Thompson. The police had publicized a picture of her leaving a pizzeria, but the private eye had traced a later photograph that showed the route she had taken.

Michelle Norris swore under her breath. This was Astria's photo, the one taken by a CCTV camera in the street a couple of blocks away from the pizza parlour. Ruby was walking with plugs in her ears and a bag slung over one shoulder. Either the private detective was a member of the forum, or he had spoken to the same people as Astria.

She read on. One of the leads the detective was following was the possibility that there was a link between Ruby's murder and the unsolved killing of the German backpacker Bertine Franck twelve years earlier. In that connection, he was tracking contacts in criminal circles in Palamós, pointing out that there had been a burglary in the town on the evening Ruby was killed.

Michelle felt certain that Ethan Mahoney had taken his information from the online forum. He was also mapping out the geography of the coastline and comparing this with weather data and sea currents to work out where Ruby's body could have been dumped.

At the end of the article, a link to a webpage in Spanish and English was included where the public could submit tip-offs.

Her anger subsided. Even though the private sleuth took credit for what the members of the forum had discovered together, perhaps it required just such a person to nudge the case along. He was someone the Catalan police had to listen to – a former colleague who represented Ruby's family.

She clicked into the webpage and opened the contact form. She put in her details, saying that she was on her way to Spain, and asked for a meeting.

'The cold has taken good care of her,' Mogens Poulsen said in his Danish accent.

Wisting fine-tuned the volume on the video link with the police pathologist. He was sitting in a conference room with a representative of the ID group in Kripos. The post-mortem had been completed and they were ready to give a verbal report.

'We expect an odontological conclusion by the end of the day,' the police officer told him. 'But other aspects mean we can assume it's Astri Arctander. That's based on a purely visual examination, including a birthmark on her neck and an operation scar below her right knee. The DNA results will come tomorrow.'

Mogens Poulsen flicked through a notepad in front of him. 'I guess the cause of death is what's of most interest to you,' he said, adjusting his glasses. 'It's actually not so easy to determine. Let me first of all say there's nothing to suggest a vehicle was involved. She has no external injuries on her body or her clothing.'

Wisting nodded. He had already jettisoned the hit-and-run theory.

'I'd expected to find hypothermic cardiac arrest,' Poulsen continued. 'But the preliminary conclusion is asphyxia. That is, suffocation through lack of ventilation in the lungs. Lack of oxygen, in other words.'

'What could have caused that?' Wisting asked.

'Some sort of respiratory arrest,' Poulsen replied. 'In the forensics field, it's usually found in cases where the nose and mouth have been covered by a hand, pillow or plastic bag, but I've a more obvious theory in this instance.'

'What would that be?' Wisting asked.

'Snow,' Poulsen answered.

Wisting moved closer to the screen. 'She was suffocated by snow? How could that have happened?'

'It's a bit too early for me to draw that conclusion,' Poulsen said. 'My main hypothesis is that her head was pressed down in the snow until she stopped breathing. She has bruises on her shoulders, back and neck to support that idea, but it can be difficult to determine the age of that kind of bleeding below the skin. I need a second opinion before I can give a final verdict.'

'Could there be any other explanation for her being suffocated in that way?' Wisting asked.

'Purely theoretically, she could have lain outdoors, unconscious, while the snow fell around her and eventually blocked her airways.'

'In that case, what would be the reason for such a state of unconsciousness?' Wisting asked.

'Hypothermia would be the most natural theory, of course, but it could also have been medically induced,' Poulsen told him. 'I need more time to exclude both of these possibilities.'

The Kripos detective leaned towards the camera and microphone. 'The other evidence supports the main hypothesis,' he said. 'Her clothes are intact and in place, but they're dishevelled, in a way that suggests some kind of tussle. Maybe even that someone sat on her while she struggled in an effort to get free.'

'What about her belongings?' Wisting asked.

'No phone or keys in her pockets,' the police investigator replied. 'She was wearing a ring and a necklace, that's all.'

'Forensically, I can't establish a time of death,' Poulsen went on. 'But from the objective circumstances of the abandoned vehicle and the subsequent snow fall, I've given her date of death as 3 December.'

'I see,' Wisting said. 'When can I expect a conclusion as to the cause of death?'

'I need another twenty-four hours, but until then I'd recommend you investigate her death as a homicide.'

They made a few practical arrangements about releasing the corpse and sending a written summary of what they had told him. When the video meeting had ended, Wisting opened the office door then slumped back into his chair. The autopsy had not provided any clear answers, making it even more critical to clarify the circumstances surrounding her death. What had prompted her journey? Where was she going? What did she know?

He had an appointment with the committee chairman in the housing cooperative where Astri had lived. Maybe he would find some answers in her apartment.

Maren Dokken appeared in the doorway with a plastic tumbler in one hand. She sat down and pushed the tumbler across the desk towards him. 'I filled it up when we came back yesterday,' she said.

Wisting looked at the tumbler. A thick black measuring line was drawn halfway up the side. The water almost reached it.

'It's evaporated by just over a millimetre in less than twenty-four hours,' she said.

He realized she was talking about the glass of water beside the sink in the summer cabin belonging to the Arctander family.

'It's warmer in your office than out in the cabin,' Wisting said.

Maren ignored his comment. 'If it was full when someone

148

set it aside, it would have taken three months for all the water to evaporate,' she went on. 'But it wasn't empty, and it's hardly likely that it was full to start with.'

'How long do you think the glass has been there?' Wisting asked.

'No longer ago than last October,' Maren replied. 'But it's more realistic to believe it has something to do with Astri Arctander. That it's from the evening she arrived in Norway.' Maren stretched out her legs. 'I think she was on her way to the summer cabin to meet someone,' she said. 'But didn't get there.'

Wisting glanced at the tumbler. Tiny bubbles had formed inside. 'We'll go out there again and pick it up,' he said, rising from his chair.

32

Username: Darby

An Australian private detective had enrolled in the forum. Hired by Ruby Thompson's parents, he had published a post offering a reward. Around the same time, Nichelle had written that she was on her way to Spain and had arranged to meet him. She had also updated the post concerning the search for Astria, reporting that the search party had found a dead woman. The post had attracted a number of comments, mostly short sentences about how shocking and tragic the death was, as well as sending condolences to family and close friends.

Line wondered whether she should write something about Astria, giving further details of what had happened, but this was information she had received in confidence from her father. That she had mysteriously driven from Palamós would only lead to speculation. She would defer writing anything at least until a public statement was made.

There were fifty-two comments on her post about the Danish girl who had been murdered in France. One of the users who had given an opinion was ApopheniaX. Despite this anonymous username, he did not hide his real identity. He was actually called Mateo, was thirty-seven years old and taught at the university in Barcelona. His username was no doubt meant ironically. Apophenia is the tendency to perceive meaningful connections between unrelated things, to discover something that actually was not there, rather as some people saw a human face in the configuration of a mountain.

He reproached himself for not having looked at cases in France, but now he had included the murder of Lone Sand in his presentation.

The single comment beneath it was brief. Someone calling herself Petra Deliro had written: *Could this be the man we're looking for?*

Underneath, there were four links, and Line clicked on the first of these. This led to a webpage belonging to a local artist, Pol Prado. He was pictured in overalls splashed with paint and a red T-shirt, his head shaven and his eyebrows thick and dark.

The text was in Spanish and English. He was portrayed as a controversial and provocative artist with a fascinating character. His works were described as subdued but at the same time full of suppressed drama.

One of the paintings represented a woman lying under a simple bed in the corner of an empty room with grey walls. The bedsheets were soaked with blood. The details were sketchily painted. The woman was curled up with her hands cradling her head and her legs drawn up. There was nothing threatening in the room, but it was easy to imagine she was hiding from whoever had already inflicted violence on her. *Esperándolo* was the Spanish title, translated as *Waiting For It*.

There were a number of bleak paintings in the same style. A skinny, naked woman stood with her head bowed and blood in her hair; in another picture a woman was on her way out through a door, into a murky darkness on the other side. There was something depressing and deeply melancholy about them. Other images had no human figures but contained the same sense of terror. A bloody meat hook hanging from a ceiling, shackles and chains attached to a brick wall, an open cellar trapdoor.

The other link was to a two-year-old news article. Line had to copy and paste the text into a translation program to make sense of the contents. An artist had been arrested and charged with kidnapping and false imprisonment, accused of keeping a female model imprisoned in his studio in Palamós. The artist had previously been found guilty of sexual assault, but this was not described in any further detail. In the case being reported, the prosecution did not proceed because the incident was part of an artistic project and the parameters had been agreed in advance.

The next link led to a report on an exhibition Pol Prado had held four years earlier. The style was slightly different, but the pictures had the same mournful undertones. The central image was a seemingly lifeless woman in a white dress lying on a wide board floating in the sea.

When Line clicked into the final link, she arrived at a similar exhibition. The style was more or less the same. They were not pictures Line would choose to have on her walls, but accusing the painter of being a serial killer felt like crossing a line. Unfortunately this was how an anonymous online forum functioned. It cost nothing to throw out crass accusations and recriminations, since you would not be called to account for them afterwards. No one pointed out the speculative nature of the comment – on the contrary, it was regarded as an interesting contribution, and subsequently links were given to interviews with the artist in question. Line spotted something Petra Deliro had not picked up. One of the exhibitions was in a gallery in the small coastal town of Blanes, while the other was in Empuriabrava. The Belgian tourist Renate Heitmann had been killed in Blanes while Pol Prado had his exhibition there, while Lea Kranz from

Switzerland was murdered at the same time as his exhibition in Empuriabrava. All of a sudden, Pol Prado's name became more interesting. One user pointed out that one of the Spanish women on the list of potential victims had herself been a painter. Another audaciously declared him now to be the main suspect.

33

Two blackbirds took off from one of the bare trees in front of the summer cabin when Wisting slammed the car door. Nothing had changed from the previous day. The house looked icebound in the snowy landscape, but it was not difficult to picture how idyllic it would be on warm summer days.

They walked in their own footprints to the entrance, Wisting leading the way. He found the key in the little metal box and let them in.

The closed window shutters dimmed the interior. Maren flicked the light switch in the hallway and moved further on into the house, with clumps of snow dropping from the soles of her shoes and forming miniature ice floes on the wooden floorboards.

The glass of water was still beside the kitchen sink, just as they had left it. Maren took a photo before pulling on latex gloves and raising the glass to the ceiling light.

'It's reduced even more, don't you think?' she asked.

Wisting had not studied it very carefully the day before. One millimetre more or less was difficult to estimate.

Placing the glass on the kitchen worktop, Maren produced a DNA kit. She swabbed the rim of the glass and sealed the sample before pouring out the rest of the water and dropping the glass into a bag for fingerprinting.

'That's it,' she said.

Wisting was not ready to leave right away. He felt as if he had left something undone, that explanations might be found in the cabin for their unanswered questions. Something that might point to whoever had been waiting here for her.

The thin floorboards creaked as he paced around. He entered the living room and opened the door into the conservatory, where it was colder than in other parts of the cabin.

Maren remained at the door behind him. The conservatory was the only place in the house from which it was possible to watch the road. The other windows were shuttered.

'Whoever was here must have waited a long time,' Maren said. 'She never arrived.'

Wisting looked around but found no trace of the person who had waited for Astri Arctander. At one end, basket-weave furniture was stacked and there was rush matting on the floor.

Outside, the snow covered everything. Their footprints crisscrossed the area in front of the cabin and they could see their unmarked police car parked on the road.

'Whoever was here must have spotted her car once they eventually gave up and left,' Maren said, reading his thoughts. 'If they didn't turn in the opposite direction at the crossroads.'

She took out her mobile to snap a photo, and Wisting moved to make space for her.

Normal practice would be to send a message or try to phone if the person you were waiting for was late for a pre-arranged meeting, he thought. No calls to Astri had been registered on that last evening, at least not on her Norwegian account. This did not mean that no one had tried to phone, merely that she had not answered or it had not rung long enough for the voicemail to kick in. However, a text message would have gone through and been recorded. And even if the person who had left the glass on the worktop had not tried to call Astri, they could have used the phone. That was what most people did when they had nothing else to do but wait. If this had been a murder inquiry, it would not have been a problem to obtain telecoms data for all mobiles located in the area. There could not have been much traffic here late on a Saturday evening at the beginning of December. Now he would have to make a strong argument for the release of that information.

Maren squinted at the photos she had taken. It struck Wisting that much of this case revolved around photographs. What had first sparked his interest had been the picture of Astri Arctander at the jetty in Stavern on a rainy summer's day.

He approached the garden furniture stored in the living room. The photo album lay on one of the chairs, where he had left it. It contained two decades of summer photos, pasted on stiff paper. Whoever had last leafed through it must have been here after the garden furniture had been taken in for winter. It was natural to think it may have been the same person who had left the glass of water by the sink. It could just have been a way of passing time, but it was also possible that the album contained something the unknown person wanted to take a closer look at.

Wisting flicked back and forth. It appeared that a group picture of the four brothers in the family had been taken every summer. The twins must be identical. Astri's father resembled them slightly, while Bernard's hair was darker and his features more rugged.

On one page, a photo was missing, leaving only the remnants of a large patch of glue where it had been displayed. The other photos on the same page were from a swimming trip. *Kloppsand, 6 July 1996* was the text below. He recognized Astri in one of them, on her way out of the water with a rubber ring around her waist. The other pictures had been taken in the same location. Wisting did not recognize any of the people in them but assumed they were members of Astri's family or their friends.

On the opposite page, there were photos taken in the garden in front of the cabin. Two of them were from a croquet match, while the others had been taken later the same evening. Coloured lanterns hung from one of the trees and the family were gathered around a set table. He was about to turn the page when he noticed a little cut in the paper, like from a sharp knife, and realized that one of the croquet photos had been trimmed.

Most of the pictures in the album had been cropped, with corners clipped so that the photos fitted. They had been pasted in at angles, partly overlapping, but this particular photo looked as if it had been cut after being glued in. One of the other pictures also looked as if it had received the same treatment. There was no incision in the paper, but he could see a slightly overlarge space on the right of the image, as if the person seated at one end of the table had been excised.

It was more than twenty years since the photos had been pasted in, and difficult to know when they had been cut, but someone had clearly been removed from these mementoes of the summer of 1996. He had no idea whether this had any significance for recent events, but he shut the album and tucked it under his arm as he left.

34

The road beside the discovery site was still closed. Maren was driving, and she manoeuvred the car past the roadblock. Sections of the carriageway had been used to deposit the snow that had been cleared. She parked the car in a spot where it would not cause any obstruction.

The crew were finishing off their work. Kittil Gram threw aside a snow shovel as he approached them. An area the size of a handball court had been hacked into the snow-covered terrain, and only a few centimetres of snow were left. The spot where Astri Arctander had been found was protected by a tarpaulin and the air was filled with the noise of a generator and hot-air fans.

One of the forensics vehicles was parked close to the open area. Wisting was surprised to see it, since he had been told they would have to prioritize other tasks.

'They've sent a guy with a metal detector,' Kittil Gram explained. 'He's just arrived.'

The forensics technician appeared behind the van, ready with his search equipment. It was one of the men who had been there the previous evening, when the body had been found.

Wisting told him about the post-mortem and that they still had no clear cause of death. 'She didn't have her phone or car keys on her,' he added.

The forensics technician turned on the metal detector. 'We'll see what we can find,' he said as he began his work.

Walking with steady footsteps, he swung the detector

from side to side. It did not take long for it to emit a signal, a distorted high-frequency sound that rose and fell depending on the distance from the hidden object.

Kittil Gram arrived wielding a shovel. He dug the snow away and found an empty oilcan that looked as if it had been lying there for a long time, but the forensics technician insisted it be placed in an evidence bag all the same.

Wisting and Maren stood watching the search continue. They did not have long to wait for another find to be made. Something metal that probably had nothing whatsoever to do with Astri Arctander. Yet another oilcan turned up, a couple of screws and a scattering of indeterminate pieces of metal. The results diminished in number as the experienced technician worked further away from the verge and in between the trees. Wisting knew he ought to return to the police station, but there was something fascinating about standing there watching the search effort. All at once the metal detector gave off another signal. The forensics technician swept the detector disc round in a circle to localize the find. The alert signal swung between various tones.

Kittil Gram stepped forward with the shovel, with Wisting and Maren bringing up the rear. Frozen blades of grass and brown autumn leaves were dug up. Then the shovel hit something metallic.

The technician laid aside the metal detector, hunkered down and picked more dead leaves away. Down in the grass, between two twigs, lay a keyring with a Volkswagen logo and a car key.

'There it is,' Kittil Gram announced.

None of the others said anything. The forensics technician returned to his vehicle and came back with a camera and equipment to mark the site. Wisting looked around. They were almost ten metres from the road. The spot where Astri had been found was about seven metres away, diagonally across to the left, closer to the road.

'How did it end up here?' Maren asked, thinking aloud in an attempt to find the answer. 'It looks as if she got lost and stumbled around before she keeled over, or something.'

'In that case, her phone and bag could also be here somewhere,' Kittil Gram suggested.

'But why was she walking around out here?' Maren wondered aloud, looking towards the woods.

Wisting followed her gaze. The area along the road was fairly open. Further back, the trees were thicker. The snow had settled on the branches, weighing them down and shutting out the daylight.

The technician had come back. Taking photos of the keyring, he dropped it into a bag and marked the discovery spot with a small flag. Then he guided the metal detector in a circle above the area to satisfy himself there was nothing more to be found.

Wisting's feet were starting to freeze, and he knocked one boot against the other. 'Phone me if you find anything else,' he said, striding towards his car.

35

Astri Arctander's apartment was located only five minutes from the E18. 'She could have managed to call in here before moving on to Larvik,' Maren pointed out.

Wisting agreed. The timeline on the evening Astri had arrived in Norway had been drawn up using evidence from the toll station transits. A brief stop at her apartment would not have caused any significant deviation in time.

The residential area seemed recently built. Despite the short distance from the motorway, it was close to the great outdoors and well screened from the road and traffic fumes.

The signage in the low-level apartment blocks was confusing. 'It must be over there,' Maren said, pointing to an asymmetrical building with protruding balconies and integral terraces.

Wisting parked the car beside a heap of snow before phoning the committee chairman with whom he had made the appointment.

'He'll be here in a couple of minutes,' he told Maren.

They stepped out, making their way along the icy path, strewn with gravel that crunched under their feet, towards the apartment block.

Wisting managed to find his bearings among all the doorbells. Astri's apartment was on the second floor.

The housing committee representative appeared, expressing his sorrow at the tragic death. 'I didn't know her, really,' he said, 'but it was a shock to hear of it all the same.'

He let them in and led the way up the staircase. 'Call me

when you're finished,' he said once they were inside. 'I'll come back and lock up.'

The apartment must be one of the smallest in the housing cooperative. Two bedrooms and a living room with an open-plan kitchen and a bathroom. It was painted in coordinating warm colours that matched the interior decor. International news magazines were scattered on the coffee table but, apart from that, everything was extremely neat and tidy.

'She hasn't been here long,' Maren said, scanning the room. 'I think there's more chance of finding something in her apartment down in Spain.' She pulled out a drawer. 'I could come down there with you and check,' she added in jest.

Wisting's response was only a smile as he picked up some receipts that lay in a basket on the kitchen worktop. Groceries. The last of these was several months old.

He refrained from saying he had already checked out suitable departures. A direct flight to Barcelona with a Spanish airline would leave on Friday morning.

They quickly realized there was nothing in this little apartment to contribute anything new to the case. The search was simply a routine step in the investigation. They opened drawers and looked in cupboards, read through a few documents and searched for names unfamiliar to them.

In one of the bedrooms, furnished as a home office, a desk was placed in front of the window. Outside, Wisting could see straight into the top of a snow-covered pine tree.

A couple of ballpoint pens and a notebook were the only items on the desk. Wisting riffled through the notebook, but only the first few pages had been used. It looked like notes from a meeting, with key words about work assignments and their allocation. Everything appeared job-related.

The drawers were tidy, with no contents out of the ordinary.

Maren opened a pair of double wardrobe doors. Nothing but clothes, carefully folded on shelves on the right-hand side, with larger items of clothing hanging on the left.

Crouching down, she moved a pair of shoes from the bottom of the wardrobe and took out a cardboard box, the original packaging for a laptop computer. A Lenovo Think-Pad. The box had a white label marked with the serial number.

'Well, at least we know what kind of computer we're looking for,' she commented as she used her mobile to take a photo.

This was the only item of interest they took with them from the search.

36

Username: Shelook

Celia sat in her underwear as she waited for her hair to dry. The *Diari de Girona* carried a lengthy article about Ruby Thompson in their online newspaper. A private detective had arrived from Australia, promising a reward. An interview with the chief investigator, Comisario Telmo Álvarez, was also appended. The first part contained only general information: he described the evidence they had secured, the sightings of Ruby Thompson, the organization of the inquiry and the contact made with her family in Australia. All of this was already widely known.

Further down the article was a barrage of questions identical to the ones circulating in the online forum. These included asking if the police had taken a closer look at the housebreaking incident on the evening Ruby Thompson had been killed and whether there might be a connection.

She scrolled up to the headline and peered at the small portrait photo of the journalist, Zita Barroso. Celia could not resist smiling. The reporter must have been in the forum and read her contribution. The idea that she had used the information Celia had uncovered gave her a strong sense of satisfaction at having excelled at something and being noticed.

The Catalan comisario's response was evasive, neither confirming nor denying anything. Nothing emerged from the article to supplement what she had published in her forum post.

The details of the sea currents were also discussed. The police had not undertaken calculations of these but felt the body had probably drifted from the north somewhere along the short stretch of coastline in the vicinity of Cap Roig.

'Have you spoken to anyone who lives in that area?' the journalist asked.

Once again the comisario avoided a direct answer and merely said they had received no sightings of vehicles or anything else on the night in question.

Her thoughts were interrupted by a knock at the door behind her. Her mother came in, carrying a Prosecure uniform shirt on a clothes hanger, freshly ironed with the sleeves well pressed.

Celia stood up and took it from her. 'You didn't need to,' she said with a smile.

'I do it for your brother,' her mother replied, moving back to the door. 'So I might as well do it for you too.'

'Thanks.'

She put on the shirt and sat down again without buttoning it. Eager to share the contents of the article in the forum, she logged on and composed a post with the title 'The Police Answer'.

She attached a link to the online newspaper and wrote a summary in English so that Nichelle and other foreigners could understand it. In addition to the housebreaking and sea conditions, the comisario had been asked about Olaf. For reasons relating to the investigation, he was unable to comment on whether the Norwegian drug dealer had been identified. Neither would he say anything about whether the rest of Ruby's clothing had been found.

A major part of the article dealt with the DNA evidence, but there was no news on that.

At the end of the interview, the journalist raised the twelve-year-old murder of Bertine Franck from Germany and drew his attention to the similarities to the killing of Ruby Thompson. The comisario replied that of course they were aware of the case, but it was less than desirable to speculate on it. He could make no comment on the other unsolved murders along the coast because the responsibility for these was in other police jurisdictions.

Celia read her post again before publishing it in the forum. Then she buttoned up her uniform shirt and prepared to leave for work.

37

The phone rang. Wisting leaned back in his chair. Garm Søbakken had called three times during the drive back from Astri Arctander's apartment. This would be the fourth time he had tried to get in touch. Wisting had avoided answering the first three times because he knew what the reporter was going to ask. Now that both Astri's family and employer had been informed, he had permission to make her name public.

Running his thumb across the screen, he put the phone to his ear and answered by giving his name.

'I'm phoning about the dead woman,' Søbakken said. 'Any news?'

Wisting told him she had been identified as thirty-two-year-old Astri Arctander from Asker. The cause of death had not been determined as yet, but there was nothing to suggest a vehicle had run her over.

'Why did it take so long for her to be reported missing?' Søbakken asked.

Wisting was obliged to inform him that she had been living in Spain and initially reported missing down there. The investigation showed she had driven from a small resort on the Mediterranean without telling her family or friends before she left.

'But where was she going?' Søbakken continued his questioning. 'What was she doing here?'

'We've not yet established an explanation for that,' Wisting replied. 'We have a number of unanswered questions and are keen to make contact with everyone who drove past the spot where she was found after ten p.m. on the evening of Saturday 2 December.'

The time had been estimated from the last toll station transit on the E18. On the stretch of road where Astri's body had been recovered, there was no electronic surveillance of any kind.

After the initial report of the van and the discovery of the body, thirty-seven tip-offs and messages had come in. Maren Dokken had recorded and sorted through them. Most were observations of the van that had been snowed in at the bus stop. The first of these sightings had not been made until the following morning. Wisting had not expected anything more. That stretch of road had little through traffic, especially during the hours of darkness. Also, there was a limit to what people noticed, even more so what they remembered after a week had elapsed. On Sundays the first bus did not run until the afternoon, either. In the course of the following week, however, many passing motorists had noticed the snow building up around the abandoned van.

One of the tip-offs was flagged. A restaurant worker who had been on his way home had phoned in to say that he had seen a dark-clad figure walking along the road around midnight. That was the closest they came to an eyewitness.

Maren had interviewed him, but nothing more had come to light than what had been reported in the initial phone call. The person in question had been walking on the right-hand side of the road in the direction of Eidsten: the witness had only seen the figure from the back, so was unable to say whether it had been a man or a woman. The sighting had been made almost exactly halfway between the location where the van had been left and the spot where Astri's body had been found. From the time the worker finished his shift, they estimated the time as some point between twenty and ten minutes to midnight. By then, fifteen centimetres of snow had already fallen and the first snowplough had been out. Later that week, the witness had noticed the van at the bus stop but could not say whether he had seen it on the Saturday night. The witness recalled no details of the pedestrian's outward appearance or whether the person had been carrying anything.

At quarter to five, Kittil Gram rang to say they had almost completed their examination of the discovery site at Manvik.

'Nothing more of interest has been found,' he said. 'Neither in the snow nor in the cleared area.'

Wisting turned his chair to face the window. It had grown dark outside.

'We should have found her phone,' he said. 'She had two. One with a Spanish number and the other a Norwegian one. Also, she had a laptop in her luggage.'

'It could be lying somewhere along the road,' Kittil Gram suggested. 'Beneath the snow. We're talking about a stretch of more than two kilometres. Starting a search would be a huge undertaking. The forensics folk suggest we close off the area we've dug up and await developments. The carriageway has been cleared of snow and we've informed the road traffic HQ that they can open the road from six p.m.'

It felt like leaving a job half finished, but Wisting realized that, as things stood, there was little more they could do.

'Of course, there could be other explanations for the phone and the laptop,' Gram went on. 'The van wasn't locked. The door had just frozen shut. Do you remember?'

Wisting did remember. He understood what Gram was alluding to, though that thought had not previously struck him.

'She could have left her luggage in the van,' Gram pointed

out. 'It was stuck there for days. Unlocked. Someone could have come by and taken her belongings.'

'But not her phone,' Wisting objected. 'Surely she'd have taken that with her when she left the vehicle?'

'Maybe it had run out of juice,' Gram suggested. 'The obvious thing would be to phone for help if you were having problems with the van.'

Wisting tried to remember whether there had been a charging point in the vehicle. There must be. She had driven such a long distance and her mobile had still been charged when she arrived in Norway.

No matter what reasoning was used, it was a break in logic that added to the difficulty of grasping the circumstances.

He sat for an hour before phoning to order a pizza. The man who took the order seemed stressed, as if he had a lot to do. To ensure the takeaway food would be ready when he arrived to collect it, Wisting took his time driving on the snow-covered roads. When he got there, he drove around the block more than once before a parking place was freed up near the entrance.

A woman was serving behind the counter. She smiled and gave him a nod of recognition. Wisting imagined it was a family-run business. The owners looked to be from somewhere in the Middle East.

He walked up and told her what he had ordered, but the woman seemed confused. 'Are you sure?' she asked.

'I phoned a quarter of an hour ago,' Wisting said.

As the woman disappeared into the kitchen, the swing doors slammed shut behind her. She spoke to someone in a foreign language before returning with a man. They leafed through a few notes before the man finally found the order. He looked around, as if searching for someone to blame, but there was no one.

'Sorry,' he said, waving the note. 'I forgot you. I'll make an express one right now. Ten minutes. You can have it for half-price.'

He vanished into the kitchen again before Wisting had time to say anything.

The phone beside the till began to ring.

'You can wait there,' the woman said, pointing to a table beside a group of teenagers engrossed in their mobile phones.

Wisting glanced at the time. 'I'll come back.'

The counter assistant was busy with another phone order when Wisting headed for the exit. The snow swirled into the small space when he pulled the door open. He drew his lapels together and decided to go for a walk.

A snowplough drove past with the blade scraping on the asphalt. Wisting moved off in the same direction, down towards the harbour.

Only one boat was moored, a small yacht with no mast, rising and falling with the rhythm of the grey sea. Something loose rolled back and forth across the deck.

He walked on, out towards one of the breakwaters. The wind was chill as it gusted in from the sea, whipping frozen beads of snow over his face.

The first winter he had worked in the police force, he had rescued a dog from drowning in the calm waters of the harbour basin. He had come driving along in his patrol car with an older officer and even from a distance they could see that something was going on. People were pointing and waving to them, and they drove up.

Ice had formed a few metres from shore and a brown Labrador was swimming in the water beyond. It was struggling to clamber on to the edge of the ice, but every time it got a grip with its paws, the thin ice gave way.

The owner, Ellinor Brink, was screaming in terror.

One of the spectators watching the drama had run out on to the jetty to find a boat, but it was tied up with chains and a padlock.

The movements of the dog in the water grew more sluggish as they watched, but it was still managing to hold its head above water. It made another effort to scramble up but slid out into the black water again. Its paws thrashed about, and it began to whimper, a terrible whining sound that cut through the air and eventually changed to desperate howling.

Wisting had grabbed an aluminium ladder he saw hanging on the wall of one of the nearby buildings and pushed it out across the ice. It reached almost far enough.

While his colleague stood on the shore and held tight, he lay down on his stomach and wriggled out, rung by rung. The ladder meant the weight was equally distributed, but the ice groaned under him all the same.

With a feeble squeak, the dog stared at him with big, trusting eyes as it made another attempt to clamber up. Its claws curled downwards, into the ice, which was flecked with blood when the dog slid back into the water again.

He was half a metre distant when the ice gave way, breaking into large floes. Wisting launched himself forward, snatching at the dog's neck and managing to grab hold of the loose folds of skin as he pulled the animal towards him. Pushing off in the cold water and clutching at one of the rungs with his free hand, he hauled himself in.

Wisting shivered at the thought of what had happened that day. He recalled how the dog had sat down beside him when they finally reached the shore, rather than running off. It had pushed its nose towards him in thanks before Ellinor Brink arrived to give it a comforting hug.

An old family pet, its name was Milos, he recalled. Two years later, it was knocked down and killed by a lorry. He had seen that in the police logbook.

He flicked some snow into the water with the toe of his shoe. He had not thought of that incident for years. Actually, it was Ellinor Brink who had entered his head, he had to admit. She had turned up in his office the same morning her son was arrested. At first he had felt uncomfortable, but the conversation had flowed easily, moving on to other subjects. He had sat for a long time with her, and when she left his spirits had been uplifted.

A pair of swans came paddling towards him through the slushy sea. Wisting glanced at his watch and realized it was time to go back and collect his pizza.

It was ready on the counter when he arrived. The assistant forgot to charge him half the price, as the man had promised. Wisting paid up without protest, thanked her and left.

His neighbours' children were playing in the snow under the light from the streetlamp when he drove up in front of his house. Balancing the pizza box as he stepped out of the car, he turned to see whether Amalie was also out playing. The big brother was chasing his little sister up the street and quickly caught up with her. He gave her a shove in the back and sent her flying into the bank of snow beside the car. Then he jumped on top of her and held her down in the snow, using his free hand to throw more snow over her.

Wisting stood watching. That was how it could have happened. Asphyxia. Suffocation through lack of air in the lungs. Insufficient oxygen.

The little girl kicked about with her legs and struck out with her arms, but it was no use. The boy sprawled on top of her was physically superior and the snow also impeded the fight. In the end she gave up and lay still.

Wisting put the pizza box on the roof of the car and strode purposefully towards them. It was not easy to decide whether the game had gone too far. He was about to shout, but the boy had eased off and taken a step back. The girl lay motionless. Then, all of a sudden, she leapt to her knees, spitting out snow, and gave a broad smile before adjusting her hat and gazing straight at Wisting. Her cheeks were bright red, but otherwise she was physically none the worse for what had happened.

'Are you OK?' Wisting asked.

The boy wheeled around and looked at him. 'We're just playing,' he said.

'I know,' Wisting replied.

'Who are you?' the girl asked.

'My name's William,' Wisting told her. 'I live over there,' he added, pointing at his house.

'I've seen you before,' the boy told him.

'I'm a policeman,' Wisting went on, without really knowing why he said that. 'And I'm also the grandfather of the little girl who lives in that house there.'

Now he was pointing at Line's.

'We have to go in,' the girl said, shuffling off in a snowsuit that was a bit too big for her.

Wisting retraced his steps. The pizza box had slid from the car roof. It had opened and a couple of the slices had landed on the snowy ground. Gathering them up, he cast a glance at the pile of snow on the opposite side of the street before he went indoors. Apart from a dent in the white powder, no traces remained of what had taken place.

38

Username: Darby

Wisting checked the website about Ruby Thompson's murder while he ate. There were several new posts, and also new members. A private detective stated that he had been hired by the Australian woman's family and offered a reward on their behalf. He was now in Catalonia and had met the leader of the police investigation. In one of the comments, a link was posted to a Catalan newspaper in which both the private detective and the police comisario were interviewed. Another link led to an Australian newspaper where the comisario's comments were repeated. Wisting took note of his name and the department where he worked.

The phone buzzed, this time a number he did not have stored in his mobile.

Wiping his hands on his trouser legs, he picked up the phone and answered. A young woman identified herself as Vanda Martens from *VG*. 'I'm calling in connection with the dead woman found yesterday,' she said. 'I understand the cause of death has not yet been established but that a hit-and-run has been excluded. What theories do you have, then?'

She must have picked up the story from the local newspaper. The myriad unanswered questions lent the death a mysterious aura that appealed to the tabloid press.

'We're working on mapping out the circumstances,' he replied.

'Does that mean you've not ruled out a crime?'

He knew any hint of a possible murder would lead to lurid headlines and that the media coverage would spread far and wide. He had prepared the Arctander family for this possibility and answered as transparently as he could.

'We're not ruling out anything,' he said.

'I hear you've undertaken a thorough search of the area where she was found?' the journalist continued, inviting further comment.

Wisting confirmed this, going on to tell her how many cubic metres of snow had been removed without progressing the case any further.

The journalist had a long list of questions, about the van and the long drive through Europe, about electronic traces and cooperation with the Catalan police. Wisting negotiated his way through them all.

The doorbell rang just as the conversation was drawing to an end, giving him an excuse to bring things to a close.

'Just one more point,' the young journalist insisted, detaining him for a moment. 'We'd like a photo of her. Have you decided to issue one?'

Wisting had cleared this with the family and been given a photo they could use.

'If we decide on that, it will be included in the next press release,' he replied. 'In the meantime, we've no reason to do so.'

He ended the call in the hallway as he opened the door.

Ellinor Brink stood on the steps, holding out a plastic cake container. 'Sorry if I'm disturbing you,' she said, 'but I'm not sure if I actually managed to thank you properly.'

Wisting was taken aback to see her and needed a moment or two to gather his wits.

Ellinor gesticulated with the cake box.

'That's so nice of you.' Wisting finally found the words. 'Would you like to come in?'

The invitation was met with a smile. 'Just for a few minutes, maybe,' she replied.

She handed Wisting the container as she kicked off her boots and hung up her jacket.

Wisting walked ahead of her into the house. He really needed to vacuum and tidy. There were a couple of empty glasses on the coffee table as well as his plate with a half-eaten slice of pizza. He snatched it away, replacing it with the cake container, and asked Ellinor to sit down.

'Coffee?'

She accepted his offer and he went to the kitchen for plates, cake forks and a cake slice.

By the time he returned, Ellinor had opened the box and taken out the plate: it was a tart with thick, yellow cream.

'There's no news,' Wisting told her, referring to her son.

'I've spoken to his lawyer,' Ellinor said. 'He phoned this morning. Trond wasn't well. He'd been to see the doctor.'

Wisting had not heard about that. 'Withdrawal pains, perhaps?' he suggested. 'That's usual in the first few days when the body's been deprived of the substances it's become dependent on.'

Ellinor nodded. 'He'll just have to get through it,' she said. 'But I didn't come to talk about him. I just wanted to express my appreciation for you showing such concern.'

Wisting smiled, ignoring her comment as he tasted the cake.

There was no more mention of her son. The conversation ran easily and smoothly on to other topics, touching on common acquaintances from their schooldays but moving on to continually different lines without bringing up work or family matters. It felt invigorating, and Wisting dropped all thoughts of Astri Arctander and the murder case.

Ellinor was the one who raised the subject of the incident with the dog he had saved.

'Milos,' Wisting reminisced with a smile.

'Do you remember his name? That's impressive.'

Wisting shrugged it off.

'I don't think I thanked you properly that time either,' she said.

'Do you still have a dog these days?' Wisting asked.

Ellinor shook her head. 'It's the first time in years,' she answered. 'I live alone and really miss it. A dog's good company.'

Wisting's phone had buzzed three times during her visit. After the first call, he had switched it to silent. The next two times it had just vibrated on the table surface. None of the numbers were familiar to him, so the calls were probably from journalists.

Now it was buzzing for the fourth time. 'That's Line,' Wisting said, drawing the phone towards him.

'Aren't you going to take it?'

'I can call her back later.'

When Ellinor began preparing to leave, Wisting got to his feet. 'Would you like your plate back?' he asked.

'I can get that another time,' she replied, but she took the cake box.

Wisting walked with his phone in his hand as he accompanied her to the hallway.

Her son was again the topic of conversation. 'Will you keep me posted?' she asked.

Wisting agreed he would. 'Did Trond ever bring things to your house?' he asked.

'What do you mean?' Ellinor asked.

It was a wild idea, but Wisting was thinking of what Kittil Gram had said about the possibility that Astri's laptop could have been stolen from the van.

'Well, we did of course find stolen goods in his own house,' he told her. 'Computers, cameras, mobile phones and suchlike, but we don't think we've found everything. I just wondered if he might have left anything in your house.'

Ellinor shook her head. 'Never,' she replied. 'He's probably sold things to get money for drugs. That's the sort of thing he's been doing, after all.'

She had put on her coat. 'What will happen next?' she asked.

'I'll go to the prison tomorrow,' Wisting let slip.

Ellinor's face lit up. 'Maybe you could take something to him?'

'Things really have to go through the prison system,' Wisting told her.

'But he'll get it faster if it goes through you,' Ellinor said.

They both knew she was right.

'What did you have in mind?' Wisting asked her.

'Just a few small items,' Ellinor replied. 'Some magazines I know he likes to read. Something to cheer him up. And maybe some chocolate. To give him some extra nourishment and energy.'

Wisting agreed. 'Pop in with them tomorrow morning and I'll see what I can do,' he said.

She thanked him and went out. Wisting waited in the doorway as she walked to her car. His phone buzzed again as he stood with it in his hand. This time the call was from Maren Dokken.

'Yes?' he answered, waving to Ellinor before he shut the door.

'I've read the transcript of the interview with Ulrik Stene,' Maren said. 'Astri Arctander's ex-boyfriend.'

'Did you spot anything?' Wisting asked.

'Yes and no,' Maren replied. 'There's no mention of him being in Palamós when Ruby Thompson was killed.'

'And was he?' Wisting asked.

'Well, it happened at Easter,' Maren said. 'He and Astri were still together then. He's posted photos from then on Facebook.'

Yet again they were talking about a photograph, Wisting thought. He understood Maren's line of thought but encouraged her all the same: 'What do you read into that?' he asked.

'He was there when the Australian girl was murdered and here when Astri died,' Maren replied. 'If there's a connection between the two cases, then he's the only common denominator that's turned up so far. He could have been the person Astri had arranged to meet.'

Wisting said nothing. He had sat down with his iPad on his knee to find Ulrik Stene on Facebook.

'What did you make of him?' Maren asked.

'I got the impression he wasn't telling me everything,' Wisting told her. 'That he was making excuses and not being entirely honest about the break-up.'

'In what way?'

'Ulrik Stene seemed very ordinary, but I get the impression Astri was an intelligent woman. I think she was much smarter than him and that was one of the reasons she chose to split up with him.'

'He was the intellectual inferior in the relationship, then,' Maren concluded.

Wisting had found the pictures she was talking about, several of them from the event on the town beach in Palamós.

'Thanks,' he said. 'I'll have to talk to him again.'

39

They had no designated breaks in the security firm HQ but ate in front of their screens at their desks. When appropriate, they could take a few minutes off to stretch their legs, but they had no lengthy spells of free time. In return they were paid for a whole eight-hour shift. Some days were so busy that they scarcely had time to go to the toilet, while other days were so quiet there was time for other things.

Celia cancelled a false alarm in Manresa, signalling to the operator opposite that she was going to have something to eat, and logged on to the website.

Astria was dead. The report had not surprised her. Many people had responded with heart emojis and expressed how sorry they were. That was not how Celia reacted. She did not know the Norwegian woman and knew no more about her than what was stated in her online posts. Celia had long hoped that Astria would turn up in the forum again, but now she was gone it also meant that the photos and her possible discovery had also gone.

Another user had just posted a lengthy comment on her death. The information was taken from a Norwegian newspaper and repeated in English. Her real name was Astri Arctander and it seemed she had been lying out in the snow and had frozen to death.

Munching on a piece of baguette, she read on. The cause of death had not yet been clarified, but the police had instigated an inquiry. The newspaper described what they called a number of mysterious circumstances surrounding the death. And no one could explain why she had suddenly jumped into her car and driven from the small coastal resort of Palamós all the way to Norway.

Comments began to appear beneath the post. Several pointed out that she had been in Palamós when she had been working on the photo project.

MrsPeabody quoted the last thing Astria had written, the night before she left: *Think I've found something interesting*.

It was from a discussion thread about the photo project and referred to the segment of photographic material she had not yet published in the forum.

Further down the comments, someone introduced the theory that Astria's death had something to do with Ruby Thompson's murder, but no one was able to identify how this might make sense.

Celia read the post again before googling the name. Astri Arctander. It cropped up in several Norwegian newspapers, but there were no Spanish or Catalan results.

She had thought the nickname had something to do with astrology and stars, but there was a simpler explanation. Using the name, it was also easy to track down an email address. Astri had a Microsoft account. This meant she also had the facility to store several gigabytes of files and images there, free of charge. All that was needed to gain access was a password.

The left-hand screen was flashing. A fire alarm at a warehouse in Torelló, but all four of her colleagues were busy.

Celia put down her baguette and donned her headset. She had four hours left before her shift was over. Tomorrow, she knew, there was a bus to Palamós.

40

Username: Nichelle

The screen, in sleep mode, turned black. Michelle Norris sat up straight in the hard seat. Her thoughts had vanished into the darkness beyond the bus windows.

There was free Internet on board. Without that, she would have been offline for the past two hours. Immediately after changing buses at the terminal in Barcelona, she had received a message from the Catalan journalist who had interviewed the private detective. On the forum she called herself Kenzie, but in reality her name was Zita Barroso and she was a well-established crime reporter.

Her profile had been set up almost two months ago, but she had published no posts and had not actively participated in any of the discussions. Now she had read that Michelle was on her way to Palamós and was keen to see her. They agreed to meet in the hotel reception the next day.

Outside the windows, streetlights began to twinkle in the dark. The bus slowed down and turned off the motorway. A sign indicated they were entering Palamós. Seven black letters on a white background.

The sight of the town's name triggered a sense of disquiet in her, the feeling of suddenly being so near making her pulse beat a bit faster.

The buildings became more closely packed, and soon there were blocks on either side of the road. Colourful neon advertising signs swept past. The street names told her they were en route to the town centre. She had booked a room in a hotel near the street where a CCTV camera had taken the very last picture of Ruby. It was not far from the pizzeria where Ruby had spent that same evening, and not far from where the bus would stop so that she could cover the final stretch on foot.

The driver manoeuvred the large bus through the streets. Eventually the sea appeared on the right-hand side, with small restaurants and souvenir shops strung along the beach. People sat on benches or were out for a stroll.

The next stop was announced. Michelle realized that this was where she should alight and hastily gathered up her belongings. When the bus stopped, she was the only passenger to get up and move towards the exit.

The engine idled while the driver removed her suitcase from the cargo space underneath. He quickly took his place behind the steering wheel again. Michelle was left standing in the warm miasma of oil and diesel before collecting her case and trundling it along behind her.

41

Username: Darby

Someone was knocking on the front door. It must be her father. Line stood up, her gaze still lingering on the computer screen. Then she tore herself away and bounded up the stairs.

Her father stood in the living room with a question in his eyes.

'She's sleeping,' Line said, gesturing in the direction of Amalie's bedroom.

Wisting crept away and peeked inside, with Line at his back. Amalie was lying with her head on the pillow, clutching a scrap of fabric in her hand.

'Has she met the new neighbours yet?' Wisting asked once he had closed the door.

Line shook her head. Amalie had watched them from the window when they were playing in the snow but had not wanted to venture out.

'They're bigger than her,' she said. 'She thinks the boy's a bit rough.'

Wisting nodded. 'I've seen them,' he said. 'Have you met the parents?'

Line began to clear toys from the living-room floor, transferring them into a box.

'Yes,' she replied. 'They haven't moved far, it seems, just to something bigger. From an apartment to a house. They both work in the same IT firm.'

'Most things have to do with that, these days,' Wisting said. 'IT.'

'I tried to phone you,' Line told him. 'But I saw you had a visitor.'

'That was why I came down,' Wisting said, taking a seat. 'Was it anything in particular?'

Line had noticed it was a woman who had emerged from her father's house, but she did not question him more closely.

'I saw that *VG* had written an article about Astria,' she said. 'They're calling her the Ice Woman. I posted an English summary of it on the website. Do you have any objections?'

She saw from his face that he was uncomfortable with the idea that she had become an active member of the online investigation group.

'Not if you don't write anything other than what it says in the newspaper,' he replied.

Tilting her head, she looked at him, realizing there was more to the case than he had shared with her.

'I don't know much more than what it says in the papers,' she said. 'Is there a link with the Spanish murder? People have begun to speculate in the forum.'

'There's nothing but speculation on my side too,' her father told her.

'But yours is a bit more informed than the speculation from someone sitting at a kitchen table in Barcelona,' Line pointed out.

The only answer she received was an enigmatic smile.

'Do you have her laptop?' she persisted.

Wisting shook his head as Line tucked up her feet on the settee.

'People believe she had found out something but she died before she had time to share it with anyone,' she said.

'In that case the answer could lie in her laptop,' Wisting said.

'Or in a cloud,' Line said. 'I keep all my files in iCloud and automatically download updated versions to whatever computer I'm working on, either my desktop Mac in the basement or my laptop. Or to my iPad. The same applies to your folk in the police. Everything you're working on is held on a server with security back-ups. Don't forget, Astria was a data analyst who worked in various locations. She almost certainly had some form of remote storage for her private files.'

It was obvious she had given her father something to think about.

'Someone at the police computer crime centre must be able to find out about that, wouldn't you say?' Line continued. 'I pay twenty-nine kroner a month for extra storage space with Apple. Check her bank statements and you'll know where to start.'

'I have printouts of her account and bank cards,' Wisting said. 'I used them to see where she'd stopped en route from Spain.'

Line felt a sense of superiority. 'Well, it's worth checking,' she said. 'Worth a try.'

42

The rest of the cake from the previous evening was in the fridge. Wisting ate a slice for breakfast while he mulled over the visit. He was usually bad at interpreting signals from women. It was possible he was misinterpreting Ellinor and she had merely wanted to express her gratitude, but he felt there was something more underlying her actions. He was looking forward to meeting her again, but all the same, the timing was out of kilter. At least if Astri's death developed in the direction he suspected it would. However, her son's problems would give them ample opportunity for future contact. He would just have to take things as they came.

Before he left for the police station, he composed an email to Michelle Norris. He should in fact have brought her up to speed some time ago. She had undoubtedly read Line's post with the account of the newspaper report, but she ought really to have a formal reply from him. The first time he had written to her she was still in Australia. The distance meant their contact seemed fairly informal. Now she was in Spain and the case had developed. Their dialogue could end up being included in the formal case documentation, and he worded his message more economically than he would have done in a phone conversation.

In the past twenty-four hours, no more snow had fallen. The main roads were clear and the asphalt surfaces dry.

At the morning meeting, they had a run-through of what had emerged in the past day or so and anticipated what they might expect over the next twenty-four hours.

'The results of the examination of the Spanish van should come in today, and her ex-boyfriend must be brought in for a fresh interview,' Wisting said.

After the meeting, he received a message from the on-duty officer at the front desk to say he had a visitor waiting down in the reception area.

Ellinor Brink got to her feet when he arrived downstairs, smiling as she approached him.

Wisting thanked her for yesterday's visit, stumbling over his words a little and feeling rather clumsy. Ellinor held out a plastic carrier bag from a petrol station.

'I brought a few things for Trond, as you said I could.'

Wisting looked at the carrier bag. To be perfectly honest, he had tried to talk her out of the suggestion but could not bring himself to say that now. He took the bag and squinted into it – car magazines and some comics as well as bars of chocolate.

'Only if you get the chance,' she said.

'That's OK,' Wisting assured her.

A woman on one of the nearby chairs glanced up from a brochure, watching them. Wisting wondered whether he should invite Ellinor up to his office but decided against it.

Ellinor was holding a pair of leather gloves in her hands. 'Will you phone me after you've spoken to him?' she asked.

Wisting nodded. 'Is there anything in particular you want me to tell him?'

'I just hope he'll listen to you,' she replied. 'That he can put everything behind him and look to the future.'

She put on her gloves and moved to the exit. The sliding doors opened automatically. 'We'll speak later, then,' she said as she left.

Wisting stood watching her go before turning on his heel. On the way back to his office he called in to see Nils

Hammer. Electronic equipment and a computer still lay on the floor from the search at Trond Brink Isaksen's home.

'No Lenovo Thinkpad among the stolen goods?' Wisting asked, even though he already knew the answer.

Hammer shook his head. 'What was left in his apartment is cheap stuff,' he replied. 'The kind of computers you can buy at Elkøp for next to nothing. They're not worth much on the black market.'

'Are you planning to interview him again?' Wisting asked.

'First I need a list of the goods he's suspected of stealing,' Hammer told him.

Wisting sat down with the bag Ellinor had given him on his lap. 'I was thinking of paying him a visit in jail,' he said. 'Is it OK with you if I talk to him?'

Hammer gave him a puzzled look.

'We're looking for the laptop and two mobiles missing from Astri Arctander's van,' Wisting explained. 'I want to ask him about that.'

'Sounds like a long shot,' Hammer said.

Wisting agreed. 'But we don't know enough about what became of the stolen goods,' he said. 'Maybe he can come up with the names of some fences, if nothing else. Anyway, I know his mother. I've promised to try to motivate him to accept treatment.'

Hammer shrugged. 'It can't do any harm, that's for sure,' he said.

Wisting thanked him. He had already informed the prison that he would be there at noon.

43

Username: Nichelle

Michelle stood with a cigarette in one hand and her mobile in the other. She had to stand immediately outside the hotel entrance to avoid losing the WiFi signal. Water was dripping from an air-conditioning apparatus on the wall above, forming a puddle on the pavement beside her.

She was the sole forum administrator and felt a responsibility to read everything posted there. Controlling the flow of information. So far there had been no need to moderate any of the contributions, but she was unsure how to react to the discussion about the local artist who had been pointed out as a possible killer. It was one of the most intense discussion threads. He was called only *the artist*, but even though his name was not mentioned, a link to his webpage and articles about him had been published.

She took a drag of her cigarette. It crossed her mind that Pol Prado was unlikely to be his real name. It sounded more like an artist's pseudonym. Anyway, it would be wrong to start censoring posts when the express aim was to elicit anything that might have to do with Ruby's murder. The forum users themselves could take responsibility for what they wrote. Mark Zuckerberg could not be held responsible for everything people wrote on Facebook, either, just because he had founded the online community.

'Nichelle Morris?'

Michelle looked up. A dark-haired woman of her own age was standing in front of her.

'I'm Zita Barroso from the *Diari di Girona*,' she said in somewhat staccato English. 'You know me as Kenzie, from the forum.'

Michelle tossed her cigarette into an overflowing ashtray, aware of how nervous she felt facing a bona fide reporter.

'Michelle,' she introduced herself, shaking hands. 'Michelle Norris. Online I call myself Nichelle, with an N.'

The journalist nodded. 'I knew that, really,' she said with a smile. 'Did your journey go smoothly?'

'It's a long trip, without much sleep. But it went well.'

'Have you had time to look around?'

Michelle shook her head. 'I arrived late last night,' she replied. 'I saw the beach and the place where Ruby was found from the bus window.' She turned and pointed at a building further down the street. 'The last photo of her must have been taken over there.'

A camera on the wall pointed down at the area in front of the entrance.

Zita nodded. 'The pizzeria is right round the corner,' she said. 'Shall we go there?'

Michelle shook her head. 'I'm meeting the private detective there later today,' she said. 'We could go to the beach bar instead.'

'That's twenty minutes' walk away,' Zita told her. 'Shall we take a taxi or would you prefer to walk?'

'I'd rather walk,' Michelle said.

On the map, she had seen where the campsite was situated. 'We can call in there on the way,' she suggested.

They walked the same route that Ruby must have taken several times. The streets were narrow and labyrinthine with run-down buildings on either side, mostly shops and restaurants.

They moved quite quickly out of the town centre, through an area filled with villas hidden behind high walls and undeveloped strips of land with dry, scorched grass. In some parts they saw lopsided foundations for buildings never completed, where weeds and tangled shrubs had taken over instead.

Zita Barroso posed a steady stream of questions as they walked. She wanted to know everything about Michelle's upbringing with Ruby. About her thoughts on the day Ruby had left for her travels and how she had learned that Ruby had been murdered.

Michelle answered with ease. It felt good to talk about everything, and it dawned on her too late that she was actually being interviewed, realizing she had been naïve about her rendezvous with the journalist. Her intention had been to meet up with someone from Palamós with whom she could discuss the case. The motivation for Zita Barroso's approach had been different.

The campsite, located behind a low wall and a hedge of dense conifers, was more extensive than Michelle had imagined. The bungalows were a collection of brown timber buildings that resembled barracks, situated immediately beside the reception, while it looked as if the spaces for tents were further away.

'Ruby stayed in number twenty-one,' Zita told her.

She led the way towards the second row of buildings as if she had been here before. Michelle recognized the place from the pictures in the police files.

The door to number twenty-one was open and a cleaning trolley blocked the path.

Zita walked up to the door, peeked in and waved for Michelle to join her.

A tied rubbish bag sat on the steps outside, but there was no one there. The little bungalow had been rented out countless times since Ruby stayed there. Cleared and cleaned. All the same, standing in the doorway felt like somehow being close to her.

'What are your thoughts?' Zita asked.

Michelle suppressed her emotions. If Zita Barroso intended to write a newspaper article, she wanted it to be about Ruby, not her.

'Let's move on,' she said.

The beach was two blocks down from the campsite, between two rockfaces. A few teenagers were playing volleyball at the water's edge. It looked as if the waves rolled in differently here from at the town beach. They broke far out and kept the same shape and size almost all the way in. Michelle put her hand to her forehead to help her see. Surfers were lying on their boards, ready and waiting for the right moment. Further out, she saw boats with colourful sails.

The beach bar looked like a large bamboo shack. A girl with braids stood behind the counter. A young couple in motorbike gear sat at one of the nearest tables, but otherwise the place was deserted.

'What would you like?' Zita asked, making it clear that she would pay.

Michelle looked at the menu displayed on the wall. Although she had not eaten any breakfast, she was not really hungry. 'Just a coffee with milk,' she replied.

Zita ordered the same for herself, and they took their cups and sat down in a corner of the deck area.

'Do you think Astria knew something?' Zita asked.

'She had certainly discovered something,' Michelle replied. 'Something she was not yet ready to tell the rest of us.'

'Why did she leave here, do you think?'

'I've no idea,' Michelle answered. 'I hope the police in Norway can find that out. That they find her laptop.'

Zita took out a notepad. 'When did you last speak to the Norwegian investigator?' she asked.

'I got an email earlier today.'

'What did he write?'

'No more than what's been in the Norwegian newspapers,' Michelle responded. 'Just confirmation that it was Astria they had found. And that she was dead.'

She had to explain how she had reported Astria missing and the contact she had had with the policeman in Norway. She heard the sound of the sea behind her, a steady rhythm of waves beating on the shore.

'What do you think really happened in Norway?' the journalist pressed on with her questions. 'It looks as if the police have ruled out a hit-and-run.'

With a shrug, Michelle had to agree the events in Norway were mysterious.

'Tell me about the website,' Zita said. 'How does that work?'

'We're fumbling our way forward,' Michelle admitted. 'But we're a small, dedicated group looking at all sides of the case with fresh eyes and from different angles than the police. We search systematically for information from the day Ruby was killed, trawling social media, finding photographs, charting movements. Many of the members have different specialisms. Astria was a data analyst, ApopheniaX is a mathematician. Others know people who are specialists in various areas and willing to contribute their expertise. A researcher in the Marine Science Institute in Barcelona, for example, has worked out where Ruby may have been thrown into the sea.'

Michelle felt her enthusiasm grow. 'Our strengths lie in a

combination of interest, intuition and an indefatigable determination to investigate everything,' she concluded.

'Of course, you knew Ruby,' Zita commented. 'I understand your interest, but why do you think complete strangers want to get involved?'

Michelle had already given this some thought. 'I don't know the members,' she replied, 'as they're anonymous, but many of them write that they've joined for the sake of the excitement. They feel they're part of a story and a community and they like banding together to solve a mystery, taking part in uncovering the layers that conceal the answer. At the same time, they're able to use skills and abilities not demanded of them in their work or daily life.'

'Couldn't you have continued these investigations from your computer at home in Australia?' Zita asked. 'Why did you have to come to Palamós?'

'I think I needed some sense of reality,' Michelle replied. 'You can't immerse yourself in everything via a computer screen. Not all the information you need is available on the Internet.'

'Such as what, then?' Zita followed up.

'Such as who Olaf is, for instance,' Michelle answered. 'The drug dealer. We haven't managed to identify him through the Internet.'

Zita Barroso nodded. 'I don't think the police have found him either,' she said.

'What did the police actually say when you interviewed them?' Michelle asked. 'What kind of impression did you get?'

'I spoke to the guy in charge of the investigation,' Zita answered. 'He was very careful not to say too much. Nothing more emerged than what I could write in the newspaper article, but I got the impression there wasn't much active investigation going on, and they're just waiting for something to turn up in the DNA records. For that to solve the case.'

'What's required for that to happen?'

Zita Barroso shrugged. 'In practice it means that the perpetrator has to strike again so they can catch him for something else.'

Their coffee cups were now empty. The girl with the braids came out and asked if they would like anything else.

'No, thanks,' Michelle replied, seizing the opportunity to ask whether Leo Pérez still worked at the bar.

'Leo, yes,' the girl replied. 'He'll be here later today. Do you know him?'

Michelle shook her head. 'We have a mutual acquaintance,' she answered, before correcting herself: 'Had.'

44

Ulrik Stene sat in the visitor's chair. Skirting around the desk, Wisting drew a chair out for himself and attended to the recording equipment. The man in front of him seemed tense. His anxiety was clear from the set of his jaw and the tight corners of his mouth.

'Sorry you heard through the media,' Wisting apologized. 'I should have phoned to let you know.'

Stene gave him a slightly sympathetic look. 'Bernard called me yesterday,' he said. 'After it was on the news.'

Wisting cast a glance at the notebook where he had listed the members of Astri's family. 'Her uncle?'

Stene nodded. 'He's the one I've had most contact with.'

'From the time when you were buying second-hand boats in Spain?' Wisting asked.

'And from the marina at Slemmestad,' Stene added. 'He works in marine electronics.'

Wisting switched on the recorder and read out the formalities before taking his seat. He began with some of the same questions as last time but angled them differently. Stene answered in the same way. His responses were not really so important. What Wisting was keen to know was whether Stene had deliberately omitted telling him that he had been in Spain when Ruby Thompson had been killed. To reach that point, he had to feel his way forward in the conversation.

'When were you last in Spain?' he asked, continuing the conversation from where it had stopped before the recorder was turned on.

'At Easter,' Stene replied.

Wisting said nothing in an effort to make him elaborate.

'At Astri's,' he added, with a faint smile. 'The whole family was there, but we had a few days on our own together after the others went back to Norway.'

'Have you given any thought to why she suddenly left Spain?' Wisting asked.

Ulrik Stene shrugged and said no more.

'Was she involved in any disputes down there?' Wisting continued. 'Could she have met someone, got mixed up in something?'

The questions failed to elicit any response.

'We know she'd taken an interest in a murder case down there,' Wisting added.

Stene sat bolt upright in his seat but made no attempt to avoid his gaze. 'A murder case?' he repeated.

'A young Australian woman found dead on the beach,' Wisting said.

'That's right,' Stene said. 'It happened at Easter, when we were there. She'd just been found when Astri was jogging past.'

'Did she talk to you about it?' Wisting asked.

'Of course. She landed right in the middle of it.'

'What did she say?'

'She thought it was someone who'd drowned, and thought that was awful,' Stene told him. 'It wasn't until a few days later that we realized someone had been murdered.'

'How did you find out about it?'

'I think it was Bernard who came home and told us,' Stene replied. 'He'd been down at the marina and heard it there. Of course, it was a major news story too. We didn't really follow much of the Spanish news, but eventually we found out more about the case.'

'Did Astri say anything about what she thought had happened?'

'No . . .' Stene answered, hesitantly. 'I think it was an English guy who'd done it. A backpacker she'd met along the way.'

Ulrik Stene was obviously not up to date with developments in the case. Wisting did not think it necessary to correct him.

'Did Astri say anything about the murder after you came home?'

Stene shook his head. 'I don't understand . . .' he said. 'You're saying that Astri took an interest in the case. How did she do that?'

'The Englishman who was arrested for the murder was subsequently released,' Wisting told him, and went on to explain about the online forum. 'Astri joined in the search for the real killer. One of the things she did was to gather photos from the day Ruby Thompson was killed.'

For a moment Ulrik Stene looked confused, and then it seemed as if something had dawned on him. 'She asked me about photos,' he said. 'I sent her a whole load.'

'When was that?'

'A month ago, maybe?'

Wisting leafed through his notes and pointed out that he had failed to mention this when they had talked two days ago.

'It didn't enter my head,' Stene said. 'It was just some old photographs.'

'Did she say what she was going to do with them?'

'No, I don't know . . . are you saying she thought I'd taken photos of the killer?'

Wisting explained how Astri had mapped out Ruby Thompson's movements and created a timeline through her last day with the help of several thousand photos she had collected.

'There was an event with lots of people on the town beach that day,' he said. 'To mark the start of the bathing season.'

Stene leaned forward. 'We were there,' he said eagerly.

'So were Ruby Thompson and the Englishman,' Wisting told him.

'I took photos there,' Stene went on. 'I sent them to Astri.'

'Would it be possible for you to send those photos to me too?' Wisting asked.

'I can send you a link,' Stene replied, indicating the computer on the desk.

He changed position in his seat again, now more uncomfortable than when he had sat down. 'But how can what happened in Spain have anything to do with this?' he asked.

'It may not,' Wisting replied, holding up his hand in warning. 'I just wanted to talk to you, since Astri was active in the discussion forum until she left Palamós.'

Stene nodded. A look of understanding replaced the confused expression he had worn. Wisting continued for another half-hour with questions about Astri. In the end he was left with the impression that Ulrik Stene was not holding back or hiding anything.

'I'll see you out,' Wisting said in conclusion, producing his pass.

Stene stopped at the door as if he had forgotten something. 'What's the name of the website?' he asked.

Returning to his desk, Wisting wrote down the address on a sheet of paper and tore it from his notepad. 'You have to register with a username and password to gain access,' he said, handing it to Stene.

45

Exactly as predicted, it had begun to snow again by lunch-time. Huge, heavy flakes that turned to dirty slush on the roads. Wisting drove in the tyre tracks left by the vehicle in front and spent the time en route to the prison making phone calls. Line was right. Astri Arctander's bank account showed that her credit card had been charged each month with a small sum to Google Commerce Ltd in Ireland for external storage of up to one hundred gigabytes of data. It took a while for him to be transferred to an investigator at the computer crime centre in Kripos who could assist him.

'We have successful experience of obtaining data from Google,' the IT expert replied. 'But it's a bureaucratic process and can take time. First you'll have to get an order from a Norwegian court and then an official request has to be sent to the Irish police. It can take a few days for it to reach the top of their pile. The processing time at Google is even longer.'

This was as expected, but Wisting heaved a sigh all the same. The information he was after was actually only a few keystrokes away and accessible from any location around the globe.

'Police work across land borders is an exercise in patience,' the Kripos investigator commented in a jovial tone.

'We've already initiated the legal process,' Wisting told him. 'I anticipate having a court order in a few hours.'

'I can give you further help once that's in place,' the computer crime investigator promised. 'Do you know if she has more than one storage subscription?'

'I see from her bank statement that she also pays for something called SkyDrive Inc. in the USA,' Wisting said. 'It sounds like something to do with IT. Have you ever come across it?'

'It's a program for security back-ups,' his Kripos colleague replied. 'It synchronizes selected files and folders on your computer to a data server, in a similar way to Google, but it's not used so much by private individuals. We've never recovered anything from that source, but we can give it a shot.'

'What about Apple?' Wisting asked. 'She has an iPhone we've not been able to find.'

'That's worse. They claim they have no access to customer data and they have no universal key or back route to data on user accounts.'

Thanking him, Wisting ended the conversation and was left dwelling on how developments in society had forced him to adapt. His job was far more complex today than when he had started out as a young detective. Social progress had accelerated at a phenomenal rate, and globalization and digitization meant it had become really challenging to pursue all the leads in modern crime. However, he still felt competent enough. Anyway, even though so much was different, the fundamental task remained the same – searching for truth and finding answers.

When he swung off the road towards the prison outside Tønsberg, the driving conditions deteriorated further. The side roads were poorly cleared, and the slush swirled under the wheel arches.

He drove up to the prison gate and gained admission without delay. A bitter wind blasted him when he stepped out of the car, and he was assailed by a flurry of big snowflakes.

A prison officer greeted him, rising from his seat behind the guardroom window at the entrance. A buzzing sound, accompanied by metallic clicks, was heard as the sliding security doors opened. Wisting moved inside, stamping his feet in the security chamber to dislodge the snow before the second set of doors opened to let him in.

The prison officer approached him. 'You're here to see Trond Brink Isaksen?' he asked.

Wisting nodded.

'We've brought him from his cell,' the officer continued. 'He's waiting in an interview room.'

'What shape is he in?'

'Physically, he's over the worst, but he's in a foul mood. It was difficult to get him out of his cell. He wants all appointments for interview to be made through his lawyer.'

'This will just be a very short meeting,' Wisting said. 'I've brought him something from his mother.' He held out the bag. 'Reading material and confectionery,' Wisting explained. 'Is that OK?'

'Have you checked it all?'

Wisting had not examined all the wrappers but felt he could vouch for Ellinor and gave a brief nod in response. That was good enough for the prison guard.

'If you think it'll improve his humour,' he said with a shrug.

Keys rattled as Wisting followed him into a side corridor and on towards the cramped interview room.

The prison officer held the door open for Wisting. Isaksen was sitting at the window, gazing out. Turning around slowly, he looked Wisting up and down. 'I'm not saying anything without my lawyer,' he insisted.

Wisting sat down, gave the prison guard a nod and waited until the door closed behind him.

'I'm not investigating your case,' he said. 'This is not an official interview.'

'What the hell is it, then?'

'We can call it a chat,' Wisting replied, introducing himself. 'I'm trying to find a computer with important contents.'

'I know who you are,' Isaksen said.

'I've been in the police for more than thirty-five years,' Wisting agreed.

Trond Brink Isaksen's name had passed across his desk numerous times in the last twenty of these, but Wisting had never before met the man in the flesh.

'Mum's talked about you,' the prisoner said. 'You once saved her dog from drowning. She told that story nearly every time a picture of you appeared in the paper or you were on the TV news.'

'Milos,' Wisting said, unable to resist a smile.

Isaksen shrugged. 'Maybe so,' he said. 'She's had a lot of dogs.'

'I spoke to her yesterday,' Wisting went on. 'She gave me something for you when she heard I was coming here.'

He placed the plastic bag on the table. Isaksen peeked into it and seemed pleased. 'Why were you talking to her?'

'She's worried about you,' Wisting told him. 'I promised to try to help.'

Isaksen gave him a sceptical look.

Wisting did not go into details. 'Detox, treatment and eventually a job,' he said. 'But it all depends on you being interested yourself. You don't need to make up your mind right now, but when you're ready I can set up an appointment with a motivator from the drug addiction team.'

Isaksen had been through numerous court cases in the past. He knew that with the haul of stolen goods the police had found in his home, he would be convicted. The easiest way to slide through the system was to confess, agree to being remanded in custody, get the case tried in court fairly quickly and start his sentence. This would also be the best starting point for a rehabilitation programme.

'One of my investigators will take it up with you at the next interview,' Wisting said, wasting no time on that. 'I want to ask you about something else.'

'You said something about a computer containing important information,' Isaksen said.

'A Lenovo ThinkPad,' Wisting clarified. 'Scarcely a year old. It costs almost fifty thousand, brand new.'

Isaksen shook his head. 'I don't know anything about that,' he answered swiftly.

Ignoring him, Wisting related the whole story – about Astri Arctander and her involvement in the murder inquiry in Palamós, about the van that had been abandoned near Manvik, and how her laptop could contain vital information.

'If her laptop ends up on the black market, how can I find it?' he asked.

Isaksen rested his arm along the bars in front of the window.

'Check out Finn.no,' was his response. 'Everything used or stolen gets sold online.'

Wisting cast his mind back to one of his first cases and the solving of a series of thefts of video players and hifi systems. On that occasion, the stolen goods had been delivered to dealers who functioned as a sales headquarters for stolen loot. Now that stage of receiving stolen goods was gone.

'Guys like me get rid of electronic items right away to people who can deliver that kind of thing, but there's more money to be made in putting them on the Internet,' Isaksen added. 'At any rate, that's where everything ends up and gets sold, but what you're looking for will have been wiped. The hard disk is almost certainly reformatted – if not, it would be easy to see that they're stolen goods.'

Wisting nodded. His hopes that Isaksen might be able to progress the case had not been high, but it had been worth an attempt. When he was ushered out of the confined space, he had to admit to himself that the purpose of his visit had not only been to ask about the vanished laptop but also so that he would have something to tell Ellinor afterwards.

46

The email with the analysis results from the examination of
the Spanish van had arrived while Wisting was on his way
back from the prison. In consultation with the forensics
technicians who had examined the vehicle, the laboratory
had prioritized the samples from the driver's cabin. A total
of eight DNA profiles had been obtained, from four different individuals. Five of these were coincident. The same
DNA profile was found on the steering wheel, the gearstick,
a seatbelt, the mouth of an empty bottle and the catch on the
glove compartment. These would all be compared to Astri
Arctander's DNA from the post-mortem.

The sample from the wheel was a mixed profile with some
male DNA that was also found on a screwdriver in the passenger footwell. Tests showed that these two profiles were
genetically connected. They did not have reference samples
from Astri's uncle, but he had been the one who had used
the van to start with, and the profile most likely belonged to
him. In addition, two DNA profiles had been found with different male sex-specific markers on the control panel of the
car radio and interior door handles. Possibly from staff members of the company that owned the van, Wisting thought.

Of most interest was the yellow beanie hat found in the
glove compartment. Using strands of hair taken from inside
the brim, a DNA profile had been extracted with an unknown
female sex-specific marker.

Ruby Thompson's DNA profile was available in the Spanish DNA register. He would have to have a comparison run

but could not risk ending up in a time-consuming bureaucratic procedure.

He had already made some necessary preparations. From the website about Ruby Thompson's murder he had the name of the investigator in charge in Spain. He had obtained his email address and had almost finished writing a message in English.

Urgent, he wrote in the subject field. *Information about the murder of Ruby Thompson.*

The contents were succinct, but at the same time as comprehensive as possible. He introduced himself as a senior police officer and explained that he was investigating the possible murder of a Norwegian woman who had been reported missing from Palamós a week earlier. He used extracts from the English news synopsis Line had composed to give an account of the inquiry and added that Astri Arctander, during the period prior to leaving Spain, had been involved in voluntary work in a community-based online investigation of Ruby Thompson's death. One of the contributions she had made was to collect photos of Ruby in order to map out her movements in the last few hours of her life. In Astri's vehicle, a yellow knitted hat had been found, of the same kind as the one the murder victim in Palamós had been pictured wearing on the day she was killed. The hat had been kept in a sealed bag and, before she had left Spain, Astri had attempted to seek advice from a Norwegian expert, the author of a textbook on criminal forensics. The hat had been routinely tested at the national forensics laboratory in Oslo and unknown DNA of female origin had been secured. The message ended by asking if Comisario Telmo Álvarez might be interested in further information to assess whether the discovery was of potential interest in his unsolved murder inquiry.

Wisting attached one of the forensic photographs of the hat and read through what he had written before pressing the 'send' button. If he had been on the receiving end, such a message would have aroused considerable interest in an investigation that was otherwise at a standstill.

He went to get some coffee but found the pot in the conference room empty. Switching on the machine, he took out his mobile while he waited and called Ellinor.

She answered at once, and it dawned on him that she had been waiting for him to phone. He should have rung her from the car as soon as he left the prison.

'He sends his love,' he said, even though her son had not actually said anything of the kind. 'He was pleased with his magazines and chocolate.'

He moved to the window as they chatted.

'How was he?' Ellinor asked.

'In much better shape than a few days ago,' Wisting replied.

'And apart from that?'

'We talked about his options, but it's too early for him to make up his mind,' Wisting answered. 'It's a process – he has to do some thinking before the time will be ripe.'

In the street below, a lorry was spreading grit on the frozen asphalt.

'Will you see him again?' Ellinor asked.

'I'm going to follow it up,' Wisting promised.

He wanted to suggest a meeting, but Maren Dokken appeared at the door. 'There you are,' she said, not noticing he was on the phone.

'I'll call you back later,' he said.

Maren waited for him to finish. 'Did you see the email from Fingerprinting?' she asked, though she realized he couldn't have done. 'About the glass,' she reminded him. 'It's just come in.'

Wisting appreciated that the tests must have yielded results. 'What have they found?' he asked.

'Prints from three fingers of Astri Arctander's right hand,' Maren replied.

Wisting looked at her before turning to the coffee machine. The coffee was ready.

'They could be old,' he said, taking a cup from the cupboard. 'From last summer, or something.'

'They're the only prints on the glass,' Maren told him. 'She's the only one who's touched it.'

Wisting lifted the pot and filled his cup. This changed things. They had thought that someone had been waiting for Astri at the summer cabin, but instead she was the one who had been there.

'Her prints were taken during the autopsy yesterday,' Maren went on. 'I asked them to compare them.'

'You already suspected this?' Wisting asked.

'It was a possibility,' Maren answered, 'that something happened to her on the way *from* the cabin rather than on the way there.'

She crossed to the cupboard above the worktop and took out a cup. Wisting could see how her shoulder injury still restricted her movement. She had been the one standing closest when a grenade exploded during what had been a patrol assignment two years earlier. The injury had prevented her from taking part in any further active service. Instead she had been transferred to the criminal investigation department. She now occupied a post that would normally have been filled by a more experienced officer with formal qualifications in investigative techniques, but Maren had breathed new life into the department. She had the kind of flair that could not be learned but was an inborn ability. She had an extraordinary skill of letting her mind wander freely when her colleagues' thinking processes had become stuck.

'Of course, it makes the question of what she was doing in the summer cabin even more interesting,' she said, pouring some coffee for herself. 'We should really go out there to search the place again with that in mind. Look for something she may have taken with her or left behind. Maybe her laptop is there.'

Wisting's phone buzzed. The number had a prefix with the country code +34. Spain.

'I have to take this,' he said. Putting down his coffee cup, he moved to the door, but stopped and turned to face her. 'Are you doing anything special at the weekend?' he asked.

'No,' she replied. 'Why do you ask?'

The phone continued to vibrate in his hand. 'I may need you to come with me on a work trip,' he replied.

47

It was a woman on the line. She introduced herself as Zita Barroso, a journalist on a Catalan newspaper.

'Palamós is one of the areas we cover,' she continued. 'I'm phoning in connection with a Norwegian woman who went missing from here at the beginning of the month. I understand she's been found dead in Norway and you're the investigator in charge.'

Wisting flopped down into his office chair.

'Astri Arctander,' the journalist added, to clarify.

The Norwegian name sounded remarkably staccato in English with a Spanish accent.

'How can I help you?' Wisting asked.

'Do you suspect something criminal behind her death?' the journalist asked.

'The circumstances are unclear,' Wisting replied. 'We're working hard to find out what happened.'

'How did she die?'

'That's something we're trying to discover.'

'So you're investigating it as a murder?'

It was difficult to explain the nuances of difference between what was categorized as a suspicious death and what as a homicide by the Norwegian police, and Wisting realized his answer would only confirm that they had launched a murder inquiry.

'Is it correct that she was found under a metre of snow?' the journalist went on.

Wisting explained the facts and details surrounding the

discovery. It sounded as if the journalist was especially interested in the temperature and snow conditions.

'Have you been in touch with the Catalan police?'

'Yes, that's only natural, since she was reported missing to the local police in Palamós.'

'Have the Catalan police provided you with information on Ruby Thompson's murder?'

The question was unexpected. He was unsure how to answer, but coverage in the Spanish media could put pressure on the police down there and expedite a response to his email.

'We're familiar with Astri's interest in the case,' Wisting answered.

'So you're aware of the online forum of which she was a member?'

It seemed the journalist already knew the answer. Wisting confirmed it. The reporter followed up with a question about how deeply the Norwegian police had delved into the website to investigate Astri's activity there.

'We've primarily obtained our information from the website administrator,' Wisting replied, avoiding the question.

'Do you know if she had come across relevant details about Ruby's murder?'

'It's difficult for me to comment on a current Catalan investigation,' Wisting told her.

The journalist's questions continued, as if she was reading them from a list.

'Have you found her computer?'

'No.'

'But she did bring it with her when she left Palamós?'

'We've reason to believe that.'

'Do you know why she left so suddenly, without telling anyone?'

'That's part of our investigation.'

'Could the answers you're looking for be on the website?'

Wisting had experience of journalists. These questions were heading in a direction where he sensed the answers might be used to create sensational headlines. At the same time, he could not deny that she was right.

'Charting her social circle and final movements are routine tasks in inquiries such as this,' he told her. 'In the case of Astri Arctander, that includes her movements and contacts on the Internet.'

He sat up straight in his chair and distractedly grabbed the computer mouse. The screen fired up and he logged in while he spoke. The recent email with the results of the fingerprint tests on the glass of water was at the top of his inbox. Opening it, he saw it also contained results of the prints found in the Spanish-registered van. Astri's prints were in two places in the cab, as well as on an empty soft drink bottle. Also, several other unidentified prints had been found.

'You confirmed you'd been in touch with the local police in Palamós,' the journalist continued. 'But have you initiated cooperation and exchanged information with the provincial police investigating Ruby Thompson's murder?'

An alert sounded as another email popped up on Wisting's screen. This was the reply from the leader of the Spanish murder inquiry.

The message was short and succinct. Three brief sentences running to two lines of text.

Send me the profile. I'll contact our lab at once. You'll have the results in a few hours.

Wisting shifted the phone to his other ear. 'Yes,' he answered. 'We've good communication with the relevant police authorities.'

48

Username: Marmot

Maren turned the computer screen slightly to make it even more difficult for anyone who came in to see it. A marmot was a species of large ground-dwelling squirrel. She typed it into the username field. Her grandfather had called her a marmot when she was little, scampering about energetically and then flaking out. She called herself Marmot in a number of places on the Internet where she needed a nickname, and also had an email address with the same nom de plume.

On the registration page, she at first added a few years to her age and pretended she was from Australia, but then changed it. If she found anything of interest on the website, she would have to be honest about how she had obtained the information. Using a nickname was fine, but giving false information would not be acceptable.

She used a picture of a marmot as her profile picture and wrote nothing about herself except that she was a public sector worker.

Anyone whatsoever could set up a profile. There was nothing wrong with that. Nonetheless, she hesitated. It felt like deception, but if Wisting intended to involve her more deeply in the investigation of Astri's death, she was keen to know as much as possible.

Her finger firmly pressed the 'enter' key. She was in.

The appearance of the webpage resembled other discussion groups she sometimes entered to look at conversations about a film or TV series, but it had a variety of functions. One of these was the option to set up your own sub-pages with graphic presentations.

Every aspect of Ruby Thompson's murder seemed to be under debate. From an assortment of posts about evidence, motive and theories, discussion threads were spun with other members contributing their points of view.

One of the posts that had attracted most comments had to do with a possible serial killer. This was not something Wisting had mentioned. Maren clicked in and began to read. A total of eight other unsolved murders had been identified with similarities to the murder of Ruby Thompson. Each case was put forward, alongside photos and media coverage. They were presented clearly and precisely, but many of the comments were speculative and it did not take long for her to abandon the thread.

Astria's death in Norway was a subject of discussion. Here the conjectures were also fired off in numerous directions, but there seemed to be widespread agreement that she had discovered something before she died.

Maren navigated forward to Astria's photo project. As she fumbled for her coffee cup on the desk, she clicked her way through Ruby Thompson's last day. Her cup was half full, but the coffee had gone cold from being left too long and she spat it back into the cup.

The series of photographs was easy to follow, a self-explanatory mapping out of Ruby's movements on the last day of her life, but it did not contain anything revealing. No one was repeatedly lurking in the background – nor was there anything else for her to latch on to.

She read the many comments without picking up that any-one else had noticed anything in particular either. The most interesting thing was Astria's own comment that she had collected ninety-seven images but had not yet posted them on the forum, and thought she had found something significant.

A new post had appeared on the home page, a follow-up to a discussion attempting to find out what Astria had been working on but had not yet shared with the others prior to her death. A user called Shelook wrote that she had examined all the posts from the week before Astria disappeared to see where she had left comments and been most active. This analysis clearly showed that she had been most preoccupied by the post about the last unsolved murder in Palamós. She had made twenty-three comments in all. One post about a drug dealer called Olaf ranked as number two with ten comments, while on other posts she had seldom made more than one or two.

Maren clicked on the link to the post about the previous murder, which was included in the serial killer theory. Almost thirteen years ago, a twenty-four-year-old German backpacker was found murdered on the same beach as Ruby Thompson. A condensed version of the case was written in English, and photos from the coverage in Spanish and Catalan newspapers were included. Bertine Franck had travelled by train from Hamburg with a girlfriend. Their plan was to visit as many capital cities as possible on the continent of Europe. They had journeyed through Amsterdam, Brussels, Paris and Lisbon and, after Madrid, their route had moved out to the coast, where they wanted to spend a few days before moving on to Rome. In the major cities, they stayed at youth hostels, but otherwise they spent their nights in a small two-man tent. In Palamós, they had stayed at the same campsite as Ruby Thompson. One Thursday evening, her friend had gone to bed early because she had a headache, while Bertine Franck had headed on her own to the beach. She never returned to their tent. Not until eight days later was her body found on the shore, stripped of her clothes and strangled.

Several contributors pointed out the same thing: Bertine was not only found killed in the same way and in the same place as Ruby – they had also stayed at the same campsite.

Maren grabbed a pen but, instead of jotting down some notes, she sat biting the end of it as she read on.

What was unusual about this case was that a Spanish/German travel magazine had interviewed Bertine Franck and her friend while they were in Madrid. The article was printed on the very day Bertine disappeared. The photo from the interview had been used in all the newspaper articles. In most of these, her friend's image had been deleted, but in one the whole photograph was printed. Bertine and her friend were sitting on a bench in the Gran Via with their rucksacks beside them.

Maren herself had sat in the Gran Via but could not recognize anything in the photo. The summer before she had enrolled at Police College, she and a friend had visited a mutual acquaintance who was studying architecture down there. They had stayed for a fortnight, and she had nothing but good memories of the trip.

Several comments on the presentation of this case suggested that the staff at Palamós Camping should be checked out since both of the victims had stayed there. Some of them had begun to make a list based on what they found online through various search engines.

Someone called ApopheniaX had proposed the serial killer hypothesis and had posted that proposition. In one comment, Astria had asked if anyone had discovered whether Bertine's clothes had ever been found. Other members responded swiftly to say they had not been able to find out anything about this in any of the newspaper articles.

ApopheniaX confirmed that this had not emerged from any of the material he had collected. In the missing-person notice issued by the police when Bertine disappeared, it had stated that she had been wearing a beige sweater, blue jeans and grey sandals. Also, she had been carrying a small haversack containing swimming gear, a towel and a couple of bottles of beer. She was wearing the sweater when she was found. It actually belonged to the friend with whom Bertine had been travelling.

In the next comment, Astria thanked ApopheniaX for his answer and asked for the name of Bertine's friend. He admitted that this was not mentioned in any of the media coverage he had read. Astria thanked him again for his reply and asked if he knew what the Spanish/German travel magazine was called, since the name must appear somewhere there. ApopheniaX had responded to say that he knew nothing more than what was printed in the newspaper articles he had posted. The name of the magazine was not cited and the picture was credited only with the name of a photo agency. A number of suggestions were made as to which magazine it had been. A forum member who lived in Madrid wrote that he knew someone who had worked in a travel agent's at that time and would try to find out. He came back with the information that *Der Spanienweg* was the most likely. A German user reported that his library in Hamm had the relevant year of the magazine in their archive, but he had been unable to find the article in question. Another German contributor wrote that he remembered the story from the German media coverage and would search for information there. Two days later he returned with an article from the *Hamburger Morgenpost*, which had carried an interview with Bertine's travel companion. Her name was Thea Weber. The article ran to two pages. She related her memories of the disappearance, the uncertainty when she was left on her own, and her encounter with the Catalan police. They had not taken the case seriously until Bertine's body was washed ashore.

Someone calling himself Ned B. asked why Astria was so preoccupied with what had happened to the clothes. Astria answered with a laughing emoji and said that she was fixated on details. *The devil is in the detail*, Ned B. had replied, but there was nothing more on what Astria had really been looking for. Below, a comment appeared in which a member had posted a screenshot from Facebook with a search result for Thea Weber, with the suggestion that Astria could write to them all. Another user commented that it was probable she had married and changed her name in the course of the past twelve years. Simultaneously, a man called Ace of Spade had resorted to dastelefonbuch.de to narrow the list down to four women who lived in Hamburg. In a final comment, Astria had written: *Thanks, maybe I'll try that.* This was the day before she left Palamós.

There was a knock and the office door opened.

Maren switched the screen image as William Wisting stepped into the room. She realized something had happened, but he was unsure where to start.

'I've just had a phone call from Poulsen in Forensics,' he said. 'They're excluding severe hypothermia and have found no traces of intoxicants.'

'That leaves only homicide,' Maren said.

Wisting did not reply, as if this was something they had actually known all along.

'You'll have to go home and pack,' he said, glancing at the clock. 'The Catalan police have just confirmed that Ruby Thompson's DNA was found on the yellow hat from Astri's vehicle. We're leaving in four hours.'

49

Username: Nichelle

The pizzeria was half full. Michelle Norris looked from the picture of Ruby on her computer screen and up at the camera behind the bar counter. It felt strange, being there, as if she were present in two dimensions at the one time.

The door opened and a man in his twenties entered and approached the counter, seemingly oblivious to being filmed. The assistant took a pizza carton from the hot cupboard and handed it over.

Michelle concentrated on the screen again. As she was early, she made good use of the restaurant's first-rate Internet coverage.

An hour ago she had received a direct message from MrsPeabody about Astria's last conversation on the Internet. MrsPeabody had asked if Astria had found more photographs, and Astria told her she had gathered another ninety-seven images that she would shortly post on the forum. The next day, Ned B. had asked if there were any new photos of Ruby. Astria had responded that she needed more time but thought she had found something significant.

That is, as you know, the last thing Astria writes, but also the last communication from Ned B., MrsPeabody wrote.

She offered the excuse that she had probably read too many crime novels, but she had noticed the last person in contact with a missing person or murder victim was always of interest in an investigation. For that reason she had tried to send direct messages to Ned B. to ask if he had been in touch with Astria outside the forum messages but had received no reply. Then she had gone back into old posts to see what Ned B. had written. He had not posted anything himself but on a number of occasions had commented on Astria's work, including asking where the last photo of Ruby had been taken, and he had participated in the discussion about the unsolved murder of the German backpacker, Bertine Franck. However, after Astria's disappearance, there had been total silence from him, and he had not responded to her messages.

Michelle checked the log to which only she had access and saw that Ned B. had been inactive in the past couple of weeks following Astria's disappearance. In his profile he had stated he was a nineteen-year-old criminology student from Madrid. A map search on his IP address confirmed that he was located there, though it was marked as an open proxy server, which usually meant the user had redirected data traffic from their real location.

What MrsPeabody had discovered was that at the time Ned B. had gone offline, a new member had enrolled in the group: Effie P. These two usernames were constructed in the same way – a first name and the initial letter of a surname. No other forum member had created a username in similar fashion. MrsPeabody thought she had found a connection. Effie Perine was the secretary of the private detective Sam Spade in the book *The Maltese Falcon*, while Ned Beaumont was an amateur sleuth in *The Glass Key* by the same author. Effie P. and Ned B.

Michelle had not read either of these books but agreed with MrsPeabody that they could indeed be one and the same person.

Effie P. claimed to be a thirty-two-year-old homemaker

from San Francisco, which tallied with the IP address as far as that went, but MrsPeabody was of the opinion that this was instead a reference to the city where the events of the novel took place.

From the log, Michelle saw that Effie P. had been logged on five or six times a day but had never written anything. However, today no activity was registered.

The door opened again, and this time it was the private detective. He shot a glance at the camera behind the counter before his eyes scanned the interior of the premises. Michelle closed the lid of her laptop and signalled to him. Ethan Mahoney came over to the table, introduced himself and sat down.

'Nice to meet you,' he said. 'I feel I know you a little after having been on the website.'

Michelle smiled. 'Good that we could meet up,' she said.

Ethan Mahoney spread his arms wide in an extravagant gesture. 'Well, we're both here, so far from home!' he said in an exaggerated Australian accent.

A waiter approached the table.

'Are you hungry?' the detective asked.

Michelle shook her head and ordered a glass of the house lemonade. Mahoney wanted something stronger.

'A gimlet,' he said, explaining the ingredients to the waiter: 'Half-part gin to half-part lime.'

'Have you had any response?' Michelle asked once they were alone again.

Mahoney shook his head. 'Nothing of any particular inter-est,' he replied. 'Most of the tip-offs probably went to the police before me, and now the senders want a chance to receive the reward if there turns out to be anything in it.'

'Have you had a look at all the police documents?' Michelle asked.

Mahoney shook his head again. 'Mr Thompson's lawyer is working on that, but I have access to some of them through Jarod Denham's lawyer in England. Mostly the same as what you have on your website. Of course, they're keen to clear it up. That would mean a complete exoneration of Jarod and facilitate support for a compensation claim.'

'So you don't have a suspect?' Michelle asked.

'Not so far,' the private detective replied. 'What about you?'

'I think we're both stuck in the same place,' Michelle told him. 'At least, from what I understood from the newspaper interview you gave, you've uncovered more or less the same as what we've arrived at in the forum.'

The waiter was back, and Mahoney refrained from commenting. 'Tell me about Ruby,' he said instead.

Michelle reiterated most of what she had told the journalist a few hours earlier before asking what Ethan Mahoney thought of the idea that the same person was behind a number of earlier murders.

'That gives a greater chance of the case being solved,' the detective said. 'With each victim, the pattern becomes clearer and it gets easier to home in on potential perpetrators.'

'The police seem sceptical about the theory,' Michelle said. 'I spoke to the journalist who interviewed the head of the investigation.'

'Naturally they're sceptical,' Mahoney commented, gulping down the rest of his drink. 'After all, it would mean they've overlooked something for sixteen years.'

'Are you planning to do some further work on that theory?' Michelle asked.

The detective put down his glass. 'I need to take a closer look at that artist,' he replied. 'And I'm going to try to find that Norwegian.'

'Olaf?'

Ethan Mahoney nodded. 'Do you know anything else about him?'

Michelle shook her head. 'No,' she answered. 'But I can't understand why he's so difficult to track down. A pale Norwegian in black clothes. And Ruby encountered him on one of her first days here.'

'That's exactly what makes him more interesting,' Mahoney said.

They sat for another half-hour discussing the case. It was good to talk to someone as familiar with the details as she was, but there was something about the private detective she did not quite take to. He was outgoing in a way that would almost certainly have appealed to Ruby, even though the guy was more than twice her age. As for her, she felt it was all a bit over the top, as if the gestures, loud voice and fixed opinions were phoney.

'What are your plans for the next few days?' Mahoney asked as he drained his third glass.

Michelle was unsure. To be honest, she really had no plans, only an idea that she would gain something from being here.

'I've just arrived,' she answered. 'I have to get to know the place.'

'Do you have any contact with Astria's family?' the detective asked.

'No,' Michelle replied. 'I've only spoken to the Norwegian policeman in charge of her case.'

'So you don't know where she lived?'

Michelle shook her head. She had not thought that far, but Astria had spent hours on her photo project. She must have a workplace. Even though her laptop was missing, there could be a few notes lying somewhere to give some clue about what had preoccupied her so much.

'Do you think she'd discovered something?' she asked.

Ethan Mahoney got to his feet and glanced at his watch. 'Difficult to say,' he replied, lifting his jacket from the back of the chair. 'Nice to meet you. I have to get on, but let's keep in touch.'

Producing a business card from his jacket pocket, he left it on the table. Michelle picked it up even though she already had his contact information stored on her mobile.

'You'll let me know if you find out anything?' she asked.

He smiled. 'I'm working for someone,' he told her. 'Above all, I report to him.'

'Of course,' Michelle replied, and was left gazing after him as he moved to the exit.

They both had the same aim by staying in Palamós, but different motivations. Everything she found out was shared online, whereas everything he discovered he would keep to himself.

At the same time, he was only one man – she had several hundred people helping her.

Once again she lifted the lid of her laptop to send a reply to MrsPeabody.

50

Username: Darby

Line checked the time. She could sit for a while longer before she had to pick up Amalie from nursery. The images slid by on the screen.

It was almost odd that no one else had already done this. The police had obviously been unable to identify the Norwegian who had sold drugs at the beach bar in Palamós. At any rate, he had not been interviewed. All they knew was that Ruby had called him Olaf, that he was around thirty years of age, had blond hair and a pale complexion and wore black clothes.

This sounded like someone who would stand out in a crowd, someone easy to recognize in a photograph. In Astria's photobank there were almost two thousand images. She had already found someone who matched the description, a pale man in sunglasses standing among the spectators at an event on the beach, but she planned to look through all the photos before finally submitting a post. She realized that imagining she might find Olaf in this way was a naïve idea and did not want to make a song and dance about it unless it produced a positive result.

There was a knock at the front door, and she heard her father shout her name.

'Coming!' she yelled back, and dashed up the stairs.

Her father was waiting in the kitchen. 'Are you home early?' she asked.

'I've just popped in for a minute,' Wisting replied. 'I'm going to be away for a few days. A work trip. I've been home to pack.'

'A work trip?' Line repeated. 'You mean to Spain?' That was the only destination she could think of.

'Yes, I just wanted to let you know.' He looked around. 'Isn't Amalie at home?'

'She's still at nursery,' Line explained. 'Has there been a development, since you're having to travel down there?'

'I'm going to meet the Catalan investigators,' her father told her.

That was not exactly the question she had asked, but she understood she would get nothing further out of him.

'Have you told Grandad?' she asked.

Wisting shook his head. 'I'll phone him from the car,' he said, heading for the door.

'Have a good trip, then,' Line said.

Her father turned around and gave her a hug before going out and closing the door behind him.

Line shrugged on her jacket and pulled on her shoes, ready for the drive to pick up Amalie. She tried to work out in her mind what the reason could be for the sudden trip and cooperation with the Catalan police. The only thing she could think of was that Astri Arctander must have discovered something of interest to the investigation into Ruby Thompson's murder. Something that had made her leave Spain but had also got her killed.

51

It was snowing heavily. Maren leaned forward and peered out through the front windscreen. The clouds above them were low and grey, but the planes were still flying.

'I took Spanish at senior high school,' she said.

'I know that,' Wisting replied. 'It's in your records.'

'Was that why you wanted me to come with you?' Maren asked.

'The language was a bonus,' Wisting answered. 'It was either you or Hammer. You've more IT skills than he has. And more initiative. I reckon you've already set up a profile and been into the website?'

She turned to face him. 'Marmot,' she said.

'Marmot?' Wisting asked.

'It's a kind of squirrel,' Maren clarified. 'Maybe I should have cleared it with you first?'

Wisting shrugged. 'Our job is to go out and seek information wherever it's available,' he said.

'Do *you* have a profile there?'

He shook his head. 'Not my own profile,' he replied. 'But I have access to one.'

An ambulance, blue light flashing, came up behind them and drove past.

'Have you found anything in there?' he asked.

'It's swarming with information,' Maren told him. 'Some of it is facts, but a great deal is speculation and wild allegation. What's most interesting is what's *not* there. The last photos Astri got hold of and what she'd found out.'

'The computer crime centre is on the case,' Wisting told her, adding that Astri had purchased external storage space from Google.

The traffic was moving more slowly. Wisting hoped there had not been an accident further ahead. He had arranged a meeting with Gerd Arctander en route to the airport and did not have much time to spare.

Astri's grandmother was eighty-nine but lived alone. He hoped she had not alerted any of her sons to their appointment. It was easier to hold someone's attention in a one-to-one conversation, and dialogue took on a different depth and intimacy. It gave more opportunity for the interviewee to open up about circumstances normally kept hidden, especially in family situations.

Maren was leafing through the photo album, which they had brought with them. 'There are no pictures of the grandfather here,' she commented.

'He died in the eighties,' Wisting explained. 'One of the sons followed him into the family business, but it's the grandmother who owns everything.'

Maren looked at a family photo of the old woman sitting with a raised glass in a wicker chair, surrounded by her closest relatives.

Further on, the traffic was moving more smoothly. Soon they turned off from the motorway, guided by the GPS. If they made it back to the road again within an hour, they would reach the airport in good time.

Gerd Arctander lived in an old villa with a spacious garden. The courtyard had been cleared of snow and, although there were three cars parked, there was still space for Wisting's vehicle.

A gust of wind dislodged some snow from the roof, which slid in their direction as they walked up to the house. Maren was carrying the photo album in a bag and Wisting had brought his thick, hard-backed notebook. Younger investigators used an iPad or a laptop, but Wisting liked to collect notes and reflections on paper. He enjoyed thumbing back through them, jotting down new ideas in the margins, underlining important key words and drawing lines of connection.

He stood near the door, noticing how distant and muffled the doorbell sounded from inside the house. A man in a knitted sweater quickly appeared.

'Come in,' he said, stepping aside. 'I'm Henrik.' It was one of the twin brothers.

Wisting responded with a nod of the head and ushered Maren in ahead of him.

'Walter and Bernard are here too,' the man told them as they moved inside. 'Fredrik's still in Spain.'

'In Palamós?' Wisting asked.

'No, he stays in Tortosa. That's three hours further south.'

The others were waiting in the living room. Gerd Arctander was dressed in black and sat at a table set with white tablecloth, a plate of open sandwiches and a selection of soft drinks.

Wisting thanked her for agreeing to meet him and introduced Maren.

'I thought you were coming on your own,' the old woman replied, dispatching her son out to the kitchen for an extra plate and cutlery.

The eldest of the men sitting at the table stood up to shake hands and introduced himself as Astri's father. The man beside him was the youngest brother.

Wisting and Maren sat down. Gerd Arctander invited them to help themselves. Wisting thanked her but left the plate untouched. He told them what had emerged from the autopsy and said that Astri's death was now being formally investigated as a homicide.

Standing up without a word, Walter Arctander moved to the window and stared out. Wisting could see his jaw muscles working.

Gerd Arctander continued to sit, ramrod straight, at the end of the table, as if unmoved by the new information. The two other sons had their eyes cast down.

'I don't understand any of this,' Bernard said. 'What was she doing?'

'She was going to Sommerro,' the grandmother said firmly.

'Yes, but what was she planning to do there?'

The question was left hanging in the air.

Walter Arctander resumed his seat at the table as Wisting opened his notebook.

'When did you close the cabin for winter?' he asked.

'The first weekend in October,' Gerd Arctander volunteered. 'It was Henrik who was down there at the time.'

Her son confirmed this. Wisting asked him to describe what closing for winter amounted to. In the main, it was a matter of tidying the garden furniture away, closing the shutters and bringing in the flowerpots.

'What about the water?' Wisting asked.

'Previously, we just had water in summer and an outside toilet,' Gerd Arctander told him. 'Now there's a public water supply and sewage facilities.'

'Have any of you been there since it was closed in the autumn?' Wisting continued his questions.

Gerd Arctander answered for all of them: 'No.'

Wisting let his eyes survey the three sons. No one corrected her.

'Why do you ask?' Astri's father queried.

'Certain things suggest someone's been there,' Wisting answered. 'We have reason to believe it was Astri.'

Walter Arctander shook his head. 'It must have been someone else,' he said. 'Surely she never showed up?'

Wisting explained about the glass and her fingerprints.

'They could have been from ages ago,' Henrik said, and a discussion ensued around the table about how irrational it would be for Astri to have left her vehicle almost three kilometres away, gone to the summer cabin and then set off to walk back to the van in the dark and the driving snow.

'She could have driven up to Sommerro,' Bernard suggested. 'Then the snow came while she was there. On her way back she realized she could go no further with the summer tyres and had to abandon the van. Then she started to walk back to Sommerro to spend the night there, but never got that far.'

Wisting admitted this was a possibility.

'In that case, the van was left with the bonnet pointing in the wrong direction,' Maren told them. 'On the way *to* the cabin rather than on the way *from* it.'

'She could have driven some distance and then turned to drive back when she realized that would be impossible, but couldn't get any further and so she had to leave the van,' Henrik suggested.

This was plausible but did not explain what she had been doing in the summer cabin or what had become of her luggage.

'Where's the van now?' Bernard asked.

'We've finished examining it, but it's still in our garage,' Wisting said.

'You haven't found her belongings?' Walter asked.

'No,' Wisting answered.

'Could they have been stolen en route?' Henrik mused. 'While she spent the night somewhere or just popped into a petrol station? The autobahn isn't safe. That would at least explain why she didn't phone when she had problems with the van.'

'Her phone was recorded in the Norwegian telecoms system,' Wisting told him.

'Did she phone anyone?' Astri's father asked.

Wisting explained he was talking about a standard message from the Norwegian telecoms operator after she had passed the border.

'We have another question concerning the summer cabin,' Maren said, taking out the photo album and placing it on the table. 'Where is this usually kept?'

Wisting knew the answer. He had spotted the empty space on a bookshelf on the wall behind the stack of garden furniture.

'At Sommerro,' Gerd Arctander replied. 'I have a few other albums there, in the wall unit.'

'Where did you find it?' Walter asked.

'It was lying out,' Maren answered.

The three brothers looked across at their mother, but no one said anything.

'We noticed a picture missing,' Maren went on, showing them the page from the summer of 1996 on which there were only paste marks left by a photograph.

'That's right,' Gerd Arctander said. 'It's been like that for a long time. That doesn't have anything to do with Astri.'

'Who was in the photo?' Wisting asked.

Gerd Arctander hesitated, and Henrik answered for her: 'It was me and a girl I was with that summer,' he said.

'She never became part of the family,' his mother added quickly. 'So I took the photo out.'

Maren flipped through to the page where two photos had been trimmed.

'Was she in these pictures as well?' Wisting asked.

Gerd Arctander nodded and looked across at her son. 'He met Hilde the following year,' she said, making a gesture with her finger to tell Maren to leaf through further. 'They married in ninety-nine.'

'What's the name of the girl in the photo?' Maren asked.

'It was just a summer flirtation,' Gerd Arctander said, sniffing loudly as she gave a toss of the head that seemed to mean she did not remember or it was immaterial.

'Vibeke,' her son replied. 'Vibeke Hassel.'

'Where was she from?'

'Hamar. They had a cabin near Sommerro.'

'Aren't you going to eat?' Gerd Arctander broke in.

'No, thanks,' Wisting said. 'We have to leave soon. We're going to Spain.'

Walter looked at him in surprise. 'Because of Astri?'

Wisting nodded.

'To Palamós?' Bernard asked. 'Is that really necessary?'

'Something made her leave there,' Wisting replied. 'I don't think the answer to whatever that was can be found here.'

The four family members remained seated, all eyes on him.

'We're going to try to find out what happened before she left,' Wisting went on. 'I'd like the opportunity to search the apartment where she stayed.'

'Of course,' Walter answered.

Gerd Arctander had a set of keys and handed them to them.

'You've all spent a long time in Palamós,' Wisting said. 'Do any of you know of a Norwegian called Olaf? Probably a bit younger than Astri.'

Walter shook his head. The others had nothing to contribute either.

'Who is that?' Bernard asked.

236

'A name that came up in connection with another case,' Wisting told him.

'What kind of case?'

'A case Astri was interested in,' Wisting clarified. 'A woman who was murdered in Palamós around Easter time.'

'The girl from Australia?' Walter asked. 'Astri was there when they found her. She was jogging along the beach.'

Wisting nodded. 'That's probably one of the reasons Astri took an interest in the case,' he said.

'But . . .' Henrik began. 'How on earth . . . ?'

'Olaf is a Norwegian who was staying in Palamós at the time of the murder,' Wisting explained. 'He's of interest in the case, but it doesn't look as if the Catalan police have managed to identify him. It seems Astri may have tried to find out who he is.'

'So you think it has a connection to what happened to Astri?' Bernard asked. 'That he could have something to do with it?'

'That's one of the reasons we're going down there to check it out,' Wisting answered.

'What's happening here, while you're in Spain?' Walter asked. 'About Astri, I mean. The funeral, and so on. We'd like to have that done before Christmas.'

'Of course,' Wisting replied. 'There's nothing to prevent that.'

He was told the funeral director they wanted to use and promised to arrange the practical details.

'You can leave the album here,' Gerd Arctander said when they were about to leave.

Wisting felt he was not yet finished with it. 'If it's all right with you, I'd like to keep it a while longer,' he said.

The old woman raised no objections, and Maren took it with her.

Astri's father accompanied them out. Wisting turned to face him when they were standing on the steps outside. 'What's the real story about Vibeke Hassel?' he asked.

Walter Arctander cleared his throat. 'It's a bit difficult to talk openly in front of Mother,' he replied. 'Maybe you could see that. But Vibeke Hassel has probably got nothing to do with this.'

Wisting waited for him to tell him the reason for the break-up.

'Henrik became ill that summer,' Walter explained. 'Vibeke infected him with chlamydia. He was pretty badly affected. A severe infection that took ages to shake off. They didn't exactly part as friends.'

There was silence for a moment or two. As snowflakes settled on Walter's hair, he shivered and said he would like to go back indoors. 'You'll ring me if there's any news?' he asked.

'Of course,' Wisting promised, giving him a farewell handshake.

The snow was falling more heavily than when they had arrived and now a centimetre-thick fresh layer had settled on the car.

They got in, and Wisting switched on the ignition. The wipers pushed the snow off the windscreen.

Maren put the photo album on her knee and browsed through it. 'What is it they say, again?' she thought aloud. 'That behind every pretty picture there's a horrific story?'

52

Username: Shelook

The road that followed the coast was bad, and the bus rocked from side to side. Celia sat on the sunny side and the warm rays slanted down from behind her, making it difficult to see the onscreen image. There were no vacant seats on the opposite side, but it helped if she sat sideways with her laptop turned round slightly.

One of the others in the forum had done the same as she had, the Norwegian woman who had written about Astria. She had searched through her photos and found four pictures of men dressed in black who could fit the description of Olaf. They were exactly the same images that she had arrived at. Two of them were of the same man, but none showed any clear facial features. Celia had thought of showing them to her cousin Leo before posting them on the forum. He might well be able to recognize Olaf in one of them.

The bus braked suddenly and swung to one side, and Celia grabbed the seatback in front of her for support. She was sitting far back in the bus and could not immediately see what the obstacle was but finally caught a glimpse of a moped at the side of the bus.

When she looked down at the screen again, she had received a new email. This one was from Daniel, who worked as a technician in the service section. She had transferred numerous calls to him from the switchboard without knowing who he was, but a few weeks ago he had been the instructor on a course she had attended. They had sat talking during the breaks and, when the day was over, he had invited her out for a bite to eat. They had met on one further occasion, but for the time being nothing more had come of it. In addition to his technician job at Prosecure, he worked on IT servicing. This was mostly a matter of helping to reboot crashed computers and retrieve deleted files. She did not know whether he had any competence beyond that, but he was the closest contact she could ask about the chances of hacking into a cloud. She had not used the word 'hack' exactly but had invented a half-true story about her family wanting to access photos that a deceased aunt had held in an online storage service.

He wrote back that it was probably possible to hack into a cloud. There were IT programs to systematically search for different letter and number combinations, but he had no experience of these. Anyway, it would be time-consuming, even when a computer program was doing all the work for you. The total number of possible combinations of characters on a keyboard was virtually endless. He suggested guessing, trying names of family pets or common passwords such as 123456, but also came up with another suggestion:

There have been many thefts of user data, he wrote, going on to refer to major hacking episodes at Yahoo and LinkedIn. *There are lists on the net of leaked usernames and passwords. Lots of users use the same passwords in several places. If you find her email address there, you can of course try with that password.*

He had included a link to a webpage with a searchable database of compromised usernames and passwords.

Celia grew excited. She clicked on Astria's profile, copied the email address she had given and pasted it into the search field, but it yielded no hits.

She herself had three email addresses. One at work, an

official personal address and a fooling-around address she used when she was keen not to leave genuine details.

She keyed them in to see if any of her passwords had been leaked. She got two results on her nonsensical address. It did not give the source of the leak, but one of the passwords was HOGwart123, and she knew she had used this for downloading films from an illegal website. The other was TeaseME6, and she blushed when she saw it – it was for a porn site.

She spent the next ten minutes searching for other email addresses used by Astria. Arctander seemed to be an unusual surname. She found an Astri Arctander listed with a company address on a PDF file of a list of attendees at a seminar. In another location she found a similar list of participants at a chess tournament, but with a different email address. This same address was also given in what looked like a record of members of a housing cooperative. This was obviously one she used.

Celia copied it across to the database of leaked information and pressed 'search'. It took its time, but eventually two hits popped up. Sommerro2010 and Sommerro2012. The same word, but with two different years appended.

The bus slowed down and turned off from the main road. She checked the time. They could be turning off for Palamós. She would soon have to pack her things and get ready to alight, but she still had some time to spare.

The sun was no longer striking the screen.

She tried Dropbox first, but that only resulted in error messages. The same applied to OneDrive, Google and iCloud, and she began to think the task was hopeless.

In her rush, she could not think what other storage service providers existed but searched her way to a list of these: Azure, pCloud, SkyDrive, KeepiT, Acronis, Backbase,

Carbonite, Livedrive, Nova, Elephant and Zoolz. All imaginative and catchy names.

The bus lurched around a corner and Celia had to tense her stomach muscles to hold on to her seat. She filled out the log-in information, copying and pasting from one webpage to the other, being rejected time after time. In the end she had tried all the ones on the list. There were probably more, but she would have to look into that later.

She shut her laptop and was about to drop it into her bag when an idea struck her. If Astria formed her passwords starting with the same word, but adding different years, that offered a number of possibilities.

She opened her laptop again and began with the major, well-known service providers. Dropbox, Google, OneDrive. She typed in *Sommerro2013* and changed the year each time she received an error message, jumping from one website to the next.

All of a sudden the screen turned black. She thought perhaps the page had locked because she had made too many attempts, but then it opened up again. She had accessed SkyDrive.

She could not remember what year she had used, but she had gained admission to Astria's cloud.

53

Wisting stood beside the glass wall, sipping from a paper cup of lukewarm coffee. A convoy of snowploughs came driving from the south, turning on to the runway, where they were manoeuvred out in serried ranks, seven vehicles across. The orange glow from their emergency lights radiated around them in the driving snow and evening darkness.

Their departure to Barcelona was delayed, but by no more than twenty minutes.

He checked his mobile again. The airport police had promised to send him the passenger lists of all direct flights from Spain for the last seven days prior to Astri Arctander's arrival in Norway. They had not turned up yet and he was unsure whether there would be Internet access on board the flight.

It was far from likely that he would find anything, but there was a chance that someone had followed her from Spain. Someone involved in her death.

The case was registered in the criminal computer system as being under investigation. This was a matter of gathering information in order to assess whether any crime had been committed, but Wisting was now really in no doubt. They were investigating a murder.

The coffee had gone cold, and he tossed the cup into the nearest rubbish bin. The boarding crew had set up behind the counter at the gate and the information screen changed status from standby to boarding as the departure was announced.

Getting to her feet, Maren looked around for her boss, and he moved across to join her. 'Have you seen the weather forecast?' she asked.

Wisting cast a glance out at the runway. 'I think it's to snow all weekend,' he replied.

'Not in Palamós, though,' Maren said with a smile. 'Fifteen degrees and sunshine.'

'Just like a good Norwegian summer,' Wisting commented.

They joined the queue along with the other passengers. The flight looked no more than half full. The others were mainly older people, the majority of them Norwegians. Pensioners travelling south for the winter.

They had seats in the same row near the front of the plane. Maren had taken the window seat, while Wisting sat in the middle. Once the boarding formalities were completed, no one was sitting on his other side, so he moved and checked his email again, this time noting that he had received the message he was waiting for. A long list of file attachments collected from various airlines.

Taking his iPad from his travel bag, he downloaded them to that device in order to read them on a bigger screen. From sheer politeness, he paid attention to the security instructions before opening the first list.

In fact, he was not really sure what he was looking for, other than something that stood out. As far as that was concerned, the lists were disappointing. They contained nothing more than surname and first name, age, sex, nationality, seat number and the code for the destination airport. What might be of interest was to see who was travelling alone and how far in advance the tickets had been bought. Whether it was a planned journey or one undertaken on the spur of the moment.

The aircraft taxied out along the runway, moving slowly

towards the start of the flight path. The captain gave instructions before the cabin lights were dimmed and the engine revs increased.

Wisting closed his eyes and leaned his head back against the headrest as the plane took off. It occurred to him that he had forgotten to phone his father to tell him he would not be at home. He would do that from his hotel. He ought to let Ellinor know as well.

The plane levelled out and headed south. Wisting turned back to his iPad and scrolled through the first passenger list. There were not so many names featured in the case that he would fail to recognize one if it cropped up. The list was alphabetical by surname. Under S, he let the list roll more slowly down the screen, but there was no STENE, as in the name of Astri's former boyfriend.

There were a number of lists, but he ploughed quickly through them all without finding anything of interest. If nothing else, the check had helped to pass the time. It was something that had to be done, regardless, even though the overview he now had in his possession was not exhaustive. If anyone had followed Astri Arctander or gone to Norway to arrive there before her, a flight with an intermediate stop and change of plane could have been the fastest alternative.

Maren had room for her laptop on her knee. Wisting glanced across at her. She had said she would read up on the case, and he recognized the forensics technicians' report from their examination of the Spanish van. From time to time she switched the screen image to a map of Europe before returning to the report.

She noticed he was watching her and gave him a fleeting glance.

'Do you have Internet access?' Wisting asked.

'Yes, but it's a bit slow,' she replied. 'I'm trying to map out her journey.'

She changed the screen image to a document on which she had listed places and times, mainly based on the discovery of receipts and movements in her bank account.

'I can't get it to tally,' Maren went on.

Wisting leaned across the middle seat. 'Why's that?'

'I'm calculating backwards from the transit across the Øresund Bridge,' Maren explained.

Wisting nodded. They had obtained pictures of the van as it entered Sweden at quarter past one on the afternoon of Saturday 2 December.

'She takes almost eight hours from Luxembourg to Bremen,' Maren said, pointing at the map. 'That trip normally takes five hours.'

'She would have to rest, of course,' Wisting said. 'Eat and sleep.'

'She bought food at the border between Luxembourg and Germany just before seven o'clock in the evening,' Maren said, pointing at the map. 'Eight hours later she spends some money at a twenty-four-hour Burger King in Bremen.'

Wisting recalled the receipt. It had been around three a.m. The next morning she had filled up with petrol on the outskirts of the town.

'She probably slept for a few hours in Bremen,' he said. 'But there could have been problems with traffic or something that caused the journey to take an especially long time.'

Although Maren nodded, she was not entirely in agreement. 'She made a stop en route between Luxembourg and Bremen,' she said, referring to a receipt from a petrol station outside Bonn. 'It's a detour.'

She showed him the map again. 'The quickest route by car is the A1 autobahn,' she said. 'It goes through the whole of

Germany. But then she goes a roundabout way that makes her journey almost three hours longer.'

Wisting gazed at her screen. She pulled up a list of reports of road traffic accidents and delays on the A1 motorway on the day Astri had driven north. There had been road works outside Leverkusen and near Wallenhorst, but no diversions and only minor delays. He imagined this was how the keyboard detectives in the online forum operated. From anywhere whatsoever in the world, through an open search field, they could review all the facts and unearth fresh information. Without a digital map and online route calculations, it would be a mammoth task to document a detour. Maren Dokken had it done and dusted before they were halfway up in the air.

'I think she stopped to meet someone,' she said. 'It would explain why she drove rather than flying.'

Wisting admitted she had a point. 'But who could that be?' he asked.

'The only thing I can think of is that it has something to do with the previous murder in Palamós,' Maren answered. 'The one twelve years ago. That girl was from Germany.'

54

Username: Shelook

On their webpage, the campsite stated that they had a WiFi network, but nothing about having to pay four euros extra per day for that service. Six if you wanted the fastest connection.

Celia logged in with the username and password she had received from the man in reception. When she was on the bus, she had pictured in her mind's eye what it would be like to step into the bungalow where Ruby Thompson had stayed. She would spend a long time just standing in the doorway, taking in the atmosphere of the room. Then she would get to know it more intimately by opening drawers and cupboards, searching for possible hiding places that Ruby could have used – almost like in a film. Opening the air vents, looking for loose floorboards, checking behind pictures on the walls, removing the mattress cover, peering into the toilet cistern – though there was really no reason to believe Ruby would have hidden anything or left something behind. She would test out the bed, sit in the chair in front of the TV and hold the same remote control that Ruby had used.

When she let herself in, she immediately recognized the room from the police photographs. Everything was in approximately the same place. But she did not spend time taking a closer look at anything. Instead she slung her bag on the floor, placed her laptop on the desk and plugged it into the power supply. As soon as she had satisfied herself that she still had access to Astria's web cloud, she allowed herself time for a toilet break. She also realized she was hungry and regretted not having bought a takeaway sandwich at the reception desk.

The folders of film footage were arranged in alphabetical order in a list that filled half the screen. The first was called *Photos*. Celia was about to open it, but something held her back. She poked a finger between her teeth, nibbling her nail and staring at the screen. What she now had in front of her should really be treated as a crime scene in order to find traces of what the last person to access it had been doing there.

She took a screenshot.

In the top-right-hand corner, it stated that 3.65 of 5.00 gigabytes had been used. The last log-in had been on 14 December at 16.47. This was while she had been on the bus. She had lacked sufficient presence of mind to record when Astria had last accessed it.

A menu choice allowed her to sort the folders according to size, date or when they had been created, amended or last opened, and alphabetically according to name as they were organized at present.

Celia chose *last opened*. The folders on the list swapped places. A folder called *Old Cases* had now landed at the top of the list.

Taking another screenshot, she went on to arrange the folders according to when the contents were last modified. That made no change to the top of the list, but she took another screenshot anyway. Arranging by when the folders had been created showed that *Documents* contained the first items Astria had stored. It looked like written material that had something to do with her work.

The cursor slid across the screen. She clicked and opened the folder filled with *Old Cases*. It contained seven sub-folders:

Bertine Franck
Carlota Belén del Cármen
Lea Kranz
Lucia Martinez
Rachel Jenkins
Renate Heitmann
Valeria Espinosa Díaz

These were the other unsolved murders ApopheniaX had found. Bertine Franck from Germany was at the top of the list, whether it was sorted alphabetically or according to when the folder was last opened.

Celia clicked in. The folder contained photos and PDF files with media coverage of the twelve-year-old homicide, much of which Celia had already seen. They were details that ApopheniaX had posted in the forum, but there was also a great deal of new information. Astria appeared to have collected newspaper cuttings from German newspapers as well. The idea that this was the folder she had last used tallied with the comments she had left on the forum. The post about Bertine Franck was the one that had preoccupied Astria most. This case engrossed her for some reason or other, perhaps because Bertine Franck had also been killed in Palamós.

She went back and opened the folder entitled *Photos*. It contained the 1,973 images from Astria's photographic project.

A door slammed somewhere in the distance and voices could be heard from the adjacent bungalow. Celia glanced up from the screen. Outside, darkness was falling. She should really switch on a light, but she continued to sit in the gloaming.

One of the folders in the main area was called *New Photos*. *Nuevas fotos*. Celia clicked into it. A grid of miniature photographs appeared on the screen. The information line told her there were ninety-seven of them.

So she had found them. She was now face to face with Astria's unpublished photos.

55

A car from the provincial police picked them up, as arranged, from the airport. The driver was a young man in a white uniform shirt who spoke good English. He had been waiting for a while but looked as if he had plenty of time and was in no hurry to make his way through the traffic.

The trip north was on a four-lane motorway. Wisting sat in the front passenger seat. It was dark outside and difficult to gain any impression of the landscape, but the vegetation looked verdant. Palm trees and smaller leafy trees were caught in the car headlights.

Mainly to be polite and appear interested, he asked a few questions about the area they were driving through. The driver explained that they were in Catalonia, where almost eight million people lived. The driver spoke at length about the language spoken there, Catalan, and the four different provinces, describing the largest cities, and tried to explain how the police force was organized. Wisting, his thoughts elsewhere, turned halfway round towards Maren in the back seat.

'I'll speak to the family tomorrow and ask whether Astri has any relatives or friends in Germany,' he said.

She had put away her laptop but sat with her mobile in her hand.

'I've found one Thea Weber in Bonn and another immediately outside the city,' she told him. 'I can try to contact them.'

'Do that,' Wisting said with a nod of the head as he settled back into his seat.

For the next few kilometres, nothing was said. The driver asked if he could switch on the radio, and there were no objections. A Spanish radio presenter broke the silence, introducing music from the pop charts.

After half an hour they turned off towards Palamós. The driver drove past the local police station.

'Comisario Álvarez will meet you there tomorrow morning at ten,' he said. 'You'll be picked up from your hotel at quarter to.'

Wisting nodded. The meeting time had been arranged, but he had not expected to be provided with transport.

They drove for another few blocks before drawing up outside their hotel. By now it was past midnight. The driver volunteered to carry their luggage in, but Wisting turned down the offer.

The hotel was an old concrete building, four storeys high, but the attractive facade had green creepers snaking along the balconies and five gold stars were displayed above the entrance.

Maren addressed herself to the receptionist and was given keys and instructions for the Internet connection.

'Breakfast at half eight?' Wisting suggested before they headed for the stairs.

She agreed. Wisting's room was two floors above hers, but he accompanied her all the way to the door before moving on to his own room. The provincial police had attended to the reservations and the rooms were of a very acceptable standard. Simple but not shabby, and painted in shades of pale grey, with soft carpets and a small desk.

Wisting set his case down at the end of the bed and kicked off his shoes. Ellinor had sent him a message while they were travelling in the car. She hoped he understood how grateful she was and how much she appreciated what he had done for her. He replied to say he was on a work-related trip and planned to be gone for three days. He would follow up the conversation with her son on his return.

It was too late to call his father. He would have to do that the following day.

In the minibar he found a bottle of Spanish beer and took a gulp before sitting down in the armchair with his laptop on his knee. He went through his emails and other messages, but there was nothing that demanded an immediate response. Then he logged into the forum.

A new post from Darby had been published. Line had gone through Astri Arctander's photos and found three people who matched the description of Olaf. That was smart thinking, but he was not keen on her becoming an active participant in the group. Somehow it did not seem appropriate.

She had received a number of responses to her contribution. The activity on the site appeared to have increased and several members had taken an interest. There were comments from users he had not seen before. The majority of the engagement surrounded the various theories about a serial killer. One post listed the nine possible victims. Nine young women who had all set off into the world with big dreams but had never come home.

Some comments contained named candidates as the potential perpetrator. The most topical was the local painter Pol Prado. Now he was hung out to dry, his full name given. It looked as if a full survey was taking place of all the digital clues he had left behind him. In a separate project, a timeline had been drawn up, going back twenty-five years. Points of intersection were found between him and four of the unsolved murders.

Reading the discussion thread was like following a developing conspiracy theory. Much of what was presented was unreliable information, published with no thought for ethics or any regard for the person under scrutiny. The subjects of Prado's bleak paintings were interpreted as supporting the theory that he was behind the killings. In one portrait of an expressionless woman with eyes closed and mouth open, the similarities with one of the murder victims were pointed out. Some felt the blank facial expression was reminiscent of the moment of death, and all that was missing from the picture was his hands around her neck.

Wisting set aside the laptop, placing it on the bedside table, and took the bottle of beer with him out on to the small balcony. The cool night air carried with it a salt sea breeze from the south. Between two buildings, he could make out what must be the seafront and promenade. Music from a bar or a restaurant drifted up.

Ellinor had not replied. Probably she was in bed, fast asleep.

Stooping forward, he peered obliquely along the hotel facade, calculating which was the window of Maren's room. The light was switched on. Most likely she was using her laptop.

Through the open balcony door, he saw that the screen on his own laptop had turned to sleep mode. After drinking the last of the beer, he went back inside and closed the lid. If anything interesting was posted in the forum, he assumed he would hear about it from Maren at breakfast.

56

Username: Marmot

Maren sat with her back to the headboard and her computer on her lap. She felt twinges in her injured shoulder. Usually, the pains set in at night if she had been sitting in front of a computer all day. They radiated to her neck and would not dissipate by themselves. She tried to limit her use of painkillers but knew if she did not take anything to alleviate it, she would soon have a splitting headache into the bargain.

She pushed her laptop away, threw the quilt aside and went to the bathroom. She found the blister pack in her toilet bag, pressed out two pills and filled a plastic tumbler from the tap. The water tasted stale and she wondered whether it was actually drinking water but swallowed anyway before creeping back to bed.

One of the two German women she had messaged while they were in the car had already answered. She was not the Thea Weber who had travelled to Spain with Bertine Franck twelve years ago and had not been in touch with a Norwegian woman called Astri Arctander.

Sending a Facebook message to the two namesakes from the back seat of the police car had been a rash move. The woman who had responded gave her date and year of birth in her profile and was four years younger than Bertine Franck. The other woman did not reveal her age, but from her profile picture she looked at least ten years older.

She returned to the forum and the post by Shelook about Astria's interest in the previous murder in Palamós. In one comment, the addresses and phone numbers of four women called Thea Weber were listed, but the search had been restricted to Hamburg, since that was the home town of both girls. Maren found three of these on Facebook but did not believe any of them was the person Astria had been searching for. All the same, she wrote a brief message to each and asked if they had been contacted at any time in the past few weeks by a Norwegian woman called Astri Arctander. If they gave a positive response, it would confirm that Astri had sought contact with the friend of the previous Palamós murder victim.

Her head began to throb, and she realized she had been too late taking her pills. She moved the pillow behind her back to rest her neck on it. In fact, she should lie down to sleep, but she felt restless.

Activity in the forum seemed to have escalated. Perhaps that was connected to the offer of a substantial reward.

An almost two-month-old post was among the ones most commented on in the past hour. A user called Opala had suggested that the guests and staff at the campsite where Ruby had stayed ought to be checked out. Now he had made use of Tripadvisor and other sources to work out a list of guests in the last year.

Maren also used Tripadvisor, a website where you could post reports and scores for hotels, eating places and various tourist attractions you had visited. She had not written very many evaluations, but when she visited somewhere new, she usually chose on the basis of what other guests recommended. She had checked the hotel where they were now staying and found it had an average of three point five out of five and was ranked number eighteen out of thirty-nine overnight accommodation providers in the area, based on 574 reports.

Opala had posted a list of forty-eight people who had stayed at the Palamós campsite in the past year. In addition he had used the same method as Astria and located thirty-four people who had published photos from the campsite on social media. Everyone had been contacted and told that one of the other guests had been murdered, and asked if they recalled any experiences or incidents from their last stay that might be relevant.

It was an ingenious kind of digital door-to-door questioning.

The police had interviewed some of the guests at the campsite when Ruby was killed, but they had limited this to the tourists in the adjacent bungalows. The investigators were probably also in possession of a comprehensive guest list, even though it was not included in the police documents published on the forum. However, Maren doubted whether the investigators had spoken to all of them.

Opala's method appeared effective. He had received seventy-four replies. Very few of these had anything to report, but three previous guests stated that they had had unfortunate episodes with the caretaker. Two women had come across him in the shower block while they were showering or getting changed, while a third had taken him by surprise in the bungalow when she returned from a walk along the beach. He had told her he was checking the fire alarm system. Later she discovered two pairs of underpants missing from a bag of dirty laundry.

None of the three knew the man's name or how long he had worked there. His age was estimated at around sixty. He could have been there when Bertine Franck and Thea Weber were staying at the campsite twelve years earlier.

One comment pointed out that the campsite in Palamós was part of a chain, and it did not take long to identify affiliated campsites in the vicinity of the locations where the other murdered women had been found. It emerged from the old media coverage that Rachel Jenkins had been staying at a campsite in Benidorm when she went missing, and the same applied to Lucia Martinez, who had been found murdered in Torrevieja more than two years ago.

Further down the discussion thread, a check was underway on all the staff members at the campsite in Palamós. The name of the owner was quickly unearthed and links to newspaper articles with photos of him were posted, including one about a tree that had toppled in a storm and crushed two motorhomes. It seemed he ran the campsite with his wife, and their Facebook pages were studied in detail, uncovering pictures of people who must be staff members, including some from what looked like a staff party. Most of them were young women, and none fitted the description of the caretaker.

It was almost fascinating to see how the online detectives managed to get everything to conform to the new theory. They chose fragments of information and interpreted these to suit the answers they wanted. That the caretaker had not been at the staff party, or at least had not allowed himself to be photographed, made him suspect. A loner who did not get along well with others.

However, it was still strange that the Catalan investigators had not undertaken more work at the campsite. That type of overnight accommodation could function as a refuge for individuals who shunned any contact with the authorities. The first summer she had worked in the patrol section in Larvik, she had gone on many excursions to the numerous campsites along the Norwegian coast and picked up wanted criminals. She particularly recalled a rapist on the run who had cycled from Drammen to Blokkebukta, where he camped in a small two-man tent.

It was nearly half past one, and her headache had worsened. Maren squinted at the screen but knew the best she could hope for was to fall asleep as fast as she could and for her headache to have cleared by the time she awoke.

57

Username: Shelook

She had studied every single one of the ninety-seven photographs. Ruby Thompson was in one of them – the yellow beanie made her easy to spot.

The picture had been taken in connection with the event on the beach, but from a slightly different angle than the photos already published. The main subject was an older woman in a swimming cap. Ruby was in the background, standing beside Jarod and Mathis. She had a paper cup in her left hand, and the photo had been taken just as she was saying something. Her mouth was open and her head half turned towards Jarod. It was impossible to read anything more into it.

Astria had written that she had made an interesting discovery. Celia could see nothing significant about the picture. It was only number one in the series and placed early in the timeline of the day of the murder. Whatever Astria had found must be in one of the other photographs.

She went through them again, letting each picture fill the screen as she studied every face and scrutinized every vehicle.

Each photo was a random segment of time, but also part of a bigger picture. There must be something she had failed to see.

It had grown late and was now half past one. She had no intention of giving up yet but had to take a toilet break.

Putting her laptop away, she took out her washbag. The receptionist had pointed out the communal shower block, less than a hundred metres from the bungalow.

Once she had locked the door behind her, she soon regretted not having thrown on a jacket. Sounds carried in the cold, raw air. She could hear low voices from a camper van and, somewhere in the distance, a clatter of glasses and the waves beating rhythmically on the shore.

Moths and insects circled around the bulkhead light above the entrance to the shared facilities. As she stepped inside, her thoughts did not waver from the ninety-seven photos. It irked her that she was unable to see or understand the information to be found there. Finding links or discrepancies was something she usually excelled at. She was good at detail and often discovered continuity errors in TV films. Like when a glass contained more water in one clip than in a previous scene because the clips had been pieced together in the wrong order. Or when an extra in the background walked past twice, heading in the same direction. But maybe she lacked the skills to see what was hidden in the photos. Perhaps it was a face Astria had been able to recognize but she herself had never seen: someone in the wrong place, or something along those lines.

She used the toilet, washed her hands and took out her toothbrush.

She was anxious to publish the photos in the forum on her return to the bungalow. Maybe someone else would be able to spot the same thing as Astria had.

She studied her reflection. Her user profile was anonymous, but if she could contribute to solving the murder case, she would step forward. Then she would actually have solved her first homicide even before enrolling in Police College. Also, a reward had been offered.

The ceiling light flickered as if there was something wrong with the voltage.

Celia spat into the washbasin.

Even though she had ferreted out Astria's password by legal means, logging into the photos and downloading them would be regarded as hacking, and that would undoubtedly prove problematic.

The toothpaste foamed up in her mouth as these thoughts churned in her head.

The discovery of the pictures was a major breakthrough, but she would really have to let someone else take credit for it. She would have to set up a new profile.

She spat into the basin again and packed her washbag. The new username had come to her by the time she was back in the bungalow. Salamander. Almost like the name of the female hacker in some Scandinavian crime novels she had read.

Before she created the new profile, she linked up to a DNS server in Stockholm so that her IP address would be traced to there. It had seemed advanced the first time she had learned how to conceal your computer tracks in that way, but a small computer program took care of everything. She had used it when she downloaded films from the Internet, but that had been before her family had a Netflix subscription.

She added ten years to her own age, ticked the box for female, stated that she was an IT technician and found a photo of a black salamander she could use for her profile picture.

Using *The Unpublished Photos* as the heading for her post, she briefly explained that these had been collected by Astria but not previously shared with the other forum users.

The upload took almost eight minutes on the slow network connection. She had expected an immediate response, but now the post had been published for five minutes without attracting any comments. Either there were no active users awake or they were busy looking through the images before deciding to offer an opinion.

Celia logged off, disconnected from the DNS server and

logged in again as Shelook. Still no reactions. She hesitated slightly before entering the comments field herself and writing *Thank you.*

Almost at once another comment appeared.

Opala: Ruby Thompson is in image IMG–7232.jpg. See nothing of interest there.

If nothing else, it confirmed that the post was visible to the others.

Celia went back to SkyDrive. Astria's storage space contained a number of folders she had not gone through so thoroughly. Nothing seemed to refer to Ruby Thompson. They looked more like different projects in connection with her work. One of the folders she had not yet opened was called *Lua.* She clicked it open and immediately understood that *lua* must be Norwegian for *gorro.* A knitted hat.

Astria had cropped the best photos of the yellow hat Ruby had worn and enlarged them as much as possible without the picture becoming blurred. She had also saved pictures of a similar hat from an online shop. The brim of the hat had a little fabric label with a woven logo from the manufacturer – Billabong.

Four more photo files were left in the folder. Celia called up the next one and felt her pulse race. It was a picture of the same hat, or at least the same type of hat. It lay in a box beside what looked like electrical equipment, squeezed down between two metal components alongside cables of various colours.

The next image showed a metal cabinet with two open doors. The cabinet appeared to be located inside a garage. On the middle shelf she could see the box with the hat as well as some protruding wires.

Celia swallowed and ran her tongue over the roof of her mouth.

In the next photo, the contents of the box had been pulled out and displayed, leaving no doubt that this was the very same hat Ruby had worn.

In the final image, the beanie had been placed in a transparent plastic bag, as if taken as evidence.

Astria's last words rushed through her head.

Need a bit more time, but think I've found something interesting.

Returning to the forum, she read the entire thread.

MrsPeabody: Have you found more photographs?

Astria: Have collected 97 photos that have not been posted yet. Coming soon.

Ned B.: Are there photos of Ruby there?

Astria: Need a bit more time, but think I've found something interesting.

When she reread it now, she saw that Astria had not really answered Ned B.'s question. He had wondered whether she had found more photos of Ruby. Astria had replied that she needed time but thought she had found something significant.

The picture of Ruby was not difficult to find. She had not needed time for that. What Astria had found had been something totally different. She had found the yellow hat.

Celia checked the metadata on the photos. This showed that all four photographs had been taken on 30 November at 18.37, 18.38, 18.40 and 18.44, the day before Astria had left for Norway. There were no coordinates to say where the photos had been taken, but it must have been somewhere to which Astria had access. At the house of someone she knew.

58

Username: Darby

Line liked to rise half an hour before Amalie usually woke, giving her some time to herself before she had to focus on the morning routine of personal hygiene, breakfast and getting dressed. A fixed pattern made the start of the day more predictable for them both, avoiding unnecessary fuss that normally resulted in Amalie being grumpy and difficult. A pleasant early morning was a method of ensuring that the whole day went smoothly.

When the breakfast table was set and the packed lunch ready, she sat down at her laptop to check her email and read the headlines in the online newspapers before logging into the forum.

There had been a tremendous flurry of activity since the previous evening, a deluge of new posts and comments. Astri Arctander's last photographs had been found: it looked as if a hacker had managed to get hold of them.

Line reached out for her teacup and drank as she read.

Ruby was in one of the photos, but from the comments Line understood there was nothing special about either that or any of the other photographs.

Line had to see them for herself and clicked her way through the series. Keeping an eye on the time, she spent no more than a few seconds on each photograph. She too could not find anything revealing or anything that seemed of any relevance to the murder case, but something was obvious from the contents of Astri Arctander's computer.

Wondering whether her father was aware of it, she sent him a text.

The profile of the person who had posted the pictures had been newly set up. A thirty-two-year-old woman from Stockholm, if the details given were to be believed.

One of the users had laid their hands on lists of results from various chess tournaments in which Astria had competed. She was highly rated and alleged to be an extremely clever woman. She had spotted something in the final series of images that no one else had succeeded in discovering.

Line made up her mind to take a closer look at these pictures after she had dropped Amalie off at nursery. She still had a few more minutes before she had to give her a shake, and she moved to the section of the forum dealing with the possibility of a serial killer. A new candidate had cropped up, an unnamed staff member at the campsite where Ruby Thompson had stayed.

The comments in the discussion thread fired off in two directions. Someone thought it more logical that whoever was behind the murder had some connection to Ruby Thompson rather than being a complete stranger. For example, someone she had met at the campsite. Others argued the opposite and insisted on the radical artist as the chief suspect.

Many of the comments were fascinating to read. Their attention had homed in on a single face. The notion that they had uncovered the killer was like a blind passion, so that despite logical defects and deficiencies they were convinced they had found the right man.

During the night, suggestions had been made as to the

identity of the caretaker. In several local authority documents linked to the inspection of water meters, the name Thiago Hernández Zapatero had emerged as the campsite's representative. In order to verify this was the correct person, they had searched for photos of him on the Internet, so that a kind of photographic identification parade could be set up for former guests at the campsite. However, no trace of him could be found online. No results from Google searches. Something that in itself was commented on as being suspicious. It was concluded that he was clearly someone who avoided attention.

Line now tried to search for the name. She was very experienced in tracing people on the net, at least in Norway, where she had access to media archives and records that were not searchable without being logged in. She tried without the middle name, but this brought up far too many hits, more than it would ever be possible to sort through. Then she looked up the Spanish word for caretaker and added it to the search text, but the language barrier meant nothing useful came of that.

She gave a sigh of resignation and felt almost a bit scared by her own determination. Like all the others in the forum, she believed she could discover or work out something no one else had managed to. A fresh Internet search was like inserting a coin in a slot machine in hopes of a huge win. There was something presumptuous about the entire enterprise. The belief that a group of online snoopers could succeed in clearing up a complex murder mystery was nothing but a pipe dream.

Her mobile buzzed. Her father had read her message and responded with thanks.

Closing her laptop, Line moved it from the breakfast table and went to wake Amalie.

59

The images had been published at 01.43, only a few minutes after she had switched off her laptop and gone to bed.

Maren clicked through them once again. Ruby Thompson was in only one of them, standing on the beach chatting to Jarod.

In another of the other beach photos, she had spotted one of Astri's twin uncles. Henrik or Fredrik. Most probably Henrik, as he was the one who lived in Palamós. Fredrik lived almost three hours further south.

In fact, there was nothing sensational about one of them appearing in one of these photographs. Ruby Thompson had been observed in sixteen photos. It was almost strange that they had not seen more of the Arctander family.

She returned to the picture of Ruby in the yellow beanie. As she saw it, Astri Arctander had two opportunities to get hold of the hat. One was that she had found the crime scene and the hat was still lying there. But it was intact and clean and bore no signs of having been lying outdoors for more than six months.

The other possibility was that Astri had found the hat somewhere the killer had left it. Either because it had been inadvertently left behind or because for some reason he had kept it safe.

She had found her way to an American thesis about serial killers, something she had read when she was writing her dissertation. One of the chapters dealt with patterns and motives. Examples were cited of serial murderers who were careful not to leave any traces, though personal possessions from a number of victims had been found in their homes. The thesis concluded that these were seldom regarded as trophies or souvenirs. Neither was the intention to use the items later to re-create the attack in their imagination. Instead it was a result of impulse, accident and chaos. In total confusion, the killer could take something that was later difficult for them to get rid of.

All the same, it would have been interesting to know where Astri had found it.

She clicked back on the picture of Astri's uncle on the beach. He was with a woman. Maybe it was Fredrik after all, since he was the one who was married.

She checked her watch. They had agreed on breakfast at half past eight. Her headache had persisted when she awoke, but now it was easing off. Hopefully, with the help of some food, it would soon be gone.

60

The sun was breaking through the morning mist as a few gulls hovered above the rooftops. Beyond, the sea shone against a hazy horizon.

Wisting stepped in from the small balcony and gazed at himself in the mirror. His shirt needed ironing before his meeting with the Catalan police, but the room was not equipped with an iron and a board. He would have to keep his jacket on.

Somewhere in the distance, a church bell was ringing.

As Wisting shut the balcony door, his father came to mind. He had seemed out of sorts on the phone, as if his thoughts had been elsewhere.

Nothing was wrong, he had insisted, but Wisting could hear that something was bothering him, something he was reluctant to talk about. At least not as long as his son was in Spain and could not chip in with anything useful. He decided to phone him again but felt it best to wait until evening or else ask Line to pay her grandfather a visit with Amalie in tow.

He went down to breakfast and found Maren already settled at a corner table with her laptop before her.

'Have you seen the pictures?' she asked.

He nodded. He had spent a restless night and had got up just before six a.m. When Line had sent him the message about the photos, he had already been studying them for an hour or so.

'One of her uncles is there,' Maren went on.

Wisting had noticed the same thing. In one of the photos from the event on the beach, one of the twin brothers was there in the company of a woman.

'Fredrik, I thought,' he said, helping himself from a coffeepot on the table. 'We can ask him later. I just spoke to Astri's father. Fredrik's coming to Palamós this afternoon. I've arranged to meet him in the family apartment at three o'clock. We should be finished searching it by that time.'

Maren reached out for a glass of orange juice. 'Did you ask about Germany?'

'Yes – as far as they were aware, she knew no one there.'

'I received a reply from a Thea Weber in Bonn,' Maren told him. 'It was the wrong one, but I've written to three others in Hamburg with the same name.'

She sat with her eyes fixed on him. Wisting realized she was holding something back.

'Penny for your thoughts,' he said.

Maren sat up straight in her chair. 'Astri Arctander was good at chess,' she commented. 'The others in the forum believe she possessed cognitive abilities that meant she'd discovered something the others were unable to see. But I was thinking it might not be that at all. Maybe she was the only one in the right situation? That her suspicions were directed at someone only she knew, someone in her own family, for instance?'

She shifted in her seat again, as if she felt uncomfortable.

'It's just a stray thought,' she added. 'But the whole family were here at Easter when Ruby was killed, with the exception of the grandmother. And they were in Norway when Astri was murdered.'

Wisting nodded.

'I know it's too early to draw conclusions,' Maren continued. 'But it does at least explain why no one in the family knew she was going to Norway. She had to keep shtum about it to avoid alerting the person she was tracking down.'

'We should be able to get a quick explanation,' Wisting said. 'The investigators down here now have Astri's DNA profile. They can compare that to the trace DNA evidence from their case and work out whether there are genetic similarities.'

Maren looked at him, sizing him up with her eyes. 'You've been thinking the same as me,' she said. 'Since before we met them at the grandmother's house?'

Wisting refrained from answering. 'There's another thing we have to look at,' he said. 'I've been trying to locate Vibeke Hassel, the woman who was excised from the photo album.'

Maren nodded.

'She died the summer after the photos were taken,' Wisting went on. 'It was listed as a suicide. I've asked the police in her home town to digitize the papers and send them to me.'

Getting to his feet, he moved to the breakfast buffet and helped himself to an omelette. Maren followed him and chose some cereal with yogurt and fresh fruit.

A waiter approached the table when they sat down again. 'Señor Wisting?' he asked.

Wisting turned his head. The man set down a newspaper and said something in Spanish.

'He says he thought you'd like to read the newspaper,' Maren translated.

Pictures of Astri Arctander and Ruby Thompson were splashed on the front page.

'*Gracias*,' Wisting replied.

The waiter gave a brief bow and withdrew. Wisting pushed the newspaper across to Maren.

'It's in Catalan,' she said. 'I don't understand much of it, but it says something about a Norwegian woman who may have taken secrets with her into death.'

Wisting leafed through to the pages cited and was confronted by two pictures of himself. One had been taken from a photo agency and the other was the one that had been printed in the newspaper at home when they were heaving the stretcher carrying Astri Arctander's body over the bank of snow. In addition, there was a similar photo of Ruby Thompson's corpse being carried from the beach alongside an inset photograph of Comisario Telmo Álvarez.

On the opposite page he saw a screenshot from the online forum with a picture of a young, red-haired woman. Michelle Norris, according to the caption.

'Did you know about this?' Maren asked.

'The journalist phoned me yesterday before we left,' Wisting replied. 'What does it say?'

Maren shook her head, obviously finding it difficult to understand the contents.

'It says the Norwegian police have come to the Costa Brava,' she finally worked out. '*El cap de la investigació noruega, William Wisting.*'

She cast a glance across at the waiter who had brought them the newspaper.

'Apart from that, it looks as if it's mostly about the website and the discussion forum,' she said. 'That Astri was deeply involved in the investigation and had made a discovery she had not shared with the others before she left Palamós.'

'What do the Catalan police say?' Wisting asked.

Maren screwed up her eyes as she struggled to find the part where Comisario Álvarez made a statement.

'They make no comment on the website or the work done by Michelle Norris,' she told him. 'He confirms they're collaborating with the Norwegian police.'

Wisting drew the newspaper towards him and studied the photographs. News spread fast, with no regard for languages or land frontiers. The picture of the snowy scene in Manvik was credited to Garm Søbakken. The Catalan newspaper had been in touch with *Østlands-Posten* to obtain the rights. Soon the headlines in the Catalan paper would be picked up by the Norwegian media. They would only have peace to work for a limited period of time, he thought, as he folded the newspaper.

61

Username: Nichelle

The website traffic had multiplied. Normally she had around three hundred individual visits and about seventy daily log-ins. Overnight, the page had registered more than 10,000 hits and almost 3,000 new members had joined. Practically all the activity seemed to have resulted from the online edition of the *Diari de Girona* newspaper. The article about Ruby and the crowdsolving group had been published just before ten p.m. the previous evening, including a direct link to the forum. Never before had Michelle seen such a huge upsurge. The new users flooded the discussions with irrelevant comments or took up topics that had already been debated to death. They all seemed keen to contribute, but the sudden outpouring of information was difficult to handle and made the forum impossible to supervise.

In need of a smoke, she took her laptop out with her to the pavement restaurant opposite the hotel. The password for the WiFi network was printed on the table menu. Logging on, she lit her cigarette and ordered an iced tea when the waiter approached.

If the translation of the Catalan newspaper article was correct, it meant that the Norwegian policeman was now in Palamós. It was far from certain that he was aware she was here too if he had not seen the newspaper or read her post on the forum.

She took a deep drag of the cigarette and began to write

an email, explaining her presence in the town, naming the hotel where she was staying and suggesting they might meet. She was unclear about what she could expect to gain from a meeting with him, but it would be interesting to talk to him after he had spoken to the Catalan detectives.

The waiter arrived with her iced tea. The ice cubes clinked as he set down the glass. Michelle stubbed out her cigarette, took a gulp and redrafted the beginning of her email. She now began by thanking him for being so helpful and obliging when she had had no more than a gut feeling that something had happened to Astria, as if to remind him she had been involved from the very start. All the same, she felt she had to offer him something that would entice him to meet her.

A taxi had parked at the nearby kerb. The driver sat with the car door open, his feet planted on the asphalt as he smoked. Michelle absent-mindedly stared at him as she pondered. Then he met her eye and she looked away, changed the screen image, returned to the forum and located Salamander's post. She clicked on the profile and wrote a direct message, introducing herself as the administrator of the site and expressing thanks for publishing the photos Astria had collected. Thereafter she carefully worded a question about the existence of other computer material that Astria had not shared in the forum, making it clear she was interested in everything, no matter whether or not it appeared relevant to the case.

Once she had sent the message, she returned to the email for Wisting and added a sentence to say she was in dialogue with the anonymous user who had posted the ninety-seven photos and that she expected an answer imminently as to whether there was any further material.

The sun had moved above an adjacent building and now slanted across the wide pavement. The waiter cranked the handle to open out the sunshade and welcomed an older married couple who had just arrived.

A new post in the forum, only a few minutes old, caught her attention. The title was *Bad Cop*.

The post concerned the private detective and was written by a new member. Someone who had adopted the name Latitude and said he was from Melbourne, back home in Australia.

There was one reason that Ethan Mahoney was a *former* policeman, he wrote, linking to a newspaper article about the resolution of a robbery on an armoured security van almost ten years ago. Three heavily armed men had stolen almost four million dollars. Armaguard, the security firm, in collaboration with the insurance company, had offered a reward of 10 per cent of the loot. This had yielded information that led to the crime being solved. Three men were convicted, and some of the robbery proceeds were recovered. A thirty-two-year-old man with a criminal background had received the reward. Later it was revealed that he had shared the money with one of the police investigators. It eventually emerged that he had used the thirty-two-year-old as an informant, and allegations were made that the guy actually had no knowledge whatsoever of the robbery but the detective had channelled details provided by various other snitches through him. At the same time, the informant was given inside information from the official investigation so that he appeared extremely credible. The accusations could not be proved, but they had resulted in the detective leaving the police force. He was not named in the article, but Latitude stated he knew for certain he was the man Flynn Thompson had hired to investigate his daughter's murder.

Michelle could well imagine this was true. Ethan Mahoney seemed less than honest. He had obviously acquired information from the forum and presented it as the result of his own investigations.

A direct message popped up on her screen. From Shelook. She was one of the more law-abiding members, and one of her significant contributions had been to link Ruby with a housebreaking incident. She wrote that her name was in fact Celia Verdadero Pérez and that she was the cousin of Leo Pérez, who had met Ruby at the beach bar. Celia had come to Palamós the previous evening and wondered if they could meet, and maybe even hook up with Leo together and hear what he had to tell them about Ruby.

Little birds were hopping around between the tables. Michelle picked up her cigarette packet and chased them away. Shaking out another cigarette, she ran an online search for a random café on the promenade and suggested meeting there at one p.m.

62

Username: Shelook

She had downloaded the photos of the beanie hat to her own computer and saved a back-up copy. This was a discovery that could lead to clearing up the whole case. Her first impulse had been to post it in the forum, but she had restrained herself. First she would have to try to come a step closer and find out where the photos had been taken.

A message from Nichelle appeared on the screen. She was keen to meet her and suggested a time and place where they could meet up.

Nichelle should know about the photos. The website was her project, and Ruby had been her friend.

She would have to wait and see. It depended on how the meeting went and what she managed to find out before that. She had four hours to go.

She wrote a short reply and used the Google map to discover the location of the meeting place. Then she typed a message to her cousin Leo to say she was in Palamós and asked if they could meet this afternoon.

There was no answer. Probably he was still fast asleep.

She clicked into the forum. Someone had just posted a link to a newspaper article about Ruby and the crowdsolving that Nichelle had set in motion. That explained the surge in activity on the site. It had almost exploded with posts and comments, both factual and false.

Her post as Salamander had received enormous attention,

but no one had gleaned anything further from the ninety-seven photos. On the other hand, a few people had discovered that Thiago Hernández Zapatero was a local plumber and not the suspect caretaker.

Celia gazed at the screen. The caretaker could not be so difficult to find. The simplest thing would be to go to reception and ask.

She looked around the bungalow and heard a low rumble from the small fridge under the worktop. She moved across to open the door. It was empty and not particularly cold.

She rocked it and dragged it forward. Big dust bunnies followed it out across the floor. It must have been ages since it was moved, maybe not even when Ruby was killed and the police had examined the bungalow.

The plug was in a wall socket. She yanked it out, pushed the fridge back in place and left the door open to let out the cold air and create the impression that it had been out of order for a while. Then she headed to reception.

The man who had checked her in the day before was behind the counter.

Celia gave him a smile when he looked up. 'Do you have a caretaker or anything?' she asked.

'Is something wrong?'

'The fridge isn't working.'

The receptionist grabbed a pen and produced a form. 'Which bungalow is it?'

She gave him the number and the man made a note.

'I'll pass that on,' he said, placing the form in a basket on his right.

'To the caretaker?' Celia asked, in the hope that she would be given a name.

The receptionist nodded, but then the phone rang and he excused himself.

Celia was almost blushing when she went out, embarrassed by her abortive attempt, and headed back to the bungalow. From the other side of the campsite she heard the sound of some kind of garden tool in operation. That could be the caretaker, but she gave up on the idea of trying to find out and instead darted back into the bungalow and locked the door.

Sitting down at her laptop, she logged on to Astria's Sky-Drive account. In addition to the folders with the ninety-seven images and the folder about the other homicide cases, there was a folder entitled *Thea*. It contained a collection of material on Thea Weber, much of it identical to the documents in the folder assigned to Bertine Franck, including the article in which the girls were interviewed together in the Gran Via in Madrid.

An Excel document contained a list of eleven different women called Thea Weber, with columns for age, residence, phone number and email address. It was obvious that Astria had searched for Bertine Franck's travel companion, but it did not look as if she had been in touch with all of them. The columns of addresses and contact information were only partially filled out.

At the foot of the list, another name was given. Thea Kleibl, listed as living in Bonn, but no phone number or email address was included.

She found a Thea Kleibl from Bonn on Facebook. The profile picture showed a woman with a broad smile and dark blonde hair. It mentioned that she was married to Fabian Kleibl and had previously lived in Hamburg.

Celia looked up the photo from the travel report in which Bertine Franck and Thea Weber had been photographed in Madrid's Gran Via only a few days before Bertine was killed. Thea Kleibl could pass for a twelve-years-older version of

Thea Weber. Astria could well have found her, but there was nothing in the folder to indicate she had made contact or why she was so preoccupied by her.

The answer could easily be only a keystroke away.

Opening the message window, she wrote that she was looking for a Thea Weber from Hamburg and asked if she could be her. Once the message was sent, she thought she should perhaps have written something about Astria. She considered writing another message but dropped the idea when she saw that Leo had responded to her earlier message. He would finish work at eight and was happy to meet her.

Capri at half eight? he suggested, adding an address.

Celia looked up the location and saw that it was a bar in the harbour area.

Great! she wrote back: *See you there.*

Her stomach was warning her she needed to get something to eat. She could also feel it in her head, as she was struggling to gather her thoughts. Before she ventured out, she wanted to check the forum, where there was a continuous stream of recent comments. Many of the new users seemed to be from Palamós, and they had begun to name the individuals in the photos taken at the beach.

She changed to the Salamander account and saw she had received two direct messages. One was from the private detective, Ethan Mahoney, who offered her 1,000 euros for all the other information from Astria's computer to which she must have access. This was around the same amount that her trip to Palamós was going to cost. She might well need that money, but it did not feel right. Anyway, it would reveal her identity.

The other message was from Nichelle, welcoming her to the forum, but she was really angling for the same thing as the private detective. She wanted to know if there was more material in addition to the ninety-seven images already published.

Part of her wanted to reveal the contents of the Thea folder, but it could rebound on her like a boomerang, because if she got an answer from Thea Kleibl, this was something she would have to share in the forum. Then the fact that she was the one behind the Salamander account could easily be exposed. The best tactic would be to wait and find out what Thea Kleibl had to say and then she could let it appear as if she had traced her single-handed.

It was now ten a.m. The sun had been beating down on the bungalow for a few hours and the air began to feel clammy. She opened a window and hid her laptop under the quilt before she went out. The cloudless sky promised a hot day.

63

They stood waiting outside the hotel for their transport. After breakfast, Maren had changed into a more formal outfit, a black suit and white blouse. It crossed Wisting's mind that the Catalan detectives might think she was his secretary, but he kept that to himself.

An unmarked police car stopped at the kerb. It was a different driver from the previous day, one with a more aggressive driving style but good local knowledge. When the traffic came to a standstill ahead of them, he negotiated his way through side streets and back alleys. At the police station, he accompanied them into reception and handed them over to a young officer who had obviously been waiting to guide them onwards.

A small, cramped lift took them up to the second floor. The meeting room was at the end of a narrow corridor and three uniformed men and one woman stood up when they were ushered in. A man in a suit at the end of the table remained seated.

Wisting first greeted Comisario Telmo Álvarez before introducing Maren. 'My colleague, Maren Dokken,' he said.

Comisario Álvarez had brought an investigator from the provincial police in Girona, while the other two were local detectives. One of them was the police officer Malak Rendón.

'We've spoken on the phone,' Wisting said.

The woman facing him nodded, confirming that she had been in charge of the case when Astri Arctander was first reported missing.

The man in the suit was from the public prosecutor's office. His tie was tightly knotted and beads of perspiration already glistened on his hairline.

They sat down, Wisting and Maren on one side of the table and the Catalan investigators opposite with their backs to the windows.

The meeting room was long and narrow with shabby floorboards and shelves of old books lining the walls. In the centre of the table there were bottles of water and a large pot of coffee beside stacks of cups and glasses, packets of sugar cubes and tiny portions of cream. Malak Rendón invited them to help themselves. Wisting took a bottle of water and poured some out for Maren and himself.

Wisting had been prepared for the meeting to take the form of some kind of trench warfare in which the Catalans would be primarily focused on hearing what Wisting had to tell them without giving anything away beyond the bare necessities. Telmo Álvarez, however, offered to open the meeting by running through the current status of the murder case.

Although his photographs did not convey it, he was a big man with a slightly roguish expression that made him look affable.

The report took ten minutes, but nothing new to them emerged.

Wisting described their case from the very first email he had received from Michelle Norris and was open about having read the contents of the online forum. The Catalan investigators listened intently without interrupting with questions. Afterwards Álvarez wanted to know whether Astri Arctander's death was being treated as murder or whether it could be put down to an accident.

'We're investigating it as murder,' Wisting replied.

'In that case, what was the motive?'

'We've excluded a number of options,' Wisting told him. 'The idea we're working on is that the motive is somehow linked with Ruby Thompson's murder.'

The Catalan investigator nodded thoughtfully. 'Do you have any suspects?' he asked.

'No,' Wisting replied, but let Maren tell them about the Arctander family.

Álvarez leaned across the table. 'So one of her uncles may have killed her?' he asked. 'And Ruby Thompson?'

'Time and place certainly permit that possibility,' Maren answered.

The Catalan police inspector remained still for a moment before sinking back into his seat. 'That sounds like a contrived theory for want of anything better,' he said.

Maren glanced in Wisting's direction. 'If nothing else, it's a hypothesis we can test by comparing the DNA samples,' she continued. 'That would easily allow us to see whether Ruby Thompson's killer is related to Astri Arctander.'

Álvarez turned to the public prosecutor at the end of the table and received a nod in response.

'Let me just remind you that the information we give in this room must go no further,' he added.

Wisting sat up in his chair, understanding that sensitive information was about to be divulged.

'We've had a biogeographical analysis conducted,' the Catalan police inspector explained. 'It strongly suggests a Middle Eastern ethnic origin.'

The room fell silent. The public prosecutor got to his feet, reached across the table and drew the coffee pot towards him.

'That means you're looking for a dark-skinned perpetrator,' Wisting said. He felt the fragile framework around his own theory collapse.

A gurgling sound was heard as the prosecutor filled his cup. 'Not necessarily,' he said, unwrapping two sugar cubes.

Wisting gazed across at Álvarez.

'It means we may not have the killer's DNA profile,' Álvarez explained. Opening a folder, he produced sheets of photographs and pushed them across the table.

Wisting did not understand what he was looking at. The Catalan captions were of no help to him. Maren moved closer.

'Hair?' she asked.

'Two single black hairs,' Álvarez confirmed. 'From inside the neckline of her sweater.'

It now dawned on Wisting. Ruby Thompson had been found partially clothed after her body had spent a night in the sea. He had expected the DNA profile to link with evidence of a sexual assault, perhaps a semen sample. What he was looking at were close-up images of the blue sweater Ruby Thompson had been wearing when her body was found. The pictures showed two strands of hair entwined in the stitches of yarn.

'The DNA profile is from a single follicle,' Álvarez explained. 'It's the only forensic evidence we have.'

Wisting sat looking at the photos of the turtleneck sweater. The most obvious explanation was that the hair came from someone pulling the sweater over their head.

He thumbed through to the final sheet in the stapled bundle, a report stating that the sweater was part of a French designer range sold in a relatively small selection of outlets in Europe, the nearest of which was located in Barcelona.

'It's a man's jumper,' Maren commented. 'Do you know where Ruby Thompson got it?'

Álvarez shook his head.

'What about the French boy?' Wisting asked. 'Mathis

Leroux? He was dark-skinned, maybe originally from the Middle East.'

'He's been excluded,' Álvarez replied.

Wisting remembered there had been something about the sweater in the interviews he had read. Both Mathis Leroux and Jarod Denham were asked if they knew how Ruby had acquired it. Neither of them had been able to answer. He had considered it a completely routine question, but now he realized there had been more behind it.

'Could she have stolen it?' Maren asked.

'We're looking into that possibility,' Álvarez replied. 'There were several thefts on the evening Ruby Thompson was murdered, but no one has listed a stolen sweater.'

'Have you double-checked that?' Maren insisted. 'Asked them specifically?'

Some of the friendliness in the expression on the Catalan detective's face disappeared, as if he resented critical questions about his investigation.

'Of course,' he answered.

Wisting quickly intervened with the question running through his mind.

'What about her boyfriend?' he asked. 'Jarod Denham was released because the DNA profile ruled him out. This evidence on the sweater means he could still be the killer.'

'Other circumstances also weakened our suspicions of him,' Álvarez explained. 'Data traffic on his computer, witness observations and telephone use gave little opportunity for him to be behind it.'

Wisting nodded, realizing these were details the investigators had not shared with Jarod Denham's defence counsel and therefore had not featured in the investigation material published in the online forum.

'Besides, he didn't have access to a vehicle,' Álvarez added.

'There's nothing to suggest the discovery site was also the crime scene. The body had probably been transported somewhere in a car, dumped in the sea and washed ashore on the beach sometime overnight.'

Wisting wondered whether they had made their own inquiries into the sea and tidal conditions or if they had relied on the information in Michelle Norris's forum.

'Have you identified Olaf?' he asked instead.

The cordial smile was back beneath the grey moustache on Comisario Álvarez's face. 'Olaf is a fiction,' he replied, placing his cup under the spout of the coffeepot.

Wisting waited until the man had filled his cup. 'He's mentioned in three different police interviews,' he pointed out.

'They invented him when they realized there was going to be an investigation,' Álvarez told him. 'Leo Pérez has admitted he was the one who sold drugs to Ruby Thompson, Jarod Denham, Mathis Leroux – and other backpackers. His case comes up in court after New Year. Our lawyers weighed up the possibility of charging the Englishman and the Frenchman with giving false statements, but cross-border cases are a bureaucratic nightmare.'

'So Olaf was never found?' Wisting wanted this clarified.

Álvarez turned to face the local police officers.

'There was someone like that here in town two years ago, but not when Ruby Thompson was killed,' Malak Rendón told them. 'When Leo Pérez needed to blame someone else for the drug dealing, he resurrected Olaf.'

Wisting nodded to indicate he understood. 'What do you know about the real Olaf?' he asked.

'We've no certain identification for him,' Rendón admitted. 'His trail has begun to go cold. According to our drugs squad, he stayed here for only a short period. They've no evidence to suggest he's been here in the last twenty-four months.'

'And anyway, Leo Pérez has admitted they used him as a template when they needed someone to pin the blame on, to escape suspicion themselves,' Álvarez added.

Wisting was reluctant to let the subject drop. 'Where did Leo Pérez get his drugs from?' he asked. 'Have you found his dealer? Uncovered the network around him?'

Malak Rendón's face took on an irritated expression. It was obvious she did not enjoy having their work or conclusions challenged.

'It's all documented in the case against Leo Pérez,' she replied. 'As we told you, it'll soon come up in court.'

'I see,' Wisting said, now addressing himself to Álvarez: 'Have you thought of going public with any of this?'

The comisario shook his head. 'We've never reported Olaf missing or publicized any information about him,' he replied. 'If a few online trolls are looking for him, that's nothing to do with us.'

Wisting leafed through to a blank page in his notebook. 'Astri Arctander had also shown interest in another murder in Palamós,' he said. 'The German girl, Bertine Franck. Of course, there are a number of obvious similarities, also with several other unsolved murders. Have you taken a closer look at that angle?'

The Catalan investigators exchanged looks. Once again it was Álvarez who spoke up.

'There have been seven other cases in the last seventeen years,' he answered. 'The factors that make these cases tricky to solve are the same aspects that may give the impression of external similarities. The victims were travelling. Foreigners killed in foreign parts. The sea and saltwater have washed away all forensic evidence.'

'So you're not considering the possibility that the same perpetrator is behind them all?' Wisting asked.

The public prosecutor at the end of the table said something in Catalan, followed by a brief exchange of words before Álvarez continued.

'We've already clarified that what's said in this room must not be shared with any outsiders,' he said. 'I'd like to remind you of that. There are elements in some of these cases that have led us to form a special group to investigate them. It's crucial that this group is allowed to work in peace. So you cannot make reference to any of what Police Officer Alcantara is about to tell you.'

The other detective from the provincial police in Gerona now took over.

'In the cases of three of the dead women, a particular discovery was made that gives us cause to believe the crimes were committed by one and the same person,' he began. 'That applies to Bertine Franck, who was murdered here in Palamós twelve years ago, but not, however, Ruby Thompson.'

'What kind of discovery?' Wisting asked.

'Pebbles had been inserted into their vaginas,' Alcantara answered.

Wisting had never heard anything like it.

'There have been other instances of this,' Alcantara continued. 'The US police had a case in the eighties in which bodies were found in the same condition. Probably done in an attempt to sink the corpses. To make them stay submerged.'

Wisting doubted this would have any practical effect and glanced at Maren, as if she might have knowledge he lacked.

'He didn't succeed,' Maren said. 'The bodies floated ashore all the same, despite the stones.'

The police officer opposite nodded. 'There's a limit to the amount of weight you can add in that way,' he commented.

'Which other two cases are we talking about?' Wisting asked.

'Carlota Belén del Cármen and Valeria Espinosa Díaz.'

Two of the Spanish women, Wisting thought. In the chronological overview of victims, they were numbers three and four.

'Naturally, the special group has looked at all the cases, but these three in particular stand out,' Álvarez explained. 'Not just in the modus operandi, but they're within a limited time period and in the same geographical area.'

Wisting pictured in his head the map that one of the forum users had drawn up. These three murders were in the middle of the long stretch of coastline.

'I see,' he said. 'Are there any other circumstances that distinguish these three cases from the others?'

'All three of them spoke Spanish,' Alcantara replied. 'The German woman too.'

'A Spanish woman was murdered in Torrevieja last year,' Wisting pointed out, but no comment was made on this.

'To return to your original question,' Álvarez said. 'There's no evidence of any connection between the murders of Ruby Thompson and Bertine Franck.'

Wisting felt far from convinced. If it were true that the pebbles really were an attempt to weigh down the bodies, then that could easily be explained in a chain of events with the same killer: in the very first case the body had floated ashore. Next time he struck, he tried to sink the body, but was unsuccessful. He made another two similar attempts before giving up. The salty sea washed away all traces regardless.

If the use of pebbles was some kind of perversion or

destructive act, the absence of pebbles in the other cases could be explained by them having slipped out again. The pebbles on the beach were round and all the muscles in a dead body became slack.

He had closed his notebook when the comisario had asked them not to take notes. Now, however, he opened it again.

'Well,' he said, 'what do we do next?'

64

The restaurant had been chosen at random, but from the table Michelle could view the spot where Ruby had been found. Down at the water's edge, she could see a man walking his dog but, apart from that, the beach was deserted.

She made eye contact with a Spanish woman with a short, practical hairstyle as she strolled along the street. Although her gaze was penetrating, her smile was disarmingly inquisitive. Michelle gave her a brief nod and the woman responded in similar style as she approached the table.

'Nichelle?' she asked.

'That's me,' Michelle replied, getting to her feet.

'I'm Shelook,' the woman said, holding out her hand. 'Or Celia, really. That's my real name.'

They both sat down.

'Lovely to meet you,' Celia said. 'I feel as if I already know you a little.'

'Thanks, me too,' Michelle answered. 'When did you get here?'

'Yesterday. I'm staying at the same campsite as Ruby. Have you been there to take a look around?'

Michelle nodded. 'I popped round there yesterday,' she said.

They were both feeling their way forward in the conversation, just like at a party or funeral where people were wary about what it was appropriate to say.

A waiter arrived to break up their chat. Michelle was helped by Celia to read the menu and ended up with a

Mediterranean salad and a glass of lemonade. Celia ordered the same for herself, as if what she had to eat was completely inconsequential.

'I must show you something,' Celia said as soon as the waiter had made himself scarce.

She produced a laptop from her bag. 'I discovered it just before I had to leave to come here,' she went on. 'I haven't had a chance to look at it more closely.'

An African street-seller was heading for their table, his arms brimming with bags and jewellery. Celia waved him away and made a comment in Spanish before flipping open the computer lid.

'It's to do with the photos,' she said, locating the Salamander post. 'The names of the image files are in the source codes.'

Celia turned the screen towards her. To avoid the sun's reflection, she leaned forward to shade it.

Michelle could smell the scent of her hair. Fresh, perhaps with a touch of salt.

'The files mainly have the standard names they're allocated automatically,' Celia explained. 'Like this one here.'

She pointed at a random file name on the list. DSCF5539.jpg. 'Or this,' Celia continued, pointing at a file further down. IMG7832.jpg.

Michelle nodded. Her own computer was full of similar filenames.

'But some of the images have been given new names,' Celia said, pointing out one of them. O_IMG0391.jpg.

'Astria has added an O,' Michelle concluded. She had done the same thing herself at times if she wanted to differentiate something in a long list of files. 'What's in the photograph?' she asked.

Celia clicked it open. It was one of the photos from the beach. Michelle squinted at the screen to see what was special about it. Ruby did not feature in it and at first glance she could not see anything else either.

She shot a quizzical look at Celia, who sat with a slightly teasing expression on her face.

'On the far left,' she said.

Michelle took another look at the picture. In the second row there was a young man with dark hair, wearing a black sweater with a brightly coloured inscription.

'Olaf?' she queried.

'Well, it is at least someone who matches the description,' Celia said. 'I think that's why she's added an O in front of the file name.'

Michelle agreed. 'Have you checked the original photos?' she asked.

'Yes,' Celia answered, almost nonchalantly. 'It's the same there. The pictures with Olaf candidates are marked with an O, but there are also some photos marked with B.'

Celia scrolled up through the list of files. At the very top she found B_DSCF3478.jpg and B_IMG4390.jpg.

'What's in them?' Michelle asked.

Celia, having already displayed the two photos side by side in a single document, now enlarged it to full-screen mode. One was from the event on the beach while the other had been taken on the promenade.

Michelle sat for a long time staring at them, moving her eye from one image to the other, without noticing anything significant.

'Do *you* see anything?' she asked, turning to face Celia.

Celia shook her head. 'I can't think of anyone whose name starts with B, either,' she said. 'Not anyone of any interest to the case, at least.'

Michelle glanced again at the photos. 'Are any of the other photos marked in that way?' she asked.

'No,' Celia replied. 'But Astria has obviously spotted something. Something that made her highlight them. Something interesting.'

They sat with their heads together, studying the two photographs, until the waiter returned.

'Oh no, olives,' Celia said with a sigh as she stowed away her laptop. 'I don't like olives.'

'Me neither,' said Michelle with a smile.

She peered across at Celia, who had begun to pick at her food. The Spanish woman reminded her a little of Ruby. She had some of the same enthusiasm and charisma, but also something else. Underlying signals Michelle was usually good at picking up. There was something about the atmosphere she created at the table that made her wonder whether Celia was the same as Ruby when it came to *that*. That she too was gay.

Celia suddenly looked up from her plate and met her eye. 'Doing anything tonight?' she asked.

Michelle shook her head.

'I'm meeting Leo at half past eight,' Celia explained. 'Want to come with me?'

'I'd love to.'

65

'Don't you like olives?'

Maren sat with a green olive on the tip of her fork. Wisting had gathered his together at the side of his plate. He had never learned to like the sophisticated taste of olives.

'Would you like them?' he offered.

Maren shook her head as she popped the olive into her mouth.

They had found a restaurant a couple of blocks from the police station. The meeting with the Catalan investigators had lasted almost three hours but had not resulted in anything more specific than agreement on continuing to exchange information.

A cat slinked around the table legs before stretching out in a patch of sunshine.

Wisting pushed his plate aside and took out his mobile. It vibrated in his hands with a call from an unknown number.

'Just take it,' Maren said, fishing out her own phone.

Wisting did so. His phone had started buzzing during the meeting at the police station. Some of the numbers – journalists – were stored in his phone memory. He would have to answer them, but not yet.

'I'll speak to the lawyers at home first,' he said.

He dismissed the call and checked his email. He also saw a couple of messages from journalists there. One was from NRK, the national broadcaster, who wanted to send a reporter and wondered how long he planned to stay in Palamós.

'*VG* have published a story,' Maren told him.

She held her phone up for him to see the headline before she went on reading.

'Most of it's taken from the Catalan newspaper,' she commented.

Wisting scrolled on through his unread emails. 'I've received an email from Michelle Norris,' he said. 'She says she's in dialogue with the hacker who posted Astria's last photographs and there may be more information available.'

Maren put down her phone. 'The answers could well lie there,' she said. 'The contents of her computer could be what nudges the case forward.'

She saw he was deep in thought. 'What are you thinking of?' she asked. 'Using information from a hacker?'

'We could at least agree to meet her,' Wisting said. 'I'll suggest our hotel at six o'clock.'

A waiter approached their table while he keyed in a reply. Wisting asked Maren to tell him they were ready to pay.

The cat sprang up and disappeared between two flowerpots. The waiter removed their plates and returned with the bill, which Wisting paid.

'Say that we need a taxi as well,' he said.

The waiter smiled beneath his broad moustache, explaining something and pointing further up the street.

'There's a taxi rank right round the corner,' Maren translated.

They followed these directions and saw the drivers sitting on a bench. An older man with a sun-tanned, wrinkled face jumped to his feet when he realized they needed transport.

Wisting produced a note on which he had written the address where Astri Arctander had lived and checked he had the keys on him.

The driver looked at the note and consulted with the other men on the bench. A few sentences were exchanged before Wisting and Maren were waved into the back seat of the car.

'*Diez minutos*,' he said, holding up ten fingers.

66

'One last time,' Line promised as she dragged the sledge back up the hill again.

Amalie held tight on the steering wheel. The tassel on her hat dangled from side to side as she sang and chattered to herself.

At the top, Line turned the sledge, sat down at the back and pushed off. They both screamed as they moved faster and faster, until Line dug her heels into the ground to brake, with snow spraying all around them. Other children, on their way uphill, laughed and leapt aside. When they neared the foot of the hill, the sledge hit a dip and bounced before ploughing into a bank of snow and coming to a sudden stop.

As Line rolled off, Amalie demanded one more turn.

'No, we're going home for hot chocolate,' Line said. 'Say cheerio to the others.'

She hauled the sledge off towards the car while Amalie waved goodbye to the other youngsters at the play area.

They were both red-cheeked, and Amalie yawned as Line strapped her into her seat. Line started the car, fired up the heating and checked her phone. *VG* had sent a news flash about a suspicious death in Norway that could solve a Spanish murder mystery.

She clicked on the story and read it through. It contained everything. All about Ruby Thompson's murder, the online forum and Astria's investigations. Even that her father had gone to Spain.

Three journalists were listed in the by-line, but Line

recognized none of their names. She could easily have written the story. Most of it was taken from a Spanish newspaper article, but she had already known all of it for several days.

It was five years since she had left *VG*, but she would have liked to be part of the team working on this.

The snow had melted on her hat and water was running down her face. She took the hat off and threw it down on the passenger seat beside her.

She would have liked to be in Spain, in all honesty, she thought. At the same time, it was far from certain that the solution lay there.

There was silence in the back seat. Line checked in the rear-view mirror and saw that her daughter had fallen asleep.

The windscreen was clear of condensation now, and she moved off, driving out towards Helgeroa.

The spot where Astri Arctander had been found was easy to locate. The police crime scene tape still fluttered along the roadside. More snow had fallen since the forensic technicians had finished their work, but the excavated area was still clearly defined.

Astri had probably been on her way to the summer cabin at Eidsten. Line had found it on the Kartverket online map pages, registered to Gerd Arctander.

She used her mobile to navigate to the cabin. It was really far more than that: it was an extensive property, containing a colossal summer cabin, surrounded by a picket fence, beneath old, gnarled pine trees.

Line drove slowly past. Two hundred metres further on, she came across a space where she could turn and drive back.

The windows were covered with external shutters. At the opening in the fence, she stopped the car and sat hunched over the steering wheel. She could see remnants of tracks in the snow where someone had trudged up to the door. Astri must have had a reason to visit the summer cabin. Something important had impelled her to drive all the way from Spain.

She took out her phone again and snapped a photo, without really understanding why. Then she drove on.

67

The Arctander family's holiday house in Spain was located north of the town, overlooking the Mediterranean. Built in the modern Spanish style, all right angles and pale-grey brick, its several storeys climbed one upon the other up the hillside. At street level, a high stone wall was carpeted with green creepers.

Wisting paid the driver and took out the keys. The black iron gate swung open with no protest from the hinges. On the inside, they could see two empty carports and a garage as well as a small, shaded garden with a swimming pool and a paved walkway leading to the entrance.

They let themselves in and followed the instructions for disabling the alarm. The air was cool, almost chilly.

From the time when Astri had signed up to the online investigation forum at the end of October until she set off for Norway on 1 December, she had lived in this vast apartment complex on her own. The room she had used was one floor up. They walked through the living room, ascended a staircase and followed a corridor to the very end.

The door was closed but not locked. The ceiling light was not working. Wisting tried the switch twice before crossing to the other side of the room and opening the curtains. The window afforded a view of the sea.

The room had an en suite bathroom and was furnished with a double bed and a desk. Everything was clean and tidy.

Maren turned on the desk lamp before pulling out the drawers, removing the contents and displaying them on the bed. There were notebooks and writing materials, folders of instruction manuals and official papers, brochures, unused writing pads, mobile chargers, receipts and an envelope containing forty euros.

They went methodically through everything without finding anything of interest. Maren put everything back while Wisting concentrated on the bedside table. They examined the room as if it were a prison cell in which the prisoner had hidden escape plans or smuggled goods. The wardrobes were examined with a fine-toothed comb and every pocket emptied. Shoes were turned upside down, bedlinen stripped and the mattress flipped.

Their inspection of the room was fruitless. Astri Arctander had left nothing to tell them what she had been doing before she had suddenly taken it into her head to travel to Norway.

They ransacked the rest of the apartment, leaving no stone unturned, but this still produced no result.

From the kitchen, a door led into the garage. The ceiling light came on automatically when they entered. There was no car to be seen, only a few garden tools, a workbench and a metal cabinet.

Wisting opened the cabinet doors. The interior contained tools, a small supply of light bulbs and batteries and a few boxes of dismantled electrical equipment.

None of this sparked any interest, but he stood there for a few moments, as if something had resonated with him.

'Pretty substantial house,' Maren commented. 'I don't think I'd have liked to live here all by myself.'

Wisting nodded. The thought that had begun to form inside his head petered out.

'Looks as if she liked it,' he said. 'She often came down here while the others were in Norway.'

Closing the doors, he walked back to the apartment with

Maren. From there, they let themselves into the adjacent unit used by the youngest of the uncles, Bernard Arctander. The kitchen drawer, where the keys to his work vehicle had been kept, contained a couple of ballpoint pens, an assortment of charger cables and a few menus from several nearby take-away restaurants.

They returned to the living room in the main apartment. Beside the south-facing picture window there was a mobile telescope on a stand. Wisting shut one eye and put the other to the eyepiece. It was directed at the marina. He adjusted the optics so that the circular field of vision became clear. The distance down to the sea must be about three kilometres as the crow flies. The telescope even allowed him to see the expressions on the faces of people moving about down there.

'There are photo albums here too,' Maren said.

Wisting turned to face her. She had taken a leather-bound album from a wall unit and riffled through it as she approached him.

She set it down on the table. The album was constructed in the same way as the ones in the summer cabin in Norway. The paper photos were pasted in and accompanied by dates and comments.

'I think this is the most recent one,' she said.

The latest photos were from something that looked like an excursion. Almost the entire family appeared to be gathered around a picnic table under an apple tree with lanterns hanging from the branches. Astri was there with her parents and what they thought must be her brother with his wife and their son. The grandmother sat at the head of the table. Bernard Arctander and one of the twins were also present.

The picture had been taken one evening in May ten years ago. It must be around then that digital photos completely superseded rolls of film and the need for development. At any rate, these were the last photos pasted in.

Maren leafed through, back in time, ending up with photos from the summer when Bertine Franck was killed.

'What date was it?' she asked.

'The 21st of August,' Wisting replied. 'She was found six days later.'

He glanced over her shoulder at a photo from the swimming pool in the garden, dated 14 August. Astri's father was sitting on a lounger. Her brother and his son were splashing about in the water. *Last swim for Benjamin. Starting school soon!* was printed underneath the picture. He must be around nineteen by now.

On the next page were photos from a birthday party. Gerd Arctander had turned seventy-seven on 25 August. In one of the pictures, she had her four sons around her.

Maren took out her mobile and photographed the page before thumbing back to the swimming-pool pictures. All four were there too. Not assembled in one image, but all of Astri's uncles had been in Palamós seven days before and four days after Bertine Franck had been murdered.

Maren took another photo before returning the album to the shelf.

'He's here,' she said, looking out.

Wisting crossed to the window. A cabriolet with its roof down had driven into the courtyard in front of the building. The driver, a duplicate of Henrik Arctander dressed formally in a suit, had stepped out.

They went down to meet him. 'We can sit here,' Wisting suggested, pointing at outdoor furniture shaded by a pergola.

'Can I help you with anything?' Fredrik Arctander asked once they were seated.

'We've done what we came here to do,' Wisting replied. 'But we're no further forward.'

The chairs were uncomfortable without cushions, and he was struggling to sit comfortably.

'When did you last have contact with Astri?' he asked.

'Last summer, in Stavern,' he replied.

'So not while she was down here in the autumn?'

Fredrik shook his head. 'I live further south,' he explained. 'Admittedly, I own some rental apartments here, but I'm trying to sell them.'

He looked as if he could not find a good sitting position either.

'It's probably true to say that after Father died and I was given sole responsibility for running the company, my relationship with the rest of the family has become a bit strained. Henrik is probably the one I have most contact with, but that's fairly understandable, since we're twins.'

'What made the relationship strained?' Wisting asked.

'Money,' Fredrik replied. 'I work in property. Buying, selling and renting, all based on the assets from our father's firm. I have the necessary expertise to run it, and none of the others had any objections. The business provides a solid profit and a good return, but the management role has also provided me with contacts and the opportunity to invest on my own behalf. The fact that my wife and I run a separate company in the same line of business has created some friction, but the truth of the matter is that none of my brothers wanted to develop the business or take risks when the chances were there.'

Wisting was surprised by what he was hearing. 'I had the impression that the family was closely knit,' he commented.

Fredrik Arctander smiled. 'Yes, of course,' he answered. 'And as long as Mother is alive, everything will continue as usual, but we all know we'll dissolve the company when she's gone and her holdings are shared out. I'm comfortable with that, but it's not so easy for Ann-Mari.'

'That's your wife?' Wisting asked.

'Yes, it didn't take long for her to get on the wrong side of Mother and the others.'

Maren took over the conversation. 'Where is she now?' she asked.

'In Norway,' Fredrik replied. 'That's to say, she's on her way down here. I've to pick her up at the airport this evening. She'll stay a few days for a meeting with a builder in Tortosa, and then we'll go home together. That's why it suited me to come here today. Of course, I don't have anything to contribute, neither here nor in Norway, but I offered to come anyway.'

'You were both here at Easter?' Maren asked.

It looked as if Fredrik had to think about this. 'A couple of days,' he finally responded. 'We had a viewing at an apartment we were trying to sell.'

'Astri took an interest in Ruby Thompson's murder,' Maren went on.

'So I understood,' Fredrik replied.

'She was last seen just before eight o'clock, and on the same evening there was a mass swim on the beach,' Maren reminded him. 'Do you recall anything from that evening?'

'That was the day we arrived here,' Fredrik told her. 'We were on the beach, but I don't remember anything in particular. Astri was out running the next day, when the body was found.'

Maren nodded. 'Did you all stay here?' she asked, glancing up at the apartment complex.

'No, that would be too much of a squeeze,' Fredrik answered. 'Ann-Mari and I stayed at a hotel down in the town. Vostra Llar.'

'So you weren't all together, you four brothers and Astri?'

'No, but we met at the hotel later that evening. Walter, Henrik, Bernard and I. From a formal point of view, it was a board meeting. We went through the annual accounts and decided on the dividend. It took only half an hour. They'd had everything sent to them in advance.'

Wisting's interest was growing. 'When did the meeting end?' he asked.

'We met at seven, so we were probably finished by half past. Bernard was unhappy, I remember. He left first.'

Wisting cocked his head as a sign that he was keen to hear what his dissatisfaction had been about. Fredrik turned on a broad smile.

'It had to do with financial expectations,' he said. 'Bernard usually gets his own way, at least when Mother is around. His behaviour can be a bit immature when things don't work out the way he wants. Walter hung around for a while, but not for very long. I stayed with Henrik and we had a beer in an English pub down by the harbour.'

Wisting wanted more information. He wanted details about movements and activities but let the conversation drift on to other subjects. The crucial questions could wait. All he knew when they rose from the hard, uncomfortable chairs was that the four Arctander brothers had been out on the same evening as Ruby Thompson and her killer.

68

Wisting sat on the hotel balcony with his phone in his hand. He had spoken to three journalists before ringing home to his father, who had seemed in better shape than in the morning. However, usually he showed interest in the cases Wisting was working on. Now he was more concerned about when his son was coming home.

It was already past six p.m., and he had received a text message from Maren to tell him she was sitting in the pavement restaurant with Michelle Norris. He went downstairs to meet them.

They were sitting in a corner on their own. Wisting recognized the Australian woman from the photos in the online forum.

'So pleased you have time to meet me,' she said.

'Thanks, likewise,' Wisting replied as he sat down. 'When did you arrive in Palamós?'

Michelle and Maren exchanged glances, and Wisting realized she had just asked the same question.

'Wednesday night,' Michelle answered. 'I'm staying at a hotel at the end of this street.'

'We read a newspaper interview with you,' Wisting said. 'I understand a lot of people have become involved. Has anyone got in touch with fresh information?'

Michelle shook her head. 'Not with anything of significance,' she replied. 'Of course, a reward has now been offered, so most of the messages have probably gone to the private detective.'

Clasping her hands, she twisted round in her seat so that she could face Wisting. 'What do you think of the website?' she asked. 'Have you had a look at it?'

Wisting nodded without saying anything about the alias he used. 'It's an excellent tool,' he said. 'It's not certain that the solution will show up there, but as long as the website is active, it'll act as a reminder to the official investigators.'

'Do you think they find it annoying?' Michelle asked.

'Absolutely, I'm sure of that,' Wisting replied. 'You're like a squeaky wheel to them, but the squeaky wheels are the ones that get oiled first.'

He flashed a smile. 'But you ought to have some guidelines,' he continued. 'Even though it's a closed forum, you shouldn't permit users to name their suspects. That can destroy the lives of innocent individuals.'

Michelle nodded earnestly. It seemed she had thought the same thing herself.

'And then I'd be careful about publishing police documents,' Wisting added. 'That can backfire on you and could lead to the police shutting down the site.'

'Have they threatened to do that?' Michelle asked. 'Have you met the detectives here?'

'We were at the police station this morning,' Wisting told her. 'They brought us up to speed. Your website didn't come up. I got the impression they ignore it.'

'Did they have anything new to tell you?'

Wisting was unable to pass on any details from the meeting but was not lying when he told her there were no new developments in the case. Strictly speaking, the information they had received from the Catalan investigators was several months old, even though much of it had been news to them.

'There's nothing to suggest they're close to a breakthrough,' he said.

A waiter approached the table and asked what Wisting would like to drink. The other two had lemonade, and Wisting ordered the same.

'Have you heard anything more from the hacker?' Maren asked when he had gone. 'Salamander?'

'Not yet,' Michelle replied. She put the straw to her mouth and drank. 'What about Astri?' she asked, replacing her glass on the table. 'Are you any nearer to finding an explanation for what happened to her?'

Wisting shook his head. That was true. At the same time, it was important for Michelle to gain the impression they were being open with her, so that she too would share information if she came across anything. He told her about the conversation with Astri's ex-boyfriend, about the meeting with her grandmother and the rest of the family and that they had just searched their holiday house.

'We have a good overview of her journey but know very little about what she did down here before she left or what happened in Norway,' he rounded off.

'She worked digitally,' Maren said. 'We think the answers may be in her computer.'

The waiter had returned with Wisting's lemonade. The ice cubes rattled as he set the glass down on the table.

'What do you know about the hacker?' he asked, taking a swig of lemonade. 'Has she accessed Astri's computer, or did she find the photos somewhere else?'

'I've no idea,' Michelle answered. 'Most probably she's taken them from a server. That's one of the things I'm trying to find out.'

They fell silent as Wisting took another sip of his drink.

'I've looked through all the images of Ruby on the day of her murder,' Maren said. 'There's one thing I was wondering.'

'What's that?'

'Her clothes,' Maren said, going on to explain: 'When Ruby left the pizzeria just before eight, she was wearing a fawn skirt with a white T-shirt tucked in, but when she was found on the beach the next day, she had a blue sweater on.'

Michelle agreed.

'There's nothing to suggest she went back to the campsite that evening,' Maren went on. 'No one saw her there, but she must have got changed.'

'She had a bag with her,' Michelle reminded them. 'It can get cold here in the evenings in April after the sun has gone down. Maybe she had extra clothes with her?'

The bag had most likely contained a change of clothing and tools for the break-ins, but Wisting refrained from commenting on that.

'I've seen the other pictures of Ruby,' Maren went on. 'Both from France and after she arrived in Palamós, but she wasn't wearing the blue sweater in any of them. Do you know whether she owned a sweater like that?'

A peculiar expression crossed Michelle's face, as if a worrying thought had struck her. Her body stiffened and she frowned before sitting up straight in her seat.

'No,' she replied. 'Do you think it might have belonged to the killer? That he dressed her, afterwards?'

Her gaze shifted from Maren and moved to Wisting.

'I don't know,' he answered, withholding the information about the strands of hair and the DNA profile. 'But that's one of many unanswered questions.'

The conversation moved on to something else. They talked about the snow in Norway and life in Australia. Michelle told them about her upbringing with Ruby and her day-to-day life. She was studying social sciences online while working in a local bar.

'How long do you intend to stay here?' Maren asked.

'A week,' Michelle told her.

She had drained her glass as they chatted and now took out a cigarette packet.

'How long are you two staying?'

'As long as we need to,' Wisting replied. 'But we have return tickets booked for Monday afternoon.'

'Then maybe we can meet up again?' Michelle suggested, seemingly impatient now to leave.

'That would be a good idea,' Wisting said. 'There are a lot of balls in the air just now.'

Michelle got to her feet but suddenly flopped back down again. 'Be honest,' she said, fixing her eyes on Wisting. 'What do you really think? Is this a case that can be solved?'

Wisting tried to weigh his words. 'I think all cases can be solved,' he said. 'This one's no different. It's not as if the police down here have no leads, and we're not searching for something mythical or illusory. The solution is out there. Someone knows something, and what you've set up might well be the most effective way of reaching out to them.'

Michelle Norris sat for a while before getting to her feet again. 'Thanks,' she said, before dashing away.

69

Username: Shelook

Celia sat in bed listening to the faint thrum from the fridge. The caretaker had been in the bungalow while she was out. He had plugged it in again and got it working. A selfish thought crossed her mind about posting his name on the forum, but in all honesty she had little faith in this being a lead worth following.

She looked down at the screen again, studied the B photos once more and felt increasingly irritated. She was struggling to see what Astria had seen, but perhaps it was not a matter of drawing some kind of logical conclusion. Astria's starting point was very different from hers — someone she knew could be in the photos.

Her Facebook profile was still online, but her privacy settings allowed only her friends to see her list of friends or her posts. There was little other information to glean from it, but she did find a line-up of family members. One brother, Morten. One nephew, Benjamin. One cousin, Merete.

Benjamin Arctander.

She clicked on his profile. The most recent posts were from friends offering condolences for his aunt's death. After that, a series of photos from ski slopes. Winter and snow, but there were also photographs from Spain.

She heard a knock at the door, and the abrupt sound startled her. Shutting the lid of her laptop, she slid it under a pillow and went to answer the door.

'Hello?' she called out.

'It's me,' came a voice from outside. 'Michelle.'

Celia looked at the time. It was no more than a couple of hours since they had parted, and they had not planned to meet again for another hour.

She opened the door and let Michelle in. 'Has something happened?' she asked.

Michelle shook her head. 'Not really, but I think I've understood something.' She looked around the room. 'Do you have a computer?'

'Yes.' Celia crossed to the bed and took her laptop out.

'Find the police photos from the beach,' Michelle requested. 'The ones of Ruby.'

They perched side by side on the edge of the bed. Celia had given the pictures from the discovery of the body only a cursory glance. She had realized that not all the police material had been published, only a sufficient quantity to give an impression of the incident. Anyway, it had seemed both unnecessary and inappropriate to study them in detail. The descriptions in the police report were more than adequate.

'There!'

Michelle was pointing at the top photo of two displayed on a document page. Ruby Thompson was lying on her side, almost in a foetal position. The blue sweater reached down to her thighs and covered her crotch. Her skin and hair were coated with sand.

'Take a copy!'

Celia copied the photo to a blank document.

'Now find Astria's B photos,' Michelle said.

These were already open in a photo-editing program. Celia placed them alongside the beach photograph.

'Do you see it?' Michelle asked. 'The blue sweater?'

She was pointing at the B photo from the beach, at a man

318

in a blue sweater standing among the spectators, moving her finger across to the picture from the promenade and pointing at a man seated at a café table with his back to the photographer. The shade of blue was exactly the same and it looked like the same man.

'Do you think . . .' Celia began, but she failed to complete the sentence.

She enlarged the image of the rubberneckers on the beach, zooming in on the man in the blue sweater, a dark-skinned man in his thirties with black, curly hair.

'It looks like the same kind of jumper,' Celia said.

'The Norwegian investigators were interested in her sweater,' Michelle said. 'They asked if it was Ruby's. They had looked through all the photos of her but hadn't seen her wearing that jumper before. I haven't either.'

Celia clicked more methodically on the sweater, studying the neckline and the sleeves.

'Ruby's sweater looks like a different size and fit,' she said. 'It's longer and narrower, almost full-length.'

'It's wet, though,' Michelle pointed out. 'I'm sure it's the same sweater. Astria must have seen it too. That's why the file names are marked with a B. B for blue.'

Celia smiled. So that was why she had failed to spot the link.

'Blue is *azul* in Spanish,' she explained, looking at the photos with her head tilted. 'Can it really be the same sweater? I mean, exactly the same one?'

'Maybe he's in some of the other photos too?' Michelle suggested.

Celia called up the post with all the photos Astria had collected and began to click through them. Michelle moved closer to look at them with her. It took a long time to download all the images. Ten minutes later, they had only gone through two hundred of them. They would not be able to examine them all by the time they had to meet Leo.

Then he cropped up again, in another photo taken at the event on the beach. The angle was better this time. He stood with his head turned towards the photographer with no one else in front of him.

Michelle leaned even closer to the screen. 'I wonder who he is,' she said.

'We can try an image search,' Celia suggested.

She opened the photo in an editing program and cropped the photo so that it only included the man in the blue sweater. Then she uploaded it to an image recognition search engine. It came up with lots of hits on dark-skinned men in blue tops, but not the man they were looking for.

'But I think you're right,' Celia conceded. 'It's the same sweater.'

She switched from one photo to the next, alternating between them. The man in the sweater did not resemble the many Moroccans who had settled in Spain but more probably came from one of the countries in the Middle East. However, in two of the photos he was with a Spanish man and woman of similar age.

The event on the beach marked the opening of the bathing season, but the tourists did not usually arrive for another few weeks. Most of the people taking part were from the local population.

It seemed far-fetched to believe the perpetrator had dressed Ruby after murdering her, but she began to glimpse a possibility, an explanation for what could have happened.

'What do you think of the housebreaking idea?' she asked. 'Have you seen the photos? Could that really be Ruby?'

Michelle nodded. 'I've had the same thought,' she replied. 'She could have stolen it.'

Celia looked up a website with historical weather data. On the evening Ruby was killed, the temperature had dropped to less than ten degrees Celsius.

'Shall I write a post about the sweater?' she asked.

'If he's from Palamós, it might be easier to find him in the good old-fashioned way,' Michelle suggested. 'We can show people the picture and ask if anyone knows him. Or we could go up to the neighbourhood where the break-ins took place and show it to residents there. If the sweater was stolen in the same area, I mean.'

Celia had come up with another idea. 'We could do it in the new-fangled way,' she said.

'What's that?'

'Use Facebook.'

Celia no longer used Facebook much these days, but people of the same age as the man in the blue sweater still did.

As Michelle seemed sceptical, Celia went on to explain her thinking. 'My aunt's in an organization that looks after stray animals,' she said. 'When they bring in a dog that's not chipped, they make a Facebook advertisement visible only to people living a few kilometres around the area where the animal was found. There's always someone who's able to identify the owner.'

'I set up a Facebook page for Ruby, but it's inactive now,' Michelle volunteered.

Celia pushed the laptop towards her. 'Open it,' she said.

Michelle logged in and activated the page. It contained little except photos of Ruby and a redirection to the online forum.

Taking back the laptop, Celia appointed herself administrator and moved to the advertisement settings. She uploaded the image and wrote a simple heading in Spanish: *Who is this?*

Underneath, she wrote a brief text about the person in the photo potentially being unaware that he might have information about Ruby Thompson's murder. A click on the advertisement would provide the opportunity to send in tip-offs.

In the next stage she had to provide the parameters for the target audience. The chances of coming across someone who recognized the man in the photo increased according to how accurately directed the notice was. Besides, it was cheaper if it targeted only a few but the most appropriate people.

She gave the minimum possible radius around the street address of one of the break-ins on 16 April and an age group of twenty- to thirty-eight years old, which she assumed would include about five years above and below the age of the man in the photograph. She decided the advertisement should reach Facebook users of both sexes and that it should be visible for twenty-four hours.

For ten euros, the advertisement would be shown 1,800 times.

'How many people live in Palamós?' Michelle asked.

'About 20,000,' Celia replied.

She raised it to fifty euros for 15,000 views.

'We can split the cost,' Michelle suggested.

With a nod, Celia keyed in her credit card information and completed the transaction.

Once the advertisement was submitted for approval, it would be posted within the hour.

70

They arrived ten minutes late. Leo was sitting on the edge of a flower trough, waiting. He sprang up when they arrived, shoving his mobile into his pocket and tossing away a cigarette.

'Hi,' he greeted them with a broad smile.

He held out his arms for a hug and took plenty of time before releasing Celia from his embrace and turning to Michelle with a question in his eyes.

'I must introduce you,' Celia said. 'Leo, this is Michelle.'

Leaving the explanations until they were seated, she headed for the restaurant entrance. Leo did not move, and instead pointed his finger at Michelle.

'You're Ruby's friend from Australia,' he said. 'I read about you in the newspaper. You were at the beach bar yesterday when I had my day off.'

'That's right,' Michelle replied.

'Let's go in,' Celia suggested, forestalling further questions. 'I'll explain.'

They were shown to a window table. Celia outlined how she had found Michelle's website and joined the online community. The conversation was in English and only interrupted when a waiter appeared to take their order.

Leo insisted they had to eat tapas and drink wine.

'Have you taken a look at the website?' Celia asked, but Leo shook his head.

'I didn't know about it until today,' he answered, glancing across at Michelle, 'when I read about it.'

The wine arrived at the table, and Leo tasted it while Celia checked Facebook on her mobile. The advertisement had been approved, but there were no responses as yet.

'Do you have any contact with Jarod and Mathis?' Michelle asked.

'It's months ago now,' he replied, pouring wine for the two women. 'Have you?'

Michelle drank from her glass. 'I've exchanged emails with Jarod,' she told him. 'He sent me a lot of documents from the case, but that was around the time I set up the site.'

'What about Olaf?' Celia asked. 'Have you seen any more of him?'

Leo took another gulp of the wine. 'No,' he answered. 'I think he was only here by chance, the same as many other people. He's probably gone back.'

'I have some photos,' Celia said, locating them on her phone. 'Could you take a look and see if it's him?'

Holding up the screen, she showed him the Olaf photos. 'They're from the day Ruby was murdered,' she explained.

Leo leaned forward to look but was interrupted by the waiter returning with their food. A long tray with an assortment of small dishes. Celia made space for him and, when he had left, she held out the phone across the table again.

Leo studied the photograph carefully before shaking his head.

'Difficult to say,' he said, helping himself to some meatballs. 'The picture quality's poor. Anyway, I only met him a couple of times, and it's ages ago now.'

'What about these?' Celia asked, showing him the other photos.

Leo shook his head. 'Sorry,' he said, tucking into the food and changing the subject. 'Where are you staying?'

'At the campsite,' Celia replied, laying aside her phone.

'In a tent?'

She laughed and shook her head. 'I've rented a bungalow,' she told him.

'You could have stayed with me,' Leo said. 'I've plenty of room.'

With a shrug of the shoulders, Celia bit into a chicken skewer.

Leo turned to Michelle. 'What about you?' he asked. 'Are you staying at the campsite too?'

She shook her head. 'I'm at a small hotel,' she replied, giving the name.

Celia was keen to shift the conversation back to Ruby. 'What do you think happened to her?' she asked.

It was Leo's turn to shrug. 'There are loads of visitors in Palamós,' he said. 'We've only got 20,000 residents here, but almost 200,000 tourists come in the course of a year. Besides, the coast here is swarming with illegal migrants. They walk along the beaches selling fake handbags and watches. I see them every day.'

He drank more wine. 'What about you two?' he asked. 'Have you come up with any theories?'

'Not really,' Celia replied. 'But a lot of interesting things have cropped up and need further investigation.'

She and Michelle took turns relating the story of Astria, the other unsolved murders, the local painter, the caretaker and all the other theories and rumours swirling around in the forum.

The hours passed and the wine gradually began to have an effect.

'I'll come with you,' Leo said when they broke up for the night.

Celia snuggled into her jacket against the chill evening air as they sauntered through the streets.

'Will I see you again?' Leo asked.

'I'll be here for a few more days,' Celia replied.

Before they parted company outside the campsite, she arranged with Michelle to meet on the promenade the following day at ten a.m.

On the way to the bungalow, she fished out her phone and checked the Facebook advertisement. Her inbox was empty, but the notice had garnered 3,000 views and a whole slew of comments. She read them as she walked. Some pointed out that the picture quality was not the best, and others gave their own interpretations, estimating the man's age and where he came from. There seemed to be agreement that the man looked Arabic. Someone asked if he was the murderer, while another expressed an opinion that all Arabs looked alike. No one came up with any specific names.

71

Vibeke Hassel died of self-inflicted poisoning, a mixture of anti-depressants and alcohol. A farewell letter running to several pages had been scanned, together with supplementary case documents attached to the email. Wisting had read similar letters. They told of inadequate self-belief, an inability to get to grips with existence, a life without purpose.

A door slammed in the hotel corridor and Wisting checked the time. Almost midnight.

Reading a suicide letter was always strange, affording an intimate insight into another person's life. Like reading someone's last thoughts.

Often there was more to be read between the lines than in the text itself. He thought he could detect that here too, especially in one paragraph addressed to someone who must be her younger sister. Vibeke Hassel wrote about how she had wept every night, and in a sense that had been OK, because it had kept her deep-seated pain at a slight distance. Then it came: *They won in the end.* After that, she praised her sister, saying how good and important she had been.

They could refer to dark thoughts or negative emotions, but the overall impression was that she was talking about an incident or situation and the individuals involved in that, who had made her feel her life was worthless.

He skimmed the other documents. Neither her sister nor any other family member had provided any explanation. The only thing included with the case documents was a doctor's statement, describing in general terms a state of clinical depression and prescribed medication.

A light knock was heard at the door. Wisting got to his feet, crossed the room and opened it a crack.

Maren Dokken stood outside with her laptop flipped open in her hands. 'You hadn't gone to bed, had you?' she asked.

He opened the door wide and let her in. 'I was reading about Vibeke Hassel,' he said. 'The woman cut out of the photo in the album.'

Maren gave him a quizzical look and Wisting shook his head in response.

'The case seems open and shut,' he answered, giving a brief account of the main elements. 'She had a history of depression.'

He sat down in the armchair again and cast a glance at her laptop. 'Has something happened?'

Maren looked around for something to sit on but ended up perching on the edge of the bed.

'I read through the Astri case one more time,' she said. 'The lab report was ready this afternoon. Have you seen it?'

'No.'

'You asked them to prioritize the samples from the driver's cab,' Maren said. 'They found DNA on the yellow beanie.'

Wisting nodded. 'Ruby Thompson's,' he said.

'Her profile's not in the Norwegian DNA register, but you got the Catalan police to look it up,' Maren continued.

Wisting nodded again. 'That's why we're here.'

Maren stood up again and turned the laptop screen towards him. 'The same profile was found in three places in the cargo space,' she said. 'It's in the final report. Ruby Thompson has been in that van.'

Wisting took the laptop from her and placed it on his knee. The lab report was loaded with information. A total of fifteen DNA profiles were located in the vehicle. Five of them belonged to Astri Arctander and had been found on the steering wheel, the gearstick, a seatbelt, the mouth of an empty bottle and the catch on the glove compartment. A further three unidentified male DNA profiles had been taken from the interior of the driver's cab. The same profiles had been identified in several places in the load area. The DNA profile from the yellow hat in the glove compartment was listed as an analysis result from an unknown female. The profile was identical to three samples from the cargo area. All the samples came from what was described as 'scrapings from rust-coloured material'. Two of these were from the floor, while the third was taken from a propeller blade. In the comment field a note had been added: 'Possibly blood.'

He looked up, thinking of the autopsy report that had described cuts and scratches, but these had been written off as injuries sustained while her body had drifted around in the sea.

'She could have sustained them while putting up resistance,' Maren said, as if reading his thoughts.

Wisting had to read the conclusion a second time. The samples from the hat and the cargo space were identical. A separate document with photographs pinpointed where they had been obtained.

'The van is a crime scene,' Maren went on. 'That was why Astri took it. It wasn't only about the yellow hat. She wanted to have the van examined.'

'She could have gone to the police down here,' Wisting objected.

'Instead she drove the van to Norway,' Maren said. 'That makes sense if she believed the perpetrator was Norwegian. That it was someone she knew.'

Grabbing his phone, Wisting rang Nils Hammer at home in Norway and came straight to the point when he answered.

'The Spanish van,' he said. 'Do you know whether it's still down in the garage?'

Hammer cleared his throat. 'It's been released,' he replied.

Wisting felt a jolt in his chest. 'When was that?'

'Last night,' Hammer answered. 'They said the examination was finished.'

'Who picked it up?'

'One of the Arctanders. The guy who works in the firm that owns it.'

'Bernard?'

'That could be right. I just spoke to him on the phone. He came after office hours. It was one of the patrol section who signed it out.'

Wisting had got to his feet. 'Can you have it brought in again?' he asked.

'In again?' Hammer repeated incredulously.

'There's been a mistake,' Wisting explained. 'It has to be re-examined.'

'I can give him a call early tomorrow morning,' Hammer suggested.

'That's not good enough,' Wisting said, explaining what they had discovered. 'We can't let anyone in the family get wind of it. You have to send out a surveillance car to trace it.'

'OK, then,' Hammer said. 'I'll report back to you as soon as that's done.'

'Excellent,' Wisting said, and thanked him. 'That's great.'

He ended the conversation and looked across at Maren.

For the first time in this case, he felt on the brink of something that might lead to a real breakthrough.

72

Username: Shelook

A streak of sunlight found its way through a gap in the curtains and touched her face. Celia moved the pillows at her back and wriggled to one side of the bed, still with her laptop planted on the quilt in front of her.

Three messages had come in, all naming the man they were looking for. Yusuf Sleman. He worked in an estate agency and lived in the north-east of the town. Celia looked him up and found other photos of him. There could be no doubt. Yusuf Sleman was the man in the blue sweater. On Facebook he was depicted with the woman from the photos on the beach. Just as she had expected, he was not from the region, but said he was from a town in the Sinai Peninsula.

Celia removed the advertisement, as there was no point in spending more money to let it run on longer. Besides, she did not want to risk Yusuf Sleman seeing it.

She had sent a message to Michelle, asking if she had seen this too, but received no response. Maybe she was sleeping late. They'd had a late night the previous evening.

She took out the map on which she had identified the locations of the three break-ins that had taken place on the evening Ruby was killed and plotted in the address of the man in the blue sweater.

He lived only three houses down from the last crime scene. From there, it was only a short distance to the campsite.

The intense emotion aroused by closing in on something significant made her flesh tingle. It was like a crossword, even though that was a bad analogy. Crosswords were boring. But if you found the solution for one word, you found the answer to several more.

Michelle still had not read her message. She wrote another one and asked how they should proceed. Whether they should send a text to Yusuf Sleman or pay him a visit. She felt the second proposition would be better.

Outside, someone fired up an engine. Celia crawled out of bed and opened the curtains. A man with a grizzled, gaunt face was busy trimming a hedge. The caretaker, presumably.

She pulled on a pair of shorts and a T-shirt. Choosing clean clothes from her suitcase, she pushed her feet into sandals and carried her washbag to the shower block. She had great expectations about what the day might bring.

73

They sat at the same breakfast table and ate the same as the previous day. Wisting had received a new message from Ellinor, but the contents were fairly humdrum. She wrote that she was tired of snow and winter and envied him being in Spain, and ended by saying she hoped they could meet again on his return.

Wisting began a reply in which he wrote that the temperature in Palamós was about twenty degrees Celsius and the sun was still shining in a cloudless sky.

'Shouldn't we let the local police know?' Maren asked. 'After all, it's their case. Their crime scene.'

'I want to make sure we've got the van back first,' Wisting answered. He finished writing his text and sent the message.

'I'll phone Hammer and see what the situation is,' he said.

Nils Hammer answered at once.

'Do you have the van?' Wisting asked.

'No,' Hammer told him. 'But I'm tracing it as we speak. It seems it was the Viking breakdown service that picked it up from here on Thursday. They put old winter tyres on it and drove it to Bernard Arctander in Asker. I've a patrol car outside the house. The van's no longer there. I'm waiting for the toll station transit info.'

'Phone me as soon as you have any news,' Wisting instructed.

He rang off and gave Maren an account of the conversation.

'That doesn't narrow down our suspicions any further,'

she said. 'It could be someone else who's used the van. Every-one knew where the keys were kept. They were accessible to everybody in the house.'

'Someone from the marine workshop could also have used it,' Wisting said, though he did not really believe that.

Maren shook her head. 'Bernard Arctander uses the van when he's here in Palamós,' she said, referring to a police statement. 'He was here when Ruby Thompson was killed.'

Wisting took a gulp of coffee before drawing his chair back from the table. 'Gather all the information you can on him,' he said as he stood up.

His phone rang. An unknown number, but with a Spanish prefix. He answered without delay and a woman introduced herself, though Wisting did not catch her name.

'Am I speaking to Señor William Wisting?' she asked in English.

Wisting sat down again. 'Yes, that's me,' he replied.

'I'm calling on behalf of el Comisario Álvarez,' she said. 'You met him yesterday. He'd like to meet you again and has suggested one p.m. Does that suit you?'

Wisting had no other appointments. 'What's the back-ground to the meeting?' he asked.

'There's been a development in the case you discussed yesterday,' the woman answered. 'El Comisario would like to give you an update. We can send a car to your hotel.'

Thanking her, Wisting wrapped up the conversation and looked at Maren.

'There's been a development,' he said. 'We've been called in for another meeting at the police station.'

'What kind of development?' Maren asked.

'We'll find that out at one o'clock.'

74

Username: Shelook

Celia pushed her laptop across the table and glanced back at the promenade. It was quarter past ten and Michelle had not turned up.

She did not have her phone number. They had only kept in touch by email and direct message on the online forum, but she had not responded to either of these.

Another five minutes went by before she phoned her cousin Leo.

'Yes?' he answered, clearing the sleep out of his throat.

Celia explained she could not get hold of Michelle. 'Did you see her back to her hotel last night?' she asked.

'Yes, or just until we caught sight of it. To the corner of the street, not all the way up to the entrance.'

'What hotel was it?'

'Hotel Trias, down near the harbour,' Leo told her.

He asked her to let him know if there was anything he could do to help. She thanked him and signalled to a waiter that she wanted to pay for her coffee.

While she waited, she found the Trias Hotel on a street map on her mobile; only six minutes' walk away. In case they missed each other en route, she sent another direct message with her phone number.

Leaving a one-euro tip on the plate with the bill, she set off towards the hotel.

It turned out to be a run-down building with a nondescript entrance. Celia approached the man behind the reception desk.

'My friend is staying here,' she said. 'Michelle Norris. Could you phone her room and tell her I'm here, please?'

'We no longer have phones in the rooms,' the receptionist replied. 'Everyone uses mobile phones.'

'I don't have her phone number,' Celia explained. 'I can go up and knock. What room is it?'

'We don't give out that kind of information,' he told her.

'But we'd arranged to meet,' Celia tried to explain. 'Something must have happened.'

The receptionist took a step back as if to take a better look at her. 'But you don't have her phone number?'

Celia could understand his mistrust. 'Could you go up and knock on her door, then?' she asked. 'Leave a message?'

'You can leave a message here at reception,' he suggested, placing a notepad on the counter.

There was no reason to believe that a note in reception would reach Michelle more quickly than a text or an email, but she scribbled a short message asking Michelle to phone her and giving her phone number.

Outside, she stood wondering how worried she should be. She did not really know Michelle but had gained the impression that she was neat and organized. That she could be relied upon. But she could not be sure. She had been tipsy when they parted company. She could have ended up in a bar, gone back to her room very late and still be fast asleep in bed.

A lorry with orange gas canisters aboard stopped in front of the hotel entrance. Celia headed around the street corner and scanned the area for a taxi. In a side street, she saw a car waiting in the shade of an elm tree. Although the driver sat reading a paperback, he confirmed that he was available.

Celia settled into the back seat and gave the address of

the man in the blue sweater. The taxi rolled slowly out into the street. The driver repeated the address to himself, puzzling over it, and then it appeared to dawn on him where he should go.

Ten minutes later she stood outside a wrought-iron gate beside a south-facing villa with a red tiled roof. A metal sign warned that the property was equipped with a Prosecure alarm. In the interior courtyard, two cars were parked, and children's toys were scattered across the lawn. All indications were that someone was at home.

A bell rang somewhere inside the spacious house when she pressed the button. Someone called out something, and a man emerged. Celia recognized him immediately. Yusuf Sleman.

He cocked his head, looking askance at her as he walked towards the gate. 'Can I help you?' he asked before he had reached her.

Celia told him her name. 'I have a strange question for you,' she said. Taking out her mobile phone, she showed him the clearest of the B-photos. 'Is this you?' she asked, holding it out to him.

Yusuf Sleman leaned forward and gazed at the picture. 'Why do you want to know that?' he asked.

'It's a long story,' Celia replied. 'But what I'm really wondering is where your blue sweater is?'

Yusuf Sleman gave her a long, searching look. 'Do *you* know where it is?' he asked.

Celia took this as confirmation that it was missing. 'Maybe,' she replied.

Yusuf Sleman opened the gate and invited her in. They sat down at a table on a paved patio in front of the house. The woman in the photographs came out to join them.

'She's asking about that blue Zeke sweater of mine,' Yusuf clarified.

The woman sat down. 'Does she know something?' she asked.

Celia was unsure where to begin. 'Has it been stolen?' she asked.

'Yes,' they answered in unison.

The woman gave some further explanation: 'I had hung it out to air,' she said, pointing in the direction of some clothes-lines. 'We'd been with some friends who smoke. The smell had clung to the sweater, so I hung it up outside. Next day it was gone.'

'We have cameras and an alarm system,' Yusuf explained. 'But not in that part of the garden.'

'Do you know who took it?' the woman asked. 'It was an expensive sweater. Hardly worn.'

Celia related the whole story and ended by showing them the photo of Ruby Thompson on the beach.

The woman could scarcely sit still. She stood up and sat down again several times, breathing heavily and repeating how dreadful it all was.

From somewhere inside the house, they heard a child crying noisily. The woman disappeared inside.

'Did you report the theft to the police?' Celia asked when they were alone again.

Yusuf shook his head. 'It was only a sweater,' he said. 'Have you spoken to the police?'

'No,' Celia answered. 'I don't think they know about it.'

'Should I report it now?' he asked. 'Or will you do that?'

Celia pondered the question. She could easily go to the police. They would undoubtedly speak to Sleman anyway, but she was the one who had spotted the connection.

'I can do it,' she said, rising from her seat.

Yusuf accompanied her to the gate. Once outside, she checked her phone again. Nothing from Michelle.

75

Username: Darby

She could not access the website. Everything had worked well a few hours earlier, but now all she could see was an onscreen message that the website was unavailable.

Line moved to the kitchen window. Amalie was playing on her own out in the snow. Lying on her back, she was chewing the end of one of her mittens as she stared up at the sky and the snowflakes drifting down towards her.

If Line found out when her father was coming home, she could clear his yard of snow so that he could drive all the way in with his car.

Amalie spotted her in the window and threw handfuls of snow up in the air. Line waved back at her. Her daughter had been outside for a long time now and was almost certainly soaked through. Soon she would start to shiver with cold.

Deciding to make some hot chocolate before calling her in, she took out the milk, sugar and cocoa powder.

It could be some kind of overload that had caused the server to crash, she thought as she stirred the pot. The number of users had exploded as the media coverage surged. The case and the forum were being discussed in Catalan, Spanish, Australian, Norwegian and British media outlets. It could easily be too much for a simple website to cope with.

When the hot chocolate came to the boil, she slid the pot from the heat and sat down at her laptop again. Something was obviously wrong. The webpage was still down. She would have to try again later.

76

'It's Hammer,' Wisting said when the phone rang.

They were sitting in his hotel room: Maren out on the balcony with her laptop on her knee and Wisting seated at the desk.

He switched to loudspeaker to allow her to tune into the conversation.

'I've had a reply from the toll station company,' Hammer said. 'There's a transit on the southbound lane near Svinesund on Thursday night, at two minutes to eleven.'

'En route to Sweden, then?' Wisting asked, mostly seeking confirmation.

'He's probably on his way back to Palamós in the van,' Hammer replied. 'If he drives as fast as Astri did, he could already be at your end.'

Wisting did the mental calculations. Astri Arctander had taken almost thirty-five hours to reach the Swedish border, including short spells of rest and sleep. Thirty-six hours had now passed since her uncle had set off on his journey.

'There's little more I can do here,' Hammer added.

'OK,' Wisting agreed. 'I'll take care of it. Thanks for your help.'

Maren had come into the room. 'He must have left just after we visited them,' she said. 'Picked up the van, converted to winter tyres, and headed south.'

'What do you have on him?' Wisting asked.

Maren glanced at her laptop out on the balcony table. 'Not much,' she replied. 'There's nothing in the records, and he's not on social media. He has his own firm, Barctander AS. Works on the repair and maintenance of boats, but we already knew that. Looks like he hires himself out to a similar firm here in Palamós, Navis Servinauta. He reported that he had moved to Spain in 2002, but he also has a Norwegian address and still pays tax in Norway.'

Wisting crossed to the other side of the room and all the way back again.

'I'll call Astri's father,' he said. 'Try to get some information from him.'

He keyed in Walter Arctander's number. 'There's no news, I'm afraid, but there's been a lot of interest in the press,' he began.

'We've picked up on that,' Walter Arctander replied. 'But we don't understand much of it. The idea that Astri might know something about the murder of that Australian girl . . . does it have anything to do with this Olaf? Have you discovered anything more about him?'

'We had a meeting with the police down here yesterday,' Wisting told him. 'Olaf's a red herring.'

'But have you discovered who he is? I mean, you should surely talk to him if Astri was searching for him?'

'It seems to be a false name,' Wisting explained. 'I can't share much information from the Catalan investigation, but they've come to the conclusion that he was a complete fabrication.'

He changed the subject to avoid further questions, instead asking about contact with the funeral directors and whether a date had been set for the ceremony.

'It's to be right before Christmas,' Walter replied. 'On 21 December.'

'We're staying down here for another few days,' Wisting said, going on to tell him they had been in the apartment and examined Astri's room. 'Will it remain empty for long?' he asked.

'No, Bernard's on his way down with the van now.'

Wisting stole a glance at Maren, signalling with his eyes that he had managed to ferret out the information he was after.

'Now?' he asked.

'He wanted to get it out of the way before Christmas,' Walter said. 'He's coming home again for the funeral.'

'Then maybe I could hand the keys back to him, down here?'

'He has his own keys, but you can certainly do that.'

'I'll phone him afterwards,' Wisting said, 'to find out if he's arrived.'

Through the years, Wisting had spoken to numerous grieving relatives. Later, they did not always remember what had been said. Often it was of no consequence. The important thing was for them to be left with the feeling of being taken care of. That they were kept informed and given the opportunity to contribute something. And so he spent some time before ending the conversation. He spoke about the interest his daughter had taken in the Catalan murder, about the nickname she used in the online forum, about the photos she had collected, and how he had been contacted when there was nothing but radio silence from her. Everything of no significance for the inquiry into her death, but that would soon be reported in the media.

He saw that Maren had become engrossed in something on her laptop while he was on the phone.

'What have you got?' he asked.

'I've had a reply from Thea Weber in Hamburg,' she answered. 'She's not *the* Thea Weber we're looking for, but we're not the first to ask her that question. Previously, there were email exchanges and phone calls.'

She read out the message, translating it as she went: 'The Thea Weber who travelled to Spain with Bertine Franck has married and changed her name. She's now called Thea Kleibl and lives in Bonn.'

'Do you have contact details?' Wisting asked.

'She's included a Facebook link,' Maren replied. 'She writes that they were friends there for years, mostly because they thought it was fun to have someone in their friends list with the same name. But then of course she changed her surname.'

Wisting checked the time. 'Our lift will be here soon,' he said.

Maren turned back to the screen. 'I've got time to write to her,' she said.

Wisting nodded, filled with a sense that they had come another step closer.

77

Username: Shelook

There was a good mobile signal, but she could not gain admission to the forum. The website was down.

Celia felt anxious. Clutching her phone, she hurried on, increasing her pace. She felt sure something must have happened to Michelle. Her thoughts raced in the direction of the worst possible scenarios. That she had been subjected to the same fate as Ruby.

If she did not hear from her in the next couple of hours, she would have to contact the police. Three p.m., she set as a deadline.

She came to a crossroads and took the left fork, beside an abandoned building site with the unfinished bones of buildings, strewn with rubbish. She checked the map on her phone to make sure she was heading in the right direction. Ruby Thompson had probably walked the same route after her housebreaking spree on 16 April. It was the shortest way back to the campsite.

The information about the blue sweater had brought a bit more certainty to the case. It provided a new lead on Ruby Thompson's last known whereabouts. Somewhere along the road ahead, she had been attacked and killed.

Celia scanned the area. The sun glittered on metal or broken glass inside one of the weed-clogged brick skeletons. The grey walls were spattered with graffiti, and iron reinforcement bars jutted out from the concrete. She had no problem visualizing an attacker waiting somewhere in the darkness here. Ruby's bag or clothes could be somewhere in this desolate area.

She peered into the bushes along the way as she walked, finding plastic, empty bottles and other types of rubbish everywhere. One thing made her stop in her tracks – a bundle of clothing tucked halfway under a wooden board. It looked like a black sweater.

The sight made her pulse race.

She found a stick, flipped the board away and poked at the dirty garment. Beside it she saw a pair of well-used gloves. On the back of the sweater, the name of a construction company was emblazoned. It was probably something discarded by one of the building workers.

Celia tossed the stick away and walked on, but she was still keen to suggest to Michelle that they should bring Leo with them and examine this terrain more closely.

Soon she arrived at a residential area and, a few blocks later, she could see the flagpoles of the campsite. Along the final stretch of road, there were countless places where it was easy to imagine an attacker lying in wait.

She turned in through the gate. On her way to the bungalow she linked up to the WiFi network but was still unable to access the forum.

Her laptop lay hidden under her quilt. Taking it out to try again, she saw she had received a Facebook message from Thea Kleibl.

The contents were succinct. She confirmed that her name had formerly been Thea Weber. *Why do you want to know?* she had added.

The message was only eight minutes old and, seeing that Thea Kleibl was logged on now, she wrote a hurried reply: *Have you recently been in contact with Astri Arctander?*

345

It only took a minute for the response to ping back: *Yes. Who are you?*

To avoid complications, Celia wrote back that she was an acquaintance of Astri's, currently in Palamós. *Astri is dead,* she went on. *I'm trying to find out how that came about. Why did she get in touch with you? Did it have to do with Bertine Franck?*

What happened to Astri Arctander? was the immediate question in return.

Celia located the link to the Norwegian online newspaper article in which there were photos from the discovery of Astri's body.

We don't know yet, she answered, attaching the link. *Some kind of accident. Looks as if she froze to death.*

Another message pinged back. Presumably she was looking at the Norwegian webpage. If nothing else, she would see Astri's name there and the picture taken as they lifted the stretcher over the high bank of snow.

Why did she contact you? Celia wrote again. *Was it to do with Bertine?*

This time it took longer for the answer to come. *Yes. Astri paid me a visit. Wanted to see the rucksack.*

Angling her head, Celia knitted her brows in consternation. She could not fathom anything about the rucksack or the visit.

She visited you? When was that? Why?

The answer and explanation slowly took shape. Messages bounced to and fro in a lengthy online conversation in which both wrote in clumsy English.

It emerged that Thea Kleibl had received a message from Astri asking if Thea knew Bertine Franck, who had been murdered in Palamós. It had taken twenty-four hours for Thea to see the message and, by the time she replied, Astri was already in the van en route to Norway. Two hours later she had been on her doorstep in Bonn.

Astri had shown an interest in the rucksacks in the picture of Thea and Bertine taken in Madrid and wondered if Bertine's rucksack had been returned after the murder. It had not. Astri wanted to know more about the rucksacks and asked if there were any other photos from their trip in which the rucksack was more clearly visible. Thea had produced an envelope of old photographs and told her that, in order to be real backpackers, they had each bought a rucksack of the same make prior to their trip. In order to tell them apart, they had sewn fabric letters on the top flap. A black B on Bertine's and a big red T on Thea's. Before she left, Astri had received a picture taken just before the two girls had set off, both of them standing with their backs to the camera, rucksacks bulging, as they looked back and waved.

Why was Astri so interested in the rucksacks? Celia asked.

The answer was swift: *She knew someone who had a rucksack exactly like it. With the same letter on it. Bertine's rucksack.*

Celia felt a surge of adrenaline rush through her body. Astri knew where Bertine Franck's rucksack was, twelve years after the murder.

She swallowed hard. It was not necessarily in the possession of the killer. Probably not. He would almost certainly have got rid of it. Tossed it away. Someone could have found it and started using it. It had been practically brand new. That was the most likely explanation. Or it could have ended up in a charity shop.

Who? she typed.

She wouldn't say, was the reply. *She was going to speak to the police first, but then I heard nothing more from her. And she didn't reply to my messages.*

There was a pause for a few moments before another message ticked in: *I've just had a message from a Norwegian police-woman. It might be about the same thing. I've answered but haven't heard anything further as yet.*

Celia leaned back in her bed. She had no idea how to respond now, but she would really have to get hold of Michelle.

78

Opening one of the bottles on the table, Wisting poured the contents into a glass and asked Maren if she would like some.

She shook her head.

They had been ushered into the same meeting room as last time but had been waiting for Comisario Álvarez for ten minutes now.

The water was tepid. It looked as if the bottles had been left out since the previous day.

'What kind of development could it be?' Maren asked. 'I didn't have the impression they were on the brink of any kind of breakthrough yesterday.'

Wisting agreed. 'But it must be something significant,' he said. 'Since they've brought us in to tell us about it.'

'Maybe it's something to do with the sweater,' Maren suggested. 'That they've found out where it comes from.'

Wisting's mobile buzzed. An unknown Norwegian number. He did not want to be talking to a journalist when the meeting began, so he switched his phone to silent mode.

They heard voices out in the corridor. It sounded as if someone was standing outside, winding up a conversation before entering the room.

Wisting looked at Maren, but she shook her head. She could not make out the Catalan words.

Then the door swung open.

Comisario Telmo Álvarez stepped in with Officer Malak Rendón at his side. Their faces wore the same serious expressions as at the previous day's meeting.

'Sorry for keeping you,' he said. 'I'm glad you could come.'

Wisting nodded expectantly as the two Catalan investigators sat down.

'We have some new information,' Álvarez went on. 'It's probably of no importance to your case, but we thought it right to let you know all the same.'

'We appreciate that, of course,' Wisting said, answering in the same slightly formal tone as the Catalan policeman. 'We would have asked for another meeting anyway,' he added. 'We have some fresh information for you also.'

'Good, let's come back to that, then,' Álvarez said.

He shuffled some papers as if reflecting on what was written on them, as if he were about to read a press statement.

'Today at 9.30 a.m., the provincial police in Girona arrested a fifty-six-year-old man, Ruben Montano, for the murder of the Swiss national, Lea Kranz, in Empuriabrava in 2014.'

Wisting found the page in his notebook where he had copied down Astri's alphabetical list of the unsolved murder cases. Lea Kranz was number three on that, and the only case in which a DNA profile had been secured.

'Ruben Montano lives in Figueres, about twenty kilometres from the spot where Lea Kranz was found,' Álvarez continued. 'As a matter of routine, we're checking to see if he has any connection to Palamós or any of the other discovery sites.'

'Figueres is one hour north of us,' Malak Rendón interjected. 'Near the French border. But so far everything points to this being an isolated incident.'

It seemed rather early to draw that conclusion, in Wisting's opinion, but he refrained from voicing that. Instead, he asked: 'What led to the arrest?'

Álvarez did not answer the question. 'The first interview has already been completed, and he has made a confession,' he said.

The affable smile was back beneath his moustache.

'Was it forensic evidence?' Wisting insisted. 'DNA?'

'A new witness came forward,' Rendón replied. 'A woman from the drugs scene the killer belongs to. The media attention in the last few days prompted her to get in touch. Ruben Montana confessed his guilt to her as long as three years ago. She had kept a recording of it. We expect to have the DNA results by Monday.'

Álvarez ran through the contents of the statement given by the drug user who had been charged. Wisting was not familiar with all the details in the case, but nothing emerged to make him doubt the confession. He crossed out the name Lea Kranz in his summary, cleared his throat and leafed through to a fresh page.

'A situation has arisen in our case that may be of great significance,' he said. 'Last night, we received the final report from the forensic examination of the service van belonging to Navis Servinauta. The vehicle Astri Arctander drove to Norway.'

He expressed himself in over-elaborate detail in order to be sure that the Catalan investigators were following what he said.

'In the analysis we had prioritized, Ruby Thompson's DNA was found on her hat in the glove compartment,' he said. 'In the later tests that were carried out, her profile was also found in blood samples taken from the cargo space.'

Having had a copy printed at the hotel reception, he now slid it across the table. It was in Norwegian, but he had used a yellow marker to highlight the four places where the same DNA sequence had been found.

'I'll have this translated into English and Spanish over the weekend,' he said.

Álvarez's gaze sharpened. 'That means the van may be the crime scene,' he said. 'Who had access to it in April?'

'For a start, her uncle,' Wisting replied. 'Bernard Arctander. But there are also other possibilities.'

He explained how the keys were kept. 'Besides, it's a company vehicle. Several other people could also have used it.'

Maren slid a sheet of paper across containing personal details. 'None of Astri's uncles has any kind of criminal record in Norway,' she said. 'But they've all spent lengthy periods of time in Spain.'

Malak Rendón picked up the piece of paper. Álvarez made a gesture with his hand, as if to tell her she should make some checks in the Spanish criminal records immediately.

'Where is the van now?' she asked.

Wisting could not hide how uncomfortable the question made him feel. 'We don't know,' he said, shifting in his seat. 'It was returned to Bernard Arctander on Thursday. He's probably on his way here with it.'

Álvarez kept a straight face as he asked: 'You mean the suspect and the vehicle are on their way to Spain?'

'He may already be here,' Wisting replied.

The two detectives opposite him exchanged a few words in Catalan. Short sentences accompanied by excited gesticulation. After the brief discussion, Rendón stood up and left the room.

'She's warning the team,' Álvarez said. 'They'll drive out to find the van. And the driver.'

The comisario also began to pack his things. 'Do you want to return to your hotel or would you rather wait here until we get this organized?' he asked. 'Then I can take you up to the major incident room once the operation is rolling?'

Wisting nodded. 'We can wait here,' he said.

79

'I've had a reply,' Maren told him.

They were still in the meeting room on the second floor of the police station, and Maren had opened her laptop.

'From Thea Kleibl,' she explained. 'She's met Astri Arctander.'

Wisting moved closer and read it for himself. The contents of the message were brief, clear and precise, as if the sender was experienced in writing reports. Following prior contact on Facebook, Astri had visited her at home in Bonn around nine p.m. on 1 December.

That tallied with the travel route and timeline Maren had worked out.

Astri had been interested in the rucksack belonging to Bertine Franck. It had appeared in a photo used by the press in connection with the murder. The rucksack was unique because it had the letter B sewn on the top flap. It had never been recovered after the murder. Astri had seen it before, apparently, though she had not said where.

Wisting raised his hand to his throat. He read the message one more time but had not finished before Maren changed the screen image. She tried to log into the online forum, but the website was still down. Instead she looked up Bertine Franck and found several versions of the photo taken on the bench in the Gran Via in Madrid. She clicked on to the one with the highest resolution, centred the segment on Bertine's rucksack and enlarged it as much as possible without the subject becoming blurred. Bertine was resting her right forearm on the bag. Her hand covered part of the top flap, but they could see the letter B.

'That makes sense,' Maren said. 'If the killer didn't get rid of Ruby Thompson's beanie, he may well have kept something from the other victims too.'

Wisting did not like the idea of a murderer who collected trophies, but the reality was that it had not been recovered after the homicide. Also, it had a very distinctive characteristic, the sewn-on letter B.

'This supports our suspicions about her uncle,' Maren said. 'Where else could Astri have come across a rucksack like that?'

Wisting agreed. It pointed to someone in the family. He tried to remember whether there had been any rucksacks in the apartment they had searched the day before but could not picture anything.

'Maybe the rucksack was also in the van when she drove to Norway,' Maren suggested. 'And the killer took it with him along with her laptop but overlooked the hat in the glove compartment?'

'Don't you think she would have shown it to Thea Kleibl if that was the case?' Wisting mused. 'To get confirmation from her that it was the same bag?'

Maren took the point. 'It could have been in the summer cabin, then,' she said. 'That could have been the reason she was going there.'

Wisting's phone buzzed again. This time it was Line calling.

'Hi,' he answered.

'Hi, Dad,' Line replied.

Her voice sounded strained, as if she was struggling to control it. 'I've been trying to phone you from the hospital,'

354

she said. 'It's Grandad. He's been taken to A&E. A heart attack.'

Wisting stood up.

'They say it's serious,' Line continued, her voice breaking. 'You have to come home.'

80

Username: Shelook

HTTP 404. The page you are searching for may have been removed, had its name changed or be temporarily unavailable because of network issues.

The man she had met at the entrance of the police station had looked like the Norwegian investigator. She could not recall his name and still could not access the forum.

On her first search for *Astri Arctander*, however, both his name and photo popped up. *William Wisting*. It was him. He had rushed out and clambered into a waiting police car.

Maybe he would be of more help than the police officer at the front desk. She had not had all the information she needed to fill out the necessary form. No date of birth, home address or address in Palamós for Michelle. Nor did she have her phone number, let alone the names of her parents and employer. Undoubtedly she could have found all these details in a Google search, but when the police-man eventually realized she was not the next of kin and had only known Michelle for twenty-four hours, he became dismissive.

She had used the newspaper article to explain the connec-tion between Michelle and the unsolved murders in an effort to convince him that Michelle could be in a vulnerable pos-ition. He did not seem to understand her concern, but in the end he had promised to contact the hotel.

The Norwegian policeman had met Michelle. He knew

the case and would be able to persuade the Catalan police to take her disappearance seriously.

Michelle had located his contact details on the Internet. She could do the same thing, or even simpler: she could just ask Thea Kleibl for the contact info for the Norwegian policewoman.

Celia had to smile to herself, knowing exactly how to capture her interest. After all, she had promised Yusuf Sleman that she would tell the police about his sweater, but hadn't specified which police force.

81

Maren felt the weight of responsibility on her shoulders. She was in the back seat of a surveillance car and had been tasked with single-handedly taking care of Norwegian interests in the investigation.

The vehicle was parked just under a hundred metres from the Navis Servinauta premises. They had a good view of all the motor traffic in and out of the fenced area, but so far everything had been extremely quiet. One of the Catalan detectives had gone up to the gate on foot but had not found anything worth reporting.

Maren grabbed the door handle. She wanted to go into the marine workshop to see for herself.

The driver was sceptical. 'You'll have to be quick,' he said. 'In case anything happens.'

'You'll be able to see me the whole time,' she assured him.

'Take this,' the officer in the passenger seat said, passing her a hand-held police radio.

Maren pressed the 'send' button and made sure she had contact with the communications unit inside the vehicle.

A boy on a skateboard turned and stared after her when she stepped out of the car. The wheels on the board clicked on the joints in the paving stones behind her.

The boat workshop was part of a maritime industrial area. Boats both old and new were stored high on huge steel racks. A vast workshop building was situated at the quayside. Maren walked some distance alongside a wire-mesh fence in order to get a better view. There was no activity inside.

She returned to the car. Surveillance had never been to her taste. She was far too impatient to simply sit waiting for something to happen. And strictly speaking, there was no reason to have three officers here.

Taking out her phone, she checked her email and messages. A Spanish woman had written to her. She was a friend of Michelle Norris, who ran the online forum, and was in Palamós to meet up with her. The previous evening they had come across new information about the sweater Ruby Thompson had been wearing when she was found. Today she had not been able to get in touch with Michelle. She was afraid something had happened but had been unable to enlist the help of the local police.

A phone rang in the front of the car. The man in the passenger seat answered. He had obviously received a message that took him aback. He turned to his colleague and said something in a quizzical tone to the caller, as if to confirm that he had heard correctly. Maren picked up the words *fuego* and *explosión* – fire and explosion.

The driver must have understood what it meant. He exclaimed wildly and flung out his hands angrily while his colleague continued on the phone. With a nod of the head, he received a message and rang off before turning to the driver and passing on the instructions.

'What's going on?' Maren asked.

The two men turned to face her. 'A vehicle fire,' said the man who had received the phone message.

'A fire?' Maren repeated.

The driver turned back and started the engine.

'Yesterday,' the other officer explained. 'The message came from the police in Germany. They were responding to the police bulletin. The vehicle caught fire on the autobahn outside Düsseldorf. It's completely burnt out.'

359

Maren slumped back in her seat.

'It was an old van,' the Catalan policeman went on. 'Probably badly maintained, and it's been driven hard in the last couple of weeks.' He shrugged. 'These things happen.'

'What about Bernard Arctander?' she asked. 'Where is he?'

'I didn't get any information on that.'

The driver executed a U-turn and headed back to the police station.

'Maybe the comisario will have more details for you when we go in,' he said.

82

His phone was about to run out of juice. Wisting had just plugged it into a socket behind the seats nearest the gate when Maren called. He had to sit hunched over to be able to talk while the phone was charging.

'Any news?' she asked.

'I just spoke to the hospital,' Wisting replied. 'His condition's unchanged. How are things with you? Have you found the van?'

He heard Maren sigh. 'Yes and no,' she said. 'The German police have reported that the van caught fire on the autobahn outside Düsseldorf. I have some photos. It's totally incinerated.'

Wisting's despairing gesture yanked the charger lead out of the phone.

'What about Bernard Arctander?' he asked, fumbling in his attempts to reconnect the cable.

'It's been confirmed that he was driving the van,' Maren told him. 'He's uninjured. Comisario Álvarez's team have spoken to the owner of the boat workshop. They had rental car insurance, so Bernard has picked up a Skoda Octavia. I have the registration number.'

'Rental car?' Wisting repeated, looking out at the runway. 'Surely the easiest thing would be to take a plane back to Norway?'

Maren agreed. 'The car's been flagged for surveillance here in Spain,' she said. 'I suppose Düsseldorf is halfway between Norway and Palamós. He could have gone in either direction.'

They fell silent for a moment, deep in thought.

'It occurred to me that you could ring him about the apartment keys,' Maren continued. 'Tell him you've arranged with his brother to hand them to him, but you had to go home unexpectedly. Find out what he says.'

Wisting glanced at the monitor beside the gate. He still had time to spare before boarding. 'I'll call you back,' he told Maren.

Bernard Arctander had both Norwegian and Spanish phone numbers. Wisting tried the Norwegian one first, but the call went straight to voicemail. The same happened with the Spanish number.

He tried both numbers again, with the same result.

The counter staff had arrived at the gate and the most eager of the passengers were lining up. Wisting was about to phone Maren to tell her she would have to try to get hold of Bernard herself but changed his mind at the last minute and called the eldest brother instead.

Walter Arctander answered immediately.

Wisting began by letting him know that a man had been charged with a murder in a small town north of Palamós, but the Catalan police did not believe it had any connection with Ruby Thompson's death.

'I'm phoning mostly to tell you I'm on my way home to Norway,' he said. 'I'm at the airport and should have spoken to Bernard about the apartment keys, but I can't reach him by phone.'

'No, there's been an accident,' Walter said. 'The van burst into flames. His phone went up with it.'

Wisting had to feign surprise. 'Is he OK?'

'He's fine, thanks. He noticed when it started to smoke so he managed to drive to a lay-by and get out before the fire took hold.'

'I tried his Spanish number as well,' Wisting said.

'That phone may be in the apartment down there, or else it was in the car too,' Walter replied. 'He called me from the breakdown recovery company.'

'How is he getting home?'

Walter sounded hesitant at first. 'Well, I spoke to him right after it had happened,' he explained. 'I don't think he'd thought that far ahead yet, but I expect he'll take a flight.'

'I see,' Wisting replied. 'My colleague is staying a few days longer in Spain. She's the one with the keys. I'll ask her to bring them back to Norway.'

They ended the conversation. The other passengers had started boarding the aircraft. Wisting phoned Maren and told her what he had learned.

'I think he's on his way here,' Maren said. 'He's eradicated all traces left in the van, but there could be other evidence down here he also needs to get rid of.'

Wisting unplugged the charger lead and coiled it up. 'I have to board now . . .' he began.

'There's one more thing,' Maren broke in. 'I got a message from the Spanish girl Michelle Norris is with down here. It seems she's vanished.'

'What do you mean?'

'She can't get hold of her and the website is down.'

'You have to go to Comisario Álvarez with that,' Wisting told her.

'They don't seem interested.'

Wisting walked towards the gate. 'Make them interested,' he said.

He stopped and let a businessman cut in ahead of him. 'Just one more thing,' he said.

'Yes?'

'Be careful.'

83

Username: Shelook

She turned the screen towards the Norwegian policewoman and showed her the pictures of the man in the blue sweater.

'I downloaded them before the website crashed,' she said.

That was not true, of course. She had downloaded them from Astria's cloud.

'His name's Yusuf Sleman,' she continued, going on to tell the policewoman about her meeting with him. 'After looking at the photos we met up with my cousin, Leo Pérez. He walked with her back to her hotel. That was the last time I saw her.'

Her words faded towards the end: her breath vibrated as it left her lungs, and it was difficult to breathe in again. She realized she was on the verge of some kind of panic attack and tensed her jaw muscles in an effort to control her anxiety.

The Norwegian investigator did not betray her feelings at all. Instead, she seemed engrossed in the photographs.

Maren Dokken.

Only a few years older than she was, but already an investigator. In a case like this.

'I'm starting Police College next year,' she blurted out.

Celia had no idea why she said that. Maybe to forge a bond or emphasize that she was not a complete amateur.

'I don't understand why they have to wait twenty-four hours before starting to investigate,' she went on. 'The first few hours are the most critical when someone goes missing.'

'I've spoken to the top brass,' the Norwegian woman explained again. 'They say they're dealing with it.'

'How will they do that?' Celia asked. Her breathing was still laboured. 'What does it mean? What are they doing, actually?'

'They've checked her hotel room,' Maren reminded her. 'Now it's a matter of gathering information to find out where else they should search.'

Celia stood up and walked to the balcony door for a lungful of fresh air. A night moth was tapping on the globe lamp on the wall. From the street below, she could hear snatches of cheerful conversation.

Maren sat down at her own laptop. 'Could you send me the photos of the blue sweater?' she asked. 'It's been a hot topic for the police here. I have to let them know.'

Celia remained on her feet, crossing her arms to hide her trembling.

The Norwegian woman got to her feet. 'Are you OK?' she asked.

'Yes, I'm fine,' Celia assured her, looking away. 'It's just too many thoughts all at once.'

Maren approached her. 'It's getting late,' she said, placing a hand on her shoulder. 'Would you like to sleep here tonight?'

Celia knew she did not like the idea of going back to the campsite.

'Wisting has only slept on one side of the bed,' the Norwegian policewoman went on. 'The room's paid for another two nights.'

Celia glanced at the bed. 'Isn't this your room?' she asked.

'I've got a smaller room a couple of floors below this one,' Maren replied. 'I thought we could use this one as a meeting room, now that Wisting has gone. But it's OK for you to stay here, and we can hook up again in the morning. Maybe we'll know more by then.'

Celia was about to accept with thanks when Maren moved to the door. 'I'll go down to reception and get you a toothbrush,' she said. 'Then you can stay here until we know what's going on.'

84

The squalling snow scudded sideways in front of the car, buffeting the bonnet. He could see the rear lights of a vehicle a few hundred metres ahead of him and drove in its tyre tracks. Apart from that, the road was deserted.

After a couple of hours behind the wheel, he turned off from the motorway, wondering whether it would be at all possible to speak to anyone at this time of night. The plane had circled above the airport for twenty minutes before the runway was cleared, and it had taken more time than usual to collect his luggage. Now it was almost two a.m. and most of the lights in the huge hospital building were off.

He found his way up to the coronary care unit, well aware that this was outside regular visiting hours.

In the corridor, he met a night-duty nurse and introduced himself in hushed tones. 'I've come straight from abroad,' he said. 'My father was admitted here yesterday. Roald Wisting?'

The nurse nodded sympathetically. 'He's had a massive obstruction in one of the coronary arteries,' she explained, glancing at the clock on the wall. 'He was operated on this morning and has had a new blood vessel inserted. A successful bypass operation.'

'So everything went well?' Wisting asked.

The answer was a smile. 'He's in the intensive care unit,' she replied. 'Nothing unusual has been reported.'

'Can I see him?'

'It's better if you wait till tomorrow. He'll be moved to a

regular ward in the morning, but he'll stay in hospital until Christmas. To begin with, he'll need plenty of quiet and rest, so we don't allow lengthy visits or too many visitors.'

'I understand,' Wisting replied.

'Sometime after half past one,' the nurse told him. 'But I'll make sure he gets the message that you've been here and you're coming back.'

Wisting thanked her and headed out to his car, tapping in a message to Line before he drove off. She phoned him back at once.

'I don't know much more than I've told you,' he said.

'What are they saying about the prognosis?' she asked.

'That I don't know,' he answered. 'But I understood everything had gone well. Maybe I can speak to the doctor tomorrow.'

'So everything's going to be OK?' she pressed him.

'They said he'd be home by Christmas,' Wisting told her, adding, in an effort to cheer her up: 'I've bought him an iPad. It's already all set up, so it'll be perfect for him.'

Line managed to force out a chuckle before they ended the call.

She must have cleared the snow from the driveway and steps. Fresh snow had fallen since then, but not enough to prevent him from driving up in front of the house.

His travel bag was on the back seat, with the photo album from the Arctanders' summer cabin beside it. He took both inside with him, setting down the bag in the hallway and placing the album on the kitchen table. He stood there, browsing through it. Twenty years of summer memories. He could not see that it contained anything other than pictures from happy times, but then he knew that this was an edited version. Something like Instagram and other social media, where only the brightest sides of life were on display.

He stayed on his feet and looked at pictures from the summer of 2009. On the left page, there was a group of family members on board a boat making its way out into the fjord. On the right-hand page, they had built a cairn on a mountaintop. The boat trip was dated 5 July, but the mountain trek was undated, though obviously not the same day. Both the clothing and the weather were different. He leafed back and forth again. Other occasions were documented on double pages. The transition from the boat trip and the mountain trek was sudden and made him think that a page of the album may have been torn out. The stiff cardboard page was perforated on one side and attached to rings, like in a ring binder. It was easy to remove pages or add in more.

The summer of 2009 was fifteen years after Vibeke Hassel had been excised from the album, so something else must have been deleted from the Arctanders' family history.

He thumbed through the entire album again, studying every occasion depicted, and found yet another point where a page seemed to be missing. From the summer of 2011.

So, in two places in the album, a page had been torn out.

A sudden noise made him look up. The weight of snow on the roof was making the house creak. The kitchen clock showed quarter past three.

The photo album provided no more answers. He shut it but decided to take it to Gerd Arctander the next day and ask her about the missing pages. He could do that before visiting hour at the hospital.

The bed was exactly as he had left it. A solitary quilt curled up on one side.

His body could find no rest when he lay down. For the first couple of hours he dozed fitfully, but by the crack of dawn he finally managed to catch some proper sleep. He did not awake until the phone rang. He checked it and saw that

Maren Dokken was calling and the time was twenty past eight, before he answered.

'They've taken out an arrest warrant for Bernard Arctander,' she said.

Wisting swung his legs out of bed and asked her to explain.

'I've spoken to Officer Rendón,' Maren told him. 'The Catalan police are charging Bernard with the murder of Ruby Thompson. He's listed as a wanted man internationally. She phoned me to get the keys for the apartment. They're going to search it and the boat workshop.'

Wisting got up. They had given the Catalan police what they needed to bring charges against Bernard Arctander. The victim's DNA profile in a vehicle he used.

'They want to be first,' he said.

'What do you mean?'

'They want to arrest him before we do,' Wisting clarified. 'If we succeed in building a murder charge in *our* case, they'd have to wait until the case has gone through the Norwegian justice system before there could be a trial in a Catalan court.'

'And now we're the ones who have to wait?' Maren asked.

'That depends on where he's apprehended,' Wisting replied. 'If he's taken into custody in Norway, the Norwegian case will take priority.'

'What if he's arrested in Germany, or some other country?'

Wisting headed into the bathroom and looked at himself in the mirror. 'All other countries will hand him over to Spain,' he answered, running his hand over his chin. 'What about Michelle?' he asked. 'Has anyone heard anything from her?'

'No,' Maren told him. 'Celia Pérez is here at the hotel. She's staying in your room. I haven't spoken to her this morning as yet.'

'What does Officer Rendón say?'

'That they're working on it, but I'm not so sure. After all, we saw how they dealt with it when Astri was reported missing.'

'I can give Comisario Álvarez a call,' Wisting suggested.

'That would be a good idea,' Maren replied. 'What should I be doing while I'm down here?'

'I'll speak to the public prosecutor to see how you should tackle things,' Wisting said. 'In the meantime you should do what you can to be included in the searches at the boatyard.'

Maren was silent for a few moments. 'It's my fault,' she said.

'What do you mean?'

'Michelle Norris found out where the blue sweater came from,' Maren replied.

Wisting listened as she related the story of how Ruby Thompson had probably stolen the garment from a clothes-line after the housebreaking spree, a short time before she was attacked.

'I gave them the information last night,' she finished off. 'The hairs on the sweater belong to Yusuf Sleman. It meant they could eliminate that DNA sample from the case. There was no longer anything to prevent them from charging Bernard Arctander.'

'You did the only right thing,' Wisting reassured her. 'But now they owe you a favour. They have to let you join the search and let you talk to the other employees. Someone who can tell us more about Bernard Arctander. We know nothing about him.'

'OK, then,' Maren said.

Wisting felt she was holding something back. 'What is it?' he asked.

'I don't know, but I suspect there's more to it. It feels as if they're keeping something back from me. I think they have information they're not keen to share. At least, not with me.'

'You're probably right,' Wisting said. 'Just make sure you stick close to them. Let them understand that locking us out will make the case more difficult for them. After all, it was our lab that produced the evidence.'

They brought their conversation to a close. Wisting completed his morning ablutions, dwelling on whether he had placed too much responsibility on Maren. But there had been no alternative. Everything would happen quickly now, and Maren would be on the spot as events unfolded.

He moved into the kitchen and inserted a capsule into the coffee machine before phoning the chief Catalan investigator. It rang for a long time, and he opened the fridge as he waited for an answer. The rest of Ellinor's cake still sat on the middle shelf. He took it out and tossed it into the rubbish bin under the sink. The phone rang out while he rinsed the plate.

The milk had gone out of date. He ate a large portion of breakfast cereal with nuts and dried fruit. Afterwards he made another unsuccessful attempt to get hold of Comisario Álvarez before going outside to shovel snow. While he was clearing away the snow, he thought of Vibeke Hassel and the part of her farewell letter addressed to her younger sister. When he had finished, he went inside and phoned her.

'This is Heidi Hassel,' she answered.

Her voice was clear and distinct, and sounded authoritative.

Wisting explained who he was. 'I'm investigating the death of Astri Arctander,' he began, and she confirmed that she was familiar with what had taken place.

'But I'm fifteen years older than her, and Astri was only little at the time we had a cabin in Stavern,' she said. 'It was her uncles I knew. I don't know anything about Astri.'

'I understand that,' Wisting replied. 'I'm calling because I'd like to speak to an outsider with knowledge of the Arctander family.'

He realized immediately that this made her feel uneasy.

'Dysfunctional,' she commented. 'Maybe they don't appear to be so, but there was something abnormal about the whole clan. I understand more now than I did then. I'm a trained child welfare officer and know how important it is to set healthy boundaries. The Arctander brothers never experienced that. Their mother controlled everything but never set boundaries. Just explained things away and smoothed things over whenever they did anything wrong.'

'It's my understanding that your sister was Henrik Arctander's girlfriend?'

Heidi Hassel hesitated before answering. 'You do know what happened to her?' she asked.

'I know she's no longer alive,' Wisting replied. 'I've read the police report on her death.'

'I mean what happened before that?' Heidi said. 'What happened in Stavern.'

'I've only heard the Arctander family's account,' Wisting said.

Heidi Hassel's voice took on a sarcastic tone. 'Exactly,' she said. 'It's a long story, but I'll give you the short version.'

The beginning of the tale was the same as he had heard from the Arctanders. A sexually transmitted disease, but it was Henrik who had infected Vibeke Hassel, and not the other way around.

'Vibeke had not been involved with anyone else for a long time,' her sister explained. 'But that's really immaterial. It was the other business that destroyed everything.'

Wisting had taken out a pen and was already jotting down notes.

What had destroyed everything had happened one even-ing when Henrik and Bernard were left alone in the cabin. Vibeke was there and Bernard had a visit from a girl of the same age. They all got drunk, especially Vibeke. Bernard and his girlfriend had quarrelled, so she had left.

'During the night, Vibeke woke up to find Bernard having sex with her,' her sister said.

Wisting asked her to say more about what had happened.

'She woke when he was pushing a boccia ball up into her, but other things had happened too. She was totally out of it when she fell asleep, so he must have been inside her without her knowing anything about it. Raped her – and it happened after she was infected, but before she knew about it herself. Bernard brought the disease upon himself. That was the only punishment he got.'

Wisting had to take time to write down everything he had now discovered.

'It wasn't reported?' he asked.

'It was a different era,' Heidi Hassel replied. 'At that time, you needed to have more credible evidence if you reported a rape. Mum and Dad spoke to a lawyer they knew but were advised to drop it. Vibeke would not emerge unscathed from such a case. She would be accused of having loose morals, of having had sex with both brothers and infecting them both with chlamydia. And there was no proof of the opposite. It was a lost cause.'

Wisting sighed audibly. The rape had taken place in the summer cabin at Eidsten. In his own police district. All the same, he had to admit it would probably have been shelved.

'Vibeke was already fragile,' Heidi continued. 'She had her own demons, but this came on top of everything else. In the end it became too much for her to bear.'

The conversation lasted for another half-hour before

Wisting put down his pen and thanked Heidi Hassel for sharing this information with him. Her statement was full of rancour, coloured by the loss of her sister, but Wisting believed her. He had no reason not to. Two points stood out as being of central significance. Bernard Arctander had committed rape before, and from experience he would protect himself from infection in any other rapes. This could explain why there was no sperm or DNA found in any of the victims along the Spanish coast.

He opened the photo album again and flipped through it to a random page where Bernard Arctander was lying on a sunbed. A sun-bronzed man with a broad smile.

The picture revealed nothing about the man lying there, but there was now an abundance of evidence pointing towards him.

85

Username: Shelook

No word had come from Michelle overnight.

Celia checked the local online newspapers, mainly to see if there were any reports of an accident or anything else to explain what had happened to her friend. She got no further than the front page of the *Diari di Girona*. The headline news was that a man had been arrested for a murder in Empuria-brava in 2014.

Lea Kranz from Switzerland, one of the victims on Apo-pheniaX's list.

Celia skimmed through the story. There had been a confession. A fifty-six-year-old man from the local region. The police were tight-lipped apart from that and would not comment on whether he would be investigated in connection with the other unsolved murders in the area.

She read the story one more time. The arrest was covered in several other online newspapers, but no further details emerged. If only the website had been up and running, she would have had someone to discuss this with. She made yet another attempt, but this resulted in the same error message.

There was a knock at the hotel-room door.

Celia pushed out her chair and tightened the belt on her dressing gown. It had lain unused in the bathroom. She had slept badly, but that was not because of the bed or the room. An unfamiliar anxiety had weighed down her thoughts and kept her awake.

She opened the door a chink to find the Norwegian police-woman there with a paper cup in each hand.

Celia held the door wide and let her in.

'I brought you some coffee,' Maren said, proffering one of the cups. 'If an Americano's OK with you?'

Celia accepted it with thanks. 'They've arrested a man for Lea Kranz's murder,' she said, gesturing towards the laptop on the desk. 'Did you know that?'

'We had a briefing yesterday,' Maren replied. 'It probably has nothing to do with Ruby Thompson or the other cases.'

'Have you spoken to them today?'

'Yes, I'm going to the police station at half past nine. There's been a development, in a different direction. I can't say very much about it.'

'What about Michelle?' Celia asked. 'Did they tell you anything about her?'

Maren looked across at the laptop. 'You still haven't heard from her?' she asked.

'No,' Celia replied. 'I got hold of Leo last night. We're meeting at her hotel later. Maybe someone else will be working there today who can tell us more.'

'Wisting is going to phone Comisario Álvarez,' Maren said. 'That will put some pressure on them, but there's a lot going on just now.' She took a sip of her coffee. 'I've spoken to the reception staff,' she went on. 'They know you're staying here. You can have some breakfast down in the restaurant.'

Celia thanked her but was not hungry.

'I really have to get going now,' the Norwegian police-woman said. 'Is that OK?'

'Yes,' Celia assured her. 'I'm meeting Leo anyway.'

Maren moved to the door and touched the handle, as if reluctant to leave her. 'I'll call you if there's any news,' she promised.

The door slid shut behind her as Celia sipped some coffee before heading for a shower. Her short hairstyle needed little attention, but she wished she had a change of clothes and a few toiletries. Sometime today she would have to go to the campsite, but it was difficult to make other plans as long as she was in the dark about Michelle.

On her way out she took another cup of coffee from the breakfast room. She should really have worn sunglasses in the dazzling sunlight, but they too were in the bungalow.

The streets down towards the harbour area were Sunday quiet, and on the eastern side of town, church bells were ringing.

She was outside the Trias Hotel ten minutes before the appointed time. Leo was nowhere to be seen but, unwilling to wait, she ventured inside.

It was a different receptionist from the day before.

'I left a note here for my friend,' Celia said. 'Michelle Norris. Has she been back?'

The man shook his head.

'I've spoken to the police,' she went on. 'She's missing.'

'The police have been here,' he told her. 'They searched her room and took her computer. I don't know anything more than that.'

Celia swallowed hard as a mixture of feelings churned within her. It was reassuring to know that the police had launched an investigation, but the knowledge that her laptop had been left in her room meant that Michelle had not disappeared of her own volition. She would not have gone anywhere without it.

'Did they say anything?' was all she could bring herself to ask.

'I really don't know anything else,' the receptionist reiterated.

Celia thanked him and went back outside again. She felt the salt tang of the sea on her face. A large bird took off from a wall on the other side of the street. Celia crossed the road and gazed down into the dark waters, where a plastic bottle and other rubbish drifted around.

The perimeter of the seafront was not high enough to prevent anyone from falling in. In some places the saltwater had caused the concrete to crumble, making the barrier even lower.

She kept a lookout eastwards along the shore. The sun glittered on the waves. At the nearest bar, a man was setting out deckchairs and parasols. Further away, children were playing.

The marina lay in the opposite direction. Masts bobbed on the waves along the pontoons. A large yacht with an older couple aboard was on its way out to sea. The reflection of the waves flickered on the hull.

Beside one of the innermost pillars of the pier, something was floating in the water. Something that only just broke the surface of the waves.

Celia began to walk towards the harbour entrance. She turned, looked again for Leo and walked on. Before she had reached it, whatever had been drifting in the water had been swept underneath the pier. She lay on her stomach and peered down at it. She could hear the water gurgle but at first saw nothing. Then she caught sight of it. A deflated swimming ring.

Feeling foolish, she was about to scramble up again when she spotted something else. Further down in the water, something reddish-brown was swaying. Its shape was impossible to make out, and it was drifting away from her.

She crossed to the other side of the pier. The sunlight made it difficult to see anything, but she eventually realized it was a stinging jellyfish. For a second she had thought it was Michelle's head and the tentacles were her red hair.

A car horn sounded behind her. It was Leo, standing beside a rusty old delivery van, waving at her.

Celia approached him.

'Have you heard from her?' he asked.

Celia shook her head and told him what she had found out from the receptionist.

'Where was it you saw her last?' she demanded.

Leo pointed out the spot where he had parted from her. The street corner was fifty metres from the hotel entrance. There were no CCTV cameras nearby.

She turned back towards the sea. A camera was attached to a pole at the marina entrance, but it did not pick up anything of what happened in the street.

Leo lit a cigarette. 'So what do we do now?' he asked.

'I need some photos for a missing-person notice,' Celia replied. 'I'll post a message on Facebook and an advert with her details on it. Ask if anyone has seen her or has any information.'

Leon slouched against the van as she took a photo of the uninspiring hotel entrance.

'My laptop's at the hotel,' she said when she had finished.

'Hotel?' Leo asked. 'Aren't you staying at the campsite?'

Celia explained about the Norwegian police detectives and how she had been given permission to stay at their hotel.

'Fine,' Leo said, stubbing out his cigarette. 'Then I'll drive you there. Hop in.'

86

At 10.45 a.m., the Catalan investigators conducted a coordinated operation. One team moved in on the Arctander family apartment at the same time as another team entered the marine workshop. Maren had been granted permission to accompany the second team as an observer, but no one paid any attention to her. All the dialogue was in Catalan and she received no explanation of any kind.

From the initial messages on the police radio, she understood the apartment was empty. The same applied to the workshop.

The owner of the marine workshop had been picked up at his home address half an hour earlier to give them the necessary access. She heard that he had spoken to Bernard Arctander after his works van had gone up in flames, but he did not know where he was now.

Four workers were employed in the firm in addition to seasonal hired hands. The Norwegian worked part-time. He was seldom in the workshop but travelled around the various marinas along the coast to carry out servicing or retrofit electronic equipment – GPS chart plotters, radar, echo sounders, autopilots, navigation equipment, music systems, intercoms and other electronic gear.

At the far end of the premises, Bernard Arctander had his own combined electronics workshop and office. It was a cramped space and Maren had to stand outside in the corridor with the owner, watching through the doorway as two Catalan investigators ransacked the drawers and cupboards

381

and shelves. A few ring binders were labelled with various years, going back ten years in time, perhaps fulfilling a legal requirement for the retention of receipts.

The older of the two police officers had found something in a folder and asked the owner about it. Maren understood it had something to do with the company van. The folder included the purchase contract and other documentation. From what was said, Maren picked up that the van had been bought new in 2009. In the past five years, Bernard Arctander had been almost the only person to use it.

They talked about theft. She learned that a *neboda* had gone off with the van. The owner pointed to the computer on the desk and said something about *vigilância* while making extravagant gestures with his hands.

Maren was unsure whether she had followed correctly and had to ask the man beside her. In a mixture of English and Spanish, he explained that the works van had been equipped with the same kind of tracking device that Bernard Arctander installed in boats in case of theft. If he had known the van was missing, he could have used the Internet to find out where it was.

The owner appreciated Maren's interest. He took a step into the room and grabbed a brochure with details of the system. It was in Spanish and Catalan, but she understood how it worked. The vehicle or boat could be located at all times via the GPS system. It was also possible to receive an alert as soon as the tracking device was on the move or if it travelled outside a geographically defined area.

'Nowadays this is integral in most new boats, but we still retrofit them on older models,' he explained.

'Does this mean that Bernard Arctander could have received a warning by phone when his niece took the van?' Maren asked.

'If that's how the system was set up, then yes,' the owner confirmed. 'He could have followed her route all the way.'

One of the investigators inside the office gave a shout. He held an opened ring binder and was leafing back and forth through several of the documents. His colleague moved towards him. Words were exchanged so rapidly that Maren found it difficult to work out what it was all about. She moved into the room to find out.

The detective was flipping through from one document that looked like a guarantee certificate for a chart plotter, to another concerning the installation of a satellite telephone. The subsequent pages contained an assortment of documentation for similar work. The two men were talking about times and places. The jobs had been done on 3 and 4 June, the previous year. All the customers had addresses in Torrevieja, suggesting that Bernard Arctander had amassed a number of jobs in the same area before driving down there. Maren knew what it was about before the older investigator mentioned her name. Lucia Martinez. She had been murdered in Torrevieja while Bernard Arctander had been there.

Maren had not believed that the Catalan investigators had put any faith in the theory that one and the same person was behind several of the unsolved cases, but they were obviously following this lead.

The man who made the discovery took out the ring binder marked 2013. Maren had the list of victims in her head and realized he was thumbing through to the time when the Belgian Renate Heitmann had been killed in Blanes.

He did not detect the same coincidence, but neither did he find any documentation to prove that Bernard Arctander had been working elsewhere at that time. In other words, his work did not give him an alibi.

The other investigator drew out an older binder to check

the contents for the time of the murder of Valeria Espinosa Díaz in 2011, but shook his head. The same applied to the murder of Carlota Belén del Cármen in Barcelona. The collection of documents did not go further back than that.

Maren crossed to the wall shelf and placed two fingers on the ring binder for the year the Danish girl, Lone Sand, was murdered in France. 'May I?' she asked.

The older investigator gave her a brief nod.

Maren took out the binder and leafed through to the month of June. A shudder ran from her diaphragm to her chest when she found papers confirming that Bernard Arctander had been in a French marina fixing a major fault in the navigation system on a Spanish offshore sailing boat the day before Lone Sand was killed.

Without bothering to ask, she simply took out her mobile and snapped a photo. Then she walked down the corridor again to call Wisting.

87

The snow was cleared from the courtyard in front of Gerd Arctander's house, but no cars were parked there. Everything suggested she was at home alone.

Wisting tucked the photo album under his arm and strode up to the entrance. He had to wait for almost a minute before the door opened. Although Gerd Arctander passed comment on his unannounced visit, she showed him into the same room where they had sat last time.

'You're back already, then?' she said when they sat down.

'I arrived yesterday,' Wisting replied.

He told her about the investigation in Palamós but not why he had been compelled to return so suddenly.

'Has Bernard come back?' he asked her.

The old woman shook her head and explained that she did not know when he was coming either. 'I don't understand why there was such a rush to take that van back down again,' she said. 'It would have gone on fire anyway, but he could have waited.'

'At least he was uninjured,' Wisting commented.

He opened the photo album that now lay on the table between them. 'It looks as if a few pages are missing,' he said, leafing through to the double-page spread with the boat trip on one side and the mountain trek on the other.

Gerd Arctander drew the album towards her and turned it around to take a look.

'That's Salsås,' she said, pointing at the photo in which they were building a cairn.

Her eyes shifted, as if searching for something. Then she flipped back and forth through the pages before deciding that Wisting was right.

'Do you know what's become of the other photographs?' he asked.

'No,' Gerd answered, appearing irritated that anyone had taken such a liberty.

'Do you recall what was in the pictures, then?'

'They were photos taken on excursions, nothing other than that.'

'Can you remember who was in them?'

Gerd Arctander leaned over the album again and peered at the photos. 'No one apart from the people you already see,' she replied.

Wisting showed the other point where a page was missing. Gerd gave a discouraged sigh.

'Have you saved the negatives?' Wisting asked.

'Yes, but they're not here,' Gerd told him. 'If no one has thrown them out, they'll be at Sommerro.'

She thumbed through the album again before continuing: 'I had the photos developed at Solberg's in Larvik. That shop is no longer there. Now all photos are digital. No one keeps photo albums any more.'

'So the negatives are in the summer cabin?' Wisting pressed her.

'I collected all that stuff in a drawer in the writing desk, up in the big bedroom,' Gerd replied. 'But they're not there now. Henrik put everything into boxes and stowed them in the annexe when he was redecorating.'

Wisting pictured the small building under the pine trees.

Gerd Arctander closed the photo album, pulling it towards her and placing her forearm across it, as if to make it clear that she intended to keep it.

'I have another photo I'd like you to look at,' Wisting said.

He produced his mobile, which contained an image of a segment of Bertine Franck's rucksack. 'Do you recognize this rucksack?' he asked, showing her the photo.

The old woman squinted at the screen. 'Where did you get that?' she asked.

Wisting sensed she thought this was some kind of test and she had to be careful how she answered.

'From Spain,' he replied.

Gerd took her time giving this some thought. 'It's Bernard's,' she said. 'You can see the B on the top flap.' She pointed at the screen.

'Do you know where he got it from, or where it is now?'

'You'd have to ask Bernard that.'

Wisting reclaimed his phone. 'I'll do that,' he replied, pushing his chair back from the table. 'I won't detain you any longer.'

If the hospital did not have bad news for him, he would have time to drive out to the summer cabin before dark.

The snow on the steps whirled in when Gerd Arctander opened the front door. As soon as he was outside, the door shut firmly behind him.

The wind had picked up in the short time he had been indoors, and hard snow pellets stung his face.

Wisting pulled his lapels together at the neck and jogged to his car, just as a BMW turned into the yard. The rigid wheels skidded in the snow before the vehicle came to a complete standstill. Walter Arctander gave him a nod and stepped out.

'You've been visiting Mother, I see,' he said, slamming the car door behind him.

'I was returning the photo album,' Wisting replied.

Walter locked the car with a click of the key. 'She'd appreciate that,' he said. 'Is there any news?'

Wisting waited beside his car. 'No,' he answered. 'Has Bernard come home yet?'

Arctander shook his head. 'I haven't heard from him,' he said, hovering hesitantly, as if making up his mind to say something. 'Is there something I should know about Bernard?' he asked in the end.

Wisting tried to look him in the eye, but the driving snow made that difficult. 'There's something I have to ask him about,' Wisting said.

'Have you spoken to Mother about him?' Arctander asked.

Wisting said he had.

'I'll have to go in,' Arctander said, moving towards the front door, but he turned and retraced a few steps towards Wisting.

'Bernard has a special place in Mother's heart,' he said. 'Always has had. I was called after our father's father. Bernard is the youngest and called after Mother's father. That made him special, for her.'

Wisting gazed at him, wondering whether the man was trying to tell him something.

'If Bernard has done something wrong, she wouldn't let you know,' he said. 'She never has.'

'What has Bernard done?' Wisting asked him.

Walter stood with his lips clamped together, as snowflakes speckled his eyebrows.

'A lot,' he said.

The door behind him opened, and Gerd Arctander stood in the doorway, arms crossed.

'Walter!' she called out through the wind and snow. 'Are you coming in?'

Walter stood with his eyes fixed on Wisting, as if seeking answers. 'But Astri was his niece,' were his parting words.

His mother shouted again. Walter turned on his heel and trudged towards the entrance.

Wisting waited until the door was shut before getting into his car, reversing out from the yard and driving slowly away.

The de-icing salt had melted most of the snow on the motorway. Wet slush splashed through the wheel arches as soon as he deviated from the tracks left by other motorists.

The car radio was on a station playing music from the fifties, sixties and seventies. Wisting switched it off. His thoughts alternated between his father in hospital and a hardening suspicion pointing straight at Bernard Arctander.

He had worked as a police officer for nearly forty years, most of these in CID. It was only seldom that a single scrap of information led to a breakthrough or a solution, or you arrived at a turning point that made everything clear. That was not how things stood now either. Major, complicated cases rolled slowly forward. They gradually took shape and direction before eventually narrowing down to a single perpetrator. Always, something pivotal turned up towards the end that suddenly forced the entire case to change course.

His phone buzzed. It was Maren. 'We've finished at the boat workshop,' she said. 'Everything's pointing to Bernard Arctander now.'

She explained how documentation had been found linking Bernard in time and place to another two of the murders.

Wisting told her about the missing photos from the album. 'I think the rucksack features in those photographs,' he said. 'The negatives are somewhere at the summer cabin. I'll go out there and get them. At any rate, Gerd Arctander confirmed that the rucksack belongs to Bernard.'

'That links him to Bertine Franck's murder,' Maren said. 'She was found with pebbles in her vagina. Two other victims were found in the same state. Carlota and Valeria. That

389

connects Bernard to those cases as well. The investigators down here already believed there was a connection.'

Spray from the car in front splattered across the windscreen. Wisting moved out to overtake as Maren added new leads to support this suspicion.

He liked her enthusiasm and thought he could recognize something from the beginning of his own career in the police force. Her experience was still limited but she had a good grasp of what investigation was all about. Also, she had shouldered responsibility when required, when he had been forced to leave.

'How's your father doing?' she asked all of a sudden.

'I'm on my way to the hospital now, but I think he's doing well,' Wisting replied. 'What about you? What are you going to do now?'

'I'm meeting Comisario Álvarez tomorrow,' Maren replied. 'Before that, there's not so much I can do. Not officially, at least.'

The answer invited another question: 'And unofficially?'

'I'll be with Celia. She's sketched out the route Ruby Thompson was probably walking when she was attacked. It goes through a deserted building site with half-finished houses. She wants to see if we can find anything there, maybe something the killer threw away. She also has a list of all the items that were stolen that night. No one knows what happened to them.'

Wisting nodded in satisfaction. The chances of identifying a crime scene were minuscule, but it was a good plan.

'Just be careful,' he said.

Maren was quick to laugh this off. 'You've already said that,' she told him, with a chuckle.

88

Michelle looked at the note with the message to phone Celia. Automatically, she fumbled for her mobile in her pocket, but of course it was not there. The police had taken both her phone and laptop. She would have to make the call from her room.

The man behind the reception desk wore a sceptical expression. She took her key and walked to the lift. Feeling grubby, she was aware of her own body odour as the lift rattled up through the floors. Her hair was lank and greasy, and her skin felt sweaty.

The lift stopped with a shudder and the doors slid open. Her room was at the end of the corridor.

The police had searched it. Her suitcase had been emptied and all her clothes lay scattered on the bed. Her bag was lying on the floor. It had been rummaged through, but the contents had been replaced. Her passport was also there. They had not taken that. She would be able to go home.

She looked around. There was no phone in the room, neither on the bedside table nor on the desk. Most of all she wanted to take a long, hot shower, but instead she went back down to reception. On a small table displaying an array of tourist brochures, there was a phone she could use.

It took a long time for Celia to answer. Her voice faltered when she heard the Spanish woman at the other end of the line.

'Michelle? Is that you?' she asked. 'Where the hell are you?'

Although they did not know each other well, there was something reassuring about hearing her speak all the same.

'Yes, it's me,' Michelle replied, 'I'm back at my hotel.'

Tears welled up in her eyes. She brushed them away, aware that the emotional reaction would come now. Her body began to shake and she struggled to breathe.

'I was arrested,' she managed to blurt out.

'Arrested?'

Michelle took a deep breath and gathered her wits. 'The police picked me up at the hotel yesterday morning.'

'But why on earth?'

'Because of the website.' Her chest felt tight again and she had to gasp for breath. 'They said it was illegal,' she croaked. 'They've taken my phone and my computer.'

'But . . .' Celia began. 'They can't just . . .' She broke off. 'What room are you in?'

Michelle clutched her head, forcing herself to think. 'Room 412,' she finally came up with.

'Stay there,' Celia told her. 'I'm on my way. There's a lot going on now. I'll tell you everything.'

89

The temperature had dropped and the wind had picked up, skimming the tops off the banks of snow left by the snow-plough and piling these into snowdrifts at either side of the road.

Wisting had both hands on the wheel. He had not been prepared for his meeting with his father. Not as he was now. The nurses had assured him he was in good shape, but he was weaker and more exhausted than Wisting had antici-pated. There were dark shadows under his eyes and his cheeks were sunken. He seemed apathetic, and his voice was full of complaint. Wisting had tried to cheer him up, but it had been difficult and it was almost a relief when one of the nurses came in and said it was time to go. He had left the ward with a dispirited sense of helplessness. The nurse had told him there was nothing to suggest his father would fail to make a full recovery. By the next day they would see an improvement, she said.

He turned off from the motorway in the direction of Lar-vik. His phone buzzed and he saw it was Ellinor. Maybe she had heard about his father's heart attack and had learned that he had come home. When he answered, he realized she had not. Her voice was as animated as ever.

'How are things with you?' she asked.

He told her what had happened, that his father was ill and he had flown home. 'But he seems to be doing OK,' he added.

Ellinor expressed her sympathy and concern. 'Was it sud-den?' she asked.

'No warning at all,' Wisting replied.

'What about you?' she went on. 'How are you?'

He appreciated her thoughtfulness. His anxiety about his father's illness was preying on his mind.

'You're welcome to drop in here,' Ellinor suggested near the end of their conversation. 'If you'd like to.'

Wisting thanked her for the invitation. 'I'm going to see Line and Amalie this evening,' he said. 'But maybe another time.'

As he passed the bus bay where Astri's van had been parked, he slowed down until they had ended their chat. The spot where the body had been found was still cordoned off, but it was almost completely covered in snow again. The police tape still hung there, twisting in the wind.

As Wisting drove on, he estimated that it would be dark in an hour's time.

A car was parked at the summer cabin, right beside the snow bank, to avoid obstructing other vehicles. An Oslo-registered Mercedes, the same model as one of the three vehicles that had been parked outside Gerd Arctander's house when three of her sons had been present.

Driving up behind it, Wisting quickly turned off the ignition and stepped out.

Melted snow had pooled on the bonnet of the car and there were footprints across the ground, the pattern of the soles not yet erased by the wind.

He squinted out at the grey landscape, blanketed in snow. It looked as if the prints first led up to the house but then backtracked and skirted round to the rear.

The wind was gusting and a loose shutter was banging against the wall. Wisting dipped his head, waded out through the deep snow and followed the tracks.

At the corner of the house, he stopped and put his hand

on the wall for support as he blinked away the driving snow. The footprints headed straight to the annexe. The door was closed, but the front entrance had been cleared. A spade had been left in the snow outside.

He trudged on. The pine trees around him swayed in the blasting wind and hard snow pellets nipped his face.

The tracks ahead of him pointed in only one direction. Although he had assumed that someone was inside the annexe, he suddenly noticed a movement on his right. The back of a man making his way down to the jetty holding a cardboard box in his hands.

The negatives.

Wisting turned around and moved out into the soft snow, straight towards him.

The man was tramping sluggishly forward, lifting his knees, and had not noticed that someone was coming after him. Hampered by the snowdrift, Wisting fell, floundered and scrambled to his feet again.

The man was now down at the water's edge, where the snow was sparser, most of it melted by the saltwater swept ashore on the wind. The jetty itself was almost completely clear. The man moved out on to it, walking almost to the very end. He put down the box and turned his back to the sea and wind.

Bernard Arctander.

He had still not clocked that he had company. Hunched over the box, he was clutching something in his hands. A lighter.

It looked as if the wind would blow out the tiny flame as fast as it flared up.

Wisting had now reached the jetty and called out to him as he tramped along it. At that very moment, the flames caught hold of the box. The contents must have been doused in petrol or some other flammable liquid. Taking a couple of steps back, Bernard looked at Wisting in confusion.

Just as quickly as the flames erupted, they were blown out by the howling wind.

Wisting walked calmly towards Bernard Arctander as the waves sloshed against the jetty supports.

Bernard kicked the cardboard box closer to the edge.

'Get away from the box!' Wisting yelled, raising his arm in warning.

Bernard Arctander gave the box another kick, and this time it hit a mooring ring that prevented it from landing in the sea.

Wisting dived forward, striking the younger man with his shoulder and shoving him aside. Bernard staggered back before roaring something at the top of his voice. He grabbed hold of Wisting and hauled him towards him, delivering a series of rapid, hard punches to his chest and stomach.

Wisting dodged free and blocked the punches. Bernard took a few more steps back before lunging towards him. Both men toppled over and lay struggling on the jetty. A leg hit the cardboard box and it capsized. Wisting watched as an envelope of photographs was snatched by the wind: a few strips of negatives fluttered out before disappearing under the waves.

Blows and kicks were aimed in both directions as they rolled around at the edge of the jetty. Wisting ended up underneath Bernard with his faced pressed down on the wooden planks. He felt Bernard's arm around his throat and heard his laboured breath in his ear. Wisting jerked his head back, but there was no room for manoeuvre. As Bernard squeezed harder, it became difficult to breathe. Wisting tried to twist out of his grip, waving his arms and straining to reach his opponent's face and find his eyes, but he could not make it. Instead he tried to use his legs. Pulling his knees up, he braced himself and pushed off, at last managing to hurl himself around.

Now Bernard was lying underneath, but he still kept his grip round Wisting's neck and finally succeeded in twisting round again.

Wisting inched his way along the jetty, clawing his fingers into the wood and pulling himself forward until he had a handhold on the edge of the timber. Screwing up his eyes, he clenched his teeth and made another superhuman effort, thrusting his body forward to lie on his side with Bernard behind him.

They were now sprawled on the very edge of the jetty timbers, with the waves splashing over them. Wisting used his body to force the man behind him even closer to the edge. Bernard resisted furiously but was jostled further out. His movements grew frantic, but he refused to release his grip on Wisting's throat. Then they both plunged into the water.

Wisting managed to gasp for air before he went under. The freezing water paralysed him. His clothes, plastered to his body, grew heavy and dragged him down.

Bernard Arctander was beside him, coughing and spluttering as he thrashed about, arms flailing, towards the jetty. Murky waves tossed ice and slush towards the steep hillside. He would find no escape route in that direction.

A gust of wind caught the cardboard box and flung the rest of the photo envelopes out into the water. Wisting manoeuvred his body towards the jetty, groping for the edge. Once he had grasped the plank, he tried to haul himself up and succeeded in planting one arm on it, but he lacked the strength to heave his body up after it. The fight on the jetty had sapped his energy. He slid into the water again and lay back, holding tightly on to one of the seaweed-encrusted jetty supports.

One metre away, Bernard Arctander was struggling to clamber on to the jetty. He jumped, managed to haul his chest above the edge and kick off, but had to give up.

Wisting, spluttering and blinking saltwater out of his eyes, took off one of his boots, leaving the other one on. In a fresh effort, he tried to clamp his legs around the support pole and hoist himself up. A wave gave him an unexpected jolt. He threw himself forward, pressing his arms and chest against the base, struggling to get as much heft as possible beneath his upper body and casting around for something to grab hold of. His nails scratched the frozen timbers. He strained every muscle but in the end had to give up. He sank back and concentrated on keeping his head above water.

For a long time he lay pitching on the waves, hoping to gather renewed strength, but gradually felt a loss of sensation in his fingers, and then his legs.

Bernard Arctander shouted something unintelligible, raising his arm and waving madly. 'Help!'

Through the veil of snow, Wisting could make out a figure on the shore but had no strength left to call out. Bernard Arctander slumped back into the waves.

The man on shore followed the tracks out to the jetty. Wisting tried to watch his movements, but his eyes slid shut. He was exhausted and did not know how much longer he would be able to keep his head above water.

However, the sound of boots on the timbers above him made him look up.

Walter Arctander now stood on the edge of the jetty. Bernard reached out an arm to him, but his brother did not move. A powerful wave made Bernard bob up and down in the water before Walter turned his back on him.

Wisting's head dipped below the waves and he swallowed mouthfuls of water before breaking the surface again with panicky movements. Walter Arctander knelt down and grabbed his jacket. Hauling him halfway up, he snatched at him again and managed to heave him over the edge.

Wisting rolled on to his back and lay for a few moments, catching his breath, before scrambling to his knees. Walter Arctander helped him struggle to his feet.

'Bernard?' Wisting asked, looking over the side of the jetty.

Walter Arctander turned and stared in the same direction. No one was there.

90

Maren Dokken entered the office, wrenching off her hat. 'Have you been eating cake in here today?' she asked, pointing at the empty plate on his desk.

With a smile, Wisting shook his head. 'It's just something I have to return after work,' he replied.

The arrangement with Ellinor had been that she would drop in to collect the plate, but then she had invited him to her place for dinner instead.

Maren sat down, rubbing her hands together.

'Cold out there today,' Wisting commented.

'It takes time to warm up, that's for sure,' she said.

Wisting nodded. The weather forecast predicted more frost and sub-zero temperatures.

The search for Bernard Arctander had continued for three days, both at sea and along the shoreline, but with no success.

'We found another envelope of photographs and some loose negatives,' Maren told him.

'But no photos of the rucksack?' Wisting asked.

'Not yet,' was Maren's despondent response.

Wisting glanced at his computer screen. 'Do you remember the light in Astri's room in Spain didn't work?' he asked.

Although Maren seemed taken aback, she nodded her head. 'The bulb had gone,' she said. 'I think we forgot to draw the curtains again.'

Wisting turned the screen slightly, making it easier for Maren to see. 'I received an email from Michelle Norris,' he said. 'She's had an email from Salamander with more photos from the server Astri used.'

He paused for a moment before opening the first image. 'All the material's been handed over to the police in Spain,' he went on. 'But Michelle wanted to send it to me too, in case they didn't pass it on.'

'And they haven't?'

Wisting smiled. 'Not yet.'

As he opened the photograph, Maren leaned closer to the screen. The photo had been taken in the garage of the holi-day house in Palamós belonging to the Arctander family.

'Do you remember that cupboard?' Wisting asked. He was pointing to the top shelf and the boxes of spare light bulbs of various shapes and sizes. 'Astri must have gone to get a new light bulb and then found something very interesting,' he said, clicking on the next photo.

The box with the yellow beanie hat.

Maren gasped.

'Probably it had been left in the works van,' Wisting said. 'Henrik Arctander has told us that Bernard had been in the garage clearing things out of it before he returned the van to the marina and flew back to Norway.'

'So it was just left in there?'

'Obviously,' Wisting replied. 'He may not have realized its significance. When Ruby Thompson was attacked, she'd changed her clothes. The photos of her in the yellow hat didn't show up until later.'

Maren nodded. 'So the Catalan investigators don't need to search for a trophy collection,' she said.

'No,' Wisting answered. 'The rucksack turned up almost in the same way. None of the brothers remember when it first appeared in the house down there, but Henrik recalled asking Bernard if he could borrow it one time he was going home to Norway. Everyone took it for granted that it was his rucksack. Later it ended up at Sommerro.'

'It must have been the rucksack that first aroused Astri's suspicions,' Maren said. 'She began to ask questions about it before she came across the beanie.'

'The hat probably gave her final confirmation.' He turned the screen back.

'The other holes are also beginning to close up,' he said. 'The toll station transit times tally with Bernard being here the night Astri was killed. The telecoms data tell the same story.'

'It's always easier to find proof when you already have the answers,' Maren commented.

'The forensics technicians have found evidence on his computer of his participation in the online forum,' Wisting added. 'He called himself Regulus.'

'Of course, he understood who Astria really was,' Maren said. 'And realized what she was about to discover.'

'They've also located the computer program for tracking the van,' Wisting told her. 'I think Astri was in the summer cabin, picking up Bertine Franck's rucksack, and her uncle attacked her when she was on her way out. Afterwards, he dumped her body near the road and parked the van out there.'

He rummaged through a pile of papers. 'We have a witness . . .' he said, finally finding what he was looking for. 'A restaurant worker who saw a figure dressed in dark clothing walking along the road around midnight. It must have been Bernard going back to his own car.'

'So then he got rid of the rucksack and Astri's belongings,' Maren summarized. 'Her phone and her laptop.'

'He most likely chanced upon the photo album with the pictures at the same time,' Wisting said, nodding. 'Or else he went back later. What he failed to think about was the negatives. It didn't dawn on him until his mother told him what I'd been quizzing her about. If I hadn't called in at the hospital first, I'd have got there before him.'

Maren stood up. 'When do you think the penny dropped for Astri's father?' she asked.

'I don't know,' Wisting replied. 'They say they never suspected anything, not until that last day. But I'm not so sure.'

'I think there were a lot of things that were never talked about in that family,' Maren said.

She hovered in the doorway, as if reflecting on what had gone wrong in Bernard Arctander's upbringing, and then smacked the door frame lightly with the flat of her hand before disappearing in the direction of her own office.

Wisting remained at his desk, writing more of the report he had promised to send to the Catalan investigation team. Not until after four p.m. did he receive the email he was expecting. Confirmation that the local authority would provide financial guarantees for Trond Brink Isaksen's drug rehab treatment.

Printing it out, he placed it in an envelope and took it with him to the car, along with the plate.

Ellinor Brink lived in an old timber villa in Byskogen. The house was decorated for Christmas with a wreath on the door and advent stars in the windows.

She gave him a welcoming hug and ushered him inside. On the floor in the hallway, there was a box wrapped in Christmas paper and tied with a red bow.

'I've got something for Trond,' she said. 'I thought you could maybe deliver it before Christmas, just like last time.'

The package looked like the first prize in a Christmas raffle. It contained comics and chocolate, marzipan pigs and bags of nuts.

Wisting smiled. He felt some reluctance at having to circumvent prison rules and routines but did not say anything.

'I brought this back,' he said, handing her the empty plate along with a bottle of wine with a carefully written Christmas label.

Ellinor accepted both with thanks. 'Just go straight into the living room for now,' she said, half turning towards the kitchen.

Wisting walked along the passageway and turned right. It was an old house with several rooms downstairs. A small dining table in the living room was set for two and a fire was burning in the hearth.

Ellinor appeared behind him. 'Dinner will soon be ready,' she said, handing him a glass of sparkling wine.

'Thanks, but I'm driving,' Wisting said.

'It's just a small glass,' Ellinor insisted. 'Anyway, you won't be driving again for a while.'

He accepted the drink. Ellinor sipped hers before heading back to the kitchen.

Wisting stood beside a wall covered in family photographs in which both Ellinor's sons featured. Two of the photos must have been taken at confirmation time. There was nothing to suggest that one of them would become a drug addict while the other would go on to be a successful financier.

Ellinor returned. 'How's your father, by the way?' she asked.

'He's a lot better, thanks,' Wisting replied. 'They expect he'll be discharged before Christmas.'

'That's good,' Ellinor answered, smiling, before going out again.

Wisting brought his glass with him into the adjoining room. It was just as snug as the first room, but more luxuriously furnished. A long table with high-backed chairs stood in the centre and old landscape paintings hung on the walls.

Beside the gable wall he saw a framed painting on the floor, propped up with the picture side facing inwards. Wisting turned it round and stood gazing at the subject, a brown speckled dog with its head cocked, looking directly at him.

Wisting felt a jolt in his gut. Putting down his glass, he picked up the painting. The artist's signature was in the bottom-right-hand corner. Arvid Steggen. It all tallied. As did the description, a shaggy mongrel with big eyes. This was the painting that had been stolen last summer. The dog theft. In one of the newspaper spreads, Arvid Steggen had been pictured with his neighbour's dog, which had been used as the model. He could see the likeness.

Ellinor came up behind him. 'Is this where you are?' she said jovially. 'Come and sit down.'

Wisting turned the painting round and gave her a quizzical look.

'Oh yes, that,' she said. 'I haven't had time to put it up on the wall yet.' She pointed to the space she had in mind.

'Where did you get it?' Wisting asked.

Ellinor hesitated, as if searching for an explanation or excuse. 'I got it from Trond for my birthday last summer,' she replied. 'He thought it looked like Samos, the last dog we had while he was still living at home. And he's right. It was a mongrel, part Border collie and part Bernese mountain dog.'

Wisting turned the picture to face him again. The local newspaper had run numerous articles on this particular art theft and it had even been covered on national media. Ellinor Brink could not have avoided knowing about it. She must also have been well aware of that when it was presented to her. All the same, she had chosen to accept it and even cleared space on the wall to display it.

He looked at her. She knew that he knew. 'I think it's stolen,' he said.

'Then Trond would never have given it to me,' she said. 'He told me he'd found it in a second-hand shop.'

She took a step towards him, peering down at the picture.

'I haven't looked at it very closely,' she said, becoming even more entangled in a lie. 'Is it by a well-known artist?'

'I'll have to take it with me,' Wisting said. 'Sorry.'

'Of course,' Ellinor replied. 'If that's how it is.' She flashed him a smile. 'Now let's sit down.'

The painting was not mentioned during dinner, but it had put a damper on the atmosphere. Ellinor had lied to him, covering up for both herself and her son. He would always come between them, and she would always put him first. What Wisting had felt for her had gone, and he realized this would be their last meeting. A relationship would have been challenging to start with. It was her son's lawbreaking and his role as a police officer that had brought them together. That would always be there as a reminder, but Wisting had nevertheless been prepared to try to make a go of things. He missed having someone in his life and had thought Ellinor could be the right person to invite in. Now he understood that he had been wrong.

When they had eaten, he told her about the municipal guarantee of treatment for her son, and then thanked her for her hospitality.

Ellinor Brink did not try to persuade him to stay. He took the painting with him, tucking it under his arm. The Christmas box was left in the hallway.

Outside, the snow had turned to slush.

Username: Darby

Wisting sat down beside his daughter.

'It's been up for over a week,' she said, gesturing towards the screen.

The new website resembled the old one. Michelle Norris welcomed users, but its aim was no longer to clear up Ruby Thompson's murder but instead to gather more evidence against the killer.

'After all, his body's not been found, so there are loads of conspiracy theories and rumours circulating,' Line explained. 'But a lot of new evidence has been gathered that's going to make it difficult for him if he ever turns up alive.'

She clicked into a message from Shelook about the sixteen-year-old unsolved murder of Rachel Jenkins in Benidorm. She had discovered a man who had bought a boat on the same day that the English tourist was murdered. The sales report had been filled out in Benidorm and signed by Bernard Arctander. A photo of the document had been posted in the forum.

Another user had got hold of a guest list showing that Bernard Arctander had spent the night in a hotel near where one of the Spanish women had been found murdered, while the Frenchman who had been helped to fix the fault in his navigation system when Lone Sand was killed had set up a user profile and given a personal account of his meeting with the Norwegian killer.

'A climbing group has identified the spot where Ruby Thompson must have been dumped in the sea,' Line went on. 'They've found her belongings there.'

Shelook had posted a group picture of four climbers from a club in Manresa. They were standing on the edge of a cliff, equipped with ropes and other climbing gear. She had also posted a photo of an insurance document that showed a loss list detailing what had been stolen in one of the burglaries on the evening Ruby was killed. Most of the items had been found at the foot of the cliff. Marmot was the first user to comment. *Well done*, it said.

'The net is closing in around him,' Line said.

A wave of her hand in the direction of the computer showed which net she meant.

Wisting sat staring blankly at what Michelle Norris had called a fifteen-inch window on the world. Then he nodded pensively. The answers were to be found out there.